ALTAMONT AUGIE

ALTAMONT AUGIE

by RICHARD BARAGER

InterloperPress

Altamont Augie
By Richard Barager

Published by
Interloper Press
3300 Vista Way, Suite B,
Oceanside, CA 92056
760-631-0016
publisher@interloperpress.com

ISBN-13: 978-0-9830661-0-1

Publisher's Cataloging-In-Publication Data
(Prepared by The Donohue Group, Inc.)

Barager, Richard.
　Altamont Augie / by Richard Barager. -- 1st ed.

　　p. ; cm.

　Includes bibliographical references.
　ISBN: 978-0-9830661-0-1

　1. Nineteen sixties--Fiction. 2. Peace movements--United States--20th century--Fiction. 3. Pacifists--United States--Fiction. 4. Soldiers--United States--Fiction. 5. Rock music festivals--United States--20th century--Fiction. 6. Man-woman relationships--Fiction. 7. Love stories, American. I. Title.

PS3602.A72 A47 2011
813/.6   2010916503

Book and cover design by Robert Aulicino, www.aulicinodesign.com
Edited by Gail M. Kearns, To Press & Beyond, www.topressandbeyond.com
Book production coordinated by To Press & Beyond
Book Cover Text: Graham Van Dixhom, Write to Your Market, Inc.

Printed in the United States of America
First Edition
9 8 7 6 5 4 3 2 1

To my parents,
Russell and Beatrice Barager,
for reading to me when I was a child.

PART I

Shall we never, never get rid of this Past? . . .
It lies upon the Present like a giant's dead body.
Nathaniel Hawthorne, *The House of Seven Gables*

CHAPTER ONE

WHAT KIND OF MAN GOES TO ONE OF THE BIGGEST ROCK CONCERTS of the sixties, manages to drown in a nearby irrigation canal an hour into the show, and is never identified? Who was this John Doe? Another hippie drifter left over from the Summer of Love, more drugged-out flotsam from the wreckage of an overwrought decade? A nutcase, one of thousands wandering the Bay Area back then? An oddball suicide, perhaps.

Such were the questions on my mind when I arrived at San Francisco's Fillmore Auditorium on an August night in 1999 for a Crosby, Stills & Nash concert. After surrendering my ticket at the door, I stepped inside the ramshackle old building and wrinkled my nose at its stale smell, a kind of drug-tinged mustiness cracking open an olfactory portal to the sixties. I passed through the dank lobby into the Fillmore's main hall, where I encountered an expansive wooden floor (sans chairs; the crowd stood), a low-slung stage with a scrim, and, to the left of the stage, a timeworn mahogany bar, one end of which sat near a rickety staircase leading to a memorabilia shop upstairs. Psychedelic concert posters hung like bunting at a counterculture parade, paper relics from the Fillmore's glory days, when the stentorian voices of Janis Joplin and Grace Slick imbued the auditorium with what I had bitterly come to believe was the meretricious ethos of their time.

I staked out a spot at the bar and ordered drinks from a square-faced bartender in a red T-shirt. It wasn't long before complacent-looking baby boomers jammed the place, seeking, I supposed, one last communal high before the withering and shrinking of early senescence got an upper hand. The ripe scent of burning hemp perfumed the air, rising up my nostrils and fogging my brain.

I was in San Francisco seeking the past—or more precisely, seeking Altamont Augie's past. I first learned of Augie two months before, when the West Hollywood post-production company I worked for assigned me to cut a trailer for the thirtieth anniversary re-release of *Gimme Shelter*, a rock documentary profiling the final ten days of the Rolling Stones' 1969 U.S. tour. The last city scheduled was San Francisco, where the Stones were to headline a free concert in Golden Gate Park, a West Coast bookend to Woodstock. But as the December 6 concert date drew near, the city council declined to issue the Stones a permit. An alternative site wasn't secured until December 4, at an eighty-acre racetrack forty miles east of San Francisco known as Altamont Speedway.

The Altamont Speedway concert was a disaster. An unexpectedly massive crowd endured cold weather, inadequate parking and facilities, shortages of food and water, and indiscriminate mayhem at the hands of the Hell's Angels motorcycle gang, including a stabbing captured on footage that became *Gimme Shelter*'s climactic scene—and Altamont's defining image.

But what intrigued me even more than Altamont's metaphoric significance as the Death of the Sixties was an obscure fatality nobody paid much attention to that day: an unidentified white male who drowned after plunging into the California Aqueduct shortly after the concert began. It struck me as one of the most futile deaths I had ever heard of, a futile death at a futile concert, symbolizing the end of a futile decade. Futility, the perfect grist for making a movie—a not-so-secret dream of mine. Along with every other L.A. trailer editor. I could pitch it as a spin-off to *Gimme Shelter*, like taking a minor character from a wildly successful novel and giving him his own story. The real-life details of which I was determined to unearth and write a screenplay about. I even had a title for it: *Altamont Augie*—a wry tribute to Bellow's *The Adventures of Augie March.* I hadn't the slightest reason to think *my* Augie—mild-mannered trailer editor Caleb Levy's Augie—would prove as enduring an anti-hero as Bellow's famous character, but when it came to movies, who knew? I was banking on my appointment with the San Joaquin County Coroner the following day to provide the reason for Augie's peculiar death, if not his identity.

As for the Fillmore, I admit I went looking for a nostalgic glimpse of the sixties. No matter how absurd the decade appeared in the century's rearview mirror, it had at least *aspired* to be relevant; my life spent duping the public into seeing bad Demi Moore movies had yet to signify even that much. The sights and sounds of the Fillmore and ageless voices of CS & N almost made me yearn to have been alive back then, back in those confounding times. And then suddenly, I was. The crowd erupted as a denim-clad Neil Young shuffled on stage to join the other three. Together they sang "Ohio," the incendiary dirge Young had written all those years ago.

I recalled my mother's description of the moment she first learned of the Kent State shootings. She and my father were newlyweds attending a performance of *Hair,* four months before I was born. Immediately after the show, with its hopeful final number still resounding in their heads, the audience was told that Ohio National Guardsmen had shot into a crowd of war protesters at Kent State University that afternoon, killing four.

Oh, how my radical father must have craved the revolution! To fill the streets with foot soldiers of the Weather Underground and Black Panthers, whites and blacks together offing the pigs and taking their country back, dismantling the war machine that was slaughtering their Viet Cong brothers and sisters. More than anything that had gone before it, Kent State confirmed my father's heartfelt belief that imperial America and its war of aggression against an innocent peasant society had to be defeated "by any means necessary," so that America could be remade into the kind of participatory democracy Tom Hayden had called for. But much had changed since then, when Kyle Levy and Jackie Lundquist were all passion and youth—and still married to each other.

A man of about fifty with a leporine face offered me a joint. "We shut down one stupid-ass war back then, didn't we brother?"he shouted above the music, nose twitching wildly. "If it weren't for us," he continued, oblivious to my age of twenty-nine, "the military might *still* be over there fighting!"

I thought of my mother's close friend Mai, whose appearance in our lives in 1980 made my mother's decade-long transformation from flower child to closet conservative complete—and killed all hope of rapprochement between my parents, already two years divorced by then over some unspeakable wrong.

Mai had escaped Vietnam in 1979, getting smuggled out of Hue City in a small fishing boat. She left behind her father, an internee in a reeducation camp, who later died from torture; her mother, who perished at sea during a botched flight to freedom; and a brother who hanged himself rather than submit to communists. Whenever Mai spoke of Vietnam, her eyes filled with tears—caused, I knew, by grief over her family, anger at the totalitarian regime that stole the soul of her country, and lingering regret over the genocide their clients, the Khmer Rouge, perpetrated in Cambodia. Mai attributed these personal and national tragedies to America's retreat from Southeast Asia—an abandonment for which she held the antiwar movement my parents were so much a part of responsible.

I waved off Rabbit-Man's proffered toke with Mai's gracious Asian face much in mind. "We forced the military out of Vietnam all right."

. . .

The following morning, I piloted my rented Accord across the lower deck of the Bay Bridge, fought past Oakland on Interstate 580, and sliced east through Alameda County toward a speck on the map called French Camp, home of the San Joaquin County Coroner's office. Altamont was right on the way. The hotel concierge had told me the racetrack was still in operation, and the surrounding area little changed over the years. I cruised against traffic through fog-smothered hills and let my mind wander to the night before, when the Fillmore, psychedelia's battered reliquary, had managed to channel the sanctimonious blather of the sixties straight from Rabbit-Man's lips to my ears.

My contempt for the era began in 1978, when I sided with my mother—by then well on her way to renouncing the New Left and all she'd previously fought for—after my parents divorced, ostensibly over her political apostasy. My father washed his hands of his turncoat wife and eight-year-old son, moved from Los Angeles to the Midwest, and signed on with the University of Wisconsin, an assistant professor of political science.

Aside from child support, he behaved as if I had never existed. I sent a raft of anguished and then embittered letters that drew no response. My mother dismissed his behavior by abstrusely saying that some things were better left alone, but years later I surmised from old letters and random comments that their marriage had ended not over political differences, but over some moral trespass my mother committed—something so egregious that she refused to discuss it. I assumed her unpardonable sin had been an extramarital affair, but by the time of my trip to Altamont, I no longer cared. I had been estranged from my father for twenty years, and the only feeling I still held for him was an intense desire to reject all he stood for. And Kyle Levy stood for nothing if not the sixties.

A few miles past Livermore, I exited I-580 at Altamont Pass, a gash in the sun-baked hills of eastern Alameda County. From there I followed Grant Line Road one-half mile to Midway Road. Just beyond the intersection, a narrow, turbid stream with cement embankments wended a southeasterly course. A trim blue sign identified the swift-flowing canal as the California Aqueduct.

I turned right onto Midway Road and traveled three-quarters of a mile to Altamont Raceway Park, the name reflecting the latest in a series of ownership changes the speedway had undergone. The road veered left and made a sharp ascent to a bluff overlooking the grounds of the speedway. I pulled to a stop at the edge of a vast, unpaved parking lot and got out to see what the burial grounds of the sixties looked like.

Apart from all the power lines and windmills, the hilly, flaxen landscape appeared remarkably similar to panoramic shots from *Gimme Shelter*. To call it uninspiring would have been kind. Lacking shrubbery or trees or greenery of any kind, Altamont was a windblown, starkly yellow place, sere and inhospitable, with a monotony of straw-like prairie grass covering hill and hollow alike. It was hard to imagine a less inviting place for a concert.

With the hum of the still-visible 580 droning in my ears, I faced east, into a mid-morning sun that nettled my skin, and a stiff, dry wind that parched my lips. The speedway's double-oval race-tracks and austere bleachers lay directly beneath me. The grand-stand itself wasn't used at Altamont, though the track served as a landing pad for helicopters ferrying in musicians and equipment. The racetrack's northern boundary sloped to a barren valley, which I knew from *Gimme Shelter* was where Altamont's stage and closest mass of fans had been. Arrayed around this low-lying area were three steep hillsides, occupied during the concert by an army of bedraggled, intoxicated youth. Beyond, within easy walking dis-tance, the California Aqueduct curled southeast toward the county line, a shimmering ribbon of water beckoning like a desert mirage.

"Excuse me! Are you Jim Wheeler?"

I spun around. A middle-aged man with a receding hairline and mirrored sunglasses waved at me from the running board of a white SUV parked next to my Accord. I waved back and walked over, meeting him halfway.

"You must be looking for someone else. I'm Caleb Levy," I said, shaking his hand. "Who are you?"

He reached into his jeans and pulled out a business card. "Marty Giampaolo. KSAN Radio, 107.7 FM." He checked his watch. "I'm supposed to meet this guy Wheeler, but I guess I'm a little early."

I recognized the famous call letters immediately. "KSAN? As in KSAN Radio from the sixties?"

He flashed a smile of little white teeth. "Back then we were 94.9 FM. Progressive rock. We're classic rock now. Trading on the glory that was."

I gestured behind me. "KSAN did a post-Altamont wrap-up show the day after the Stones concert here in '69 that's quite a part of Altamont lore. I've listened to it. The DJ that hosted the show tried his damnedest to make sense out of what happened that day. I forget his name."

Giampaolo shaded his forehead with his hand and nodded. "Stefan Ponek. His picture is all over the place at the studio. How did you get ahold of KSAN's Altamont broadcast? It's proprietary— at least until the re-release of *Gimme Shelter* comes out this year. Excerpts from it are loaded onto the DVD as a special feature."

The blue madras shirt he wore was beginning to stain at the armpits. I adjusted my stance so he wasn't facing directly into the sun and gave him an omniscient smile. "I know. The post-production company I work for in L.A. is doing the trailer. I'm the editor."

"No shit!" he said, slapping his thigh. "Small world. What made you come all the way out here?"

"I thought seeing Altamont in person might help me edit the trailer. How about you? Why are you here?"

"I'm the station's marketing director. KSAN wants to sponsor a thirtieth anniversary concert here on the same date as the original—December sixth. They're even trying to get the Stones. So far they want nothing to do with it. The track manager is supposed to give me a tour of the grounds and hear my pitch. I'm hoping he gives me a history lesson, too. I was twelve in 1969, so other than what little I've heard about the guy that got stabbed, I don't know much about Altamont."

The details of the calamity that transpired in the desolate scrub around us some thirty years before were as familiar to me as if I'd been there myself. "I've done quite a bit of reading about it, and I've watched *Gimme Shelter* half a dozen times. I'd be happy to give you the CliffsNotes version if you're interested."

For the next fifteen minutes, the overweight, balding, perspiring marketing director of what was once the most influential rock station on the West Coast listened in rapt attention to my condensed history of the Altamont Speedway concert. "After Golden Gate Park fell through as the preferred site," I told him, "an unfavorable agreement—at least for the Stones—was struck with Sears Point Raceway near Sonoma. But at the last minute, San Francisco attorney Melvin Belli negotiated a better deal for the Stones with Dick Carter, owner of what was then called Altamont Speedway. Apart from concessions, Carter offered Altamont for free, hoping publicity from the concert would land him lucrative contracts in the future for similar events. Carter told Belli he had eighty acres of land that could accommodate one hundred fifty cars per acre. Assuming four passengers per car, they figured he had adequate parking for fifty thousand—the upper end of the range the Stones estimated might attend. They announced the change in venue from Sears Point to Altamont on local radio—KSAN, probably—at four p.m. Friday, one day before the concert.

"Soon after, long caravans of vehicles began streaming east out of San Francisco and Oakland, intent on claiming spots near the stage the following morning. Tens of thousands slept outdoors at Altamont that night in near freezing temperatures. By first light, all available parking had been taken by the advance guard of a crowd that would swell to over three hundred thousand—six-fold more than what Carter had been told to plan for. New arrivals were forced to park along the shoulders of access roads, forming twin columns of autos and vans stretching ten miles back. They covered the hilltops like a swarm of locusts."

"So whose brilliant idea was it to invite Hell's Angels?" Giampaolo asked, trickling sweat from his brow.

"That came from a free concert the Stones gave in Hyde Park the preceding July," I replied, "when the English Hell's Angels stood in as security without any problems. The Stones assumed the same would hold true at Altamont, but the San Francisco and Oakland chapters were a different breed than the London version. The Stones supposedly hired them for five hundred dollars of beer."

He mopped his forehead with the sleeve of his shirt and shook his head in amazement while I described the scene.

"The Angels took up positions on and around a four-foot-high stage, to 'protect' the fifteen bands scheduled to perform that day. The mistake was failing to hire someone to protect the audience. Squads of bikers waded into the crowd swinging lead-weighted pool cues to create a buffer zone around the stage. Anyone who came too close to or, God forbid, actually touched one of their precious motorcycles, got waled on.

"From noon to four, the bands preceding the Stones—Santana; Jefferson Airplane; the Guess Who; Joe Cocker; Crosby, Stills, Nash & Young, but *not* the Grateful Dead, who stayed in their trailer rather than expose themselves to the violence—bravely played on while the Angels pummeled the crowd and anyone attempting to intercede. They even knocked Marty Balin of the Jefferson Airplane out cold when he tried to stop a scuffle that broke out during the Airplane's set."

"Love Jefferson Airplane," Giampaolo said, playing air guitar.

I grinned and went on. "When the Stones finally came on

around five, things really got ugly. Having coped with sleeplessness the night before, lines for portable toilets running blocks long, bad trips from impure LSD foisted on them by San Francisco pushers, and waves of assaults by the Angels, the crowd surged the stage in frustration. The Angels counterattacked, splitting skulls and busting noses while a befuddled-looking Mick Jagger asked, 'Brothers and Sisters! Why are we fighting?'

"It all came to a head during 'Under My Thumb,' when a black teenager from Berkeley named Meredith Hunter pulled a revolver from inside his long green coat. The Angels fell on him, with one of them driving a knife into his back. Hunter died while the Stones played on. Though no one realized it at the time, the camera crew shooting *Gimme Shelter* got it all on film."

He thumped me on the shoulder, a good-natured whack. "That was one hell of a tutorial, my man. They should hire you to narrate the DVD."

A jet-black pick-up skidded to a halt thirty feet away amid a swirl of dust. A man with a moustache and cowboy hat hollered out from inside the cab. "Which one of you is from the radio station?"

Giampaolo told me to call him if I needed any additional background material from KSAN and promised to get me tickets if Altamont II ever came together.

After his corpulent frame disappeared into the truck, I traipsed Altamont's dusty grounds for over an hour, stopping at key locations to visualize what it must have been like: the famous groups and seminal music, the casual nudity and drugs, the Mad Hatter chaos and bloodshed. Pundits called it the Death of the Sixties, Xanadu Lost, the Betrayal of Woodstock, *Kristallnacht* for the Age of Aquarius. Others less given to such hyperbole called it a poorly organized concert marred by high-profile violence, a sad postscript to the sixties, perhaps, but not a requiem.

What had Augie thought of it all, I wondered, and what made

him charge into the California Aqueduct about the time Marty
Balin got cold-cocked? A sudden urge to cool off? A tantrum over
bad seats? His girlfriend in someone else's sleeping bag, maybe.

The brooding ghosts of Altamont yielded no answers to my
questions, but I returned to my car certain the San Joaquin County
coroner would.

· · ·

I got back on the interstate and within minutes escaped the
scorched hills of Altamont for the lush plain of the Central Valley.
Soon a sign informed me that I was entering San Joaquin County.

I discovered the jurisdictional wrinkle in Augie's case a month
earlier, when I called the Alameda County Sheriff's Department in
search of a coroner's report. A gravel-voiced lieutenant by the
name of Gustafson explained that although Augie may have *entered*
the California Aqueduct in Alameda County, his body was *recovered downstream, in San Joaquin County.* He referred me to
Sergeant Amanda Pershing, a San Joaquin County deputy coroner
whose annoyance at my subsequent call melted when I told her I
was doing research for a screenplay. She promised to locate the
report and review it with me in person, mentioning before we
hung up that many John Does were later identified.

French Camp was a gritty hamlet five miles south of Stockton,
buried in a hot, fertile valley that called itself the Nation's Salad
Bowl. The San Joaquin County Sheriff's Department resided in the
town's most attractive building, a two-story structure of ocher concrete and jade glass that could have passed for a contemporary art
museum. I parked in the visitor's lot and sauntered up a bleached-
white sidewalk that cut a swath through the compound's rolling
lawn. I registered with a guard in the lobby and was directed down
a narrow hallway to my left.

Amanda Pershing, a chunky woman in her thirties with short

dark hair and liquid brown eyes, met me in the reception area. I
followed her through a maze of glass cubicles to a cluttered metal
desk near an open window. Her lopsided hobble drew my attention
to a built-up orthopedic shoe on her left foot. She sat down in a
heap behind the desk and directed me to the chair in front of it. A
small splotch of coffee marred the front of her plain white blouse,
which she left unbuttoned at the collar. "So you're Caleb Levy. I pictured you older, forty maybe."

An uncomfortable moment passed with her staring at my face.

"You have aqua-colored eyes," she finally said, her voice tinged
with wonder.

I fidgeted and cleared my throat. "Greenish-blue is what's on
my driver's license."

"No, they're aqua. Bushy hair, big shoulders, and aqua eyes. I
bet you surf."

"I don't even skateboard."

She scowled, as if her mistaken discernment were my fault,
then brightened again.

"They shot *Cool Hand Luke* near French Camp, you know. I've
seen it three times. I thought you might be interested. Being that
you're a screenwriter and all."

I raised my brow. "A deputy coroner that watches prison movies?"

She blushed. "I have a crush on Paul Newman. Anyway, I found
the case you called about. Before I tell you about it, though, I'm
curious to know why you're so interested in this guy. He seems like
kind of a loser."

"Exactly. Even more so than the loser concert he was at. Both
utterly futile. That's what my screenplay is about. Futility."

Seeming satisfied, she pulled a worn leather journal from the
shelf above her and thumped it onto the desk.

"Back then, fatalities in the county were recorded in this." She
tapped the cover with her finger. "It's called a State Book. I cross-
matched the case numbers of all deaths filed between December of

1969 and April of 1970 with our John Doe index. After I found a match, I searched our microfiche for the medical examiner's report."

"Microfiche?" It sounded like something from the silent movie era. "Our files weren't digitized until the eighties. Neither were anyone else's," she added, reading my mind.

I winked to make up. "I forget there really was a time we didn't have computers. If he died in December of '69, why search cases from 1970?"

"Because the date entered in the State Book is the date the case was *filed*. For John Does, the filing date was usually a month or two after the actual death."

She drew a manila folder from her desk drawer and waved it in the air. "So, here's what we had on fiche. I'll summarize it for you."

She said that at approximately 12:50 p.m. on December 6, 1969, during a rock festival at Altamont Speedway in Alameda County, a white male in his early twenties wearing jeans, a blue work shirt, love beads, and an earring was observed by a state police officer to have climbed a chain link fence running parallel to the California Aqueduct. After ignoring the officer's warning, the man slid feet first down the Aqueduct's concrete embankment into the canal, whereupon he swam to the middle, struggled, and sank, sucked under by the canal's powerful current. His body surfaced two hours later in San Joaquin County, which therefore handled the case.

"Because entry into the canal was witnessed to have been voluntary," she continued, "the medical examiner chose not to do an autopsy, relying instead on an external examination of the body and blood toxicology samples. The tox screen came back positive for lysergic acid diethylamide—LSD. The cause of death was determined to have been accidental drowning, with hallucinogens probably impairing the victim's judgment. The medical examiner speculated from the lack of identification on the victim's person that he was a vagrant, but we'll never know. His body was never claimed. This one's still a John Doe, a thirty-year-old cold case."

There wasn't much more to say. I thanked her for the time she had spent on an obscure death of little interest to anyone but me, and asked her to call me in the unlikely event something else turned up. She gave me a copy of the report and joked about playing herself in the movie while escorting me out.

I headed back to San Francisco unfazed by Augie's enduring anonymity. My fascination with him had from the beginning been motivated not by some altruistic impulse to rectify a nameless death, but rather by a vengeful desire to write a screenplay laying blame for Augie at the feet of my father's beloved New Left. That such a script might seem more a denunciation of the sixties than a repudiation of the father who forsook me didn't trouble me in the least. The sixties and Kyle Levy were one and the same to me. What better way to discredit him than by casting Augie as a hapless sixties Everyman, his freakish death and presumably feckless life an inevitable result of the dissolute decade the New Left helped spawn?

There was no requirement that *Altamont Augie* be a scrupulously accurate film biography. I had been prepared all along for the possibility that despite my efforts to unmask him, Augie might remain Augie, his identity a mystery, his life unknown. With that now the case, I would simply invoke plan B: make it all up. Imagine Augie's life rather than discover it—except the ending, of course, which was already more absurd than anything I could ever invent.

The farther I drove, the more appealing the notion of fabricating Augie's life story became. It would give me artistic license to portray him the way I wanted, a victim of his time, seduced by the siren songs of communal love and universal understanding and then sacrificed on the altar of unfettered personal freedom.

I exited the upper deck of the Bay Bridge and inched toward Union Square fully committed to writing the fictional *Augie*. My antipathy, it seemed, had finally found the voice it deserved.

. . .

A week later, long after everyone else had gone home, I sat in muted light in my editing bay viewing a gallery of still photos included as bonus material with the *Gimme Shelter* re-release. A half-empty can of Pepsi and foil wrap from a burger I had consumed littered the console. My collection of action heroes—Batman, Superman, Green Lantern, and more—stared down at me from every nook and cranny, twelve-inch plastic figures from a parallel universe I longed to inhabit. After surviving the usual gauntlet of clueless studio executives—most of whom didn't know Digibeta from a beta test, but insisted, like dogs pissing on a tree, on putting their mark on my work—my trailer had been accepted much as I submitted it. With one exception: the studio insisted that I use some of the stills in my final cut. Much as I hated to admit they were right, it wasn't a bad idea. Adding them gave the trailer a doomed look my original cut had lacked.

Since returning from Altamont, I had made little progress at inventing Augie's life. Rendering a suitably flawed protagonist without creating a one-dimensional caricature of sixties self-absorption was harder than I thought. What redeeming qualities to bestow on a man who drowned in an irrigation ditch high on LSD? I had begun to think that scrapping *Altamont Augie* in favor of a scathing *roman à clef* of my father would be an easier, if less subtle, way of unburdening myself.

I readjusted the ergonomically perfect black leather chair I had talked our producer into buying for my temperamental spine and then dragged a group of stills from my selects bin to the end of my sequence. I hit play and my timeline streamed across my playback monitor, allowing me to study the photos on a larger screen. Many were of the humongous crowd in the hours before Altamont began, gamboling in the feeble sunlight leaking through the morning haze. I clicked through them one by one, people blowing bubbles, throwing Frisbees, making love, peeing in the weeds, and getting high. Even then the scowling faces of the Angels—an early beer buzz and the pressing crowd slowly raising their ire—cast a foreboding pall over things.

One of the photos caught my attention. It centered on a fat man running naked through the crowd, ass-cheeks flapping like a bulldog's jowls. In the background sat a couple on a blanket. The girl, a blonde in a floppy orange hat and checked poncho, appeared to be pointing at the obese streaker, whom her longhaired companion ignored in favor of staring at the girl. Something about her seemed familiar, the crook of her wrist or tilt of her chin. I zoomed her face—the bodacious grin, the freckled cheeks, the lustrous skin as yet unblemished by time—and used my sharpening tool to remove the graininess.

I pitched forward in my chair and knocked over my Pepsi at the first jolt of recognition; it was my mother in full bloom, a hippie goddess of twenty-two with a nimbus lighting her face.

Once the shock of seeing her subsided, hurt and resentment set in. She attends a historic concert they make a famous documentary about and never once mentions it to me? What was up with that?

I turned my attention to the dark-haired man beside her, his besotted gaze proof enough that whoever he was, he adored Jackie Lundquist. Because the file had been imported at such high resolution, it took me a moment to enlarge his image, but once I had, Amanda Pershing's clipped voice sounded as clearly as if she were standing behind me.

A white male in his early twenties wearing jeans, a blue work shirt, love beads, and an earring.

.   .   .

My mother responded to my agitated phone call by arriving within the hour. I met her in front of the converted Queen Ann our trailer company occupied and let her in. Now a Century City condo specialist with carefully tended hair worn shorter than mine, my mother at fifty-two had that attractive but startled look women of a certain age get from one too many facelifts. The jaunty confidence of the counterculture princess in the photo at Altamont had given way to the jaded acceptance of an aging beauty who somehow knows she will spend the rest of her life alone.

Why this was so had never been clear to me. There was no shortage of older Westside players asking her out—granted, most of them having already driven off a wife or two with their inexhaustible needs, but still. Perhaps she was so successful at selling condos—selling the illusion that was California, she liked to say—that she just wasn't desperate enough to put up with a man as set in his ways as she was fast becoming in hers. Yet I'd often wondered if the maliciousness of my father's old crowd after she broke with them politically had left her permanently scarred, forever mistrusting of new intimacies? Even from my child's perspective, the vituperation they heaped on her was stunning to behold.

She openly declared for Reagan in 1980—a coming-out precipitated in no small part by her new friend Mai's eyewitness account of what life with Uncle Ho was really like. To discredit her, they spread rumors that my father had left her because she was a closet lesbian, and Mai her lover. They sent hate mail accusing her of turning her back on the poor in favor of the lily-white rich—even though some of them had by then become rich themselves. They called her a gullible sellout, hoodwinked by a former actor whose reckless Cold War posturing was going to start World War III.

But through it all, she never wavered, never became embittered, never gave up. She raised her son alone and became self-sufficient—something many of the women in her old peer group paid lip service to but never managed to achieve. They should have cheered her fierce maternal instinct, lauded the fine feminist example she set, a woman on her own, no manly aid—life on HER terms, not HIS. They never did, but I didn't care. She was father and mother to me, guardian and nurturer, mentor and friend. She was my hero—then and still.

I rearmed the security system and led her back to my bay, where not a smear remained of the Pepsi slick her spectral appearance on my monitor had caused. Her spotless white tennis shoes squeaked as she walked across the hardwood floor. She sat expressionless in a powder blue jogging suit during my preamble about the *Gimme Shelter* re-release and trailer, but blanched and looked away when I got to Altamont's anonymous drowning victim. I selected the still of her and the unknown man I'd named Augie on my timeline and pushed in as far as I could. Though the enlargement was slightly blown out and heavily pixilated, there was no mistaking her.

"You never told me you were at Altamont. Who was the guy next to you?"

She let loose a broken ululation—the kind of *cri de coeur* mothers usually reserve for dead sons—and came out of her chair. She threw herself around me, wiping out an entire shelf of action heroes on the way. Her nails dug into my shoulders with such force I had to pry them loose on account of the pain. I held her in my arms until she cried herself out, the sleeve of my shirt made sopping wet by her tears.

"His name was David," she said, looking more like the girl in the photo than she had in years. "David Noble. I met him when it was still all music and miniskirts. Before it all went so wrong."

PART II

Rightly to be great
Is not to stir without great argument,
But greatly to find quarrel in a straw
When honor's at the stake
—Shakespeare, *Hamlet*

CHAPTER TWO

David Noble peered down Northrop Mall, the University of Minnesota's main pedestrian thoroughfare. Lined by red brick, neoclassical buildings with limestone trim and colonnaded porticos, the mall was bounded on the south by Coffman Memorial Union and on the opposite end by Northrop Auditorium, where David now stood. Leafy oaks and maples scant weeks from flaming into conceal foliage shaded broad sidewalks fronting the handsome buildings. A pair of droning mowers glinted in the morning sunlight, lifting the sodden scent of dew-laden grass off the mall's inner rectangle of lawn.

Swarms of students clotting Northrop Mall that first day of fall quarter looked nothing like the year before, when David was a wide-eyed freshman numb with gratitude at escaping the series of foster homes that pockmarked his youth. Back then, the mod revolution emanating from London's Carnaby Street had yet to strike Minneapolis with full force. Coeds with bouffant hairdos wore knee-length gingham skirts, white blouses, and fuzzy sweaters left dangling from their shoulders. And the men wore button-down shirts tucked securely into belted pants, their hair slicked with pomade.

But the earnest faces and conventional clothes of 1965 were the last vestiges of conformity their soon-to-be-dismayed parents would enjoy before the shocking laxity came. A year later, with hemlines higher and hair longer, the students on the mall bore bemused, mischievous looks on their faces, as if gauging how much more fun they could get away with before shedding the chrysalis of youth to fly wet-winged into the tempest.

The women now wore tweed skirts and mid-calf boots, or flared bell-bottoms over square-toed shoes. Hair swept up at the crown flowed shoulder to waist, soft and natural—or else was chopped short, like Twiggy's. Frat boys in hip-hugging slacks with wide cuffs wore print shirts splashed with color, and grew their hair long over their collars, void of oil or sheen.

So far 1966 reminded David of a ride on Cyclone, the wooden roller coaster at Excelsior Amusement Park, where he had been just twice in his life: once with the fourth of his seven sets of foster parents, and again a week ago with Jackie Lundquist, whom he met registering for fall classes. The entire country seemed awash with color and sound, consigning the bland, staid Eisenhower years to Rotary Clubs and smoke-filled VFW Posts. Pop culture churned out new delights weekly, and David, eager to put his bleak foster years behind him, welcomed them all—Mary Quant miniskirts, white go-go boots, flash cubes, color broadcasting on all three networks, and static-free radio.

But above all, he loved the music: the soul-searing, mind-bending music that not only expressed what he felt, but defined who he was. Blues, soul, folk rock, pop rock, and psychedelic rock—music by the young for the young, laying down a generational demarcation so absolute as to be a virtual Berlin wall. There were groundbreaking albums from the Beatles and Bob Dylan and a torrent of innovative singles: "Wild Thing," "Summer in the City," "Walk Away Renee," "Paint It Black," and the most unlikely hit of all, "The Ballad of the Green Berets," a song about patriotic sacrifice by Staff Sergeant Barry Sadler.

Yet despite the fashion and music and movies that made him

glad just to be alive, he knew that darker forces were welling to the top of the societal caldron. So far that year alone, Richard Speck had stabbed eight student nurses to death in their dorm in Chicago and a lunatic named Whitman had gunned down thirteen from a clock tower in Texas. And Vietnam was a mess, with the draft looming over everyone like a scythe.

He brought his gaze to rest on a throng of students halfway down the western promenade, in front of Walter Library, where Jackie had instructed him to meet her. A lone speaker at the foot of the stairs engaged the audience while a girl in a gray sweatshirt handed out fliers. David weaved down the crowded walk, working his way closer. He spotted Jackie toward the back of the crowd, looking monochromatic-hip in a brown mini with matching boots and a brown cashmere sweater. Her long blonde hair, restrained in front by a checkered headband, fell to mid-spine. David strode over and tapped her on the arm.

"What's all this about?"

She turned to him, a long-legged girl with pouty lips and lapis blue eyes. Fair of complexion and lightly freckled, she possessed a devastating blend of midwestern wholesomeness and centerfold wantonness that made it easy to see why two summers before she had been named Miss Robbinsdale, the Minneapolis suburb she was from.

"I'm so glad you came," she said, taking his hand. "They're handing out leaflets for a teach-in a few weeks from now at Coffman Union. The guy talking is in SDS. His name's Kyle Levy. I met him in history class."

"What's SDS?" he asked, drowning in her eyes.

She cocked her head, quizzical. "Are you serious? Students for a Democratic Society. They're against the war. Kyle's so smart. Listen."

The object of her praise had intense dark eyes and messy black hair that tumbled over his brow and ears. Bony of shoulder and slouched of stance, there was nothing physically compelling about him, though his voice was another matter. The rich baritone issuing forth from his whippet-framed body suggested inner strength, some determined core. David studied his angular face—the sloped nose, the pointed jaw—while he spoke.

"Let me set you straight about Vietnam," Levy said, jabbing his finger at them. "We're not there to protect the South Vietnamese from communism. We're there to make South Vietnam an American colony, one that trades our currency and welcomes our companies. The grand aim of this 'neocolonialism' is to bring enough nations under the protection of the U.S. military to impose a *Pax Americana* on the world."

He waited a beat, scanning the crowd like a bird of prey. "Article 3 of the Geneva Accords called for an internationally supervised election to unify Vietnam under one government. It's widely accepted that Ho Chi Minh would have won such an election. But with America's blessing, South Vietnam's President, Ngo Din Diem, prevented a vote from ever taking place. And America was *party* to the accords. So here we are, a decade later, still propping up Diem's illegitimate government. And we have the audacity to say we're protecting South Vietnam from communist invaders? But for American neocolonialism, there would be no South Vietnam to defend!"

David could tell by the disconcerted faces around him—like children on Christmas Eve who blundered across an uncle climbing into a red Santa suit—that Levy had hit his mark.

"Many young Americans can't vote yet," Levy said, changing cadence. "But we can die, can't we? Over three thousand already. And for what? American imperialism, that's what! Say no to war!" he shouted, his face a mask of righteous anger. He drew raucous agreement, fists in the air, shouts of "Right on!" and "Tell it like it is!"

A black-edged frisson shot through David, a quavering sense of dread the likes of which he had never felt before. An instinct so primeval he had no name for it surged inside him, and Barry Sadler's solemn hymn about the Green Berets thrummed inside his head. Clear and on key, the chorus of the divisive song rolled off of his tongue, above the din.

Stunned silent, the flock of students turned to Levy, waiting to see how their impresario would respond. His ebony eyes locked on David. "Not exactly progressive rock," he said through a thin smile, "but to each his own, brother, to each his own. Come to our teach-in and maybe you'll see things differently." He filled his hands with pamphlets and began working the crowd one-on-one.

"That was very uncool," Jackie said with a stern face.

David snapped out of his fugue and shrugged. "It just came out of me."

"It's embarrassing."

"I'm not embarrassed," he said, looking around to see who was.

"Well, I am. People will think I like that stupid song."

He made an open-palmed gesture in Levy's direction. "What 'people' are we talking about here? The guy with the big voice?"

Jackie stared, hand on hip, incredulous. "I go out with you one time and you're laying this possessiveness trip on me? Go away. You're upsetting me."

"Cripes, what are you getting so worked up about? And it's not a stupid song. I teared up the first time I heard it."

She crossed her arms and tossed her head. "You are such a dip. We have nothing in common."

Her dismissive tone unsettled him. "Does that mean you won't go out with me Friday?"

"Don't you have an ROTC meeting to go to or something?" She turned and walked away.

• • •

Left flummoxed by her outburst, David moped past Smith and Kolthoff Halls—a green-eyed, marble-bodied nineteen-year-old who walked with a deliberate, forward-leaning gait—as if bracing for another of life's blows. With unfashionably short hair, a strong brow, and a defiant cleft chin, he had a face that could have been limned and framed for West Point, a shining example of the ideal cadet.

He trundled across a footbridge that arched over Washington Avenue and entered Coffman Union, an Art Deco–style student building that included a bowling alley, billiard room, a myriad of grills and study areas, and a ballroom that once hosted Benny Goodman and Glenn Miller. He took the stairs to a second floor lounge and sprawled on a dilapidated wing chair to figure out how to go about changing Jackie's mistaken belief that he was a dip— short for dipshit, he knew from the hazing he had endured last summer, the only college boy on a city roofing crew. Did she think he was a dip for tearing up over "The Ballad of the Green Berets" or for singing it when he did?

It came as no surprise to him that Jackie, cosseted by her prosperous father, had a vastly different perspective on what the military was fighting for than did he, a forsaken child subject since birth to "foster drift"—the term caseworkers applied to throwaways like him who bounced from family to family without ever engendering an adoption. The same capitalist system Levy and Jackie blamed the war on had funded his scholarship, giving him at least a scrabbling chance in life. Unlike them, David didn't loathe the bourgeoisie; he aspired to it. Its very existence gave him hope he might yet overcome the oppressive anonymity of his deformative years and distinguish himself.

The classics he had turned to for solace during his bereft childhood (reading voraciously behind wood sheds, up in trees, or under covers with a flashlight) had left him convinced that compared to Hugo's Paris or Dickens's London, twentieth-century America was a paragon of fairness and opportunity. *Pax Americana*—the rest of the world should be so lucky. He was proud to have sung out on his country's behalf.

But none of that would be of any use in getting Jackie to go out with him again. He fretted that maybe she'd spotted something about him she didn't like during their first date at Excelsior a week ago. Since David owned no car, Jackie had driven. She arrived at the steep-roofed, big dormered home in Dinkytown, where he rented a room, in a red Mustang convertible her father had bought for her when she graduated from high school. They took off with the top down and KDWB wide open, Jackie's wind-whipped hair a mess. She gunned it to eighty-five when they reached Highway 12 heading west, singing at the top of her lungs to the Cyrkle.

Her unchecked exuberance and the rush of her hurtling machine swept him into the moment. He sang along, as untroubled and joyously alive as ever he'd been. So it went the entire day, Jackie in the lead, racing from one attraction to the next like a child on a sugar high, even though she'd been to Excelsior countless times before—including the night the Rolling Stones played the park's ballroom in 1964. At the time she didn't like them, she confessed, wasn't yet ready for their snarling brand of rock.

Together they staggered through the Barrel Walk, where they fell tumbling like a load of clothes in a dryer, navigated the Fun House's undulating gunny sack slide and distorting mirrors, and rode out Cyclone's stomach-tossing plunges again and again, Jackie's sheer, reckless zest an irrepressible force.

What made her insist on Excelsior for their first date? Had she somehow sensed its special meaning to him?

The only other time he had been there was with foster mother Number Four—a hopeless drunk who drove off a bridge and died a week after she took him there. He had longed ever since to be like all the rest of the children he saw at the park that day—normal kids having fun without the grinding worry that went with being a serial foster child, always waiting for your walking papers, never knowing when the current gig would end and you'd be packed off to someone new, someone even worse. How could she possibly have known that he loved Excelsior the way most children loved birthdays? And how was it that at nineteen, she hadn't outgrown the goofy delight of having air blown up her ass in a Fun House? He had never met anyone like her, had never known anyone with her insatiable appetite for thrills, for kicks. For life. She was like an impish, mirthful changeling—in a temptress's body.

He recalled the exact moment he fell in love with her—at the corn dog stand, after she'd consumed her third that day, the air around them heavy with the aroma of deep-fried batter and the corner of her mouth dotted with mustard. She took his arm, seized by yet another impulse, another craving. "Take me on the Ferris wheel," she urged.

The request surprised him. It didn't seem like a Jackie kind of ride, more something her parents might have done—while she rammed ten-year-olds at bumper cars. He dabbed her face with a napkin and smiled. "Why that ride?"

She took his hand and mugged while singing her answer.

Though he knew the lyrics to Freddy Cannon's ode to amusement park love by heart, he had never known if a place called Palisades Park really existed or not, and if it did, where it was. But whenever he heard the song on the radio, he pictured couples all across the country necking in tunnels of love, falling for each other in amusement parks just like Excelsior. That was it. He was done, a mess, dead-bang drunk in love before they even got to the top of the Ferris wheel, where, swaying to and fro sixty feet above ground, she finished him off with a long, slow kiss glazed in cherry lipgloss.

He stared at the study lounge's coffered ceiling and thought of a maxim he once heard about getting your lover to forgive a quarrel: invite her to some activity you will surely detest, but that she will surely enjoy. If sufferance was what Jackie required, so be it. Maybe sweet forgiveness would follow.

. . .

For penance, he invited her to a cult film at the Campus Theater—*Un Homme et une Femme*—followed by a pot party on Huron Avenue. He half hoped she would reject the offer, but instead she complimented him on his open-mindedness and said she'd be at his place by seven Friday evening.

She parked her Mustang out front and they walked the ten blocks to the theater, located at Oak and Washington. Even amongst the cavalcade of hipsters streaming inside, Jackie stood out: white headband, silver stretch top with matching tights, plastic white mini, flat-heeled white boots. David wore a black turtleneck and corduroys, but with his short hair and athletic build he looked more like the burglar/hero of the television series *T.H.E. Cat* than a London mod.

Fragrance, though, was a standoff, David redolent of Brut, Jackie's hyacinth-and-jasmine Fidji preceding her down the aisle. The movie was about a widow and widower who fell in love after becoming friends, but who then failed to consummate their love on account of the woman's guilt over her deceased husband. Hailed for its avant-garde camera angles and transitions from black-and-white to color to sepia, the film struck David as typically French: beautiful, but useless. What was its point—that celibacy was the purest expression of grief? He kept his opinions to himself. Jackie was enthralled, and gave him full credit. Maybe next week they could see *Thunderball.*

The party, to which he had scrounged an invitation from a neighbor by promising to bring a foxy chick, was in a ground floor unit of a three-story apartment building, two blocks east of the theater. After passing cursory inspection at the door, they stepped inside a darkened living room, the only contents a shabby blue sofa, a poster of Lichtenstein's *Whaam!* and a stereo playing "Eight Miles High" by the Byrds. Candles strewn about cast a wavering light over fifteen or so students in all manner of dress: frumpy skirts, tattered sweaters, a boy in a jacket and tie, a girl in a checked mini and bowler hat. A fuzzy blanket on the floor accommodated eight. The remainder milled about, grooving to the music.

On the couch, a vacant-faced preppie tapped a bongo wedged between his knees. A stringy-haired campus pothead named Dexter lay couchant on the blanket, expertly fashioning joints with a roller donated by the Loring Park pusher who sold him the grass—at a price equivalent to five dollars per dozen joints, Dexter informed them. He passed each one around as it came on line. Soon a drug-laced miasma clouded the unventilated room, its musky smell clinging to clothing and hair alike. David took Jackie by the hand and squeezed onto the blanket next to his neighbor Paul, a florid redhead.

Paul offered her a hit. "David wasn't kidding about bringing a fox, was he?"

She winked and cupped a hand around the joint, dragging deeply, cheeks puckered by the ferocity of her effort. Lungs duly inflated with hooch and blue eyes glistening, she passed the smoldering cigarette to David like a precious baton.

Though it may have looked otherwise from his stiff-fingered pinch of the half-consumed joint, his marijuana maidenhead had already been claimed. One Saturday last summer, after David had finished tacking down the last shingle on a side job re-roofing the duplex down the block where Paul lived, Paul met him at the bottom of the ladder with a lighted doobie. Under his neighbor's tutelage, he drew smoke and held it till it burned.

"Inhalation hits your brain faster than IV," Paul assured him, like a car salesman touting a Corvette over a Barracuda.

He felt the promised buzz within minutes. His body tingled,

and by the time the once-fat joint had been reduced to a skimpy roach, he understood things he had never even considered before: how ten thousand Greek hoplites enveloped three hundred thousands Persians at Marathon; that the long, slow death march of the English monarchy began in a meadow named Runnymede; how Rousseau begot Marx. He climbed back up to the roof and stood at the edge, contemplating what it would feel like to leap into the crepuscular splendor, high above it all, seeing the full chromatic spectrum with blinding clarity, as if his foveae were three times their normal size. Only Paul's hysterical laughter kept him from plunging off the roof like a drunken platform diver, yanking him back to the here and now in time to turn away and crawl back down the ladder.

What David learned from the experience was that the mildly hallucinogenic effect marijuana had on most people was for him not so mild.

He avoided it now by holding the acrid smoke in his mouth, then blowing it out in a plosive gust after an appropriately descriptive interval. The rest of the room toked away for real, and as their eyes reddened and tongues loosened, he heard reference to something called the New Left. He joined their free-flowing dialogue enough to gather that the New Left, of which Students for a Democratic Society seemed an integral part, was a movement of young radicals committed to a new communist paradigm—presumably without the Stalinist purges. But when talk turned to Vietnam, which everyone in the room but him seemed obsessed with stopping, he tuned out to check the scene around him.

Dexter presided over the magic blanket like a dazed magus speaking runic phrases, his disciples frantically recycling every ratty-looking roach. And Jackie sucked each communal joint and quaffed the sweet, red wine being passed around with the determined zest of a rat in a Skinner box, a serious case of the munchies the only force capable of distracting her. She scrambled to her feet and yelled to no one in particular, "Victuals, people! I need victuals!" before charging off to the kitchen, blonde mane trailing like a palomino's tail. During her absence, interest turned from Vietnam to music.

David felt a gush of relief and chimed back in, engaging Dexter in a debate over the comparative merits of Simon and Garfunkel's "Sounds of Silence," which Dexter claimed was an album of sublime importance, and the Beach Boys' "Pet Sounds," which Dexter dismissed as surf crap.

"'Sloop John B' is hardly surf music," David argued, "and if you ask me, 'Pet Sounds' is way more complex than 'Sounds of Silence.'"

Dexter shook his head. "Simon and Garfunkel are poets, man."

David persisted, wagging a finger in the air. "Yeats is a poet. Simon and Garfunkel are singer-songwriters. Besides, if you're into the poet thing, 'Sloop John B' was lifted from a West Indies folk song made known by Carl Sandburg."

Dexter rose up on all fours and squinted in disbelief. "Do I even know you?"

Jackie reappeared with her headband askew and fragments of orange pulp clinging to her chin. "I take full responsibility for him," she said, giving Dexter a cocky grin. "What can I say? He's cute."

"To you maybe," Dexter mumbled. "He's a redneck to me."

She knelt beside David and ran her fingers through his hair and murmured in his ear. "Dexter's getting on my nerves. Take me back to your place."

Thirty minutes later, he guided her up the stairs of his duplex and across the threshold of the dimly lit rented room he'd furnished during a one-day spree at a local consignment shop. An oaken, rolltop desk with a keyless tambour sat opposite a nicked-up, three-drawer maple bureau and matching bed.

Right up to the moment she stuck her tongue in his mouth and began dry-humping him, there was nothing he wanted more than the slim thighs of Jackie Lundquist wrapped tightly around him. But her boozy breath and insistent grinding triggered an unseemly vision of foster mother Number Six, greedily sating herself on his sixteen-year-old body, a succubus sending him to class in the morning with the smell of her on his face and fingers, drenched in shame, her policeman husband clueless. Yet for all his compunction, on the nights she didn't come to him, he lay awake hoping she would, the creak of a floorboard enough to make him achingly hard.

It ended only when her husband came home early from a night shift and discovered his fleshy, thirty-eight-year-old wife astride their surrogate son, breasts flailing. David recalled the concussive report of the shots fired from the enraged man's service revolver, the bullets narrowly clearing her lolling head before slamming into the wall behind her.

His erection flagged. How to explain that ever since Number Six, he no longer trusted the feral passions of the night? "Come back tomorrow when it's light," he whispered through a soft kiss. "The first time's better that way."

CHAPTER THREE

She did come back. In the week that followed, they spent every possible moment sequestered in David's meager room, where he employed all the carnal wisdom the voracious Number Six had imparted to him: where to touch a woman and how, when to talk dirty and when to shut up, when to murmur the L word. "You're really good in bed," Jackie told him after a particularly satisfying bout of lovemaking, the two of them side by side between the sheets. A wisp of smoke snaked into the air behind them, strawberry incense burning in an ashtray of Buddha she had placed on his dresser, filling David's bedroom with its cloying scent. "The way you make love is different from other guys. You don't rush, and you seem so . . . practiced. Did you have an older girlfriend or something?"

David at first refused to credit Number Six. In his mind, any debt owed her for having transformed him from a bumbling teenage paramour into a proficient adult lover had been more than requited by the frequent—and unfailingly noisy—gratification Number Six had enjoyed as a result.

"Older, but not exactly a girlfriend. It's not something I really want to talk about."

Jackie sat up in bed. "Was she a prostitute?" Their rumpled top sheet fell partially away, draping her like a toga. Her left breast lolled free, her large areola a splash of cinnamon dotted by a tumid nipple. "Come on, I need to know what I have to live up to here."

He propped up on one elbow and told her the whole lurid truth, concluding with a blistering indictment of the scow of a caseworker who had handed him over to a predator like Number Six in the first place. And who later yanked him back to that despicable youth shelter on Portland Avenue before placing him with his final set of foster parents, religious lunatics who insisted he attend daily Mass to save himself from the perdition Number Six had damned him to.

"You banged your foster mother?" A look of adulation crossed her face, as if his seduction at the hands of Number Six were some bawdy rite of passage he should be proud of, a defining moment conferring worldly credibility on him, sexual cachet. It was David's first glimpse of his new girlfriend's utter disbelief in consequences.

He dropped his gaze. "There's nothing in life I'm more ashamed of."

"I don't believe in shame," she volunteered, "Shame was invented by religion to control human impulse. I like my impulses. My greatest fear is failing to satisfy every last one raging inside me. What else is there?"

He studied her face and gave a wry smile. "You sound like Wolf Larson in London's *Sea Wolf*," he chided. "The meaning of human existence summed up by Man's need to fill his belly."

She dabbed the tip of his nose with her finger. "Wolfie baby was right. Whether by striving to master them or striving to indulge them, our urges determine us. What's your greatest fear?" she asked, her cobalt eyes dancing. "Not getting all A's?"

"Dying as anonymously as I was raised," he said without hesitation.

She looked sad, about to cry, but then abruptly changed the subject by sweetly suggesting that he audit the history class she was taking that quarter. "So we can spend more time together."

"Not the one Levy's in, I hope?"

Her innocent expression soured. "What does that matter? I just think you'd like Professor Devlin, that's all. He tells the whole story."

"What do you mean, the whole story?"

"Both sides. America's not all Yankee Doodle and Betsy Ross, you know."

He snorted. "How do you give both sides of the Louisiana Purchase? Teach it in French?"

Jackie reached over and slapped him, dislodging the sheet from her shoulder and puddling it across her stomach and thighs. "By asking what Thomas Jefferson asked, smarty—if the Louisiana Purchase was constitutional? That's what makes Devlin great. He gives alternative perspectives."

David rolled his eyes. So that's what this was about, that most distaff of urges, a woman's desire to change her lover. It was a campaign Jackie had begun tentatively at first, by gently prodding him to grow his hair out to avoid looking out of place, and then more assertively, by telling him to stop saying "cripes" and "jeez" all the time, because it sounded so Minnesota. And now this. "I don't know how many more 'alternative perspectives' I can handle these days."

"Then how about this?" she cooed, inching the sheet from her lap. "Can you handle more of this?"

Her tight blonde tangle left him mesmerized, a charmed cobra unable to strike. She broke the trance by reaching between his legs and stroking him. He climbed atop her knowing he would register for underwater gargling if she asked him to, but a moment after his triumphant explosion, an old fear encroached.

How long would it be before Jackie Lundquist, like his mother long ago, made him anonymous again?

• • •

A gloomy layer of stratus hung low over the Minneapolis sky-line, scraping the Foshay Tower and foreshadowing the savage winter to come. David made it halfway across the pedestrian deck of the Washington Avenue Bridge before the sky opened and spewed a cold autumn rain, dousing his uncovered head and saturating the three-dollar serge shirt he had bought at a surplus store in Dinkytown. Soaked jeans clinging to his thighs, Jack Purcell tennis shoes squeaking, he cleared the bridge with a shiver and scuttered over to Blegen Hall, a four-story, contemporary classroom building on the university's fledgling West Bank campus.

The class he had come to audit—"Nineteenth-Century American History: The Era of Manifest Destiny"—was on the third floor. He bolted up the stairs two at a time and ducked into a restroom to towel off before going down the hall to room 308, where he spotted Jackie in the fifth row of a packed class of forty. She motioned to an adjacent desk she had saved by laying an umbrella across it. David shuffled over and gave her a kiss, her cheek soft and warm against his chilled lips. He settled beside her with his skin beginning to itch from his wet shirt. Outside, a staccato of windblown rain beat against the metal-mullioned windows.

Kyle Levy sat two rows in front of them, wearing a green plaid Pendleton shirt. He twisted in his chair and shifted his gaze back and forth from Jackie to David, his face expressionless, his black eyes cold and hard. After a moment, he gave David the barest of nods—which David acknowledged with the barest of smiles.

Thomas Devlin began his lecture by writing on the blackboard "Manifest Destiny: Divine Duty or Land Grab?" A thickset, ruddy-faced man with whorls of silver hair and knobby hands, he wore a herringbone jacket and wing tips that made him look like an interloper from another era. David noticed in the course syllabus Jackie lent him that Devlin urged his students "to learn to think in a historical context." He learned from Devlin's lecture that while journalist John L. O'Sullivan had coined the *phrase* Manifest Destiny in

1845—in support of the annexation of the Republic of Texas—the *idea* could be traced to the Monroe Doctrine, with its warning to Europe to stay out of the Western Hemisphere. It was argued at the time, Devlin related from behind his lectern, that enforcement of the doctrine was best achieved by consolidating North America under one flag, to establish a buffer against Great Britain. To illustrate the sentiment, he pulled a pair of reading glasses from inside his jacket and read a quote from a letter John Quincy Adams had written to his father.

"'The whole continent of North America appears to be destined by Divine Providence to be peopled by one nation, speaking one language, professing one general system of religious and political principles, and accustomed to one general tenor of social usages and customs. For the common happiness of them all, for their peace and prosperity, I believe it is indispensable that they should be associated in one federal Union.'"

He set his glasses and notes aside and paced with his hands clasped behind him. "By 1843, the public's perception of the United States as a virtuous nation destined by God to spread liberty and democracy was well-entrenched, and the fulfillment of Manifest Destiny had become a moral imperative.

"But not everyone agreed. Opponents of Manifest Destiny believed that it sprang more from a dangerous mix of nationalism, racism, and religious zealotry than from concerns over self-defense. They complained that politicians like Andrew Jackson had promulgated the 'Divine Providence' theory in order to justify expansionist policies motivated by jingoistic greed." He stopped beside the lectern and placed a knotted hand on top of it. "This controversy has never been settled, even as Manifest Destiny continues to influence American foreign policy today." His limpid gaze and steady voice offered no clue as to his own beliefs.

"In the moments we have left, would anyone care to comment on the relevance of Manifest Destiny in this thoroughly modern—or should I say mod—year of 1966?"

Levy's hand shot up ahead of half a dozen others, attracting Devlin's clear blue eyes. "Yes," Devlin said, singling him out. "Go ahead."

Levy's resonant voice reached into every corner of the room. "Manifest Destiny remains relevant because it laid the foundation for a century of American colonialism—starting with the Spanish American War, and continuing today in Vietnam. As for justifying it by claiming Divine Providence, I doubt the genocide we perpetrated against Native Americans was God's bidding."

Devlin nodded and said, "The tragedy suffered by our indigenous population is without a doubt the dark side of Manifest Destiny."

David waved his arm in the air. Jackie shot him a look, but Devlin encouraged him to speak.

"What was the alternative?" he queried to the back of Levy's head. "To remain confined to the thirteen original colonies until Britain or France or Spain gathered an army large enough to revoke the Constitution? And what about the good we've done? Would an intact Cherokee Nation have been up to D-Day?"

Levy spun around, his face clouded and dark. "By annexing Texas at the point of a gun, Manifest Destiny gave us another slave state. Then it gave us Teddy Roosevelt, and his dreams of an American empire. And now Vietnam—all in the name of spreading our 'special way of life.' Don't you think it's time we learned that democracy can be encouraged, but never imposed?"

"Right on, end the war!" a student shouted. "Out of Vietnam!" others echoed.

David stared at Levy's choleric face and waited for the amen chorus to die down before responding. "Jefferson said that 'The tree of liberty must from time to time be refreshed with the blood of patriots and tyrants.' The French weren't peering into the Atlantic in 1944 in search of a little encouragement, you know. They were praying to God for an invasion fleet flying the stars and stripes from its masts."

A wave of assent equal in volume to an opposing cascade of jeers roiled the room, but Devlin reasserted control before it got out of hand. "I'm afraid we're out of time, but I want to thank the two of you for making my point. As everyone can see, the debate over Manifest Destiny is alive and well."

David glanced at Jackie like a puppy that had chewed her favorite slippers. She stared back with a look of distaste. "You sounded like a commercial for the John Birch Society. How did you get like this?"

He shrugged. "A lot of people think like I do. You just don't seem to know any of them."

Someone tapped him on the shoulder from behind. "Sorry for interrupting, but our paths seem to keep crossing, don't they?" It was Levy, composed and smiling, extending a conciliatory hand. "I'm Kyle Levy."

David swallowed Levy's insubstantial hand in his oversized roofer's grip. "David Noble." He dialed up enough pressure to make it clear that he could grind Levy's delicate bones into a dislocated mess if he chose to. He searched Levy's face for signs of discomfort, but encountered only the molten intelligence of his eyes. He released his grasp. Trying to intimidate Levy physically was pointless, he concluded. That wasn't how war with Kyle Levy would be waged.

Levy crooked a finger at him. "You're a damn good debater, you know that? You knocked that Jefferson quote out of the park."

David gave a short, scoffing laugh.

"What's so funny?" Levy asked.

"Baseball jargon coming from you. Doesn't seem like your thing."

Levy brightened. "Are you kidding? I love the Twins."

"You do, huh?" David said, unconvinced. "Who's their second baseman, then?"

Levy swatted the air with one hand, like shooing flies. "I know the whole line-up, and their batting averages too: Mincher, .251;

Battey, .255; Allen, .238; Killebrew, .281; Versalles, .249; Oliva, .307; Hall, .239; Uhlaender, .226; and the pitcher, Kaat, won-lost record 25 and 13."

David felt Jackie's reproach boring a hole into the side of his flushing face. "Jeez, I would never have guessed, I mean, man, I feel like an idiot!"

Levy gave a quick, forgiving laugh. "Hey, everything's cool. My father has season tickets. Let me know if you want to go some time. Later on," he said to Jackie before leaving.

Jackie crossed her arms and smirked. "So, do you need any help?"

"With what?" David questioned, suspicious.

"Removing your foot from your mouth," she said, using both hands to effect a pretend extraction. "Aren't you mortified?"

"I don't care if he does like baseball. Why does he want us to lose in Vietnam? I don't get him."

Jackie shook her head in disbelief. "I don't get you. All this anguish over winning or losing a war, this archaic sense of national pride. You're like a character out of those ridiculous Walter Scott novels you like so much, some kind of throwback." She paused and furrowed her brow. "There's a better word for it, though. I just learned it in anthropology class." A look of glee came over her, like a child finding her Easter basket. "Atavistic, that's it! I'm sleeping with an atavist!"

. . .

That night at his desk, David's mind wandered from his American lit assignment to his exchange with Jackie. Maybe she was right about him being an atavist. Maybe some random juggling of nucleic acid had occurred during his formation in his mother's womb, some critical translocation causing a few crucial alleles to hark back in time.

He fingered the edge of his desk's raised tambour and considered her reference to Walter Scott. There was no denying that he loved *Ivanhoe* and all its chivalrous trappings: duty and sacrifice, nobility of deed, reverence for womanhood. But stories like that were out of favor now. All anybody talked about in American lit was *The Catcher in the Rye*—required reading, maybe, but a book that left David conflicted.

He liked Salinger's writing, and the story, too, but Holden Caulfield's disdain for the traditions of the prep school hot shots that Caulfield dismissed as phonies and hypocrites struck David as a deliberate affront to the chivalrous values Walter Scott's classics had been founded on. Their professor had said that *The Catcher in the Rye* was a book about personal authenticity: what about tradition and duty and honor did Holden Caulfield find so inauthentic?

Jackie, of course, didn't see it that way. She regarded *The Catcher in the Rye* as one of the most important books in twentieth-century literature—and *Ivanhoe* as chauvinist propaganda, intended to trick young men into fighting and dying for old men in power. Phoniness was out, she told him, being "real" like Holden Caulfield was in.

But in an odd way, her efforts to change his beliefs about such things made David feel like he mattered to her, like he wasn't just passing through her life. Why else would she bother to fight with him about it? She made him feel visible, identifiable, as if he were on the verge of a life he actually belonged to. David had even asked her about bringing him home to meet her parents, but Jackie had said that the prospect of her father—a real-estate attorney whom she characterized as hopelessly at odds with her over the war—and her boyfriend toasting General William C. Westmoreland at the Lundquist family dinner table was too gross to even think about.

Even so, he reflected before returning to his studies, since meeting Jackie he no longer felt anonymous. And because of it, he would have sat through an all-day screed on dialectical materialism

if she'd asked him to—or even the teach-in she insisted on dragging him to the next Saturday.

. . .

The day of the teach-in broke crisp and clear, a glorious
October morning. A crowd of about five hundred spilled onto the
lawn in front of Coffman Union, toting thermoses, coolers, and
picnic baskets. Weekend traffic raised a muffled, Dopplered hum
off nearby Washington Avenue, while across the Mississippi the
downtown skyline etched a ragged silhouette into a beryl sky.

A podium flanked by two long, wooden tables rested in the
middle of a plywood stage. A clutch of speakers sat at the tables,
inspecting the crowd and its plethora of signs: In Your Heart, You
Know It's Wrong; Out Of Vietnam; White Skin=II-S, Dark Skin=I-
A; and many more. Jackie led David to an open patch of ground up
front. Braless in a gossamer blouse, her long hair unadorned, she
unfurled their blanket and chattered at a dizzying pace, barely able
to contain herself, like a fan expecting the home team to win big.

To give the event some context, David had taken time that
week to read about the New Left. It drew its name, he had discovered, from a 1960 communiqué entitled "Letter to the New Left," in
which the author had advocated a "new" leftist agenda, one dealing
less with traditional proletariat concerns and more with the
human dysfunction caused by capitalist societies.

Surprisingly, he had observed, the New Left seemed even more
hostile to traditional liberals than to conservatives, who, by virtue
of Goldwater's landslide defeat in '64, the New Left viewed as irrel-
evant. He even came across a New Left position paper blaming
Harry Truman for starting the Cold War, which the article's
authors disparaged as "a tragically flawed coda to Henry Luce's despicable 1941 *Life* magazine article on 'The American Century.'"

Of the dozen speakers taking the podium that day, eleven were faculty members. The twelfth was Kyle Levy, representing SDS, which had organized the teach-in. Talks ranged from the specific to the arcane, everything from an attack on the Monroe Doctrine by an associate poly sci professor to a defense of solipsism by a philosophy emeritus, with condemnation of the draft a common thread. David grew restive as the forum wore on. He found it a one-sided affair, unleavened by even a single competing perspective. He longed for the reasoned, impartial voice of Thomas Devlin, someone with the intellectual honesty to at least explore the possibility that winning in Vietnam might be better than losing.

The same cold, clabbered shudder he felt the day he first tangled with Levy in front of Walter Library swept over him again. Only this time it was less nebulous than before. He feared for his country.

A red-haired sociology professor named Perkins ratcheted up the rhetoric by zeroing in on Lewis Blaine Hershey, the widely loathed director of the Selective Service System, whom Perkins accused of rigging the draft in favor of privileged college students. "Students who stay in school past the age of twenty-six can avoid the draft legitimately with a II-S student deferment," he said, "while everyone else has to either flee to Canada or contrive to flunk their induction physical. Why should people of color and the underprivileged be disproportionately called on to fight this war?" He closed by raising his fist and shouting, "In your heart, you know it's wrong!" eliciting a roar of applause and a flurry of sign waggling.

David glanced at Jackie, whooping and yelling with the rest of them, her color rising, her voice angry, so alive, so impassioned: so dangerous, this spasm of partisan lust. He turned away, her protestor's face too much to bear, the silky cheek he'd stroked, the garnet lips he'd kissed, so twisted now, so foreign.

Levy went next. He stalked to the podium with his shirttail fluttering in a late-morning zephyr, his black hair rumpled, his face flinty and grim. "I'm here to talk about napalm." His mike-aided voice reverberated with sureness and moral authority. "Napalm is a sticky, flammable gel that our military uses to clear helicopter landing zones in Vietnam. It's composed of 25 percent gasoline, 25 percent benzene, and 50 percent polystyrene. Napalm burns at two *thousand* degrees Fahrenheit, and adheres to whatever it comes in contact with.

"Human beings hit with a napalm blast die by either burning to death or suffocating from the carbon monoxide it produces. Those unlucky enough to survive run off screaming with the stuff clinging to them, melting their flesh as they go." He let the image linger, the wind rustling through partly shorn trees the only sound.

"I mentioned they drop napalm to prepare landing zones," he resumed, his tone somber. "But what's near landing zones? Villages. And what's in villages? Children. *Ramparts* predicts that thousands of Vietnamese children will fall victim to napalm attacks this year alone, many maimed for life, their bodies permanently disfigured."

David peeked over his shoulder at the faces behind him. Levy had them cringing, appalled at their own country. He unfastened the microphone and strode from behind the podium, black eyes blazing, a matador unsheathing the killing stroke.

"The sole supplier of military-grade napalm is a company in Midland, Michigan. Dow Chemical. You know what else Dow makes? Saran Wrap. So they're pretty good at getting things to cling. When asked about making something as horrible as napalm, the people at Dow say they're just being good corporate citizens by helping the war effort. But the 'good Germans' who helped stoke the Nazi war machine thought they were patriotic citizens, too.

"From this day forward, let the 'good Germans' at Dow Chemical be exposed for what they are—killers of children! Countries that wage inhumane wars risk becoming inhuman themselves. I implore you all: stand up, stand down, or stand aside, but do not stand for Dow!"

Chants of "Down with Dow!" cascaded off the front of Coffman Union and down the mall. Jackie got to her feet and yelled in unison with the others, "Down with Dow! No more war! Down with Dow! No more war!"

David stood and took her face in his hands, his choice made, the consequences already unbearable. "I have to go." He blinked back tears before stepping away.

She gaped and asked, "Are you all right? Go where?"

"To the nearest recruiting station to enlist in the Marine Corps."

Her turn to blink back tears. "What about us? What about killing children? Didn't you hear what he just said?"

"I heard him. He's the reason I'm enlisting." David turned away and began elbowing his way toward the street.

Jackie tore at her hair and stamped her foot. "I hope you come home in a body bag!" she screamed after him.

CHAPTER FOUR

DAVID WALKED NINE BLOCKS EAST, TO A STOREFRONT MARINE Corps recruiting office that had been the target of a number of recent protests. The jingle of a bell over the door announced his arrival. A lone recruiting officer manning a metal desk stationed in the center of the room rose to greet him. He wore a long-sleeved khaki shirt with matching tie and sky-blue trousers edged with red striping. Proud-faced marines on a picture-board behind him snapped off crisp salutes and presented arms, their eyes aflame with the values printed in bold at the bottom of the display: Honor, Courage, Commitment.

The officer introduced himself as Sergeant Philip Beale, a gray-eyed, straight-spined man with a bosom full of ribbons and a busted nose that was so deformed David wondered how it still drew air. After seating David in front of him and determining his intent to enlist, Beale reviewed the different options available. With the ramp-up in the war, he explained, the corps had begun offering two-year enlistments in addition to the traditional four-year commitment. David chose the two-year option, which Beale seemed to have expected.

"You need to know that as a two-year enlistee," he said in a practiced voice, "you'll be trained only as a basic infantryman, without benefit of the specialized instruction our four-year men later make great use of in civilian life."

Four years sounded like twice as long a possibility to get killed. "I understand. I'll stick with two years."

Beale asked why he had chosen the Marine Corps over other branches of service.

"Because I want to fight for my country. I know I'll see action with the marines."

Beale's taut face softened and his squared shoulders sagged. "Joining the Marine Corps isn't about being prepared to *fight* for your country, son. It's about being prepared to die for your country. I've been to 'Nam. It is an unsafe place."

His words took David by surprise. For all the talk on campus about high-pressure, dishonest recruiters, it felt more like Beale was trying to talk him *out* of joining. An adolescent tug of gratitude pulled at his stomach. He wished he'd had a father like Philip Beale, someone to watch out for him, to remind him to use a rubber and not drive home drunk.

"I appreciate the warning, but my mind's made up. I'm in."

Beale shrugged and reached for a packet of papers on his desk, his obligation fulfilled. "Very well." He handed the papers to David. "These are legally binding documents committing you to two years in the United States Marine Corps."

After he had read and signed them, Beale told him to go home and get drunk. So he did, at Stub and Herb's near his apartment—after which he threw up and passed out.

He took his induction physical three days later, leaving bare-footed tracks in the powder they laid down to check inductees for flat feet. They swore him in with the serviceman's oath.

> I do solemnly swear that I will support and defend the Constitution of the United States against all enemies foreign and domestic; that I will bear true faith and allegiance to the same; that I will obey the orders of the president of the United States and the orders of the officers appointed over me, according to

regulations and the Uniform Code of Military Justice.
So help me God.

And that was that. He departed Wold-Chamberlain Field at
10 p.m. on October 15, aboard an American Flyers charter packed
with anxious new recruits like him, bound for San Diego. Not even
the gathering roar of their takeoff could silence the fell scream still
ringing in his ears: "I hope you come home in a body bag."

. . .

His plane touched down in San Diego at 1:30 a.m. Drivers met
them at the baggage area and herded them onto transport buses for
the short trip to the Marine Corps Recruit Depot (MCRD), adjacent to Lindbergh Field. After a brief document check at the base's
entrance, a cinder block of a sentry wearing crisp, short-sleeved
fatigues and a shit-eating grin waved them through and then gave
them the finger.

"Your ass belongs to the corps now, you dumb bastards!"

David's bus wound its way in caravan with the others through
a warren of pristine streets and byways swathed in mellow street
light. Sculpted shrubs and climbing espaliers hugged the sides of
pastel buildings with clay tile roofs and arches and graceful
pilasters. And there were palm trees everywhere, their broad fronds
undulating as though in a Hollywood beach movie. It was all too
seductive and he knew it. His heart flailed and his palms grew
clammy as they pulled to a stop in front of a two-story building of
Spanish design with a sign staked in the lawn: Restricted
Area/Receiving Barracks/Keep Out. He closed his eyes and exhaled.
Save the trembling and cottonmouth for Vietnam, he told himself,
not a postcard-gorgeous base in California. Fear of the unknown,
that's all this is. The place looked like paradise, for cripes' sake, not
boot camp. How bad could eight weeks in San Diego be?

As if in answer to his question, the bus doors lurched open and a pair of enormous marines in forest green uniforms and brown Smokey the Bear hats burst inside.

"Get up, douche bag!" one of them yelled at a lanky towhead up front. Before the boy could move, the marine yanked him to his feet, punched him in the stomach and heaved him out the door. The two of them emptied the bus seat by seat, making sure not a single recruit exited under his own power. The larger of the two collared David, dragged him up the aisle, planted a black-booted foot on his rear, and propelled him out the door. He hit the ground in a heap and tore his pants and gashed his knee, ashamed by his lack of resistance. A third marine circulated amongst the battered jumble of recruits outside the bus, kicking at those too slow to get up and bellowing, "Scumbags! Maggots! Get your sorry asses on the yellow footprints and keep your maggot mouths shut!"

David scrambled to his feet. On the asphalt in front of the receiving barracks were rows of yellow footprints painted in formation. He raced over and occupied a set, one of seventy-five new recruits jostled and shoved into rank for the first time.

The human side of beef that booted him off the bus stepped front and center, skin lathered, thin lips drawn and menacing. A pair of tiny, knobby ears protruded from his huge skull like Mr. Potato Head parts. He glared, daring them to breathe. "I'm Sergeant Westbrook," he said with a languid drawl, "your platoon commander. And you are what is known in this part of the country as *cucarachas*—cockroaches for those of you that flunked high school Spanish." A chill crawled up David's spine even as his cheeks grew hot with resentment.

Flanking Westbrook were the other two Visigoths who participated in the mugging. He introduced them as Sergeant Garland, a bull-necked, square-jawed man with thick arms and saurian eyes, and Sergeant Mills, who towered over the other two in black-framed oval glasses that made him look like some kind of predatory owl.

Westbrook called the platoon to attention and marched them

to the front door of the receiving barracks, above which hung a sign he made them read aloud as a group.

To be a Marine

You have to believe in:

Yourself

Your fellow Marines

Your Corps

Your country

Your God

Semper Fidelis

David stood in formation while the three drill instructors ushered groups of five at a time inside the receiving barracks with a kick in the seat or swat to the head. "Move, Goldilocks!" Mills yelled at a chunky blond boy, "or Papa Bear's gonna crawl up your ass!" Once inside, David submitted along with the others to a team of barbers, who sheared him nearly bald. He felt sad and diminished, like Aslan shorn of his mane. From there he queued up for initial issue and surrendered his civilian clothes in exchange for a green utility coat, matching trousers, cap, skivvies, socks, and a pair of black field boots. Next came bucket issue, where he received a metal bucket full of equipment termed 782 Gear: canteen, cup, cover, meat can, knapsack, haversack, shelter tent, tent poles, pegs, soap, shaving gear, towel. He was then given a seabag and told to place his bucket inside the bag.

He slung it over his shoulder and staggered under its weight, then steadied himself and set out with the rest of his platoon on a quarter-mile hike to the billet area, located on the southwestern edge of MCRD's parade grounds. He ploughed through street after street of identical steel Quonset huts to the one he was assigned to, marked by a boulder with his platoon's number stenciled on it in white: #2012. The inside of his hut was as ascetic as a monk's dorm: concrete floors, two long rows of double bunk beds, the biting smell of antiseptic in the air. Nothing else, no pictures or paintings, no rugs or plants, no furniture of any kind. It was like a sterile metal tomb, made all the more sepulchral by the drill instructors' strict prohibition against talking. What was the point of that? How were they supposed to develop the famous marine camaraderie he'd heard so much about if they couldn't even talk to one another?

Mills followed them inside to assign them their beds and show them how to make a bunk the marine way: green woolen blanket drawn tight as a tick. After stowing his seabag and bucket issue in a wooden storage chest at the foot of his bunk, David joined the rest of his platoon outside in the predawn darkness to await further orders, his knee crusted and throbbing, his sleep-deprived brain struggling to process the avalanche of information being thrown at it. He let his mind wander to the snug, waiting bed he had just prepared. An order for sack time couldn't come soon enough.

He startled at the sound of loudspeakers blaring reveille. Scores of green-clad recruits emerged from billet huts up and down the block to assemble and march to mess hall to the chant of their drill instructors: "Hwan, Hup, Threep, Fo, Yo, Lef."

His stomach sank with despair as Westbrook kept them in formation long after the others disappeared. "I wanna make sure all those hungry *men* get to mess hall before you little *boys* do. In case there's not enough chow to go around. While we waitin', I need a show of hands from those of you who came here by way of the draft." A thin smile traced his jowly face, like a prison guard depriving the inmates of food and sleep—and reveling in it. Sadist.

A few hesitant arms poked skyward. Westbrook—his ears ridiculously small—registered a look similar to what a child molester might have elicited from a district attorney. "You mean to tell me you buckets of puke lacked the courage to *enlist* in the Marine Corps? You had to be *drafted?*"

The trio of DIs fell on the smattering of hapless conscripts among them like vultures on carrion, punching them in their stomachs and calling them pussies, then demanding push-ups while the rest of the platoon was made to mock them. "Draftees,

draftees, momma's little draftees!" David yelled with the others, loathing himself for doing so, loathing Westbrook more for choreographing it. What did all this humiliation have to do with becoming a marine?

It was light out by the time Westbrook released them to breakfast, after Garland and Mills taught them how to stand at attention—toes at forty-five degree angles, head up, chin in, chest out, thumbs along their trouser seams—follow basic commands, and report to an officer. At least it was something other than pointless degradation.

They marched to mess hall veiled by a morning marine layer and entered the white clapboard building double file, passing beneath a sign over the entrance that read, "Take All You Want, But Eat All You Take." The tantalizing odor of sizzling bacon made David's stomach rumble and his mouth water. As instructed, he held his tray perfectly level between his chin and waist and side-stepped down the buffet line, extending his tray in complete silence at each serving station. After loading his plate with French toast drizzled in maple syrup, slabs of crispy bacon, piping hot coffee, grits and hash browns, and freshly squeezed orange juice, he sat with his platoon at their designated table.

He found the clank and clang of metal trays and silverware unaccompanied by the usual hum of table talk unsettling; even at meals they were not allowed to speak. He made up for the lack of conversation by making eye contact with the recruit across from him, a Slavic-looking kid with an ugly scar curving like a worm over his left cheek. This is fucking weird, their eyes agreed.

They spent the rest of the morning on MCRD's parade grounds—an immaculate asphalt lake known as the Grinder. The fog that blanketed them earlier burned off by ten, and a bright yellow sun climbed an azure sky stippled by commercial jets departing Lindbergh Field in steep-incline take-offs, the engine roar intermittently drowning out the drill instructors' deep male voices.

The intricacies of drill and the art of synchronized pacing—left foot forward, each step thirty inches, arms swinging in metronomic rhythm—did not come easily, and the DIs harried them for it at every clumsy turn. Their frequent missteps seemed a particular affront to Sergeant Garland, a third-generation Frenchman from New York, David later learned, and a purported descendant of the Marquis de Lafayette. After yet another disjointed march from one end of the Grinder to the other, Garland went after a timorous-looking recruit named Hawkins.

"You march like a retard, Jethro! No retards in the marines. Gimme twenty push-ups!"

Hawkins hit the pavement and struggled up and down in an awkward, lurching rhythm, his gangly frame ill-suited to the task. Garland dropped to one knee beside him, his reptilian eyes cold and hooded, his massive forearms tense. "You pansy-ass hick! I let you off easy and this is what I get? Twenty more—on your knuckles. If you can't do 'em, the whole *platoon* gets knuckle push-ups!"

Each upward thrust off the Grinder's hard blacktop ripped new tears in the boy's bony knuckles. He grunted and groaned, his hands soon bloodied. Garland crouched over him, maniacal, taunting. Hawkins caved, hitting the deck and staying there.

David's insides knotted in revulsion. Something elemental was being taken from them, some essential part of their being methodically stripped away, annihilated. Dignity, he supposed, but that wasn't quite it. It was worse than that, intended to deny their very existence. His gaze found Westbrook's, questioning the need to shame Hawkins further. Westbrook scuttled over and crowded against him.

"You makin' cow eyes at me, bitch? You got a *hod*-on for me?"

He let his gaze meet Westbrook's for a second time. My name is David! The words shouted inside his head. Westbrook's hand shot up and fastened round his throat with the grip of a lock-jawed bulldog. David raked at his arm, but Westbrook forced him to his knees and showed his battle face, teeth bared, eyes full of mayhem. "I catch you eyeballin' me again, boy, they'll carry you off on a stretcher. The Marine Corps is only as strong as its weakest link. You unnerstan' me, puke?"

He managed only a gurgle. Westbrook turned him loose. He sucked air, a paroxysm of strident whooping. He finally said in a cracked voice, "Sir! Yes, sir!"

Westbrook spat on the ground and put a hand to his ear, as if straining to hear some far-off noise. "I believe I heard this maggot request permission to do twenty knuckle push-ups to satisfy the debt incurred by the platoon on behalf of the *other* maggot." His head snapped back toward David. "Permission granted!"

Starry-eyed and wheezing, David pumped out twenty knuckle push-ups, his gristly roofer's hands impervious to the Grinder's baked asphalt. He wobbled to his feet, careful to avert his gaze.

"It appears the platoon's debt has been satisfied," Westbrook declared. "Five minutes to use the head and reconvene. Fall out!"

Seventy-five recruits with full bladders and bulging rectums sprinted to a brick building fifty yards away. Since there weren't near enough urinals and toilets to accommodate them all, lines formed rivaling a women's restroom at a Beatles concert. Bashful bladders jammed things up even more. David licked his abraded knuckles and waited his turn. He had to shit, but there were no stalls in the latrine, only a row of open toilets—all unoccupied, the prospect of grunting out a crap in front of new platoon mates completely unappealing. He settled for a pee instead and arrived back at the Grinder with time to spare, a satisfying bowel movement nothing compared to the relief of keeping Westbrook off him.

He passed the afternoon marching and running through MCRD's myriad streets and roads under a withering sun. The drill instructors sang cadence while running beside them. David liked hearing the DIs sing the colorful stanzas. It made them seem almost human.

After evening chow came more marching and more exercise. David maintained by taking a fantasy plunge in the nearby Pacific. Make it through the day, he told himself over and over. Just make it through the day. He imagined himself slicing head-long into the cooling spume, waves breaking over his back, a briny film on his skin.

It was well past dusk when Mills finally sent them to the billet area to shed their dirty utilities, put on shower shoes, and march to the head to shower and shave. Afterward, David fell into formation with a white shower towel draped around his neck and fresh skivvies on. His knee ached, his throat felt like someone had tried to rip his larynx out, and the grit in his sleepless eyes grated like sand. He waited for the order to fall out, two glorious words that would send him to his warm, dry bunk for some desperately needed sleep. But instead of releasing them, Mills exercised them till David's every pore seeped; then he made them roll around in the dirt. Only then did he dismiss them, once again forbidding them to speak inside the billet hut.

He crawled into his bunk coated with sweat and grime but too tired to care; he hadn't slept in thirty-six hours. The lights in his Quonset hut blinked out and "Taps" whined over the loudspeaker, bringing his first day in the Marine Corps to a merciful end.

Exhaustion swept him to the edge of oblivion, but a dissonant snivel prodded him back awake. From somewhere in the vast dark-ness of the hut came the disquieting sound of a young man cry-ing—not over what had been done to him, David understood, but over what had been taken from him: his identity. The pathetic weeping made him wonder what the toughest among them must surely have wondered that night.

What the fuck was I thinking?

CHAPTER FIVE

REVEILLE WAILED AT 0500. MILLS BURST INTO THEIR BILLET HUT and hollered, "Get your maggot asses out of bed and at attention! You have one minute until physical therapy begins!"

David cursed and reached for his boots and utilities. Exactly sixty seconds later, he began grinding through set after set of jumping jacks, squat thrusts, and sit-ups, his muscles stiff and aching from the day before. "I like PT indoors instead of out," Mills said, his Poindexter glasses at odds with his ursine frame, "so that I can see sweat pooling on the floor beneath you. PT ends when the puddles hit six inches in diameter."

After that it was a predawn run with flashlights, followed by morning chow and rifle issue. Once they had been taught how to secure and store their weapons, they reassembled in front of the billet huts for Westbrook's morning address. David thought Garland looked even more unhinged than yesterday, pacing and cracking his knuckles and muttering to himself. After Westbrook finished speaking, Garland ordered a big, thick-chested recruit by the name of Zbikowski back inside the billet hut.

David recognized him by the jagged scar carved across his cheek and the pissed-off expression indelibly plastered on his face as the guy he sat across from in mess hall the day before. Garland followed him inside, making sure to prop the barracks door open behind them. The sickening whack of bone on flesh carried out the door, followed by a stream of vile epithets from Garland. Zbikowski's stifled groans grew more submissive as the battering went on. Each one ripped a hole in David's heart, sapped his will to resist, leaving him wilted and drained, demoralized by Zbikowski's thrashing, even this monster of a recruit made timid by the DIs. Westbrook winced and made mocking facial expressions through-out the entire beating, which lasted no more than five minutes, but seemed to David to go on forever.

Zbikowski emerged first, staggering into rank like a whipped puppy, half-doubled over but without a mark on him. Garland sauntered out after him, calm and serene, as though coming out of Sunday service. More than a few heads bowed in front of David, dispirited as he was at the sight of the defeated Zbikowski.

David got the message. Submit—or else.

. . .

He lined up for PT the next morning in a foul mood. The DIs were in his face from dawn to dusk, his muscles felt as though he'd been pummeled with a stick, and, having yet to overcome his reticence at taking a dump in front of a crowd, his bloated abdomen had pitched and griped all night long. MCRD was getting to him in ways he wouldn't have thought possible just seventy-two hours before. He'd been snookered. This wasn't boot camp; this was Dante's Ninth Circle of Hell. He toyed with the notion of doing something egregious enough to get kicked out, but later that day, an even better way out of MCRD presented itself—the possibility of a medical discharge.

After making them clean the Grinder on hands and knees with toothbrushes, Westbrook marched the entire platoon to sickbay and put them in formation outside the entrance. A slender navy lieutenant came out to talk to them. The pair of gold-braided stripes on the sleeve of his laundry-fresh white uniform gleamed like rays of hope to David, tangible proof that a power higher than Westbrook still existed in the world.

"From time to time," the doctor said, adjusting the visor of his barracks cover, "we discover recruits at MCRD who have concealed medical problems in order to avoid being rejected by the Marine Corps. This is a serious issue." He walked over and stood beside Westbrook. "Medical conditions that make you incapable of performing in the field can endanger fellow marines. This is unacceptable, and now is the time to come clean. Anyone who thinks they may be unfit for active duty is to come inside for an evaluation." He gave Westbrook a wary glance and disappeared back into the building.

Westbrook's pained expression made clear his disdain for the order he had been given. "Step forward if you think you have a medical problem that might disqualify you from the Marine Corps."

A handful of recruits came forward. David waited in rank to see what would transpire. "And what grave ailment might you have?" Westbrook asked the first recruit he came to.

"Sir! The private has syndactyly, sir."

Westbrook took a step back, looking alarmed. "What the hell's that? Some kinda VD?"

"Sir! The private was born with his fourth and fifth toes joined, sir."

"Shit, half the marines in 'Nam don't even have toes no more! Git back in rank. Next!"

"Sir!" a second recruit tried. "The private has asthma attacks, sir!"

Westbrook's expression turned helpful, concerned even. "Next time you have an attack, try holdin' your breath till it passes. Works every time. Next!"

A stocky, brown-skinned recruit named Martinez pleaded his case. "Sir! The private has a gland problem, sir."

Westbrook raised his brow. "Gland problem? What kinda gland problem?"

"Sir! The private lacks thyroid hormone, sir."

Westbrook fingered the brim of his hat and circled the hopeful recruit. "*Hor*-mones, huh? Son, I'm gonna ask you a question 'bout *hor*-mones that every marine worth a damn needs to know the answer to. You get it right, and you'll go inside to see the doctor. Fair enough?"

Martinez stared straight ahead. "Sir! Yes, sir!"

"If the need arose, how would a resourceful young recruit like yourself go about makin' a *hor*-mone?"

"Sir!" Martinez said, crestfallen. "The private doesn't know, sir."

"Don't pay her! Ha! Now git back in rank," Westbrook said, slapping him on the shoulder.

The rest of the ailing recruits melted back into formation. David returned from sickbay still trapped inside the Ninth Circle of Hell.

•   •   •

The next morning, a compact Marine Corps major in winter service uniform and garrison cap showed up unannounced on the Grinder, accompanied by a civilian in a jacket and tie. The officer pulled Westbrook aside to talk while Mills and Garland herded the platoon into formation, the two of them wearing hangdog faces and acting cowed. After a few minutes, Westbrook returned to address them with both visitors at his side.

"It seems one of you has lodged a complaint with his congressman alleging verbal and physical abuse by us drill instructors here at MCRD," he said to the platoon with a wounded look. He gestured toward the civilian. "This man is part of a congressional investigation into the treatment of Marine Corps recruits during boot camp. He's going to ask some questions that I expect you to answer in forthright fashion," he said, staring hard at Zbikowski.

At a curt nod from the major, he marched Mills and Garland to the other end of the Grinder, well out of earshot. David shot Zbikowski a questioning glance, getting a barely perceptible shrug in return.

The civilian investigator walked their ranks with a youthful spring to his step. A trim man of about forty, with sloped shoulders and close-cropped black hair, he asked recruit after recruit if any of them had ever been struck by a drill instructor. Though there wasn't a man among them who hadn't been, each and every one responded exactly the same. "Sir! No, sir!"

Undeterred, the investigator continued, coming eventually to a gawky North Dakota draftee named Burson, who David knew had lost his student deferment on account of poor grades. "Have your drill instructors ever hit you?" he asked.

Burson swallowed hard. "Sir! Yes, sir! Yesterday Sergeant Garlund knocked me to the ground and kicked me in the ribs. Without provocation, sir."

The man set his feet and drove a short uppercut into Burson's stomach, doubling him over. "Good, you slime bucket stoolie!" he yelled before rabbit punching Burson. "That's what a maggot like you deserves for snitching on fellow marines!"

He wheeled away from Burson and paced their ranks. "I'm Major T. J. Pettigrew, United States Marine Corps," he roared, "and that's *nothing* compared to what will happen to the rest of you if you ever betray a commanding officer! Do I make myself clear?"

David responded in unison with the rest of the platoon. "Sir! Yes, sir! One, two, three, four, I love the Marine Corps!"

• • •

In the waning moments of David's sixth day inside the Ninth Circle of Hell, with an orange sun dipping fast over the Pacific, Westbrook paced their ranks in front of his billet hut.

"About this time," he said, "recruits often get quite horny. Start thinkin' 'bout their girlfriends, maybe gettin' a stinky finger in the back seat at the drive-in movie. Gentlemen, I beg you: Do not catch pussy fever. No good will come of it." He squared up in front of them and shook his head. "Sure as death and taxes, you'll start wonderin' if she's faithful; she ain't. Chances are, she's already bangin' either your best friend or your worst enemy, depending on which she thinks'll hurt the most."

He squinted and searched their faces for a sign his scabrous warning had hit home. "Why would she do such a thing, you ask? Because she's pissed off you chose the Marine Corps over her, you dumb bastards!" he yelled, moving down the line. "By the time you leave boot camp, she'll have forgotten she told you she loved you, and by the time you get to 'Nam, she'll have forgotten what your dick looks like. And by the time you *leave* the Marine Corps, why, she'll be knocked up with someone else's baby!"

He paused to savor their pain, the hideous visions careening inside their heads. David silently cursed him for conjuring an image of Jackie pregnant and swollen, her breasts pendulous with milk that would nourish another man's son. He gagged back an urge to upchuck.

"Do not despair," Westbrook resumed, like a preacher dispensing salvation. "I have the cure for your broken hearts: selflessness. For to be selfless is to be free of one's self. And dwellin' on one's self is the root of the problem, thinkin' you *deserve* this or that young girl and that your best friend or worst enemy don't. Only selflessness will protect you from the green-eyed monster of jealousy, inoculate you 'gainst the vagaries of love."

He kicked the ground and went on. "And how does one become selfless, you may wonder? By being broken down, reduced, till you shed your individuality, with all its enfeeblin' wants and needs. You must become anonymous, an extension of somethin' greater than yourself." He looked skyward, hands clenched, chest heaving. "The United States Marine Corps!" After a moment he sighed and said, "And that, gentlemen, is how you avoid catchin' pussy fever. Platoon dismissed."

Once David got past all the porno-flick imaginings of Jackie with other men, he hit his bunk that night strangely comforted by Westbrook's crude trope. In his raw, Huey Long sort of way, he had given them the secret for surviving MCRD. And for David, more so than most, it would be easy. He was already anonymous. He had no self to shed.

·   ·   ·

The following morning, the sky was murky and the air moist, the bracing coolness a welcome tonic during drill on the Grinder. David's muscles had stopped throbbing and his strength and endurance were improving daily, his body annealing in the crucible of boot camp. Surviving the Ninth Circle of Hell, he realized, was more a mental challenge than a physical one, the hardest part by far learning to cope with the mind games the drill instructors played. And as he constantly reminded Zbikowski, there was one thing even Westbrook couldn't do: stop the clock. No matter how bad things got, the DIs had only eight weeks to break them. Then it was on to Camp Pendleton for Basic Infantry Training—no day at the beach, but more practical than punitive.

Westbrook mentioned something called T-1 after they returned from a break for head call. David grew instantly wary. Every time a DI hit them with new terminology, some bad shit usually went down. After the fifth or sixth reference to the next day being T-1, Zbikowski got up the nerve to speak. "Sir! The private requests to have the meaning of T-1 explained, sir."

Westbrook acted shocked. "You mean you don't know?" He turned to Mills and Garland. "How could we possibly have over-looked telling them about T-1?" Mills and Garland shook their heads in dismay at the oversight.

Westbrook spun back around, beaming like a suitor unveiling an engagement ring. "Why gentlemen, T-1 is genuine Marine Corps lingo for training day number one. Your eight weeks of boot camp officially begin tomorrow. I do hope this past week of *orientation*, while not countin' toward your time in the Marine Corps, has nonetheless been beneficial in preparin' you for the more arduous days that lie ahead."

David's knees buckled. Westbrook had not only stopped the clock, he had rewound it. The cruel trick of T-1 prized away any hope that had begun to take root in his heart. He reset by one week the internal calendar he kept to mark precisely the day he was eli-gible for discharge from the Marine Corps, then conveyed a tele-pathic message to platoon commander Westbrook: Fuck you and the whore that birthed you.

•   •   •

After evening chow three days later, Mills told David to report to duty hut, a Quonset hut used by the drill instructors, one of whom was required to sleep in the billet area each night. David reported according to protocol. Standing sideways outside the hut's screen door, he reached overhead with his outside arm and slapped the flat of his hand above the threshold three times.

"Center," Westbrook called out from within.

David rotated ninety degrees, so that he faced directly into the hut. "Sir! Reporting to duty hut as ordered, sir."

"Permission to enter granted."

David stepped inside. A group of metal storage lockers sat against the wall to his left. In front of him, a stack of papers and a cup full of pens rested on top of an unoccupied wooden desk. To his right was a single bunk, its olive green blanket crease-free. The far side of the hut was a mirror image of the half he had entered, and contained a similarly positioned bunk and desk.

Westbrook sat behind the desk, his green utility jacket open at the collar, his shaved head uncovered. His huge skull looked like an alabaster world globe, the cranial indentations and ridges corresponding to the planet's oceans and continents. David paced to the front of Westbrook's desk and stiffened to attention. He trained his gaze several feet over the vertex of Westbrook's head.

"Sergeant Mills informs me that you have yet to comply with my order to write once a week to your family. Considerin' your otherwise high level of performance so far, I find this puzzlin'."

David bit the inside of his lip. Demerits for insufficient letter writing. What was next, extra kitchen duty for not brushing his teeth? He stared straight ahead, his forehead moistening in the tyrannical silence that followed.

"Private Noble," Westbrook finally said, "where were you conceived?"

"Sir?"

"Where—were you—conceived?"

David flushed. "The private doesn't know, sir."

"And why not?"

He studied the corrugated steel wall of the hut. The lower half of his field of vision detected no movement, only Westbrook's probing stare. "The private was raised in foster homes, sir. Many foster homes."

"The personal nature of this conversation makes lookin' at the bottom of your chin most unsatisfyin'," Westbrook said, his voice soft, tender even. "Permission to make eye contact granted."

He looked into Westbrook's deep-set hazel eyes, furtively at first, then hungrily, desperate to understand how the same man who had throttled him to the brink of collapse could have the capacity to ask such a humanly curious thing. *Where were you conceived?*

It was brilliant, really. For if David knew, it meant that either his parents had told him, indicating he came from an open, loving family and was likely to be emotionally stable, or that he had figured it out for himself, implying that he was shrewd and inquisitive. And if he didn't know, it suggested that he either came from a psychologically constricted family where such matters were never discussed, or that he lacked intellectual curiosity—unless of course he had been orphaned, in which case Westbrook learned something altogether different about him. Genius. Pure genius.

He lingered in Westbrook's eyes, amazed that this unyielding martinet cared enough about him to ask such a question.

"Don't you have *anyone* to write to?" Westbrook inquired. "Some cousins or an aunt or uncle, maybe?"

David shook his head. "No, sir."

"No girlfriend?" Westbrook asked, tugging at an undersized ear.

"I *had* one, sir, but she didn't take my joining the Marine Corps all that well. We haven't spoken since."

Westbrook pondered a response, then slapped the top of his desk and said, "You need to start writin' to her."

"What about pussy fever, sir?"

Westbrook smoothed his tie and cleared his throat. "In this particular instance, pussy fever is a risk we gonna have to take. In the future, I may need to temper my remarks about becomin' anonymous. I meant to recommend it during boot camp—not as a permanent condition. This young thing you're sweet on . . . what's her name?"

"Jackie, sir."

"Jackie. All right, then. It would make me happier than the Holy Ghost if you would please write to Jackie every week you are in the Marine Corps. There is no sadder thing on God's green earth than a marine in battle with no one back home to even know he's there."

David coughed to get the lump in his throat under control. The man he had pegged for a monster was Virgil in disguise, shepherding him through the Ninth Circle of Hell. It made him want to bawl. "Sir! Yes, sir!" he answered with a thick voice.

Westbrook donned his Smokey the Bear and rose up to full height, his face turned hard as blue granite. "If you tell anyone about makin' eye contact with me, I'll toss your orphan ass into correctional custody for a week. Dismissed."

· · ·

By the third week of camp, the training curriculum at MCRD shifted to skills acquisition—especially involving their rifles. The marine rifleman, David heard time and again, was the fundamental fighting element of the Marine Corps, upon which all else depended. Day after day he worked at close order drill, the *Manual of Arms* indispensable, his M-14 his closest companion. The drill instructors demanded that he sleep with his rifle, be able to disassemble and reassemble its trigger mechanism blindfolded, and, by order of Westbrook, "know it more intimately than yo' girlfriend's snatch." His rifle became a part of him, an extension of his body, like another appendage.

Marksmanship training occurred during the fifth week in camp, at Edson Range at Camp Pendleton, some fifty miles north of MCRD near the town of Oceanside, with its long pier pointing like a finger toward Japan. David memorized the Rifleman's Creed his first day there.

> This is my rifle. There are many like it, but this one is mine. It is my life. I must master it as I must master my life. Without me my rifle is useless. Without my rifle, I am useless. I must fire my rifle true. I must shoot straighter than the enemy who is trying to kill me. I must shoot him before he shoots me. I will. My rifle

and I know that what counts in war is not the rounds
we fire, the noise of our burst, or the smoke we make.
We know that it is the hits that count. We will hit.

My rifle is human, even as I am human, because it
is my life. Thus, I will learn it as a brother. I will learn
its weaknesses, its strengths, its parts, its accessories, its
sights, and its barrel. I will keep my rifle clean and
ready, even as I am clean and ready. We will become
part of each other.

Before God I swear this creed. My rifle and I are
the defenders of my country. We are the masters of our
enemy. We are the saviors of my life.

So be it, until victory is America's and there is no
enemy.

He learned the principles of trigger control, sighting, and firing his rifle in classroom lectures. Actual rifle practice—"snapping
in"—took place at the firing range, where he was made to hold
each position for painfully long periods of time, to develop muscle
memory. He left Edson Range and returned to MCRD a sharp-
shooter—able to kill at distance with a single shot, five hundred
yards without a scope.

He did his writing on Sunday afternoons, during free time,
which wasn't free at all, but allotted to washing and ironing clothes,
spit-shining boots, cleaning rifles, and sewing buttons. His letters
to Jackie made little mention of their short-circuited love affair. He
had pussy fever bad enough the way it was—no need to make it
worse by writing about it. Instead, he recounted in excruciating
detail exactly what went on in boot camp, so Jackie would know
what it took to become a marine. He didn't care if she agreed with
what he was doing, but he wanted her to respect him for it, to
understand the difference between the slogans she chanted and the
ones Westbrook did. He wrote, too, of the stringent requirements
he had to meet in order to graduate to Basic Infantry.

*To be promoted, I have to demonstrate competence
in four main activities: marksmanship, drill test
(marching in formation while performing the Manual
of Arms), an academic exam, and a physical readiness
test—consisting of a three-mile run in full combat gear,
followed by a water survival test. Non-swimmers receive
no leniency; anyone caught placing a hand along the
side of the pool gets stomped by a DI wearing leather
boots . . .*

Though he didn't expect Jackie to wish him luck—she had not
yet deigned to answer a single letter—he found that writing about
the tasks helped him visualize completing them, like Hercules imag-
ining success in the Twelve Labors. The last letter he sent from boot
camp spoke to a particularly special milestone: the day he was measured for and issued his olive green service uniform, complete with
pisscutter—what marines called their soft, brimless garrison caps.

*I found myself unprepared for the numinous pride
wearing my uniform for the first time provoked. I hardly recognized myself in the fitting mirror: my shoulders
bigger, my chest deeper, my silhouette accentuated by the
sharp creases and tapered fit of my uniform. This sacred
swath of clothing made me realize that what matters
most to me now is the loyalty, devotion, and love of my
fellow Marines, young men touched to their very core by
the ancient notion of chivalrous honor: atavists, every
last one of us.*

• • •

Graduation Day, December 15, 1966. Four platoons of recruits
lined up in front of the base theater in bright sunlight, their families three deep in the shade on the theater's stairs. It was a day
David would never forget: his platoon's colors fluttering beneath

an eggshell blue sky; the splendid glint of the drill instructors' swords; the gloss of their rifles, slicked the night before with a fine coat of oil and carefully placed in the DIs' duty hut lockers, so that not a mote of oxidation would be visible at final inspection; the battalion commander telling them they were the tip of the spear, their nation's warriors. And David making private first class, a distinction bestowed on just seven of the seventy recruits Platoon 2012 graduated.

Yet for all that, the ceremony left him bittersweet, for among the proud families gathered beneath the half-moon sign that said Marine Corps Post Theater, there were no lusty cheers directed at David, no misty-eyed, pining gazes fastened on him. He graduated alone, his letters to Jackie unanswered, his accomplishments at MCRD unacknowledged. It was only after all the fawning families had gone home that his ambivalence began to ease.

Late that afternoon, Platoon 2012 stood in rank one final time before boarding buses for Camp Pendleton and Basic Infantry Training. He wondered what Westbrook would say. Would he smile? Make a joke? Tear up? How would this rough-hewn slab of a man standing impassively before them say goodbye?

"Now that you are marines," Westbrook began, "you may wonder if my attitude toward you has changed, if my asperity has perhaps softened?" He glared at them from beneath his Smokey the Bear. "It has not! Knuckle push-ups. Ready, begin!"

David hit the ground and carried out the last order Westbrook would ever bellow at him. Sweat poured from his brow onto the warm asphalt below, until a puddle exactly six inches in diameter had formed.

CHAPTER SIX

ON THE EVENING OF JANUARY 2, 1968, DAVID AND FELLOW privates Linton Beauregarde and Rocco Colucci lay concealed in a thicket outside Khe Sanh Combat Base's concertina wire. On loan from Bravo Company to Red Sector that night, the trio was tasked with manning the Hanging Tree, a forward listening post located at the top of a small ravine near the southwest corner of the combat base. David licked his lips and peered into the moonless night; he saw only the vague flutter of waist-high elephant grass and the indistinct outlines of small trees. Beyond lay triple canopy jungle, a black hole even in daylight. He shivered—and not just from the brisk highland wind locals called the Hawk.

The situation map at Khe Sanh had been deteriorating ever since he arrived two weeks before, by C130 airlift. The solitary black dot in the middle of the map representing forces of the 26th Marine Regiment was getting harder and harder to find amongst an encroaching sea of communist red. Elements of four NVA divisions numbering between twenty to forty thousand troops were thought to have infiltrated the Khe Sanh area, including the storied 304th, conquerors of the French at Dien Bien Phu in 1954.

Like Khe Sanh, Dien Bien Phu had been a remote, air-supplied mountain outpost near the Laotian border. And the French garrison at Dien Bien Phu had been surrounded, besieged, and slaughtered by the very same general now commanding the entire North Vietnamese army, Vo Nguyen Giap.

Conclusive evidence that Giap intended to attack Khe Sanh was still lacking, but it made perfect sense to David that he would. The day before, a marine patrol sweeping the Rao Quan Valley had discovered freshly dug bunkers and several weapons caches—though as of yet, no enemy troops.

A nudge to his shoulder interrupted his thoughts. "Over there!" Beau whispered. He pointed to a penumbra so evanescent David had to practically imagine it into existence. He squinted out over the gently canted terrain. One moment the shadows seemed human in form, the next more like a stand of trees waggling in the wind. He poked Colucci in the ribs and directed his attention to the area in question.

"Trees," Colucci murmured in his thick New York accent. "Nothin' but trees."

"Trees my ass!" Beau hissed. "Trees cain't walk. You're on the radio, David. It's your call."

David wasn't at all certain the diaphanous silhouettes Beau and Colucci were arguing about merited a call to their radio pit back at the base, but it wouldn't be the first time the scrawny redhead from Atlanta had seen things—the glimmer of a distant waterfall along the Rao Quan River, a python coiled around a tree limb—the rest of them hadn't. If Beau saw something, something was there.

He picked up their field radio's bulky black handset and in a barely audible voice alerted the operator on the other end that they had seen movement up front. He broke off without waiting for a reply.

Any doubt about the reliability of Beau's vision was soon dispelled. The silhouettes came closer—constant, definite, fleeting adumbrations no more. David counted the shapes mingling in the long grass and bamboo, six in all, bearing weapons and pacing off distances. He raised the base again. A reaction team would be deployed, he was told, but if things got hot before help arrived, they were to do whatever was necessary, even if it meant revealing their position.

He replaced the handset and pressed his belly tight against the earth. Even after nine months in-country and countless firefights, his bowels still churned and his heart still slammed against his chest. He sighted his M-16 and slowed his breathing, the way he had been taught at Edson Range: . . . what counts in war is not the rounds we fire . . . it is the hits that count.

He was tempted to cut loose, gun them down before they came any closer, but the job of a listening post was to remain undetected, to report on what was happening beyond the perimeter. What if these were sappers sent to cut Khe Sanh's wire to clear a path for a battalion-sized assault force close behind? If their LP exposed itself too soon, the opportunity to discover such an attack would be lost. Yet if they waited too long, they might be overrun. The dilemma of LP duty was always the same: when to hold and when to fold.

The discipline and fire control pounded into him in boot camp—and the experience he had gained fighting throughout the previous year in Quang Tri Province—prevailed. He jabbed Beau and shrugged. Beau spread his fingers and bobbed his hand up and down, voting to hold fire. David turned to Colucci, who shook his head and held up a hand, as if stopping traffic. That was it, then. They would hang tough and wait for the reaction force.

Fifteen minutes later, illumination flares launched by mortar squads inside the base popped into the sky. The canisters drifted toward earth, suspended from parachutes and swaying in the wind, casting an inconstant, sinister light. Despite the flares, which on account of Khe Sanh's winter cloud cover were less effective than usual, the half-dozen enemy fighters were no longer visible.

A voice rang out left of the LP, announcing the arrival of the reaction team. "Identify yourselves, goddamn it! Identify your-selves!"

The pop and crackle of AK-47 fire erupted from the area where David had last seen the intruders, sending green tracer rounds arcing through the night. Almost simultaneously, the reaction team unleashed its own barrage. He flipped his M-16 to full automatic and squeezed the trigger. "Let 'em have it!" he yelled. Beau and Colucci joined in, pouring fire into the fray.

The fusillade from the reaction force coupled with the burst from their LP ripped through the night like an invisible saw. Within minutes all fell silent, no return fire. David popped in a fresh magazine and kept his rifle trained while the eight-man reaction team swept the area beneath the stuttering light of the flares. They found nothing and returned to base empty-handed, leaving him and the others frustrated at the enemy soldiers' apparent escape.

They stayed behind at the LP to serve out their shift, but at first light Beau insisted they go out to the fire zone to inspect it themselves. "Unless them gooks figured out how to walk through lead, there's just *gotta* be stiffs out there."

The brief but intense salvo unleashed into the fire zone the night before had left trees snapped in half, bushes denuded, and elephant grass cut short, as if by a machete. The three of them walked into the heart of it and found what they were looking for: five green-uniformed NVA officers lay rigid in the grass, their bodies full of bullet holes, their bamboo-handled Chicom grenades never withdrawn. Their belts—red leather with chrome buckles bearing a communist star—had been cut off them and their map pouches removed, presumably by a survivor, whose blood trail they followed until it disappeared into the tree line, heading southwest.

There was little doubt in his mind as to why six high-ranking NVA officers would risk coming within two hundred meters of a marine combat base. They had been sent to reconnoiter, measure distances for artillery fire, and map out attack routes.

General Giap, it seemed, was about to try to reprise the glory of Dien Bien Phu.

● ● ●

David cleaved to his usual routine that morning—shit, shower, and shave, followed by mess hall. Shaving came first. He sat down on a wooden ammo box in the front of his foxhole along the base's eastern perimeter and filled his dented steel helmet with water drawn from his canteen. He then put a pinch of C4 explosive into a vented C-ration can placed beneath his helmet and lit it. C4 burned hotter and faster than the useless heat tablets they issued.

He scraped away at his stubble without the aid of a mirror in a five-foot deep fighting hole configured like an H, with the posterior limb covered by a roof made of cargo pallets and metal airstrip matting. Sandbags and soil-filled ammo boxes stacked on top of the matting provided reinforcement. The open anterior limb of his foxhole was connected to trench works that encircled the entire base—the first line of manned defense behind the spools of concertina wire, trip flares, and antipersonnel mines that marked Khe Sanh's outermost perimeter. The transverse segment of his fighting hole, flimsily roofed by a single layer of metal matting, functioned as a covered passageway connecting the front to the back.

He finished a letter to Jackie before paying a visit to the shitter, an outhouse consisting of a partially enclosed wooden toilet seat perched over a fifty-five-gallon steel drum with its top cut off. He laughed out loud when he passed by a "new guy" with a shitter burn on the way there. New guys—or fucking new guys, if they were assigned to your squad—were recent arrivals who lacked combat experience. New guys drew the worst duty: filling sandbags, pulling night watch, and burning the shitters—the daily task of sanitizing the base's makeshift outhouses by dumping diesel fuel into the massive steel receptacles and burning the human waste within. Inevitably, some impatient new guy would peer down the barrel of a shitter filled with diesel fuel to see why the lighted wick he tossed inside had not yet ignited the contents. The moment he did, flames would shoot up from the bottom of the drum and scorch his face in the red, blistered pattern characteristic of a Khe Sanh shitter burn.

He arrived at the shower—a steel drum with its top cut away and its bottom riddled with bullet holes and suspended above a crude wooden stall—about the time Beau did. Beau shed his utilities, stepped inside the wooden stall, and positioned his bony white body beneath the bottom of the drum. Khe Sanh's rich, pigmented soil had stained his hands, face, and extensor surfaces an even darker shade of red than his pubes. A thread of silver dangled from his left wrist, a bracelet he never removed. David carted a five-gallon jerry can of water drawn from a nearby water buffalo—a large tank of communal water mounted on a single-axle trailer—up a ladder leaning against the side of the steel drum. He then hoisted the can over the top edge of the drum and dumped all five gallons inside. Water percolated out the fenestrated bottom in a rough approximation of a shower stream.

"Ah, so good!" Beau moaned while lathering and rinsing. "It's almost enough to make me forgive you for the First Minnesota."

David came down the ladder and paused before heading back up with a second jerry can. "What are you talking about?"

"If it weren't for you Scandihoovian boys on the second day of Gettysburg," Beau said, rubbing his hands across his eyes like a squeegee, "ole Marse Robert would have taken Cemetery Ridge. And if he'd taken Cemetery Ridge, he would have defeated Meade at Gettysburg and marched on Washington. Lincoln would have had to sue for peace and end the war on Confederate terms: no 'Four score and seven years ago,' no Grant at Appomattox, and no goddamn Sherman puttin' my Atlanta to the torch."

He shook himself like a wet dachshund and went on.

"Longstreet had the Union artillery battery on Cemetery Ridge in his grasp, but the First Minnesota stepped into the breach like a pack of blue-bellied devils. *Eighty percent casualties*—highest of any Union regiment the whole war. Changed the course of history. Them farm boys must have been either real brave or real stupid—or both. When it comes to infantry, one's the same as the other, I reckon."

David put down the jerry can and laughed. "You know why you Rebs didn't take that hill? Not enough food. Ever look at photos of the Confederate army? Most sorry lookin' starved bunch of soldiers I've ever seen. And you look just like 'em, like a scrawny red rooster."

Beau glared. "How 'bout you quit oglin' me and haul your ass back up that ladder to pour the rest of my shower?"

After swapping roles, they headed down the base's main byway, an east-west dirt road running parallel to and south of Khe Sanh's thirty-nine-hundred-foot airstrip. Walking west in light morning fog, they passed an *ontos*—a tracked vehicle mounted with half a dozen 106mm recoilless rifles—and a wooden shanty with a metal roof and rows of sandbags laid tight against its outside walls. A red wooden sign on the front of the building had a skull and cross-bones painted above white lettering that said, Recon: The Eyes and Ears of the 26th Marine Regiment. Next they passed a cluster of tents with open entry flaps and layers of sandbags piled high from stake to stake. Inside each tent, dirt steps descended to underground bunkers, the roofs of which were fortified ten feet thick with sandbags, ammo boxes, and metal sheeting. A few hundred feet farther down the road's northern shoulder, they came to mess hall, a wooden hut with a corrugated metal roof. Four silver tanks along the east wall fed propane gas to stoves inside, where marine cooks served up hot chow.

David loaded his plate and sat across from Beau at one of the hut's long wooden tables. Colucci joined them a moment later. He wore no shirt beneath a sleeveless flak jacket, showcasing a broad, matted chest and thick biceps. Dark, volatile eyes and the black brush of his moustache made the big Italian look like an enforcer for the Mafia. In between mouthfuls of scrambled eggs and bacon, the three of them discussed the orders that had been issued in the wake of their firefight at the Hanging Tree the night before.

"NVA officers doin' night recon means one thing," Colucci said. "We're gonna get hit and hit hard. So what do they tell us to do? Dig more trenches. Fuck that shit. I didn't join the Corps to fill sandbags. Marines are trained to attack."

"I'm with you," David said. "Lownds should turn us loose, not hunker down and wait to get pounded."

Beau weighed in after a swill of coffee. "Why risk a ground assault into the jungle? We got infantry units on top of all the key approach hills and 175mm artillery support from Camp Carroll and the Rockpile. And big-time air. I say let Charlie attack. Our fly boys'll put a world'a hurt on their gook asses."

"You're forgettin' one little detail, General Beauregarde," Colucci said, his fork stabbing the air. "The *crachin*. It ain't no coincidence they're doin' this during monsoon season. Air support ain't jack without visibility." They argued back and forth and cleaned their plates, but as they got up to leave, Colucci had the last word. "The brass is using us for bait. We're nothin' but fuckin' minnows on a hook."

. . .

David split off from the other two and continued on to a pair of conex boxes—steel containers with doors in front that had been adapted to serve as Khe Sanh's PX and post office. A large green generator providing electricity to subterranean command-and-control bunkers clattered nearby. So accustomed to it had he become, he barely even noticed the hybrid stench of diesel fuel and excrement polluting the air, another new guy burning a shitter. He paused outside the PX and looked across the airstrip, which was dominated by Khe Sanh's tallest structure, a fifteen-foot, square-shaped control tower made of wood framing and metal siding. Five rows of dirt-filled, red-painted wooden ammo boxes stacked on the roof formed an observation platform. "Welcome to Khe Sahn" was written in yellow across the boxes' eastern-facing sides. And below this, tacked to the roof's tarp-covered fascia, hung another sign: MATCU 62 Airfield Operations (Marine Air Traffic Control Unit).

The makeshift tower was the first thing David had seen after walking down the ramp of a C130 cargo plane two weeks before. But the dumpy tower and hellish red landscape of the Khe Sanh plateau, stripped of vegetation and marred by trenches and gun pits and concertina wire, had left him unprepared for the sylvan beauty around him.

Northwest of the base, a string of cordilleras rose out of the piedmont like a distant caravan of green-furred camels: Hills 881 South, 861, 861 Alpha, and 558, so named for their height in meters. On clear days, few in number during winter monsoon conditions marked by the fine, milky fog the French had called the *crachin*, marines gazing north of the base saw the conical emerald peaks of Hills 950 and 1015, the latter known as Tiger Tooth Mountain to locals. Khe Sanh's eastern perimeter fell precipitously into the lush Rao Quan Valley, with its southeasterly wending river. An old French coffee plantation lay south of the base and beyond that Route 9, a dirt road running from Ca Lu to the Laotian border and controlled by the NVA, causing Khe Sanh to be supplied solely by air.

David picked up some soap and toothpaste in the PX before stopping at the base mailbox—a wooden ammo carton placed on end with a hole on top to deposit mail. He reached inside his flak jacket to the front of his utility shirt and withdrew the letter he had composed earlier. Though he had long ago given up on receiving a reply, he had continued to write to Jackie throughout his nine months in Vietnam. He had no idea if she read his letters or threw them away without opening them, but it had taken him only a few weeks in-country to realize that Westbrook had been right: there was no sadder thing on God's green earth than a marine in battle with no one back home to even know he's there.

The letter he dropped through the slot of the crude mailbox had been written over several days, so made no mention of the fire-fight at the Hanging Tree the night before.

> *Dear Jackie,*
>
> *Happy New Year! I'm in a place called Khe Sanh, below the DMZ near the Laotian border in the Vietnam high-lands. Don't bother looking for it on a map—it's so remote it might as well not even exist.*
>
> *Southwest of us along Route 9, a dirt road that passes for an east-west thoroughfare in this part of the country, is a cluster of aboriginal villages inhabited by a tribe of Bru. The Bru live in grass-roof houses built on stilts, have no written language, and are the most honest people I have ever met. Their teeth are stained deep maroon from chewing betel nut for its euphoric effect—bet even you aren't hip to that one yet!*
>
> *I've learned quite a bit of local geography during the forced wanderings we call patrol. There are two types of rain forest around Khe Sanh: double canopy jungle on mountain slopes, single canopy at lower elevations. Double canopy jungle consists of an upper layer of trees eighty feet in height and a second layer growing "only" to fifty feet. Their combined density so limits sunlight pen-etration that very little ground cover grows beneath it, allowing unimpeded foot traffic by NVA infiltrating across the DMZ. The jungle in the immediate vicinity of*

our base is single canopy: small trees, bamboo, and elephant grass. Single canopy jungle provides excellent cover
for pythons and king cobras—and our enemy.

Our combat base is a blight on the Garden of Eden, a
man-made gouge of bunkers and trenches and artillery
emplacements. I sleep in something called a hooch—an
underground hut with a roof made of wooden timbers
fortified by layers of sandbags. Our beds are cots on the
ground or canvas stretchers suspended from the ceiling by
ropes. We nail parachute canopy to the timbers to prevent
dirt from sifting onto our faces while we sleep. It sounds
pretty spartan, but I can sleep anywhere, anytime. Next
time I'll tell you about our shower—it makes the hooch
seem like a five-star hotel! Only 106 more days until my
hitch in 'Nam is over, but who's counting?

You wouldn't believe the scenery here, though. Our
base is on a plateau surrounded by cloud-ringed mountains and river valleys teeming with wildlife. We've
already encountered several elephants and even a tiger
while patrolling east of the base along the Rao Quan
River.

This was no slack-jawed, scrofulous Como Park Zoo
tiger, but a magnificent wild animal, with orange striping as bright as a pumpkin. And proud! My God, how
haughty he looked, his massive head cocked our way, his
haunches rippling in dappled sunlight. The glory of such
a beast. If I should die here, in this mountain paradise so
foreign, I want to die the way that tiger lives: untamed,
my head unbowed.

Anyway ... this place is like you. Wild and beautiful. I
know I'm the one who left, but I miss you so much it
hurts to even write about it. I think about you every day.
My fellow marines keep me alive, but you make me want

to be alive. I felt whole when I was with you. For the first time in my life, I mattered to someone. I'm tired of being anonymous.
I love you.
Semper Fi, David

CHAPTER SEVEN

DAVID CRAWLED ON ALL FOURS TO THE ROOFED-IN REAR OF HIS fighting hole. His meager belongings were laid out on top of a wooden ammo box: three pairs of green tube socks and a like number of skivvies; an extra set of green utilities; poncho; a notebook with random jottings and Jackie's address and phone number; bottles of bug juice; a P-38 can opener; halazone tablets to sterilize the water in his canteen, and make it taste like bilge; and yellowed paperbacks of *The Count of Monte Cristo* and *Sometimes a Great Notion*. He brought the latter with him to the front of his foxhole and sat down on his "porch chair"—another ammo box—to read and get his mind off things.

Earlier that day, he had helped transfer the first wave of India Company wounded from the tarmac to Charlie Med, the base aid station. India Company was part of a 3rd Battalion blocking force deployed to Hill 881 South and Hill 861. 2nd Battalion (2/26), which arrived three days earlier and increased Khe Sanh's troop strength to six thousand, had occupied Hill 558 along the Rao Quan. India had spent the last twenty-four hours trying to dislodge an NVA unit of unknown size discovered the day before, January 19, on the ridgeline of 881 North, a sister hill a mile distant from India's position on 881S.

A patina of blood filmed the ramp of the first medevac copter David had boarded, causing him to lose his footing on the way up.

Marines fresh from the fight lay stricken in the belly of the copter, raising a chorus of morphine-blunted moans. "Corpsman! For God's sake, Corpsman!" Blankets covered the faces of those who were too far gone to save.

He worked as fast as he could, every minute sacred, lifting blood-soaked, crumpled bodies onto canvas stretchers and then loading them onto flatbed trucks for the short trip to Charlie Med. A young lieutenant with milky blue eyes and loops of intestine spilling from a rent in his abdomen asked over and over about his platoon. "Did they take the ridge, are they all okay?" *The tree of liberty must from time to time be refreshed with the blood of patriots and tyrants.* He eased the dying lieutenant onto the cold, hard bed of the truck and told him that his boys had not only captured that ridge, they kicked ass and took names.

He read from Kesey's novel in fits and starts, distracted by the din of combat. F-4 Phantoms screamed in filtered sunlight overhead, pounding the ridgeline on 881N with five-hundred-pound bombs and napalm strikes, raising distant plumes of smoke. A 105mm howitzer with Ban Shee painted in red on its barrel blasted away from a gun pit just west of David's foxhole, as did the base's 155mm guns, targeting the same ridgeline as the Phantoms. An echo and then a distant, thudding impact followed each of Ban Shee's booming discharges, like a massive M-80 cracking off loud and crisp on the Fourth of July.

He looked up every few minutes to scrutinize the elephant grass beyond the eastern perimeter of the combat base, which was bounded by an escarpment that plunged to the Rao Quan Valley below. A flutter of white, northeast of the airstrip, caught his eye.

He shouted to the adjacent foxhole. "Beau! You see that?"

"Jesus H. Christ, I see it! It's a gook with a white flag!"

Word went quickly up the chain of command to Bravo Company's commander, Captain Kenneth Pipes, a compact man of about thirty with intelligent hazel eyes and a sculpted face. Pipes assembled a fire team of David, Beau, and Colucci and took them out to investigate. They made contact five hundred yards outside their wire.

"Marine *dai uy*!" Pipes called out, using the word for captain. "Marine *dai uy*!" His jaw tensed in anticipation of a response.

His words seemed to bolster the vacillating enemy soldier's confidence; he moved closer, waving his white banner like a flagman at a stock car race. He wore a mottled green tunic, faded green pants neatly cuffed over canvas boots, and a sun helmet with a narrow brim. A silver star on his collar indicated a rank of lieutenant.

Their fire team moved in on him, Colucci covering while Beau disarmed him and David accepted his white flag. He was the size of a seventh grader, with delicate folds of skin tenting the corners of dark, skittish eyes. David caught the woodsy smell of campfire smoke wafting off his tunic. They escorted him back behind their wire and waited near David's foxhole for marine intelligence to arrive.

Soon Gunnery Sergeant Max Friedlander of the 17th Interrogator-Translator Team came on the scene. Friedlander, a lank, stolid man with sunken eyes and a long nose, assumed custody of the prisoner and herded him toward a waiting jeep. David scrounged a biscuit from his foxhole and offered it to the man as he filed past. He consumed it in two bites and clasped David by the arm.

"*Cám òn*," he said, flashing a mouthful of crooked teeth. "*Cám òn*."

How savage war was, David thought, that a simple act of kindness might elicit such astonished gratitude. "You're welcome." He nodded and lowered his eyes.

·   ·   ·

At 0500 the next morning, David lay asleep in his platoon's hooch, a hundred yards west of his foxhole. A small candle flick-ered in an empty tin can, shedding barely enough light for marines coming off watch to grope their way to stretchers suspended from the ceiling or cots placed on the ground. The only sounds inside the red clay cavern came from snoring soldiers or rats rustling through parachute canopies lining the hooch's fortified ceiling.

He had hit the hooch just after midnight, edgy and anxious. Several hours earlier, Colonel David Lownds—their regimental commander—had placed the entire combat base on red alert. Captain Pipes told Bravo Company at a hastily called briefing that the defector who surrendered to them that afternoon had claimed Khe Sanh would be attacked that very night. The enemy plan, according to the defector, called for the NVA 325C Division to attack Hill 861 north of the base, while the NVA 304th Division attacked from the west, along Route 9 through Khe Sanh Village, where only two ARVN (Army of the Republic of Vietnam, or South Vietnamese Army) platoons and a single platoon of marines were stationed. Shortly before David bedded down, he learned that Kilo Company on Hill 861 had detected sappers in its wire and was taking rocket and mortar fire—just as Captain Pipes said the defector had predicted.

A series of thumping explosions and ground-shaking judders rocked his cot and swayed the overhead stretchers, rousing him from his sleep.

"Incoming!" he yelled, fully awake in an instant.

"Get to the trenches!" Colucci called out from the cot beside him.

David jostled his way up the packed hooch's sandbag staircase with Beau and Colucci behind him. They emerged to a thunderous symphony of rockets and artillery and mortar, each with its own distinctive sound. He crouched low to the ground and sprinted toward the perimeter, M-16 tight in hand. A multitude of coruscating explosions flashed like sparklers in a darkened room, temporarily blinding him. Shrapnel filled the air with a deadly whisper-and-hum, zinging to the ground all around him. He made it to his foxhole without getting hit and scrambled to the back, beneath his fortified roof.

The sonic signatures of the weaponry raining down on them were easy for him to identify: the hum and screech of 122mm rockets, nine feet in length and weighing 125 pounds; the whiz and massive blast of 152mm artillery; the whistle of 82mm mortar. His foxhole shimmied from the impact of shells landing nearby and then exploding with a sharp bang. Those landing farther away cracked like thunderclaps. Each whump generated an oxygen-sucking shockwave, jarring the roof of his fighting hole and pouring sand and clogs of red dirt onto his helmet and shoulders.

He hung on, slouched in the back of his foxhole. More and more incoming landed along the southern edge of the airstrip that ran from east to west across the base. He inched to the front of his foxhole and risked a look toward the runway. Numerous small fires and one huge one raged inside the base's main ammo dump. The voices of marines struggling to extinguish them were drowned out by powerful secondary explosions that occurred as the array of ordnance stored in the dump began to ignite: beehive (flechette) artillery rounds; 105s and 155s; mortar and illumination rounds; 106 recoilless; C-3 explosive; and CS—tear gas.

An inverted fireworks display lit the night, glorious starbursts originating from the ground instead of the sky above. When added to enemy incoming, the reverberations were painful. He covered his ears, but smoke laced with tear gas billowed across the eastern third of the combat base and stung his eyes, making them pour water. Flechette rounds buzzed overhead, a thousand steel arrows flung by unseen hands impaling the sandbags that rimmed his foxhole.

He settled into the rhythm of the attack, using lulls to poke his head up and scan the perimeter for signs of a ground assault. None came, and daylight brought the usual fog, mingled with smoke from the fires. Periodically a new cache of ammo would cook off, spewing jagged metal at varying angles and velocities, like a pitcher mixing up throws—curve ball, slider, change-up, then a fastball, high and inside.

At 0930, a blast exponentially greater than any before rocked the base, disgorging a blood-orange fireball over the ammo dump. A massive shock wave sucked David out of his foxhole and deposited him supine in front of his trench, the wind knocked clean out of him. The ammo dump convulsed, belching black smoke that fouled the air and spitting pieces of shrapnel long as swords in all directions, hissing sickles that reaped a bloody harvest. He fought for air as a tremendous black cloud of debris swirled toward him, threatening to land on him like Dorothy's house on the Wicked Witch. He dove into his foxhole and crawled beneath its covered passageway just before a mountain of hot wreckage crashed down along the base's eastern perimeter and filled their trenches.

David lay motionless, panting, one ear trickling blood. What a fool he'd been to compare boot camp to the Ninth Circle of Hell. The Inferno was here, at Khe Sanh.

•   •   •

The men of Bravo Company emerged from their fighting holes after the conflagration at the ammo dump finally spent itself and encountered a sea of debris and unexploded ordnance. David dodged sporadic flurries of incoming—the telltale sounds of enemy muzzle blasts sending him scurrying for cover—while helping his unit gather the widely strewn wreckage into huge piles of rubble.

The destruction of the ammo dump left them without sufficient munitions to defend the base. With Route 9 shut down by the NVA, re-supply would have to come by air—a daunting task complicated by the cratering of their airstrip during the artillery attack. To make matters worse, an NVA ground assault on marine and

ARVN positions at Khe Sanh Village had begun—the western attack the defector had warned of.

But not all the news was bad, he knew. Kilo Company had beaten back the assault on Hill 861. Enemy losses were heavy, Kilo had reported, with dozens of NVA strung like scarecrows in their wire. And despite the overcast skies, wave after wave of A-4s, F-4s, and A-6 Intruders were unloading 500-pound bombs and snake and nape—250-pound snake-eye bombs and canisters of napalm —on the NVA's 304th Division southwest of the combat base. Forward air controllers had spotted long columns of wounded being carted toward NVA sanctuaries in Laos.

During one of their breaks later that afternoon, David felt restless. "Beau! Colucci! Come on. Let's see what's still standing."

Together they wandered the base to assess the damage. The first thing he noticed was their loss of creature comforts: mess hall non-existent, their shower a charred pile of lumber, their hooch caved in by a direct hit. The lister bags, the canvas containers of water suspended on tripods where they filled their canteens, were shot full of shrapnel. And the eastern half of the airstrip was gouged full of holes, as if giant bowling balls had been dropped on it. The only structure left untouched was the shitter.

"Figures the bastards would hit mess hall and spare the shitter," Colucci grumped. Red clay caked his utility pants and mat of chest hair and his left eye was swollen shut. "We're gonna be eatin' C-rats morning, noon, and night."

Beau shucked a piece of shrapnel onto a pile of debris and gestured toward the nonstop explosions occurring southwest of the base. Black smears streaked his freckled face and several fiberglass panels were missing from the torn pockets of his flak jacket. "Whatever attacked Khe Sanh Village last night is gettin' the crap bombed out of it."

Colucci made a sour face and spat. "Fucked-up war with fucked-up leaders—on *both* sides. Ours send us into the middle of the jungle with our hands tied behind our backs, and theirs pretend they're fighting a war of liberation when freedom for anybody is the last thing on their minds."

Beau pointed skyward. "Ain't no hands tied this time. There's fighters and bombers stacked five layers thick up there, every one of 'em just itchin' to blast away."

Colucci grunted, unimpressed. "In the meantime," he said, in his best Little Italy voice, "we're sleepin' in trenches with no hot chow, no water, and no fuckin' ammo."

David gave him a shove to the shoulder. "They got some licks in, but now we know where they are. Charlie won't exactly be sitting in the lap of luxury, either."

That night, after standing watch straining into the elephant grass, he bedded down in the open front of his fighting hole. The covered rear made him claustrophobic. He laid a blanket on the ground and slipped his field jacket on to fend off the cold highland night, but before he could fall asleep a half-hearted enemy rocket attack began. A few landed nearby, spraying shrapnel over the perimeter and setting off trip flares. He checked their wire one last time to make sure it wasn't full of sappers and lay back down to sleep, only to be awakened by raindrops the size of cherry tomatoes splattering his face. Water tumbled from the sky in pleated sheets. He crawled beneath his roof, drenched from head to foot, his fighting hole filled with water.

He pulled his poncho on and shivered.

Why was he lying in a trench risking getting his ass shot off in a monsoon when everyone else his age was smoking dope and having sex? 'Free love' the magazines and papers had taken to calling it. Free meaning what, exactly? That before there had been a fee? After nearly a year of fighting for ground they gave back as fast as those who died claiming it could be buried, David had grown frustrated with the war. There were never any decisive battles, no Gettysburgs or Midways, nothing to make him believe his side was winning.

And worse was the lack of commitment to winning, the bombing pauses they granted and sanctuaries they tolerated. He had come to suspect that winning in Vietnam depended more on what happened back home than on the battlefield. Yet Khe Sanh, he sensed, would be different. From what he'd heard, the air attack that day had been savage. Good on ya, flyboys, as Beau would say. Good on ya. Maybe this one time there would be no rules of engagement. Maybe this one time they would let them do what marines were trained to do.

Destroy the enemy.

CHAPTER EIGHT

DAVID AWAKENED AT FIRST LIGHT. THE WEATHER HAD CLEARED OF late, and the improved visibility made their air strikes more effective, suppressing enemy shelling and allowing repair of the airstrip. C-130s replete with provisions and ammo landed several times a day. And reinforcements had arrived—one thousand from 1st Battalion 9th Marines, deployed southwest of the base to the Rock Quarry, to block the NVA 304th Division; and South Vietnamese ARVN Rangers the day before, on January 27, with their red berets and round, resolute faces. They dug in along the eastern perimeter in front of Bravo Company's position south of the airstrip, bringing Khe Sanh's troop strength to seven thousand—half stationed at the main combat base, the rest dispersed on key hilltops.

Colonel Lownds's strategy, David had learned in company briefings, was to permit the enemy to surround Khe Sanh in order to learn the location of key NVA assets such as ammo dumps, staging areas, artillery positions, and trench works. Once committed, the NVA could not easily abandon their infrastructure, and were vulnerable to counterattack by artillery and air. As a consequence of the encirclement, however, Khe Sanh had to resupply exclusively by air—over one hundred tons of provisions and ammo *per day* to sustain the main combat base, another thirty to forty tons per day to maintain the hill outposts. The combat base resupplied primarily by C-130s, the hill outposts by helicopter, with each subject to intense antiaircraft and mortar fire. Mortar magnets, Colucci called them.

He made a cup of instant coffee with water from his canteen, using a dash of C-4 to heat it. He had stopped adding halazone because of the brackish taste, so the coffee tasted pretty good. For that, he accepted the trade-off: a nasty case of the drizzling shits from drinking unsterilized water. He allowed the caffeine to jolt him fully awake before removing the liner of his helmet and employing it as a basin to sponge off and brush his teeth. Next he consumed a canned C-ration of ham and eggs that smelled like moldy hay and tasted like curdled milk before meeting with Beau and Colucci outside Beau's foxhole.

"Ramirez got zapped last night," Colucci said. "An eighty-two dropped right on top of him. Never even made it to Charlie Med."

Beau threw his helmet to the ground. "God*damn* him!" His red brush of hair flashed like the comb of a combative rooster. "I *tole* him his roof didn't have enough sandbags!"

"That's bullshit," Colucci said. His open flak jacket draped his bare torso like a knight's tabard and his stevedore arms hung like clubs at his side. "When it's time, it's time. Ain't no fuckin' *sandbag* gonna save your ass."

After debating whether or not a more diligently constructed foxhole might have spared Ramirez, they set about morning chores: ammo and water runs, shoring up trench works damaged during the night, transporting wounded to Charlie Med. David glanced at his watch. "Eight forty-five," he said.

Colucci snorted. "What the fuck are you, Big Ben?"

"He's tryin' to tell ya how much time we got to move around before the *crachin* burns off and the gooks hammer us again," Beau said, "but I guess you city boys are a little slow on the uptake."

They finished up chores just before ten and reconvened near the airstrip to wait for a new guy named Cavanaugh to return with their daily allotment of water. Though replacements for casualties or marines ending tours of duty arrived daily, there never seemed to be enough to keep pace with losses. The stuttering rumbles of the first enemy salvo of the morning left David feeling gratified he had taken time the day before to instruct Cavanaugh on the fine art of muzzle blasts. New guys didn't know shit about muzzle blasts, had no clue that their loudness and clarity were determined by the angle of the gun barrel in relation to the target. David could discern the type of weapon being fired and the time to impact by the sound of its discharge: 152mm artillery had a distinctive pop and a range of ten miles; 122mm rockets had a reedy echo and the same ten-mile range; 82mm mortars made a loud "chonk" and had only a two-mile range. And a 61mm mortar gave a hushed "tong," with a range so short the enemy mortar squad that fired it was usually within visual contact. He could even tell where on the base enemy incoming was going to land—and take cover accordingly. "A keen sense of hearing is essential to surviving Khe Sanh," he preached to Cavanaugh.

Cavanaugh appeared to have been a quick learner. He plunked down the two five-gallon jerry cans of water and cocked his ear to the sound of the barrage. Once satisfied that the shells were going to either fall short or pass overhead, he resumed his trek back toward the eastern perimeter.

David nearly leapt out of his skin and waved his arms. "Get away from the generator!"

Cavanaugh nodded and kept walking, his shoulders sagging from the weight of the filled jerry cans. David jumped up and down and yelled, but it was pointless. Cavanaugh couldn't hear him above the rattling hum of the generator. He couldn't hear *anything*, not even incoming.

He cursed himself for not having warned Cavanaugh to steer clear of Khe Sanh's diesel-powered generators and took off at a dead run. Another plosive burst of artillery sent a chill up his spine. The muzzle blast was clear and distinct. It had Cavanaugh's name on it. He ran as close as he dared, motioning for Cavanaugh to hit the deck and shouting at the top of his lungs, "Get down! Get down!"

Cavanaugh finally grasped his warning and threw down the jerry cans to run for cover. David crouched behind a pile of debris and looked on as the shell exploded with a tremendous bang. It blew a huge crater in the ground and sent shards of metal corkscrewing in every direction. A piece of shrapnel the size of a Frisbee sliced into the still-upright Cavanaugh's throat; it lifted him off the ground and pitched him on his back with blood spewing five feet into the air. He was gone by the time David reached him, his head clinging to his shoulders by a few cords of frayed tissue, on his face a gruesome rictus.

David paced back and forth in front of Cavanaugh's lifeless body, arms thrown up in the air, the same phrase tumbling out over and over.

"Fucking new guy!"

•   •   •

Daybreak, February 4, found David, Beau, and Colucci on Hill 861 Alpha. They arrived the day before, by CH-46 helicopter, part of a small unit sent from the combat base to reinforce two hundred marines from Echo Company. Captain Earle Breeding deployed their late-arriving group as a reserve force in support of Echo's northwest perimeter, marked by a token tangle of concertina wire strung with C-rat cans. Echo had only recently occupied 861A—critical to the defense of Hill 861, in turn critical to defending the combat base itself—so most of their efforts had gone into digging trench lines.

It was a dawn unlike any David had ever witnessed, a gift from the goddess Aurora he would never forget. A shock of light fell out of the eastern sky and bathed the matinal mist swirling around him in soft opalescence, with nary a sound to distract from the splendor. And across the Rao Quan, a pair of green spires rose out of the shimmering vapors like steeples at Valhalla, twin peaks as yet unmarred by human destruction. The only blight on the godly tableau lay to the southeast, where the ugly plateau of the combat base sat like a festering scab.

He spent the day burrowing into 861 Alpha's rich red umber; by nightfall he was tied into Echo's existing trench works, with Beau and Colucci dug in beside him. He fell asleep exhausted but satisfied, his twelve hours of shoveling having constructed a trench that would withstand at least an indirect hit, if not a direct one.

They were awakened just past midnight and told that NVA sappers were jangling their C-rat cans at the perimeter. Moments later, explosions from Bangalore torpedoes used to blow gaps in their wire rocked the night. A burst of mortar banged all around, pinning David in his trench. AK-47 fire and RPG rounds, too, the sounds of men screaming and shouting. Flares popped and fire support from the surrounding marine hill outposts bracketed 861A's northern slope, a thunderous suppressing barrage, churning the earth to within a few hundred yards of their perimeter.

Breeding ordered their reserve force to the front. David scrambled out of his fighting hole, running low and hard. Illumination rounds flashed off heavy fog, visibility five feet one moment, thirty the next. They crossed over a patchwork of bomb craters and split into two groups. One formed a line of defense around a 60mm mortar crew, the other continued to the perimeter. He arrived at the front beneath the strobe of flares to find NVA marauding through their trenches, some wearing marine helmets and laughing. One of them flipped a grenade inside a bunker and celebrated after it exploded. David squeezed off a burst from his M-16 and dropped him beside the wrecked bunker.

He jumped into the trench and moved down the line in fits and starts, getting small and hugging the bottom, then popping up and taking out anything in his way. Soon he came on a marine fire team attempting to extract some wounded back to Echo's aid station. He loaded a fresh magazine and provided cover while they dragged a pair of fallen marines up the hill and returned for more. During the second extraction, he began taking AK-47 fire, bullets pounding the dirt beside him. He crabbed back the other way to avoid being cut off. Two NVA appeared at the lip of the trench in front of him. He swung his gun to his shoulder, but they raised theirs first.

A burst of M-16 fire ripped into them and toppled them into the trench. Beau appeared with pointed gun. David's legs went wobbly. He reached for the side of the trench to steady himself, staggered by the narrowness of his escape—and a sudden burden of eternal indebtedness.

Beau grabbed him by the arm and pulled. "You crazy-ass Yank! Fall back to the gun pit. We're gettin' overrun!"

He hauled himself out of the trench and double-timed it to the gun pit with Beau and linked up with what remained of Echo's shattered line.

NVA streamed over the trenches behind them. The gun crew leveled its mortar tube and blasted away, their own shrapnel hissing in their faces. David chucked grenades until his shoulder ached, one after the other, *kaboom, kaboom, kaboom* into the bomb crater in front of him. They held on, hurling grenades and firing 60mm mortar on the horizontal, emptying magazine after magazine, turning back an assault they had no business turning back. Finally, after a blood-soaked eternity, Breeding reinforced their position and the battle slowly turned.

They readied a counterattack just before dawn. David crouched with the others, awaiting the order to go. When it came, a chilling sound from right beside him carried up and down the line: *Woe—hoo—ee! Hoo-ee! Hoo-ee! Woe—hoo—ee!* Beau, giving the Rebel Yell. Others picked it up, David too, halting at first, then full-throated and furious, a fulsome cry that would have unnerved Genghis Khan himself.

He charged down the hill, exhilarated, transported, every synapse firing. They tore into the bewildered NVA with rifle butts and knuckles, a face-splitting, throat-grabbing melee. *Woe—hoo— ee!* The NVA retreated, leaving scores of dead heaped in trenches or tangled in Echo's wire. At first light, whole squadrons of F-4 Phantoms roared overhead in search of stragglers.

David paused to look around, aware of the significance of what they had done—holding critical high ground—but uncertain how to acknowledge it. He thought of the day he first heard Kyle Levy speak against the war. This time, he knew, he would not sing alone. His sweet voice rang out over the bloody slope, strong and sure. It spread quickly, hundreds of them singing "The Marines' Hymn," right through to its final verse.

> *If the Army and the Navy*
> *Ever look on Heaven's scenes,*
> *They will find the streets are guarded*
> *By United States Marines.*

It reverberated down every hollow and up every peak, a unified, masculine voice that would not yield, would not succumb, would not be another Dien Bien Phu.

·   ·   ·

A CH-46 ferried in two squads of fresh reinforcements and flew David's weary detachment back to the combat base. After grabbing a couple of hours of sleep, he met up with Beau and Colucci near Beau's foxhole. The sky had gone surly gray, as if contemplating whether to dump another monsoon rain on them, the kind of smothering deluge that made it seem like the very air they breathed had turned to water.

Colucci stood flat-footed in the middle of the trench, hirsute, scowling, the front of his torn and dusty flak jacket gapped open. Beau slouched against the back wall smoking a Lucky Strike, glabrous and gaunt, his baggy, red-stained utilities appearing capable of walking down the line without him. As if David's, reeking of diesel and sweat, were any better.

Colucci broke out laughing after David hopped into the trench beside them. "You gonna wear them fuckin' things?" he asked, pointing. "They look like diapers."

David hitched up the bulky green nylon trunks he had pulled on over his utilities and shrugged. Marines at Khe Sanh had suffered so many below-waist shrapnel injuries that Colonel Lownds had insisted on passing out flak pants—padded trunks that fit over their trousers and looked like, well, diapers. But who gave a shit, considering what they were protecting?

"I'll remember that, Colucci, when you're in Charlie Med getting shrapnel picked out of your nuts."

Beau flicked ash from his cigarette. "Hell, Rock likes them corpsmen fiddlin' with his balls, don't ya Rock!"

Anyone else would have been eating red clay after a crack like that, but not Beau. Everyone liked him—even Colucci. Beau had a soothing sang-froid about him during firefights that kept everyone else's ass from puckering. Military savoir-faire seemed bred into him, a fundamental trait of his southern heritage, David supposed.

Colucci glared. "If lettin' somebody pluck my balls with a tweezers would get me outta this fucked-up war, it might be worth it. We fight by Marquess of Queensberry rules, give back what ground we take, and put a bombing pause in effect whenever the commies start to squeal.

"And if that ain't screwed up enough," he continued, like a New Yorker carping about City Hall, "they tell us the reason we're here is so South Vietnam can be free. What kinda bullshit is that? If I'm gonna risk gettin' my nuts shot off in some Asian jungle, it better be over keepin' *America* free—not a buncha ungrateful gooks."

Beau took a drag off the remains of his cigarette and ground it into the trench beneath the heel of his boot. "We *are* fightin' for somethin' worth dyin' over," he said, "but LBJ ain't talkin' about it. We're fightin' for honor, reputation, our good name: what other nations think of us. These things matter greatly, to people *and* to countries."

Colucci backhanded him on the arm. "What the fuck are you, Aristotle or somethin'? Countries fight wars for lots of reasons, but honor ain't one of 'em. Take your hero Lee, for instance. What honor was there in fightin' for slavery?"

"That's not why Lee fought," Beau replied, intense as a grad student defending a thesis. "He never liked slavery. He fought on behalf of Virginia, to defend the honor of his native state. Same reason I'm fightin'—to defend the honor of my country. At least that's what I thought when I enlisted. Halfway through Parris Island, though, I realized what I *really* joined up for was the respect and approval of the men around me. It ain't love of country that makes men die for one another—it's the willingness of men to die for one another that makes for love of country. *That's* what honor is."

Something stirred in David, an ineluctable truth laid bare by a southern philosopher with a twelfth-grade education and parents named Woodfin and Annabelle. Human beings craved affirmation, acclaim, the endorsement of peers—the kind of personal validation a serial foster child might find elusive. Where better to seek it than this defiant aerie of Khe Sanh?

"Beau's right," he said. "When we counterattacked down that hill, I didn't care whether I lived or died, only about the man next to me, about not letting him down. The rush and glory of it was intoxicating."

He left out how good his rifle had felt in his hands when he split open the face of a flat-nosed young gook, like cracking a bases-loaded triple with a Louisville Slugger, the thrill in your palms when the ball leaps off the fat of the bat.

Beau fired up another Lucky Strike and nodded. "Ol' Marse Robert said this: 'It is a good thing war is so terrible, otherwise we should grow to love it too much.'"

Colucci rolled his eyes and groaned. "Oh, Christ, I can't *take* no more'a this. You sound like one of them Baptist ministers, right before they slip a hand in your pocket and take out a month's pay." He trudged back to his fighting hole, shaking his head and mumbling as he went.

David laughed and turned to Beau. He wanted to thank him for saving his life, tell him he loved him like a brother. Instead he took him by the elbow. "The next time you write home, you tell your parents you've got a blue-bellied devil from the First Minnesota watching out for you."

Beau grinned, ear-to-ear freckles, Huck Finn in fatigues. "I will, David. I surely will. And judgin' by the way you tore into Luke the Gook this mornin', I'm gonna be damn near invulnerable."

That evening, before the sun winked goodnight over the Laotian mountains, David sat on an empty ammo box in his foxhole and wrote to Jackie. His letters lately had skipped the use of endearing salutations, so as to avoid making his longing for her worse—pussy fever still, after all this time.

> *This letter is about one of my platoon mates, a redhead from Atlanta. He's exactly what you'd expect a southerner to be like—and not at all what you'd expect one to be like. His name is Linton Beauregarde, and yesterday he saved my life . . .*

CHAPTER NINE

David hunkered down as the siege wore on. The NVA overran the Army Special Forces Camp at Lang Vei along Route 9, bringing them to within two thousand yards of Khe Sanh's western gate, while B-52 Arc Light strikes and napalm blasts that erupted into fiery popcorn balls—barbecues, Colucci called them—struck ridge after ridge in retaliation. The idyllic piedmont around Khe Sanh slowly transformed into a savage, cratered landscape, with huge swaths of lush highland jungle completely denuded. And the combat base resembled a deserted Martian plain, red and desolate, all life driven underground.

The daily grind began to wear on him. The nights were chilly and the days foggy and rainy, their sunless gloom adding to the dysphoria of sleep deprivation. He dozed when he could, but, due to the relentless incoming, never for long. And to make matters worse, fire support bases at Camp Carroll and the Rockpile routinely exploded star shells over their perimeter, to light things up and reveal enemy formations that might be massing for an attack on their wire.

He lived like a burrowing animal, caked with red clay and blood and smelling of sweat and diesel. He ate the same skimpy C-rats three times a day, with barely enough water to wash them down, and hadn't showered in a month. To move about, he slunk

from trench to trench as they all did, half-crouched, head up, eyes
roving for cover, ears attuned for that one perfectly registered
round that would splatter him like a dropped goblet of wine. Word
of their unique peripatetic style even got around to marines at
other bases; they named it the Khe Sanh Shuffle, as if it were a popular dance.

Weighing on him, too, was the steady attrition going on
around him, each morning a few more either dead or whisked away
by medevac to treat injuries suffered in the preceding night's bombardment. Fully half the men in his platoon when he arrived were
gone, replaced by new guys bearing newspapers and magazines
from home. He was surprised to learn from them that Khe Sanh
had become a media sensation, the lead segment on the nightly
news. Letters from home—never for David, of course; at mail call
he got bupkis—had also begun to mention the nation's growing
preoccupation with Khe Sanh.

Colucci's mother wrote that President Johnson had referred
to them during a speech in California as "... that little brave band
of defenders who hold the pass at Khe Sanh ..." A CBS film crew
had even shown up and prowled around, taking shots of the
charred carcass of a C-130 transport hit by rocket fire while
attempting to land.

With rare exceptions, the newspaper and magazine articles he
read seemed to have been written from a common template: they
drew parallels to Dien Bien Phu; mentioned the Khe Sanh Shuffle;
referred to NVA Commander-in-Chief Giap as a "brilliant strate-
gist"; and concluded that the cut-off, starving marines at Khe Sanh,
outnumbered six to one, were on the verge of a catastrophic defeat.

David didn't see it that way, not even after February 23, when
the NVA fired off an estimated 1,300 rounds of mortar, artillery,
and rocket fire, their heaviest bombardment yet. It went on all day
and all night, his fighting hole rocking and pitching like San
Francisco in '06. He got no sleep, was too skittish to eat, and was

practically buried alive when an 82mm mortar caved in the front of his trench and blasted a huge plug of dirt down the passageway of his fighting hole.

But after digging out the next morning, during the usual lull in shelling due to the *crachin,* he and Beau and Colucci marched over to one of Bravo Company's mortar pits and etched Fuck You onto the 81mm shells the gun crew would be firing that day. To make sure the gooks read their little love notes, they wrote on the shells' tail fins; the tail fins of mortar rounds almost never exploded. Later on, as the mist and fog began to dissipate, the three of them formed up outside their trench and thrust their fists in the air with middle fingers extended, so that the first thing enemy forward observers would see the morning after laying a horrific bombardment on the base was three marines flipping them off.

They held their pose and yelled epithets—"Ho Chi Minh fucks sheep!"—right up to the last possible moment before diving into their trench with the first rounds of the day whistling overhead, laughing, so broke up they couldn't talk, weeks of stoic suffering and deprivation upchucked in a spasm of manic laughter. Until there was nothing more to expel, geysers of fear and frustration spewed empty.

They manned their posts until a break in the shelling came, the NVA gunners needing to take a leak or eat a bowl of their wormy rice. David wandered over to Colucci's fighting hole with Beau behind him. Colocci lay on his back in the middle of the trench, staring at the gunmetal sky above, his flak jacket open. Small clods of red clay clung to his bloom of chest hair like berries on a bush.

They sat down beside him and poked at the rich red soil, saying nothing, their earlier mirth replaced by a creeping wistfulness. Beau sighed. David shook his head. Only Colucci seemed able to give voice to it.

"I wanna go to a game at Yankee Stadium again," he said, still looking up at the sky. "Smell the peanuts and Cracker Jack and hear

Bob Sheppard on the PA: 'Now batting for the Yankees, the center fielder, Number 7, Mickey Mantle, Number 7.' That's how he always does it, says their numbers twice. Been doin' it like that for sixteen years, every time, exactly the same way.

"And I wanna sink my teeth into a ballpark hot dog, the relish and mustard all mixed together, smeared on my chin, vendors all around me shouting, 'Cole beer, here! Cole beer!' I wanna hear the crack of the bat and see the ball arcing toward the fence, wondering if it's gonna make it out. I want that to be all I worry about, a ball makin' it over a fence."

He sat up and looked from David to Beau with a plaintive face, like a foundling in search of his mother. "I just wanna see the Yankees again."

Beau grinned, comprehending completely. "I can jus' see you, Rock, Yankees hat on, wipin' the foam from your face after takin' a long pull off a cold one. Tha's great, man, tha's just great."

David nodded his acknowledgment of the truth Colucci had articulated, the yearning deep inside every marine, up and down the line, to do the one thing—besides getting laid—thirteen months in 'Nam made them want to do—a different thing for each of them, to be sure, yet not really different at all.

He gave Colucci an affectionate sock to the shoulder and volunteered his own secret longing. "I want to walk across campus when the mall is deserted and it begins to snow—plump, beautiful snowflakes floating down from the sky, silent and cool and white. That's what I want, the kiss of a snowflake on my cheek."

"Nice," Colucci said, tugging his thick, black moustache. "Very nice." He turned to Beau. "How 'bout you? What do you wanna do when you make it back?"

Beau lifted the brim of his helmet off his face and gave a dreamy smile. "I wanna shoot the Hooch on a hot summer day."

David looked at Colucci, who wore the same baffled expression he did. "You want to down shots of moonshine?" he asked Beau.

Beau laughed and shook his head. "Shootin' the Hooch means goin' inner tubin' down the Chattahoochee River. We start off north of Atlanta, not far from where I live, and float down the river in inner tubes. Powder blue sky, greenish tint to the water, oak and chestnut branches hangin' over the river, smell of honeysuckle in the air—so gorgeous and peaceful. But with a purpose to it. A righteous purpose. There's even a poem about it, a famous poem, *The Song of the Chattahoochee*, by Sidney Lanier. Not that you two ignorant Yanks probably ever heard of it. Damn inferior northern schools; don't teach nothin' bout the South 'cept slavery."

He was right, David had never heard of the poem, and neither had Colucci, judging by the blank look on his face. Beau stared off into the distance into triple canopy jungle, his freckled face pensive and soft. He spoke in a low, lyrical voice.

> *Out of the hills of Habersham,*
> *Down the valleys of Hall,*
> *I hurry amain to reach the plain,*
> *Run the rapid and leap the fall,*
> *Split at the rock and together again,*
> *Accept my bed, or narrow or wide,*
> *And flee from folly on every side*
> *With a lover's pain to attain the plain*
> *Far from the hills of Habersham,*
> *Far from the valleys of Hall.*

He came out of his trance and directed his gaze to David. "There's more, but I only memorized the first stanza."

It was a loving paean to the natural wonder of the river—David could almost hear the trill and chirr of the forest, the sough of the wind through its branches. "It's beautiful," he said. "But what do you mean it has a *righteous* purpose? How can a river be righteous?"

"'Cause it's fulfilling its duty to Nature, bringing sustenance and energy and beauty to the land it runs through. That's its purpose. Its duty. Just like this is our purpose. Our duty. To *our* land."

The distant pop of artillery, followed by the whiz of incoming shells, ended their session, but later that day, David used his K-Bar knife to etch an inscription onto his canteen. It was an inscription that had begun to show up on canteens all over the base—including that of Beau, whom he suspected of originating the phrase, though Beau denied it.

"For those who fight for it, life has a special flavor the protected never know."

* * *

A few days earlier, at Bravo's weekly briefing, David had learned from Captain Pipes that an aerial observer (AO) had spotted parallel approach trenches furrowing towards Khe Sanh's eastern and southern borders. According to the AO, the southwestern trench ran along 680, the access road coming up from the old French coffee plantation; the southeastern diggings tracked north from Route 9 before fanning out to the eastern end of the airstrip.

"I welcome those enemy trenches," Pipes said. "For nine hundred thousand reasons I welcome them."

"Sir?" David asked.

"Each B-52 winging here from Anderson Air Force Base carries eighty-four 500-pound bombs and twenty-four 750-pounders," Pipes explained. "They attack in cells of three, five cells deep. That's nine hundred thousand pounds of weaponry per Arc Light. And now, thanks to those trenches, we know exactly where to unload it. Hello-o-o-o Charlie."

He reached into the upper left-hand pocket of his utility jacket and removed a wrinkled page of paper. "This is a copy of a translation from a diary of an NVA soldier captured by one of our hill outposts. If this is what Charlie's life is like already," he said, waving the page in the air, "you can imagine what it will be like now that we have his address." He read it to them.

> I joined the army to liberate my brothers in the South from oppression. I expected them to rise up to greet us, but they have not. The war here is nothing like I imagined. Half the men in my battalion have died from American air raids or malaria. Our rice and salt are gone. We live on taro leaves and manioc. Dissension is like dysentery: it spreads quickly. Three hundred soldiers from Group 926 deserted last week after a B-52 strike that made our livers ache. The political cadres tell us the Americans are weak, that they take drugs and listen to subversive music and have no will to fight. The cadres lie. The Americans are killing us, and I fear we will all die in this cruel, desolate place.

If reading some gook's diary was a stunt to boost their morale, it worked. David was glad to hear that the NVA were suffering and dying; so was his side. Now if only they could lay their hands on some of that subversive music and drugs.

Pipes went on to say that captured diaries weren't the only intelligence coups they had scored lately; top-secret technology had given them another. "Ghetto blasters," he said, smiling. "Boom boxes. Night before last, some of the boys in the combat operations center picked up something a little different than the Armed Forces Radio Service (AFRS) they usually listen to—the NVA fire-direction network. They had a *Chieu Hoi* interpret for them. It's the real deal. Anybody with a Panasonic can hear NVA gun instructions whenever they please."

His face turned hard as tempered steel. "The next time their gun batteries prepare to fire, Colonel Lownds is going to call an Arc Light on them. We'll call it Operation Panasonic," he said with a wink. "Make 'em holler while we listen in."

. . .

At 0800 on February 25, David, Beau, and Colucci lined up on Khe Sanh's southern perimeter, part of two reinforced squads tasked with hunting down an enemy 82mm mortar that had caused disproportionate damage to Bravo Company's ranks with its uncanny shooting. Their forty-seven-man patrol was under the command of Second Lieutenant Donald Jacques, a fair, slender man in his mid-twenties.

David fell into formation so weighted down with ammo he felt like a pack mule. Bullet-laden bandoleers crisscrossed his chest, twenty-round magazines jammed his cartridge belt, and a nylon pouch slung over his shoulder bulged with grenades.

Despite the usual mist, visibility was better than usual. They departed through a lane in their concertina wire and proceeded to the garbage dump south of the base, where they discovered an NVA approach trench, about three feet wide and a foot deep. They followed it west across a narrow stream and up the face of a tree-lined ridge. A fire team consisting of David, Beau, Colucci, and a raw-boned Texan named Willard descended the southern slope of the ridge and led the rest of the patrol to a dirt road slanting southeast, toward the old French coffee plantation.

Three NVA soldiers appeared a few hundred yards down the road, as if conjured out of the morning vapor. They stared at the marine patrol like deer fixed by high beams before bolting across the road unscathed. David's fire team gave chase, trailed closely by the rest of the patrol, all of them eager to make someone pay for the month-long pounding they had endured. David crashed through a wall of bushes lining the road, traversed another trench line, and burst into an open rice paddy. The other three joined him and fanned out, with Willard walking point.

The rest of the patrol entered the rice paddy behind them. AK-47 fire erupted from all sides. Willard spun and went down, pitching his rifle into the air like a drum major tossing a baton. David hit the ground and returned fire. Chicom grenades exploded. Men screamed. He worked his way back to the trench line and rolled into it along with Beau and Colucci and the rest of the patrol.

At first they were able to suppress the enfilade engulfing them, but the *bup-bup-bup* of a machine gun somewhere to their right drove a swarm of bullets into them. Men fell in clusters, cut down in a classic, U-shaped ambuscade. David flung two grenades at the yakking machine gun while what was left of their patrol maneuvered back toward the dirt road.

Lieutenant Jacques stood tall, shouting orders and directing fire. He radioed the base for artillery support, then organized David, Beau, Colucci and a few others into a rear guard to cover the patrol's retreat. They dragged or carried their injured but left their dead where they fell, in violation of their most hallowed credo. Their abandonment left David appalled, but it was a wrong he had no way of putting right. They were in danger of being slaughtered to the last man.

Mortar fire from the base began dropping in, bracketing the kill zone they had been lured into. A tank from the Rock Quarry blasted away in support, too, gouging holes and spewing dirt into the air. An enemy weapons cache ignited somewhere in the hidden NVA trench works, shaking the ground beneath David's feet. The ensuing shockwave nearly burst his eardrums. The barrage from the combat base temporarily diminished the ferocity of the ambush and facilitated their retreat, but when they reached the garbage dump road, they began taking fire again. Jacques ran from man to man, telling them that a relief force from First Platoon was pinned down and couldn't get to them.

"Get back any way you can!" he shouted. He directed them to a tree line on the ridge, windmilling his arm like a third base coach sending the tying run home, but an eruption of machine gun fire put him on his back, a crimson font pumping from each groin.

David started toward him, but Beau held him back. "He's wasted! Get to the ridge before we all die. They're all over us!"

He took off for the tree line with Beau at his heels, ducking and covering his way to a thicket at the base of the ridge. He dove into it with small arms fire whistling all around him, kicking up dirt and snapping off branches.

"I'm hit! I'm hit!" Beau cried out behind him.

David wriggled over to him. A round had caught him flush in the face, entering his right eye and exiting the side of his head. He withdrew a dressing from the first aid kit strapped to his back and clamped it over the socket where Beau's eye had been. Beau clawed the air with his right hand and kicked the ground with his right leg. His left side lay still as stone.

"They shot me in the eye! Oh, Gawd, the gook bastards shot me in the eye!"

David pressed his face close to Beau's and nearly gagged at the warm, biotic smell of the ichor seeping from his wound. "Listen to me! I'll get you out of here, even if I have to drag you every inch of the way."

Beau's good hand clenched a fistful of David's utility jacket. "No! I'm zapped and you know it. Gimme my weapon and git outta here!"

"I'm not going anywhere." David got to his feet and slipped his hands beneath Beau's shoulder blades and into his armpits to haul him away, but a burst of AK-47 fire drove him back on his belly.

"Let him go! He'll never make it!" It was Colucci, grabbing him by the collar, tugging him toward the ridgeline. "He would want you to live. Come on!"

Beau moaned, incoherent, so pale now. Before David left, before he surrendered to his craven instinct of self-preservation, he withdrew Beau's .45 from his holster and placed it in his right hand. He then lifted his paralyzed left hand off the ground and set it on his stomach. As he did, his eyes were drawn to the engraving on Beau's bracelet.

Too bad, oh, too bad!

.   .   .

It would take three hours of crawling on their bellies through heavy vegetation to make it back to base. Colucci—helmet missing, forehead cut and bleeding, his face set in a New York snarl—had to coax him forward every inch of the way, talk him out of going back at every turn. Once he even tackled him and pinned him to the ground after David had taken to his feet and started back the other way, crashing through bushes like an enraged bear.

His guilt consumed him, made him delirious. "Too bad, oh, too bad!" What did it mean? That it was too bad Beau had died? Or that it was too bad David had abandoned him? And in either case, how had his fey bracelet known? It was shameful enough that he had left a fellow marine behind, but to leave behind a fellow marine who had saved his life, whose life he had pledged to watch over in return . . . He felt like a snake, slithering away from all that was warm and human, a cold-blooded serpent with no regard for anything but itself.

He couldn't stop thinking about Beau, his eye streaming down his cheek, the stench of it rising off his disfigured face, the agony in his voice: My God, my God! Why hast thou forsaken me? But it was not God who had forsaken him. It was his pal David, his Yankee buddy, the big talker who squirmed away to save himself like Peter denying Jesus before the cock crowed. He had left his friend to die alone, with a pistol poised to put a bullet in his brain; no way Linton Beauregarde would ever be taken alive.

For Beau was a man, in all his fearless glory, come round to the sharp side of life, the cutting side, no room for wiggle, no margin for error, where blade met flesh and women cried and dying soldiers looked to the sky and gasped in wonder. Beau was the stuff they loved once, in Greece and Rome—and antebellum Atlanta, where dogwoods bloomed and women curtsied and gallant men wore long swords.

How many marines before him had died on unkind soil such as this? How many thousands had Wilson and Roosevelt and Truman and now Johnson sent into battle, never to return? But never in vain. Not once in vain, since that first marine flag had flown, the one with the yellow background and Don't Tread On Me stenciled beneath the coiled rattlesnake. "A rattlesnake never sur-renders," Westbrook had told them, while explaining the flag's sym-bolism. "And neither do marines."

By the time he and Colucci crept back through their wire, stag-gered and bloodied and out of their minds with grief, it was Lyndon Johnson's troubled face that squatted in David's mind. For it was Johnson who would determine whether Beau had died in vain or not; Johnson who would decide if Beau's death mattered; Johnson, a commander-in-chief more conflicted by the day, send-ing waves of B-52s to punish Hanoi one moment, and envoys to beseech her the next.

Before entering the safety of the base, he paused at Khe Sanh's western gate and faced east, toward America.

"Turn us loose!" he yelled, shaking his fist like a madman. "Turn us loose, goddamn you!"

CHAPTER TEN

As if the month hadn't been long enough, with the *crachin* limiting their air assault to just five clear days, 1968 was a leap year—one extra day for David to survive. NVA approach trenches that last day of February had crept to within four hundred yards of Bravo's perimeter. Just past nightfall, his reconstituted platoon, a mélange of new guys and war-weary short-timers, mustered north of the airstrip for report. The base was being put on high alert, a blond lieutenant with tragic eyes and a Nordic face told them.

"Charlie's approach trenches have been completed," he said, "and tonight he intends to use them. Intel says a regiment-sized assault force has crossed the Laotian border and is moving up Route 9. They expect a massive ground attack. They've got numbers on us, but we're gonna fight like hell. We're going to hit their assembly areas along Route 9 into Khe Sanh Village, and on the access road coming up to the base south of the garbage dump." Even their new guys knew the garbage dump road was where Bravo Company's Ghost Patrol—so named because twenty-six of them never returned—had been ambushed four days earlier.

All available weaponry, the lieutenant told them—175mm guns at Camp Carroll and the Rock Pile; Khe Sanh's 155mm and 105mm artillery and 4.2-inch mortar; and A-6 intruders dropping five-hundred-pound bombs—would be simultaneously brought to bear on the enemy's approach routes. "They're coming at us in numbers, but if we can break up tonight's attack, momentum will swing our way."

The ground shook as a thunderous explosion and brilliant flash of light to the west signaled the start of the air attack.

"That's just a taste of the hell we intend to visit on them tonight," he said. "But in case they overrun our perimeter, here's the contingency plan. Every man still able to fight is to lie face down in the trenches as if dead. Let the momentum of their attack take them deep inside the base. Wait for the high sign; then rise up and attack the enemy from behind. Kill every last one of 'em. God willing, I'll see you all at dawn."

David returned to his foxhole less than inspired by the back-up plan. It sounded desperate, too far-fetched to succeed. He readied his ammo clips, placed his hand grenades in neat rows on top of an ammo box in the front of his trench, and waited in the still highland night for things to begin, his fighting hole as dark and somber as a confessional.

It had been four days since Beau died, and he had yet to get over it. He barely ate and snapped at everyone—except Colucci, whom he'd grown closer to. No one else understood how bad it had been, how exposed they were out there. He couldn't stop thinking about Beau, the intolerable propinquity of his rotting, unclaimed corpse and still-lingering soul. Out there, just beyond their wire, in plain view.

"Too bad, oh, too bad!" An inscription Beau had never once mentioned on an amulet that had failed, that left his bones bleaching in an Asian jungle instead of keeping him safe. "Too bad, oh, too bad!" David didn't give a shit if the gooks did attack. He wanted them to. He'd take a dozen with him and wouldn't have to be alive when Beau was dead. He didn't deserve to be alive. Beau had saved *his* life, not the other way around. Colucci was right. In 'Nam, no good deed went unpunished.

The thunder of Khe Sanh's guns put an end to his grieving. The base cut loose with everything it had: four deuces; 155s; 105s, too, Ban Shee banging away for all she was worth, belching and heaving her big shells nonstop.

An inappropriate peal of laughter filtered through the din, marines cackling all along the line, like at a Bob Hope show. It was infectious, a contagious mania rolling through their ranks. David laughed along with them, though there was nothing risible about a regiment of gooks hiking over from Laos to kill them all.

"What's so funny?" he called out to Colucci, who had moved into the foxhole vacated by Beau.

"They never told us what the high sign was!" Colucci shouted back between belly laughs.

• • •

A volley of automatic weapons fire erupted along the perimeter at 2130, in the vicinity of the 37th ARVN Rangers. F-4s screamed overhead, fast-movers dropping ordnance as close as they dared. David tensed and flipped the selector switch on his M-16 to full automatic, but nothing came his way. The fighting near the Rangers went on for some time before slackening. Word came down the line that the NVA had made it to their outer wire before being repulsed with heavy losses. Two hours later they tried the same spot again, with the same result. A third and final attempt came at 0315. This time it fell apart before even reaching their wire, cut to pieces by a wall of sustained fire from the ARVN trenches.

Though the base's air and artillery counterattack went on all night, dawn came without David having fired a shot. Banks of fog billowed up from the Rao Quan River as he went out on recon detail to examine the area that had been assaulted the night before. It was like walking through an open-air abattoir, bodies every-where, with swarms of huge green flies buzzing from corpse to

corpse like drunkards at a feast. Mangled NVA frozen in all manner of positions filled the shallow enemy approach trenches: some
crouched, as if ready to spring into action, others flat on their
backs, their skulls riddled by fléchette rounds. Many died clutching
wads of dynamite lashed to bamboo sticks, sappers with crude
Bangalore torpedoes they never came close to using.

David turned to the ARVN Rangers and pumped his fist. They
cheered and waved back, their hatred fully fungible with his.

•   •   •

March wore on like the month before and the month before
that. The quotidian sameness of it was suffocating: morning, noon,
and evening shelling; morning, noon, and evening C-rations.
David's skin turned the same color red as the clay he was burrowed
into, and the cold and damp tipped his ears with chilblains. He
shaved sporadically, no longer wore skivvies under his utility
pants—they had all rotted away and disintegrated—and hadn't
bathed in longer than he could remember. His thick thighs and
sturdy calves melted away, his once solid frame like that of a grey-
hound. Maybe he'd open a fat farm when he got home, get overweight housewives to drop thirty pounds by eating nothing but
C-rats—especially the ham and lima bean version marines called
"ham and motherfuckers."

He was sick of living in a hole and sick of the snipers that
picked them off one by one, never a day without someone dying,
and now Beau dead, too, and Colucci a short-timer, only a day to
go before his magic carpet ride back to the States. He was sick of
the monsoon rains that fell in pewter sheets, thrumming into
them like automatic weapons fire and leaving their foxholes ankle
deep in water, until the sky quit weeping long enough to bail out.
And David was holding up better than most. At least he had yet to
"accidentally" shoot himself in the foot, or take his boots off at

night and smear his toes with peanut butter to entice one of Khe
Sahn's millions of rats—the biggest, nastiest, most aggressive he'd
ever seen—into biting him so he could be medevaced out. And
Jackie—would her hard-hearted silence never end? Was she even
alive? Maybe she died in a car accident, or got cancer, or drowned
in one of the ten thousand lakes Minnesota's license plates bragged
about.

One thing *had* changed, though: the weather, and decisively so.
Where February had cloaked them in chalk-white obscurity, March
brought clear skies. Planes stacked so thick they were in danger of
running into one another circled the battlefield like sharks smelling
blood. The improved visibility enjoyed by their pilots so increased
their effectiveness that the NVA's grip on Khe Sanh finally began to
loosen. Intel reported that elements of the 304th Division had
pulled back to the southwest, and elements of the 325C Division
had retreated toward Laos. With the siege weakening, limited patrols of the fecund valleys around the base had even resumed.

On March 17, David's squad went outside the wire for the first
time since the ambush of the Ghost Patrol, one of three fire teams
led by Sergeant Henry Wilcox, a long-faced West Virginian with
cold gray eyes and an eczematous complexion. They struck out
east of the base with the morning fog beginning to break up and
headed down a ravine that led to the Rao Quan Valley, where they
were to probe along the river to determine the extent of the NVA
withdrawal.

After winding down a steep, wooded trail, they reached the
river bed by noon. The southeasterly flowing Rao Quan—in summer a glorified stream, but in monsoon season a swift, swollen
river—was greenish-taupe in color and thirty yards across. Thick
cover hugged either bank. They had just begun to work their way
north when the screeching whine of an enemy rocket passed overhead. Except it wasn't a rocket. It was a jet engine, whose sound
signature was similar to a rocket's, but that included a faint basso

profundo as well. David spotted an F-4 banking their way. Puffs of anti-aircraft fire from the Badlands across the river dotted the sky.

Something was wrong. The plane was flying too low. Its engines stuttered and then it yawed crazily and burst into flames. First one and then a second parachute appeared, the pilot and radio intercept officer having blown their canopies and jettisoned out of the flaming aircraft. The first chute drifted south of their patrol and touched down short of the river. The second, with an aviator strapped to an ejection seat dangling in plain view, floated right over them before disappearing into a small valley on the other side of the Rao Quan. The abandoned plane rolled on its back and nose-dived out of sight toward Hill 1015. An explosion sounded a moment later.

Wilcox raised the base on the radio and gave the downed pilots' approximate locations. Soon a column of smoke wafted up south of their patrol, like when a new pope is named. It drew a low-flying chopper from the base, its blades glinting and beating a steady flap-flap-flap into the air. A second chopper began scouring the other side of the Rao Quan, but with no telltale smoke to guide it, the airman either dead or too badly injured to pop his distress canister, it cruised back and forth in vain over the lush riparian landscape.

Wilcox appealed over the radio for permission to break off their recon mission to rescue the second pilot. "A chopper is useless where he went down," he argued. "Nowhere to land. We can be there in fifteen minutes." After some back and forth, he won authorization to go after the pilot. They were about to ford the river when the base came back on the radio and warned that the chopper had spotted a force of about thirty NVA a half-mile north of their position, heading their way along the opposite side of the Rao Quan. The chopper withdrew to base to avoid attracting an even larger enemy force while Wilcox cobbled together a plan to deal with the NVA patrol. It called for one of them to serve as a decoy.

David volunteered. "Only way a guy can get a bath around here," he said.

They dispersed according to plan. Two fire teams double-quicked downstream to lay an ambush. The third, led by Colucci, concealed itself along the Rao Quan's western bank, across the river from where the second parachute had gone down. With the rescue team in place, David shed his weapons and gear and waded into the river; he dove in headfirst when the water line reached his thighs. A shockwave of cold washed over him, momentarily turning his rib cage into a motionless bellows. He allowed the fast-moving current to scrub him free of his gamy smell before stroking across to the other side, where he crawled into the bushes to await Colucci's signal.

Wilcox's plan called for David to scramble into the river in plain sight of the approaching NVA patrol, as if he were the downed pilot attempting to make his way back to base. He was to then lure the NVA downriver, where two fire teams lay in wait to take them out. In the meantime, the remaining fire team would slip across the Rao Quan, retrieve the pilot, and return to base. The ruse presumed that the enemy patrol's desire to capture or kill one of the pilots who had bombed the crap out of them that morning with snake and nape would be strong enough to make them chase after David and blunder into the ambush. A Puff AC-47 gunship was available to clean up if things went sour.

It took about twenty minutes for the NVA to arrive in their vicinity. Colucci gave a clandestine wave as they came around the bend and turned inland to sweep the valley where the second parachute had gone down. David charged out of the bushes and splashed into the river fifty yards ahead of two NVA soldiers walking point.

"*Dúng lai!*" they yelled, shouldering their rifles. "*Dúng lai!*"

He corkscrewed into the water and dove toward the middle, where the current was strongest. He opened his eyes and let it take him. The turbid water made him feel secure, safe even. He surfaced long enough to risk a glimpse behind him. The NVA patrol was running along the bank, gaining on him, a hated pilot almost in their grasp. They spotted him and fired an AK burst that kicked up spray a foot in front of him. He dove under again. The water closed over him, eddies swirling every which way, their net force vectoring him forward, ever forward. He bobbed up and ducked back under two more times, luring them downriver the same way the Ghost Patrol had been lured down the garbage dump road that awful day. A half dozen of them closed the gap and barreled into the water after him. The remainder clustered at the bank and cheered.

A fusillade of automatic weapons fire resounded out over the water, David's signal to swim to the Rao Quan's west bank for all he was worth, the trap sprung. The frontal salvo of the fire team hidden on the east bank left every one of the NVA who had entered the water floating face down, the current taking them downriver. David reached shore as the fire team concealed along the west bank enfiladed the NVA gathered on the opposite side of the river. He scrambled over to their position and grabbed an M-16 and began firing as if it were a snapping in exercise at Edson Range.

They kept shooting until the base notified them that Colucci's fire team had located the pilot and gotten him back across the river to a safe LZ, at which point Wilcox broke off the engagement and led the rest of them back up the same trail they had taken that morning. A Puff came growling out of the sky with turrets blazing and tore what was left of the NVA patrol to pieces.

That night on base, the tale of what went down along the Rao Quan that afternoon grew more fantastic by the hour, but David drew little comfort from the praise. Come morning, Colucci would be on the first chopper out and David would be only a bullet away from dying more alone than when he arrived at Khe Sanh.

· · ·

Jackie Lundquist jerked to a stop in front of a newsstand on a slushy March afternoon, fresh from a war protest she had proudly helped organize. The latest edition of *Newsweek* reached out and grabbed her by the throat. "The Agony of Khe Sanh," it said on the front. The cover photo was of two marines cowering on the roof of a bunker in front of a spectacular explosion, a towering orange shell-burst that sent a whirlwind of molten debris high overhead. She passed a wrinkled dollar bill to a grizzled, half-blind old man behind the register and accepted, with an unsteady hand, two quarters in change. Ten minutes later, she stepped inside the potpourri-scented apartment she shared with Liz Bodine and yanked off her boots. She sat at the kitchen table without removing her coat or scarf and slid the magazine from her bag, her heart thumping in her chest.

Four pages of color photographs accompanied a lengthy cover story. Of the photo essay's many eidetic scenes—the firefights and explosions, the blood-red soil of the trenches, the far-off stares of begrimed, weary faces—there was one she could not take her eyes off. It was a shot of Khe Sanh's medical-evacuation staging area during a North Vietnamese artillery attack. In the foreground, a wounded marine swaddled in a brown woolen blanket lay supine on a stretcher on the ground. His right arm was splinted, and a glass IV bottle rested between his legs. A fellow marine in a combat helmet and flak jacket straddled him on all fours, protecting the injured soldier the way a she-wolf might a defenseless cub. The caption beneath the photo said, "Marine shields wounded comrade from enemy mortar barrage."

After considering the photo's tender heroism at some length, she cupped her face and sobbed, a violent keening that rattled her shoulders and seemed to emanate from her very womb. And she did something else, too, something her SDS brothers and sisters, she knew, would surely not abide.

She picked up pen and paper and wrote to her marine, careful to avoid staining the page with her tears.

• • •

At 0730 on March 30, all of Bravo Company—three rifle platoons and a weapons platoon—lined up at Khe Sanh's southwest
gate to conduct the marines' first offensive operation since the
siege began. David stamped his feet like a racehorse impatient to
run. He had his helmet strapped tight, his flak vest buttoned, and
his cartridge belt cinctured snug around his waist. A canteen of
water dangled from each hip.

Under the command of Captain Pipes, they were to attack
down the dirt access road known as 680 and assault the same
network of trenches that had ambushed the Ghost Patrol. The
offensive's primary objective: drive the NVA battalion occupying
the trenches away from the combat base and back toward Route 9.
A protective box of artillery support would walk them up to enemy
lines; air support targeting NVA staging areas to the rear would
prevent reinforcement.

Though David was the only one left in Bravo who had actually
been on the Ghost Patrol, he knew that the replacements around
him, many of whom had never been in so much as a firefight, were
as anxious as he was to avenge their predecessors. With thick banks
of fog swirling in front of them, they struck out across their wire
and advanced undetected to the access road. A rolling artillery barrage commenced at 0800. Five minutes later, Pipes gave the order
to fix bayonets. David had seldom used his bayonet in combat—"If
yer close enough to stick 'em, yer close enough to shoot 'em!"
Westbrook had preached—but this one time he yearned to.

They moved southeast down the dirt road and made it almost
to the first enemy trench line before the concealing wall of fog lifted
and betrayed their presence. Even though their artillery assault had
pulverized the trenches, they took immediate fire: RPGs, machine
guns, the constant pop of AKs. Bullets sang past David's head while
mortar rounds fired straight up out of their tubes began dropping
all around him.

His platoon attacked the NVA right flank, advancing bunker by bunker, aided by marine specialists using satchel charges to blast holes in enemy breastworks. He and his squad poured through one such breach and were able to envelop an entire trench full of NVA. David fired on full automatic until there was no one standing as far down the haze-locked trench as he could see. They moved down the line to consolidate their position, but ran smack-dab into an NVA relief force arriving from the opposite direction. The two groups closed on each other before either had time to fire.

David picked out a flat-nosed gook with a battle rictus on his face and drove his bayonet into the notch above the man's sternum, grinding through bone and gristle. The enemy soldier fell limp on his blade, pithed like a frog. He dislodged his bayonet from the man's neck like an irate angler shaking an unwanted bullhead off a hook, jerking him to and fro in a spray of red before dumping him lifeless on the ground.

They tore through the NVA relief force and out the other end of the trench, where they encountered a group of marines drawn up in a half circle, fending off twenty or thirty NVA. Several marines lay motionless on the ground. Captain Pipes stood over them, bareheaded, flak jacket off, blasting away with his .45. "We're here to claim our dead, you bastards!" he yelled. The left side of his chest was stained with blood. David's squad poured a murderous cross-fire into the fray and helped Pipes beat back the assault.

So it went for the next four hours, a close-quarters rumble with bayonets and knives and pistols and rifles. It ended when there were no more NVA left to brawl with.

David would later learn that Bravo Company destroyed an entire NVA battalion that day, killing 115 enemy soldiers—among them a battalion commander, whose futile plea for reinforcements had been heard on marine radios. He would also learn that early in the battle, a mortar round had exploded in the middle of Bravo's command group, killing their radioman and forward artillery observers, and embedding a piece of shrapnel inches from Kenneth

Pipes's heart. Pipes had responded by leading his crippled command group forward and personally directing fire support—actions for which he would win a Silver Star.

But before the triumphal body counts and tales of valor began, David and the rest of Bravo Company tended to their *real* objective—recovering the remains of the Ghost Patrol.

He found Beau right where he had left him, a pile of tawny bones vestured by a tattered uniform, the right side of his skull pierced and splintered. David longed to make him whole again, redivivus and new, but the starkness of Beau's paltry remains put a harsh end to such fantasy. He hung his head and wept before slipping Beau's bracelet off his withered radius and pocketing it—a keepsake Beau's family would surely have treasured, but that David needed even more. He then lovingly gathered his friend's remains into his haversack and rejoined his platoon.

Beau was going home.

* * *

David left Khe Sanh on April 15. The day before, marines attacking from Hill 881 South had raised the American flag on 881 North, where India Company first engaged the enemy. What had begun seventy-seven days before was finally over.

He set his gear down in front of the twin-rotor Sea Knight that would carry him on the first leg of his journey out of Vietnam and looked around one last time. A rush of images seared his brain: the sign on the ramshackle control tower that said Welcome to Khe Sanh; the metal skeletons of shot-up choppers and planes; the spools of concertina wire and miles of trenches; the incarnadine soil that seeped from his pores like blood; the defiled highland jungle, its lush green pelt a bombed-out mosaic of black and brown. Who would ever know what went on here, the nature of their sacrifice? Who would care?

He hauled his pack up the ramp and sat down against the Sea Knight's cold metal frame. He closed his eyes and let the chopper ascend to cruising altitude before reaching into his front pocket to touch the only things that mattered anymore.

Beau's bracelet, and his letter from Jackie Lundquist.

PART III

And discord raging bathes the purple plain;
Discord! Dire sister of the slaughtering power,
Small at her birth, but rising every hour,
—Homer, *The Iliad*

CHAPTER ELEVEN

DAVID ROUNDED THE CORNER OF SIXTH AND HENNEPIN STREAMing with sweat. Traffic crawled, horns honked. Drivers cursed. Even in the gloaming, the July heat was oppressive, a humid pall smothering the city—the *country*—like a plastic bag pulled tight around its neck. As did everywhere else, Minneapolis simmered, the conflagration of Martin Luther King's assassination in April having given rise to the tense grief of Bobby Kennedy's murder in June.

Moby Dick's—where Jackie had insisted their reunion take place—was in the middle of the block, next to a flophouse called the Rand Hotel. A smiling white cetacean on a blue sign over the entrance promised patrons A Whale of a Drink. Across the street, the Gopher Theater advertised its latest movie on a sidewalk marquee, *2001: A Space Odyssey.* The inside smelled of mold and tobacco and wasn't much to look at: a long bar with red leather stools, a single pool table in back, an unvarnished wooden floor. Tendrils of smoke clung to the ceiling.

David felt out of place, his collared shirt and too-new Levis at odds with the crowd's hip dishevelment. He ordered a Pabst from a gargantuan bartender with tattooed arms and a ginger-colored beard and sat down at the bar to wait for Jackie while the jukebox played "Itchycoo Park."

That he was drinking beer and listening to rock and roll instead of spending the last few months of his enlistment at a cramped stateside billet had been Defense Secretary Robert McNamara's doing. McNamara had denied a request to increase the Marine Corps' size, but with compulsory combat time limited to thirteen months, the Corps was dependent on new recruits (rather than repeat tours of duty) to maintain troop levels in Vietnam. His ruling had forced the Corps to adopt an early release program in order to avoid exceeding its authorized numerical strength.

After being discharged, he had retrieved his furniture from storage, leased an apartment near Stadium Village, bought a '63 Buick Skylark, and got his old job back at the roofing company. Only after registering to enroll in school in the fall did he go looking for Jackie. He showed up at her home in Robbinsdale the last week in June, hoping to surprise her.

She lived in a snug two-story made of English brick, with an assortment of conifers strewn about the front yard and a flag draped over the threshold in anticipation of the Fourth. A genial man with neat blond hair and eyes an even deeper blue than Jackie's answered his rap on the door.

"Are you the David from Vietnam?" Pete Lundquist asked, after they exchanged introductions.

"Yes, sir. I was discharged this month."

Lundquist slapped him on the shoulder and grinned. "I can't tell you how proud of you I am. Young men like you give me hope our country hasn't lost its mettle."

He looked away to swallow a sudden lump in his throat. It was the first time since returning home anyone had acknowledged his service to his country, the first time his short hair and reflexive use of the appellation 'sir' had elicited something other than unease— or outright hostility. He pulled himself together and stammered something about it having been a privilege.

Jackie was living in Dinkytown, her father said, with a roommate named Liz Bodine. He left with her phone number and a standing invitation from Pete Lundquist to drop by anytime for dinner and a strong drink. He had called Jackie the following day, so here he was, sitting in a downtown dive with his heart in his throat, hoping to pick up where they had left off.

"Hello, David," a voice beside him said. A psychedelic rendering of Jackie stood before him, wearing a tie-dyed T-shirt knotted above the naval and bell-bottom jeans with fringed cuffs. Her hair hung wild, a gilded mat tumbling over her shoulders. A peace symbol dangled from a leather thong looped around her neck, and a slightly wanton look graced her face. It was a look he had never gotten over, a look that for nearly two years was all he had thought about.

The sight of her left him in smithereens, all hope of self-control and hiding his emotions gone. He scrambled to his feet and knocked over his Pabst, sending a rivulet of beer halfway down the bar. She giggled and reached for a napkin while he apologized to a threesome of longhairs in the splash zone. The one closest to him, a squat redhead with a Fu Manchu, gave him a contemptuous look and failed to acknowledge his apology.

"I said I'm sorry," David challenged.

One of Fu Manchu's buddies intervened, a slender blond in granny glasses and a leather vest. "It's cool, man, it's cool," David said. "Accidents happen."

He gave a curt nod and turned to Jackie, his face on fire with embarrassment.

"Is it safe to sit next to you," she asked with a coy smile, "or are you going to give me a beer bath, too?"

What he wanted to give her was a hard time about failing to answer his letters until Khe Sanh, but spilling his beer had put him on his heels. He shrugged and ordered two Singapore Slings while she climbed onto the stool next to him. "It meant a lot to hear from you," he told her. The words came out with more feeling than he intended.

"I guess I finally got over being jilted for the Marines," she replied, holding his gaze. "I'm sorry for what I said that day at the teach-in. You know I didn't mean it." A look of remorse clouded her face, then was gone.

"I forgave you the minute you said it."

Her eyes moistened and she took a gulp of her drink, as if steeling herself against their past—a past that had given him hope when hope was in short supply. "You need to know right up front that I'm still against the war." Her expression hardened. "Now more than ever. Some of the things I've done in the name of peace would probably appall you."

"Some of the things I've done would appall you, too," he said, softly. "Why don't you go first?"

He got pleasantly hammered while she reconstructed the last twenty-one months of her life. He learned that she was on track to graduate the following spring with a humanities degree: "I wanted to major in something relevant, not waste my education acquiring capitalist skills like my father. Can you imagine devoting your life to real estate? I mean, my God, how shallow!" That she regarded the use of hallucinogenic drugs as a sacred obligation: "Mind expansion is humanity's best hope for avoiding annihilation." And that the rioting in black ghettos—only sportscasters called them Negroes anymore, she told him—was a welcome sign of racial awakening: "Like Baldwin said, 'God gave Noah the rainbow sign/No more water, the fire next time!'" She admitted to having joined Students for a Democratic Society, and proudly recited the contents of a pamphlet she had helped craft in support of a student strike on campus the previous April. "It is time for us to attack the cancer that plagues our society. Too many martyrs are dying in the streets of our cities and in the jungles of Vietnam."

"What 'cancer' are you referring to?" he asked, struggling mightily to ignore the line about gook martyrs.

She seemed astonished he didn't know. "Why, white American

hegemony. The System. It's what's driving all the anger. Did you know there were more than seventy campus protests the first two months of this academic year alone? People want change and they're running out of patience. I can't *wait* for the Democratic Convention in Chicago next month. You ain't seen nothin', yet," she added, in an odd patois that defied classification.

He swilled the rest of his drink and let the gin take him. The girl he loved appeared to have become a radical, but he didn't care. The taut, bisque skin of her midriff made his balls tingle. He had waited eighteen months to be cured of pussy fever, and he wasn't about to let her daffodil political views get in the way. He flashed a drunken, helpless smile, as if the recondite things she spoke of were too much for him to comprehend. "What I really want to know," he asked, "is whether your mind has expanded enough to date a marine?"

She set her drink down and folded her hands. "That's why I agreed to see you when you called. I wanted to tell you face to face. I'm in a pretty heavy relationship with Kyle Levy."

David felt like he'd been skinned alive, flensed in a place called Moby Dick's. *Chances are, she's already bangin' either your best friend or your worst enemy, depending on which she thinks'll hurt the most.* Westbrook had that right.

"I'd sooner have a Punji stick rammed up my ass than think of you with him." His voiced thickened. "You know, those sharp stakes the Viet Cong smear with feces and try to impale us on? Those 'martyrs' in your fucking pamphlet?"

A song he had never heard before began to play, Eric Burden singing a cappella. The crowd cheered in recognition and broke out the usual slogans.

"War is not the answer! Peace now!"

The lyrics and liquor transported him to the morning the Ghost Patrol had marched to eternal grace. He stood and scanned the bar, his breath coming in ragged gulps. The song played on.

"Damn right they'll die!" Fu Manchu shouted above the music in his direction. "If it takes mothers losing their sons to stop it, the more the better!"

David grabbed a beer bottle and swung it backhand at Fu Manchu's head. His mouth burst open like a ripe tomato, making a bloody jack-o'-lantern of his face. His friends stepped in to defend him, but all they managed to do was rip David's shirt off his back and divert his fury to them. He drove one headlong into the bar and turned to confront the other, the blond in granny glasses. David broke his nose with a chopping right hand. "Maybe tonight *your* mother will be the one to cry," he growled into the boy's busted face.

The Paul Bunyan of a bartender ended things by thumping him on the back of the neck with a blackjack and pitching him out the door. He tumbled onto the sidewalk and skidded to a stop near the curb. Barhoppers and theatergoers sidestepped him and shook their heads in disgust, taking him for a drunk being given the bum's rush for brawling—which was exactly what he was.

"You're an animal!" Jackie screamed in his face before walking away. "A fucking animal! They should never have let you out of the Marine Corps!"

.   .   .

Jackie made it back to her apartment by eleven. Liz and her boyfriend Kevin, a pudgy, curly haired jokester with a nagging squint, were snuggled on a sofa bed in the living room, watching Johnny Carson on a small color television. An overstuffed armchair sat in one corner of the room, a bookcase filled with textbooks and novels in another. Martin Luther King, Janis Joplin, and Bobby Kennedy gazed down from posters on the wall, avatars of their incandescent streak in time.

"I hope you enjoy all the time you'll be spending in the kitchen," she said, before sticking her tongue out at Liz.

"I bet her a week of washing dishes that David the marine would end up sleeping here tonight," Liz explained to Kevin, shaking her head. "I can't believe I was wrong. She never wears that top without getting laid." Liz had long straight hair, tiny corms of breast, and a sparse, lithesome frame. Where Kevin was witty and hyperkinetic, she was understated and serious, antipodal of him in every detail.

"Maybe showing her stomach was supposed to make him suffer," Kevin offered. "You know, like in *Lysistrata*?"

Liz gave a short, piercing laugh completely incongruous with her languid personality. "Girls say 'no' to boys who say 'yes' to war, something like that?"

Jackie walked over and turned off the television. "The night was a disaster. A total freakin' disaster. I need to get high. Put some music on."

Kevin rolled off the sofa and riffled through a stack of albums leaning against the stereo while Liz switched on a pair of lava lamps. Jackie went into the kitchen, where a mobile of a brilliant green parrot swayed over the table. She retrieved a bag of pot from its hiding place inside a bowl of potpourri and returned to the living room. Kevin loaded Cream's *Disraeli Gears* onto the turntable while she sat cross-legged on the floor with Liz and rolled joints, like sisters baking bread.

A wave of peace descended over her after the first few lung-searing hits. She stared at an aquamarine globule of wax rising inside the nearest lava lamp and said, "He actually got *thrown out* of Moby's for fighting. Can you believe it? It was disgusting."

"What did you expect?" Kevin chided. "He's a trained killer."

She related the circumstances of David's wig-out with "Sunshine of Your Love" playing on the stereo. Afterwards, the three of them traded tokes and debated the cause of his savagery for close to an hour, filling the room with a pungent haze. Kevin contended that hearing "Sky Pilot" had triggered a flashback to Vietnam; Liz maintained he went berserk because he found out Jackie was balling Kyle Levy. Jackie suspected a little of each, but whatever the reason, she wanted no part of it. She *had* a boyfriend.

Kyle was an enlightened visionary fighting to change the world. David was a brute forever warped by Vietnam. She and Kyle saw the world exactly the same. She and David were opposites with nothing in common.

At a sign from Liz that it was time to get lost, she said she was tired and headed for the bedroom, as it was Liz's month to sleep on the foldout. She brushed through the curtain of gold beads that had replaced their bedroom door and paused to consider the woven orb of willow and twine suspended over her bed. The Ojibwa called it a dreamcatcher; it caught bad dreams and let the good ones in. Come morning, it would be chock-full after the night she had.

She changed into a summer nightie and walked over to her dresser. A tapestry with a black butterfly superimposed on concentric circles of orange and green covered the wall behind it. She scrounged around inside the top drawer of the dresser for a Quaalude—the Whore Pill, Kyle called it, on account of its reputation as an aphrodisiac.

Deservedly so, she thought half an hour later, her hand between her legs. She rubbed faster, turned on by Liz's moans in the next room. A jumble of lubricious fantasy danced across her mind, but as she fingered herself over the edge, a single, unbidden image swept away all else: that of David at Moby Dick's, his naked torso beaded with sweat, like a marble sculpture in the mist, his muscles rippled yet smooth, straining to defend the honor of his fallen comrades.

It made her gasp.

CHAPTER TWELVE

DURING THE WORKWEEK, IN THE BLISTERING HEAT OF THE ROOFS, his rage dissolved like a Fizzies tablet in a warm glass of water. But come the weekend, without the sunstroke of his job to sedate him, his anger became a bilious abscess pointing inside him. He had returned to a country where a novel glorifying an antiwar march *(The Armies of the Night)* was a best seller, where Viet Cong flags flew from university buildings (at Columbia that April), and where crude verse extolling black street crime ("Up Against the Wall, Motherfucker!") was praised as poetry. Whether his fury sprang more from the realization that much of his generation now regarded military service as shameful and draft evasion as admirable or more from losing Jackie to Kyle Levy was hard to say; all he knew was that America was in flames and Jackie was balling the guy with the kerosene.

For relief he resorted to drinking and brawling in downtown bars. Sometimes he went alone, sometimes with a coworker off the roofing crew named Wisniewski, a towering, meaty Polack who had avoided conscription on account of a heart murmur—a condition with no discernible effect on his capacity for either hard work or hard liquor. The combination of David's pent-up rage and Wisniewski's natural belligerence seldom failed to produce a fight, but to David's surprise, the feel of a cheekbone shattering or nose splaying beneath his sandstone fists assuaged him less than did the taste of *his* blood, the crash of knuckles against *his* face. Maybe the Catholics were right: it took mortification of the flesh to still a howling soul.

One night they wandered into a bar on First Avenue called the Outer Limits. Waitresses in halter-tops and hip huggers toted drink trays up and down the aisles while a band played "Fire" by Arthur Brown. A small dance floor in front was packed. They nabbed a pair of stools and ordered drinks from the nearest bartender. Wisniewski lit up a cigarette that managed to send smoke up David's nose no matter where he placed his ashtray. "Lotta spades in here," he said. "Hope they don't torch the joint. You know, get confused and think they're on Plymouth Avenue or something?" Wisniewski had slept with a loaded shotgun ever since Plymouth Avenue in North Minneapolis burned to the ground the summer before. He said he wanted to be ready in case a crowd of darkies ever tried to cross the Lowry Avenue Bridge into "Nordeast," the working class neighborhood where Wisniewski lived.

David surveyed the bar. It wasn't so much a racially mixed crowd as it was a crowd with racially mixed couples, black dudes with white chicks and the reverse, too, hippy-looking guys talking to black girls with hoop earrings and monster Afros. Even the band was interracial and played music from interracial groups, like Sly and the Family Stone and the Chambers Brothers. He lost himself in the music and people watching, but when Wisniewski disappeared after their third round of drinks, he braced for what would surely come next—a fracas with Wisniewski in the thick of it, David's cue to join in and maul someone.

Sure enough, he spotted Wisniewski's big frame and sun-whitened hair in the middle of a commotion on the dance floor. But he wasn't fighting—he was dancing, if you could call it that. His brown, weathered face wore a smitten look as he lumbered around the floor with a short, big-breasted black girl in a red tam and sequined top. She snapped her fingers and popped her shoulders in perfect rhythm to the beat, trying to teach Wisniewski to do

the same. His disjointed attempts to emulate her—like a bear paw-
ing at a swarm of bees—delighted the crowd, young black men
in silk shirts and tight pants laughing and slapping palms with
Wisniewski, who didn't seem to mind at all.

At song's end, he pointed in David's direction and bent low to
say something in his diminutive partner's ear. She laughed and
pulled one of her friends over by the elbow. A moment later, a slender girl in a paisley pantsuit headed David's way. He took off for
the restroom, but she stepped in front of him and blocked his
escape. She had hollow cheeks, glossy ebony skin, and dramatic
streaks of eyebrow that gave her a feline look. The top of her Afro
came even with his eyes.

"I bet my girlfriend I'd have you dancing before the break," she
said with a confident smile.

"Maybe I don't like to dance." He knew he would look every bit
as lame as Wisniewski if he let her talk him into it.

She looked him up and down, his short hair and white T-shirt.
"Stanley Kowalski knock-off like you? Sugar, you're dyin' to dance!"

He stifled a look of surprise and burst out laughing. She put a
hand on her hip and scowled. "What? Tennessee Williams only for
white people?" She let him stammer and turn red and feel like a
racist jackass before showing some mercy and explaining that she
was an actress at the Guthrie Theater. "We're in rehearsal for *A
Raisin in the Sun*," she said. "We open next month."

David knew the play well, had studied it in American lit class
and been required to memorize the line the title came from.
Though two years had passed, he remembered it still. "'What happens to a dream deferred?'" he recited. "'Does it dry up like a raisin
in the sun?'"

She gave a broad grin and shook her head. "Stanley Kowalski
wouldn't have known that one."

"What?" he said, pretending to take offense. "*Raisin in the Sun*
is only for black people?"

She looked down and bit her lip. "I guess I deserved that, didn't

I?" She looked up, her chocolate-drop eyes curious. "But how did you know that?"

"I'm an English major trapped inside a roofer's body. I go back to school in the fall."

"What's your name?"

"David. What's yours?"

"Lorella." She pointed at his hair. "Were you in Vietnam?"

He held her gaze and nodded.

"So was my brother Vincent. He enlisted the day he turned eighteen." A sudden sadness in her eyes said Vincent never made it back.

David took her by the hand. "Let's make good on that bet of yours."

They hit the floor to a song by Sly and the Family Stone commanding them to dance. The song made him feel good inside, a celebration of the simple vibe of youth, even though he was a terrible dancer and the brothers laughed and jived with him the same as with Wisniewski.

He liked that he was dancing with a black actress named Lorella and that he wasn't fighting, and that there was a place like the Outer Limits, where the music bound them all together like a soul brother handshake. He danced out the set—joyous, mindless dancing that made him forget his anger. Before they went their separate ways—Lorella to finish blowing off steam with her friends, David to finish getting obliterated with Wisniewski, whose views on miscegenation had evolved considerably as the evening progressed—she grabbed hold of his wrist and twisted it to the light, so she could read the engraving on the bracelet he had taken to wearing.

"What does it mean?"

"I don't know."

"Well, where did you get it?" she persisted, frowning.

"It belonged to a friend of mine who died in 'Nam. He wore it all the time. Now I wear it. To remember him."

She clutched his forearm. "You need to find out what it means. He would want you to know. I'm sure of it."

He reached out and laid his palm against her soft coil of hair, the warm, springy feel of it. "I will. I promise I will."

. . .

It was easy, once he thought about it. Beau had known more about the Civil War than anyone he ever met. And of the Civil War, Beau had talked most about Gettysburg—and Lee. It was inconceivable that the engraving on his bracelet could be related to anything else.

He sought the cryptic phrase's meaning in the claustrophobic stacks of Walter Library, where he passed much of the following day in a dusty carrel on the third floor, flipping through one neglected Civil War tome after another. It was late afternoon by the time he came upon a four-volume set entitled *R. E. Lee: A Biography*, by Douglas Southall Freeman. Freeman's sweeping account of Gettysburg left him covered with gooseflesh: the fateful troop locations; the First Minnesota, averting Union collapse on Cemetery Ridge; the doomed majesty of Pickett's Charge across that parlous meadow, forever symbolic of the Lost Cause. And Lee's reaction to Pickett's failure: "Too bad, oh, too bad!" the first stone of the Confederate sarcophagus, clearly laid.

He had found what he was looking for, the provenance of the expression on Beau's bracelet, but he read on, taken with Freeman's riveting narrative. What followed, Freeman wrote, was Lee's finest moment. He climbed atop his horse Traveller and told his discalced army that it was all his fault, that Longstreet had been right and that he, Lee, had been wrong. It was Lee's willing assumption of blame, Freeman asserted, that transformed him from a defeated Confederate general into an eternal paragon of honor—for North and South alike.

Too bad, oh, too bad!

Beau would of course have understood the deeper meaning of the phrase, and now so did David. The loss of Jackie was no one's fault but his own; he was the one who had joined the marines, not her. And the nation's flagging support of the war? No point in blaming ordinary citizens for the failure of their leaders. The country wanted out of Vietnam because it was costing more in blood and treasure than people were willing to bear for a war the politicians were uncommitted to winning.

Kyle Levy and the New Left, however, were another matter. David could no more excuse their actions than Atlanta had Sherman's.

He had a sudden need to talk about Vietnam, a desire to share his thoughts on the matter with someone. But whom could he trust? It was times like this that he missed having a father—even Westbrook would have sufficed. Then it came to him. Someone had already extended an invitation to him to talk about Vietnam. Someone sympathetic.

He phoned Pete Lundquist that night and told him he had decided to take him up on his offer to shoot the shit over a stiff drink.

· · ·

The red Buick with whitewall tires parked in her parents' long, macadam drive was not a car Jackie recognized. Her father had mentioned inviting someone to dinner—a client or friend, perhaps.

She returned home from campus less and less often these days. With her two older sisters married and living in other cities and in no rush to have grandchildren, she found her mother increasingly melancholy and resentful. Her misty-eyed reminiscence about Jackie's childhood—the Wonder Years, before little Miss Robbinsdale up and joined the revolution—was getting to be a drag. That's what she gets for investing so much of her life in her children, Jackie thought, as she pulled in behind the Buick.

She entered unannounced through the unlatched side door. The kitchen smelled of cloves and sage, her mother's favorite flavorings. Karen Lundquist looked up from a steaming kettle on the stove, her thick brown hair pulled back in a loose bun, a white apron cinched around her spreading waist. "Oh, hello dear. I was worried you might have forgotten." Her mother's way of telling her that pot affected short-term memory. Those *Reader's Digest* articles again. How long before she'd warn that birth control pills caused strokes?

"It's not even five yet," Jackie said, already annoyed. She walked across the room and grazed her mother's cheek with a kiss. It felt dry and powdery, like a dusty canvas. Someone closer to death than to birth, which was what was so unsettling. "Whose car is that in the driveway?"

Her mother smoothed her apron and gave a mawkish smile. "Your father wants to surprise you. They're in the study."

She shrugged and headed to the other side of the house to meet the mystery guest—whoever he was. Her mother's extra rouge and short-sleeved, pink polyester dress left little doubt as to gender. She trooped through the living room, with its heavy furniture and kitsch portrait art, and down the hall to her father's wainscoted refuge. She rapped once and opened the door. He was at his desk, against a backdrop of leather-bound books, his treasured Easton Press collection. He had a tall drink in front of him—a Tom Collins, probably—and a stinky Dutch Masters cigar between his teeth, fouling the air. In a wing chair angled in front of him sat David Noble, a sheepish grin on his face, the same pellucid drink in hand.

"What are you doing here?" Jackie asked, running a hand through her hair. She felt suddenly frumpy, no eyeliner or lipstick.

And the gunnysack of a dress she'd worn, something to plant tomatoes in.

"Pete invited me to dinner," he answered.

"*Pete?*" she said to her father. "He calls you *Pete?* What are you,
bowling buddies? Did it ever occur to you to check with me before
inviting my ex-boyfriend to dinner?"

He set his cigar in a heavy glass ashtray and held up his hand.
"Whoa, whoa, I'm the one who pays for groceries around here,
remember? Not to mention tuition and rent. My invitations are
veto-proof."

"Economic leverage to bend your children to your will. There's
always that, isn't there? And you wonder why Peggy and Michelle
moved away after they got married. Fine. Invite Lyndon Johnson
for all I care. But you have no right to deceive me into being here."

"You're comparing me to Johnson?" David protested.

"Stay out of this," she snapped. "This has nothing to do with you."

He furrowed his brow. "Huh?"

The look on his face, like a tolerant husband befuddled by his
bitchy wife, made her soften. "Are you growing your hair out?" she
asked, noticing its fullness.

"I got tired of fighting," he said.

She walked over and ran her hand through it, like a barber
checking for length. The thick brush of it tickled her palm, like the
coat of a camel, the ones she used to pet at Como Park Zoo when
she was little. "It looks good. Don't cut it."

"Sounds like a bombing pause to me," her father said, stubbing
out his cigar and rising from his chair. "Let's eat."

They adjourned to the dining room, where Jackie slipped into
a mellow, accommodating mood, tranquilized by the spicy
Châteauneuf-du-Pape her father cracked open—and the 'lude she
had dropped before leaving her apartment. Drugs were the only
way to keep from pulling her hair out and screaming over her
parents' obliviousness toward what was about to go down, the

dismembering of society, the White Man done, the Rainbow People rising.

She took a bite of her mother's sage-rubbed chicken and stole a glance at David, the play of muscle beneath his open-collared shirt, his nut-brown face and intrepid chin. His presence at the table seemed to complete something in her parents. It was fascinating to watch, her mother fawning and heaping his plate, her father's pride at his combat record, one of the heroes of Khe Sanh. And David basking in his praise, the two of them meant for each other, a father who lacked a son and a boy who probably still longed to be one.

So different than when Kyle had dinner with them—the one time he did. Kyle was nothing like the son her parents had always wanted, more like the one they were grateful they never had. Her father had broken out the Châteauneuf-de-Pape that night, too, but the evening had pretty much ended when Kyle called the papal mitre worked into the glasswork of the bottle "a symbol of Christian oppression"—not the thing to say to a man who ushered at St. Christopher's every Sunday.

But the lily-white, Mousketeer world of her parents was an invention of the fifties, propaganda she and Kyle were trying to take down, a mask to be melted so America would reveal her true face: separate washrooms for blacks; the military-industrial complex; Lucy and Ricky cheating on each other. Tomorrow she was leaving for Chicago with Kyle and, unlike Lucy and Ricky, they would not be sleeping in separate beds. They would be marching and screwing and getting high at the Democratic National Convention. All she had to do was hold her tongue for one more hour.

She might have done it, might have made it out the door in peace if her father hadn't started in during dessert. "Have you ever heard of YAF?" he asked David.

David looked up from his second piece of homemade cherry pie. "What's YAF?"

The hated acronym roused her from her torpor. "A club for fascist dorks," she said ahead of her father.

He scowled before responding. "Young Americans for Freedom. It's the conservative antidote to SDS. They ought to call it SCS—Students for a *Chaotic* Society."

"There's a YAF chapter on campus," Jackie said dismissively. "Nobody with a brain pays any attention to them. They're just a bunch of short-haired Goldwater groupies."

"Like me, you mean?" David said, pushing his plate away.

That *wasn't* what she meant, but now he had that look on his face, like when he went berserk at Moby Dick's, his jaw all twitchy and eyes all hard and cold. That *soldier* look.

"A student group that wants to win in Vietnam, huh? I just might have some interest in joining a group like that."

Her face got hot and her eyes bugged wide open. She couldn't help it. The thought of him with those . . . those . . . those people. "You can't be serious. YAF is creepy."

"Oh, I see. Your student group is wonderful, but the one I'm interested in is creepy, is that it? You sound like what I was fighting against in 'Nam."

"You don't know what you're talking about. SDS advocates peace. YAF is for war. What more is there to say?"

He pursed his lips and nodded. "Nothing more to say at all," he replied, sarcastic, cruel even. "Unless of course you happen to believe it's necessary to stand up to communism and fight. But fighting communism isn't your thing, is it? You'd rather fight real threats to our way of life, like ROTC programs or Dow Chemical."

She balled up a napkin, plunged it into a glass of water and launched it, plastering it against his cheek.

"Stop it!" her mother yelled. Her father, having started it all, said nothing.

David wiped his cheek with the back of his hand. "Can we continue this in private?"

She knocked her chair over and stormed into the study. She

waited until he had closed the door before going at him with both arms flailing, clouting him about the neck and shoulders. "You should never have come here!"

She took a step back and measured him for more, but instead of hitting him, threw her arms around his neck and kissed him— as insistent and unrestrained a kiss as ever she'd given. He kissed her back, the stubble of his beard rough against her face, the hands that could snap her neck in an instant cupped over her shoulder blades, drawing her against him.

"Follow me home," he said. She felt the ache in his voice, the rise in his crotch.

"Okay," she said, breathless. "Okay."

She tried to tell herself it was the Whore Pill talking, but she knew it wasn't.

CHAPTER THIRTEEN

THE BLACK BEAUTIES JACKIE DROPPED AT THE DINER SHE AND KYLE
stopped at for breakfast—bacon and eggs, with a side of hash
browns rimmed in orange grease—kicked in with a vengeance.
They filed over the bridge at the Jackson Street ingress to Grant
Park with her heart pounding and her mind lit up like a pinball
machine. Revved up on speed. Speeding toward Armageddon. A
cardboard sign scrawled in magic marker at the park's entrance
said it all: Welcome to Prague.

It might as well have been.

Ranks of hefty, gimlet-eyed Chicago policemen girdled the
park, truncheons dangling from their hips, their short-sleeve shirts
and riot helmets the same powder blue as the pristine sky above.
Pigs. Waiting for an excuse to move in and crush them the way the
Soviets had crushed Dubcek's Prague Spring the week before. And
across the street black-booted National Guardsmen, standing three
deep in front of the Conrad Hilton Hotel. Brown shirts. Daley's
minions.

She latched onto Kyle's hand and followed him toward the old
band shell in the center of the park. MOBE's antiwar rally was set
to begin at 3 p.m., timed to coincide with the presentation of a
peace plank at the Democratic Convention several miles southeast
of them, in the International Amphitheatre. His lithe frame snaked

a path through the gathering crowd, jean jacket billowing, hiking boots half-laced. His eyes were as wild and black as his hair, her radical boyfriend at his most appealing, his most dangerous—though she was glad she had talked him into leaving his backpack full of bricks and nail-studded golf balls in the hotel room. Kyle was energized by the looming confrontation. His booming voice hailed this way and that, an insider in the thick of things.

Last March he had even attended an SDS strategy session at a campground outside Chicago, organized by Tom Hayden and Rennie Davis. The purpose of the meeting had been to get David Dellinger's MOBE—National Mobilization Committee to End the War in Vietnam—on the same page as SDS and the Yippies of Abbie Hoffman to protest Lyndon Johnson's nomination.

But Johnson's renunciation of his candidacy and Kennedy's assassination changed things. The intent now was to provoke a violent response from Daley and link it to Hubert Humphrey, the Democrats' certain nominee and their last standard bearer of liberalism, the outdated Cold War political ideology that had gotten them into Vietnam in the first place. In order to destroy liberalism and replace it with the politics of the New Left they had to first destroy Humphrey, by ripping the Democratic Party apart in Chicago and thereby tilting the election to Nixon. In the fascist state that was sure to follow, the thinking went, the country would turn to the New Left to lead the revolution. Jackie was hip to the strategy of it all, but still . . . Nixon?

They ground to a halt at the foot of a hill topped by a bronze statue of a Civil War general named Logan. A memorial to a Union general she had never heard of in a park named after Grant; another little absurdity for Abbie Hoffman to poke fun at—if he made bail. Poor Abbie. Busted for public indecency that morning for having written the word Fuck on his forehead. How bogus could they get?

But then again, Tom Hayden had been arrested two days earlier for letting the air out of a police cruiser's tires. She and Kyle had arrived that same night, after driving all day to get there. And wasn't *that* a long, torturous trip, having left David's apartment at 3 a.m. saddle sore and bow-legged, David at her nonstop for three solid hours. How long had it been since he'd been laid, anyway? Didn't he ever visit any of those Vietnamese prostitutes she was always hearing about?

Kyle had showed up at seven, all clueless and affectionate, making her feel bad—sort of. Men had to realize that with free love came certain risks. Kyle had balled more than his share of SDS ingénues, doe-eyed girls away from home for the first time, infatuated with meeting someone who had actually broken bread with Tom Hayden. Well, from time to time she got some on the side, too—though there was no need for Kyle to know about it. Least of all this thing with David, which was bound to pass. She just hadn't gotten him out of her system yet, that was all.

Jackie estimated there were in excess of ten thousand in attendance. Dellinger and Davis and then Bobby Seale spoke. Kyle listened with a black transistor pressed against his ear, awaiting news of the delegates' vote on the peace platform at the convention. Later on, Allen Ginsberg, as he had at every rally that week, led them in a monosyllabic incantation intended to hypnotize—or civilize, or exorcise—the police into refraining from violence.

"*Ohm . . .*"

Word on the vote came down late in the day. The crowd stirred, a susurrus before the squall. "What?" she asked. "What's happening?"

Kyle gave her a wicked smile, like the day she told him David had joined the marines. "They voted it down!" he shouted. "The bastards voted it down!"

Delegates from their own party had adopted a platform that supported the war. Dellinger reappeared and urged them to march to the amphitheater in protest. Was he joking? No march through Bridgeport, the neighborhood Daley lived in, the source of his power—*Mordor*—had the faintest hope of getting underway.

Tom Hayden took the mike. Jackie thought he looked like Kyle, his unkempt hair, his hard-edged, maniacal face. "If we're going to be disrupted and violated," Hayden told them, his voice throbbing with rage, "let the whole stinking city be disrupted and violated. I'll see you in the streets!"

She waited at the base of an oak tree while Kyle and a half dozen others jostled their way to a flagpole near the band shell. They lowered the American flag and replaced it with a square of red cloth. The police lobbed canisters of tear gas into the park and charged the flagpole, clubbing everyone in sight. Jerry Rubin grabbed a microphone and urged everyone to "Kill the pigs! Kill the pigs!" A phalanx of blue in riot gear and gas masks hacked Rennie Davis to the ground on their way to restoring the flag. Kyle somehow made it back to her, gagging and choking through a fog bank of tear gas while police in tight formation skirmished with disorganized bands of demonstrators, pummeling their outraged young faces into bloody masks. It turned into a rout.

She and Kyle fled with the rest of them, stopping from time to time to yell, "Pigs! Motherfucking pigs!" But there was nowhere to go. National Guardsmen had moved into blocking positions on the Congress and Balbo Bridges along Michigan Avenue. She followed Kyle's lead and reversed course with her eyes stinging and lungs burning. Adrenalin and speed coursed through her in equal parts, propelling her like a mixture of oxygen and rocket fuel. They ran north, narrowly evading the roving packs of police that were taking down stragglers. The Jackson Street Bridge was the only exit left unguarded; they joined a tattered mob and streamed out of the park like the English at Dunkirk.

She and Kyle broke off from the pack and returned to their hotel on Clark Street, six blocks away, where they popped more black beauties and grabbed a quick bite to eat in anticipation of spending the night in the streets. Jackie voiced no objection when he strapped on his backpack of crude weaponry, like a boy with stones marching grim-faced to confront the firedrake. She felt proud and fiercely loyal. Kyle was every bit as brave as David, maybe more, considering his lack of guns and training.

They returned to the fray just as Ralph Abernathy's Poor People's Campaign rolled down Michigan Avenue with three covered wagons and six mules. Word got around that PPC, unlike everyone else, had a permit to march to Convention Hall. A caravan of demonstrators, Jackie and Kyle among them, fell in behind the train of mules and got as far south as the Hilton before the entire procession ground to a halt at the barricades in front of the hotel.

A lengthy delay ensued, for which Jackie, newly buzzed on speed, had no patience. The television cameras mounted over the awning caught her attention. She took up a megaphone and shouted out a chant that would come to define the entire convention. "The whole world is watching! The whole world is watching!" she yelled, like the varsity cheerleader she once was. Kyle blew her a kiss and retreated into the shadows with a handful of other backpack-toting hardliners to ready a counterattack for the assault they knew would be coming.

The police allowed the PPC marchers to pass, but no one else. Someone broke a water balloon across the shoulders of a husky cop manning the foremost barricade. Except it wasn't water. Jackie caught a whiff of urine in the air. "Piss!" she yelped with glee. "Pig piss!" The rest of the crowd joined in. "Pig piss! Pig piss! Pig piss!" The officer glared at her, his thick Slavic face, his red pig eyes.

They closed ranks and attacked the minute the last covered wagon disappeared, waves of them crashing into the crowd with truncheons flailing. The beefy monster who got doused with urine made straight for Jackie. "I'm gonna split your skull, you hippie bitch!" he shouted at her.

She threw down her megaphone and ran, afraid—really afraid—for the first time that week. There was no telling what Pig

Piss might do to her if he caught her. She ditched him in the chaos and raced to where Kyle and the others were flinging bricks and nail-studded golf balls. It had no effect on the rampaging police. They tear-gassed and beat and maced anyone in their path, mindless of the cameras recording it all. She and Kyle got funneled into a group of demonstrators and onlookers on the sidewalk in front of the Hilton. A throng of police launched a frontal assault at the same time that another squad came around the corner and smashed into them from the right. The combined weight of the two-pronged attack squashed the whole straining mob against the plate-glass window of the hotel bar with such force that it finally gave way.

Jackie fell onto the floor inside, the window behind her shattered and gaping. She scrambled to her feet with shards of glass dangling from her hair and sweater, like icicles from a tree. Cops with flared nostrils and bared teeth streamed in after them, straddling demonstrators and patrons alike and clubbing them silly.

"Come on!" Kyle called out, taking her hand. He led her through the bar and into the hotel lobby in flight from a lone pursuer. Jackie risked a look over her shoulder. It was Pig Piss, his face the color of raw sirloin.

"You little commie slut!" he yelled.

They burst out the door of the hotel and down the front walk with Pig Piss right behind them, but the street in front of the Hilton had been cleared and sealed off by National Guardsmen. They spun around, trapped, with nowhere to run. Pig Piss stepped off the curb and swaggered toward them, smacking his billy club into his palm. Kyle jumped in front of her and pointed up at the cameras on the hotel awning. "Stay away from us. You're on TV."

"Good," Pig Piss said. "Then I can watch reruns of me fuckin' you up."

He hit Kyle between the eyes with his nightstick, dropping him like he'd been shot. Jackie screamed. Pig Piss grabbed her by the hair and raised his baton overhead, his lip curled, the rank smell of urine rising off his dampened shirt.

The blow never fell. Instead he stuck his face in hers and gave a long, mocking "*Ohm* . . ." before turning her loose and walking away.

• • •

The campus chapter of Young Americans for Freedom met every Thursday evening in Room 310 of the Social Sciences building, a twelve-story brick tower on the West Bank with long rows of tightly packed, white-trimmed windows. David arrived five minutes early for the group's second meeting of the new fall semester. He helped himself to the powdered donuts and coffee that were available in the hallway outside and grabbed a seat in the back of the classroom.

The few women there weren't much to look at, mostly plain, with hairdos like their mothers. One in a dress, another in a blouse and skirt, a couple more in jeans and sweaters. That was it, and every last one of them wearing a bra, nothing like the sea of unrestrained bosom jiggling down the mall every day. And the males in the room were just as square, wearing pressed slacks and collared shirts or suits and ties, even.

Almost all of them had hair shorter than his, now that he was growing his out, Jackie having more than a little to do with that. Her influence on him grew in direct proportion to the number of times she slept with him—never enough, but better, *far* better, than never at all. Pussy fever, cured at last.

He had joined YAF the week before—a romance-killer he hadn't yet mentioned to Jackie—in an effort to help stem the pacifist tide rolling across campus. The Democratic Convention seemed to have persuaded scads of previously neutral students that the New Left and SDS were right about the draft and the war and the repressiveness of government. It had also made Jackie and Kyle Levy into campus celebrities. What, he wanted to know, was so heroic about getting your ass kicked on national TV?

The president of their chapter was a full-cheeked, effervescent knock-off of Howdy Doody named Robert Beldon, complete with freckles and oversized ears. He called the meeting to order and asked new members to stand for recognition. David and a dozen others got to their feet. He half expected to hear them sing "Ta-ra-ra Boom-de-ay," but they politely applauded instead. Beldon thanked them for "enlisting"—a word choice David could have done without—then gave a brief talk on the origins and mission of YAF. He was surprised to learn that the formation of Students for a Democratic Society and its Port Huron Statement in 1962 had been in part a response to YAF and something called the Sharon Statement, a single-page manifesto issued during YAF's founding in 1960 at Sharon, Connecticut, at William F. Buckley Jr.'s family mansion. Beldon read it aloud as a heater groaned in the background, the nights already turning cold.

"' . . . We, as young conservatives believe . . . That the forces of international Communism are, at present, the single greatest threat to these liberties; That the United States should seek victory over, rather than coexistence with, this menace; and That American foreign policy must be judged by this criterion: does it serve the just interests of the United States?'"

The document resonated greatly with David. The need to prevail in Vietnam was what had motivated him to join YAF in the first place—though Beau's homespun homily had taught him what was *really* at stake there. *We're fightin' for honor, reputation, our good name: what other nations think of us. These things matter greatly, to people and to countries.* Beldon's enunciation of YAF's strategy for the coming year, however, left him cold. It called for more of the things that national YAF leaders had done in the past, like when they picketed Firestone's corporate office in protest of Firestone constructing a rubber plant in communist Romania, or when they held a mock trial at Georgetown that found international communism guilty of crimes against humanity.

Beldon reminded him more of Howdy Doody each passing minute, his every twitch and jerk choreographed by puppeteers at YAF headquarters in Washington in service of the same tired nostrums they had tried before. Didn't they grasp the importance of confronting the New Left more directly by challenging SDS on campus?

When he finished, Beldon, to his Howdy Doody audience participation credit, asked if any of the new members had comments or questions. At the risk of sounding officious, David stood and spoke his mind. "I think we should try something different. Let's take it to SDS, give 'em a taste of their own medicine."

The room erupted with a loud cheer. *Say kids, what time is it? It's Howdy Doody time!* The odd collection of Brylcreemers around him appeared willing, eager even, to try fighting his way, the marine way: to attack.

Beldon grinned, all gap-toothed and Howdy-like. "You seem to have touched a nerve. Any ideas on how we start?" he asked.

"We hold SDS accountable," David answered.

. . .

The following evening he met Jackie outside the Campus Theater—closer to his place than hers, but she didn't seem to mind the longer walk—to see *I Love You, Alice B. Toklas*, a romance about a square lawyer, Peter Sellers, who falls for a gorgeous hippie with a talent for baking marijuana brownies. A month had passed since Jackie followed him home from her parents', and even though they had seen each other steadily ever since, Jackie staying the night more often than not, she had kept right on seeing Kyle Levy as well, and no apologies about it. Fine, David told himself, standing in line for tickets. Maybe he'd see someone else, too. But he knew he wouldn't and it only made him irritable to think about it. And who the hell was Alice B. Toklas, anyway?

"She was Gertrude Stein's lover," Jackie told him inside, in response to his question about the eponymous title. "Famous enough for that, but more so for creating *The Alice B. Toklas Cookbook* and its recipe for Hashish Fudge."

"Oh, I get it," he whispered. "Well, at least it isn't about a *marine* falling for a hippie girl. That would be *too* far-fetched." She dug an elbow into his ribs and told him to watch the movie.

Afterwards they ambled hand-in-hand through Dinkytown, where on every block hero-worshiping zealots in green army jackets and faded jeans called out in recognition of the campus darling from the Chicago convention, the girl who had faced down the pig on TV. "Hail the Radical Queen!" they would shout, using the *nom de guerre* they had given her. One of them, a long-faced boy with pimples and wavy hair who reminded David of Eddie Haskell, even reached out to touch her on the arm as they walked by. "The whole world was watching *you*," he said, a lovesick look on his face. She batted her lids and smiled and thanked him, but her studied embarrassment and the self-satisfaction in her voice made David realize that her beauty pageant days had never really ended.

All that had changed was her wardrobe. She looked more like a cover girl than an activist, a model on the runway sporting this year's hottest style, radical chic, in thigh-length leather boots and a mini-length woolen coat, her ragged blonde hair spilling over her shoulders like a waterfall. Jackie was an SDS dilettante, he assured himself, not a true believer.

She veered off into a head shop called the Glass Pipe, dragging him into a countercultural netherworld of sensory overload: Janis Joplin singing "Ball and Chain," artwork in vermiculate patterns of purple and yellow, and a blast of patchouli that made him want to gag. "Don't you just love their incense?" Jackie asked. She had a cloying look on her face, pious almost.

"There's probably no smell on earth I detest more."

She dropped his arm as if he were leprous. "How can you say that? Everyone loves patchouli."

He recalled the mound of enemy corpses outside their wire after the failed NVA assault on their trench line at Khe Sanh, the buckets of patchouli oil they poured over them to cut the stench of their putrefaction. "Not everyone," he said, leaving it at that.

A blowsy, jean-jacketed shopkeeper with a chain looped around his neck stood behind a glass counter stocked with a farrago of paraphernalia: bongs, glass pipes, rolling paper, roach clips, incense, and lighters. He wore a button that read No Hope Without Dope. Behind him were dozens of tightly rolled posters in square open bins. Clint Eastwood looked down from a movie poster tacked to the wall, wearing a serape and smoking a cigar; to Clint's left, a rack full of bright yellow *Zap Comix* comic books were on sale. An empty album jacket to "Cheap Thrills" by Big Brother & The Holding Company—the album playing on the stereo—rested on top of the counter. David pointed to a caption on the album's comic book motif cover: Live Material Recorded at Bill Graham's Fillmore Auditorium.

"I'd love to see a concert there, someday."

Jackie made a disparaging, fricative sound. "Pfff. Don't you think a pilgrimage to the mecca of acid rock would be a waste for someone who doesn't even smoke pot?"

The shopkeeper frowned. "Doesn't smoke pot?" He sounded affronted, like an English teacher learning one of his students didn't like Shakespeare. "We can remedy that, my man." He nodded toward the back of the shop.

"Does it really matter whether you drink it from a bottle or smoke it from a bong?" Jackie asked, pressuring him to get with it, get hip: *conform.* "You get high either way. Try it, just this once."

David gave an inward smile. Never was the pressure to conform more intense than when applied by a nonconformist. But at least now he understood the point of the god-awful incense. If patchouli could cover up the smell of rotting corpses, it could camouflage the smell of pot in a head shop, too. He looked at her in the smoky light, her blue eyes beckoning, the oval of her mouth an unspoken promise.

Pure seduction.

Maybe if he got high with her she'd dump Levy and things would be like they used to be, before he joined the marines and ruined the closest thing he'd ever had to constancy, to an *identity*. He could be like Peter Sellers in the movie they just saw, walk away from everything he believed in—for love. She already had him growing his hair out and dressing all proletariat in dungarees and brogans—why not become a pothead, too?

He might have done it, might have smoked a big fat one with her, if not for nearly jumping off a roof the last time he tried it. At least with booze he could gauge things, tell when he was getting shit-faced, too near the edge. "No thanks," he said to the shopkeeper, "but I appreciate the offer."

They left the head shop and moved on to a place near Jackie's apartment called the Quadratic Equation, a lively pub with wooden floors strewn with peanut shells. After their second pitcher of beer, he told her he joined YAF.

"You can't be serious." Her face was pinched, her eyes hard, the night clearly ruined.

"As a heart attack," he told her.

"What's with you? Do you sit around thinking of things to join that you know will make me insane, first the marines and now this? Am I supposed to just accept you belonging to an organization that represents everything I hate?"

"No more than I'm supposed to accept you sleeping with Levy."

Her eyes probed his face. "Tell me something. If I stopped seeing Kyle for you, would you drop out of YAF for me?"

He thought it over, getting rid of Levy in exchange for jilting Howdy Doody and the Brylcreemers. He didn't take long to reply. There was one thing he would never do: sully the honor of Beau by quitting the fight for Vietnam.

"No," he said, fingering the bracelet on his wrist. "I wouldn't."

CHAPTER FOURTEEN

Jackie was out the door and headed to campus by 9 A.M. She pulled her jacket snug around her and shivered. It was a crisp October morning with an unbroken blue sky.

She wanted SDS's blockade of Walter Library to go well in the worst way. Kyle had been surly and negative ever since she told him David was back in her life. He needed a confidence booster, something positive to latch onto. The only child of an overindulgent Jewish mother—and a father who was senior partner at a big accounting firm—Kyle wasn't used to sharing. He wanted Jackie to himself, and in that regard was identical to David—and men in general.

Well, times had changed, and for that they had Ayn Rand to thank. Jackie actually had little use for Rand, save one glorious exception: Rand's sexual unshackling of women. On this the Randians had it right. A woman was no man's possession, and therefore free to sleep with whomever she pleased.

And for the time being, sleeping with two men was what pleased Jackie. She loved them both, but in different ways, David on a visceral level, Kyle for his mind. When she peeked into the future, though—which she did on only the rarest of occasions, much preferring the here and now, because that's all you really had when you got down to it, the *moment*, everything else either already gone or perhaps never to be—it was Kyle she saw herself with. David was a crush she couldn't get over, a drug she had to have, but she owed her moral awakening, her place in the movement, to Kyle. She and Kyle were more than lovers. They were revolutionaries hell-bent on changing the world.

She arrived at Walter Library about the same time as the others, thirty in all, more than enough to clog the building's narrow vestibule and block all ingress until the forewarned local press appeared. The idea was to shut students out of the library for an hour or so to show them—and more importantly, show the public watching the news that night—how it felt for black students to be shut out of the university's curriculum. In April the African American Action Committee had called on the university to establish an African Studies program. The request went nowhere, but Kyle saw in its rejection an opportunity for SDS to make common cause with black student groups. Kyle believed that non-violent protest had run its course, and that to get to the next phase— replacing the country's corrupt capitalist-imperialist system with a more equitable Marxist-Leninist one—insurrection was required.

He and others in SDS like him viewed the Black Panther Party as the logical vanguard of any such rebellion. The Panthers had seen the methods of Martin Luther King stall; they understood that America was still a racist society. Many of them—Huey Newton, Eldridge Cleaver, Bobby Seale—had already called for armed revolt as a means to establish a more racially inclusive government. For Kyle, currying favor with black student groups was a necessary first step in a courtship designed to wed the New Left to the Black Power movement. The Panthers would be the spear of the New Left's revolution, the shock troops they needed to take the streets.

Kyle organized the blocking party and led them inside wearing protest clothes—a gray sweatshirt, jeans, and hiking boots. Jackie stayed outside with the sign brigade. Her job was to get on

camera, be the face of the movement, its fetching Radical Queen.
TV crews arrived fifteen minutes later, with a crowd of students
beginning to swell on the library steps—some stymied from getting inside, others mere onlookers, no dog in the fight. A commotion near the corner of the colonnaded building attracted her
attention. She walked over to check it out. A group of construction
workers in sleeveless tees and hard hats were filing through SDS's
checkpoint at the side entrance. She shrugged and walked away.
She had no problem with letting a bunch of workers pass; it was
students they wanted to disrupt.

The sign brigade was getting ready when a scuffle broke out in
the front vestibule, shouting and shoving, a real scrum. The SDS
blocking party suddenly reappeared, as if regurgitated by the building. The force responsible for their ejection came out after them:
the same horde of construction workers that minutes before had
been at the side entrance. Gangs of shorthaired geeks materialized
on the sidewalk, some snatching signs from the SDSers and snapping them against their knees, others raising placards decrying
human rights abuses—*by Hanoi.*

Still others handed out pamphlets. Jackie plucked one up and
read it; it made her stomach clench. SDS was being routed by a YAF
counterprotest, with local media catching every minute of it. She
had heard of such things on the West Coast, Stanford and the like,
but not here, where YAF was practically moribund. How had they
known about SDS's blockade? And who were the construction workers providing the muscle to break it up?

The answers to her questions came a moment later, when
David appeared on the steps of the library like Hector confronting the Greeks, his hair windblown and free, his jaw all heroic
and resolute. A white-haired bear of a man sidled up beside him.
Jackie knew in an instant it was the brawler off the roofing crew
David had mentioned last summer—Wisniewski, that was his
name. She recalled with horror the previous Friday, when she had

bragged to David of SDS's blockade scheme, his newly minted YAF membership never crossing her mind. David had turned their pillow talk against her by recruiting his roofing buddies to smash the blockade.

She scanned the tangle of displaced SDS protestors and found Kyle straining at the periphery, his face like an Edvard Munch painting, screaming something at David. David just laughed. Jackie looked away.

Everything was *not* copasetic.

• • •

Her *mea culpa* lasted all through the afternoon and into the night, and still it wasn't enough. Kyle glared across the kitchen table, his black eyes baleful, no forgiveness in sight. An ashtray with a pair of smoldering joints sat halfway between them. Overhead, a sweet-smelling cloud of smoke hovered like cumulus on an August day. Jackie sifted through a bowl of potpourri and with a nervous fillip sent a dried petal flying onto the linoleum. She waited for the pot to mellow him out, but he just kept it up.

"You need to understand the seriousness of this," he said, hands flat on the table, face solemn. "It's not that you're seeing another guy. It's that you're seeing a guy who's *on the other side.* You gift-wrapped an opportunity for him to get their YAF propaganda on TV. Why? It makes me question your loyalty to SDS."

She would rather have been called a two-timing whore.

When David joined the marines, it left a hole in her she couldn't fill, a void nothing penetrated—until the day Kyle invited her to a demonstration against the draft. The crowd was small by protest standards, at best a hundred, gathered on the plaza in front of Northrop Auditorium, between Johnston and Morrill Halls. Kyle was at the center of things, cajoling with his rollicking baritone, orchestrating with his hands, his pea coat unbuttoned despite the

November chill. He quoted Muhammad Ali—"I ain't got no quarrel with them Viet Cong"—and then introduced three young men carrying tongs and cigarette lighters. They burned their draft cards while a pair of shivering, mini-skirted brunettes walked back and forth carrying signs that read Girls Say Yes to Boys Who Say No.

Jackie learned from a pale, auburn-haired girl standing next to her that the purpose of the tongs was to allow the draft cards to be burned completely rather than partially so, as would be the case if held between thumb and forefinger. A favorite tactic of undercover FBI agents, the girl explained knowingly, was to retrieve remnant corners to use as evidence. After their draft cards had gone up in flames, Kyle led the defiant chant that was spreading like wildfire across the country's campuses. "Hell no, we won't go! Hell no, we won't go!"

The summoning roar of his voice and the look of purpose—of *sanctity*—on his face drew Jackie forward. She stepped beside him and joined in, self-consciously at first, then with abandon, yelling at the top of her lungs, for the first time not just watching a demonstration, but actually taking part in one. She felt transported, like passing through the wardrobe to Narnia. And an amazing thing happened. The black hole caused by David's departure was gone, filled up. By faith. Faith in the power of protest, the power of dissent. Faith in Kyle Levy and the New Left.

She joined SDS on the spot. That was all it took back then, no papers or dues, just your word. By the weekend, they were sleeping together. The attraction for Kyle was physical, fantasies of blonde gentiles come true, he admitted. For Jackie it was about something quite different: validation. She didn't want to be little Miss Robbinsdale anymore. She was a college girl, a woman of substance—not some dolt of a beauty queen. She wanted to be taken seriously, be accepted by the movement, so she could contribute to its cause of establishing a just and colorblind society. And there was no one in all of radical Minneapolis whose validation mattered more than Kyle Levy's.

So she set out to make a name for herself in the New Left. That she was Kyle's consort aided greatly, but even so, it was slow going. SDS, she was dismayed to learn, was a sexist organization, completely oblivious to the predominance of men on its key committees and absence of female speakers at high profile events. For the better part of two years all they gave her was distaff work, the fetching of coffee, the answering of phones, the sorting of mail—nothing of any consequence. Until Chicago, when Pig Piss's hair-pull made a celebrity out of her: the Radical Queen.

Maddening to be trading on her looks again, Miss Robbinsdale redux, but it had finally put her on equal footing with the boys, made her what she had been striving to be—a bona fide radical who only happened to be a woman. But she had never stopped needing Kyle's approval, his acknowledgment of her intellectual worth. His validation. Which was why his condemnation of her over the Walter Library fiasco was so devastating.

He stubbed his joint out in the ashtray and rose to his feet with bits of dried herb clinging to his sweatshirt. "How could you be so fucking *stupid*?" he asked, before walking out the door.

Jackie ran into the bedroom and threw herself on the mattress. She wept a soft, forsaken lament made all the worse a half hour later, when Liz and Kevin returned from dinner and filled the apartment with the sound of their affectionate lovemaking.

•   •   •

David sat in pajamas at the kitchen table, a cup of coffee in his left hand, the phone pressed to his ear with his right. A milk-streaked bowl with a few surviving Cheerios clinging to the rim rested beside a plate stippled with crumbs from a blackened piece of toast. The Sunday paper lay in disarray at his feet. "North Side Lanes?" he said, taken aback. "Uh, sure. I'll meet you there at one." Considering that Jackie hadn't spoken to him in nearly a month, he

would have met her at a beauty parlor if she'd asked him to, but
still—a bowling alley?

He cleared the table, showered and shaved, and inspected himself in the mirror. His hair came halfway down his neck now,
Jackie's influence, to be sure, and he liked it. The hardness of his
torso pleased him, too, thanks to a summer on the roofs and the
twenty push-ups and sit-ups he did each morning—even without
some bug-eyed drill instructor to dog him.

After pulling on a pair of jeans and a sweater, he slipped into
his bomber jacket—the *dernier cri* of the protest crowd, oddly
enough—and made it out the door by half-past-twelve. He took
Washington Avenue downtown and then maneuvered onto West
Broadway before turning north on Lyndale. Traffic was sparse, the
sidewalks empty, everyone getting ready for the Vikings and Lions
on TV. It was a game he had looked forward to all week; he had
even stayed up late studying the night before to free up time to
watch it. He wondered briefly if Jackie's sudden urge to clear the
air an hour before kickoff spoke to some instinctive female ani-
mosity toward the watching of sports by men.

For three weeks she had neither taken his phone calls nor
answered his letters, the last one pure begging, not a shred of self-
respect on the page. He felt bad about having violated her confidence—lovers' confidence, no less—in order to sabotage SDS's
blockade, but, all the same, he had no regrets about it. And this
despite the risk of losing her when it felt like he was finally getting
the upper hand on Levy, the communist who had stolen his girl
while he, David, was off fighting communists. SDS had to be
confronted—even if it meant pissing Jackie off. Vietnam was being
lost not on the battlefield, where the NVA had yet to win a major
engagement, but at home, on college campuses. Nixon may have
won the election, but the New Left was winning the fight for
public opinion, the drumbeat for peace at the expense of victory
growing louder by the day. What good was peace born from a self-

inflicted loss harming national honor? *These things matter . . .*

North Side Lanes was located near the corner of Lyndale and Lowry, not far from suburban Robbinsdale, in a single-story brick building with stone-mullioned windows and a pitch roof. He pulled into the rear parking lot and went inside. The sound and smell of the place hit him first, while he waited for his eyes to adjust to its artificial twilight: the thump-and-roll of a ball flying down a lane; the explosive clatter of pins; the confused scent of cigarettes and lacquer. A plethoric woman in a yellow bowling shirt with crossed pins embroidered over the pocket stood behind a counter. Stacked in bins behind her were rows and rows of bowling shoes sorted according to gender and size. Twenty feet removed from the counter sat a metal rack replete with bowling balls, in front of which stood Jackie, busily fitting her fingers into one ball after another. David walked over to her.

"So we're actually going to bowl?" he asked.

She spun around, the Radical Queen in bowling garb, wearing black slacks and espadrilles and a loose-fitting paisley blouse, her hair gathered behind her in a long ponytail. "I decided that crashing a twelve-pound ball into a bunch of maple pins was a more appropriate way of displacing my anger than slugging you in the mouth," she said, overly cheerful.

He mumbled something self-deprecatory and turned to the business of picking out a ball and shoes. Once they were properly outfitted, he paid the grump behind the counter their rental fees and followed Jackie to a lane in the far corner of the building. They bowled a couple of practice frames—Jackie gawky and lurching, clearly not her sport—before turning to the real business at hand.

"Here's the deal," she said, standing at the ball return with one hand atop her Lady Brunswick. "If you win, nothing between us changes and I'll never bring up Walter Library again. But if I win, you agree to a new set of rules in our relationship."

He went weak-kneed with relief and had to refrain from kissing her. Though he was no great shakes as a bowler, Jackie was obviously worse, struggling during warm-ups just to keep her ball out of the gutter. She had decided to excuse his treachery, let bygones be bygones. This was her way of forgiving him without losing face.

"Ladies first," he said, sitting down to keep score and wait his turn.

She positioned herself on the right side of the lane, hoisted her red-speckled ball to her chest, and stepped into a smooth, four-step delivery that dropped a hook ball right in the pocket, scrambling all ten pins for a strike.

"I used to bowl in a father-daughter league," she said in response to his stunned expression. "We even won a few championships."

"How few?" he questioned.

"Six, I think. Seven at most."

She racked up strikes and picked up spares like Dick Weber, crushing his pride more completely every frame. This wasn't forgiveness; this was vengeance. She beat him by thirty pins and when he demanded a rematch she beat him again, 196–159. "You set me up," he accused after crediting her final ball, the whipping complete, his ass kicked at bowling by a *girl.*

She sauntered back from the foul line triumphant and regal, the swag of her hips, the toss of her ponytail. "And now you're going to have to live with it," she taunted. "Like I did after *you* betrayed *me.*"

As Westbrook once warned, paybacks were a bitch. Jackie's new rules proved to be only slightly less restrictive than a penitentiary visit. "SDS isn't a female-friendly organization," she explained, "and I've worked too hard to see my reputation ruined because I have a thing for someone in YAF. If I'm going to keep seeing you, we have to be more discreet, like we're having an illicit affair or something. We'll go to out of the way places where no one from SDS is likely to be."

He balled up their score sheet and threw it into an open-mouthed metal bin. "You mean like Memorial Day remembrances and Fourth of July celebrations?" He had betrayed her and these were the consequences. He would be her dirty little secret, denied legitimacy, nameless and faceless—*anonymous*—to all but her.

Stunning, how a woman knew, always knew, a man's most vulnerable spot, like Delilah with Samson's hair. It was too much to ask. He would break up with her, end it, move on. There were plenty of women on campus who would be happy to date him. He had seen them when he walked into class, the tossing of hair and batting of lashes.

But the others failed to excite him like she did. His last thought before falling asleep and his first upon waking was of her warm breath on his face, the soft crush of her body, her moist scent. As bad as the new rules were, banishing him to the shadows of her life, the prospect of being without her was even worse. "I accept with one condition," he said. "That Kyle Levy knows we're still seeing each other." Hiding their love for Jackie's political expediency was one thing. Hiding it for Levy's sake was quite another. *That* he could not tolerate.

"Fine by me," she said. "It's my reputation in SDS that I'm concerned about—not Kyle's ego." She retrieved her ball from the return and held it in front of her, hands locked beneath it, her shoulders bowed by its weight. She flashed the magnanimous smile of the victor and said, "I'm feeling much better about us. Would you like to have dinner at my parents' house tonight?"

David rose to his feet and shrugged. "Why not? At least I won't have to hide in a dark corner."

"Good," she said. "My mother's making cassoulet. I told her yesterday to expect you."

CHAPTER FIFTEEN

BEING RELEGATED TO SECRET LOVER STATUS HAD ITS FRINGE BEN-efits. It charged their lovemaking with the thrill of forbidden behavior, like a Hatfield sleeping with a McCoy. They even invented a game to heighten the arousal. They discovered it one evening in his apartment, with Buffalo Springfield's "Rock and Roll Woman" playing on the stereo and a second bottle of Blue Nun lying empty on the living room carpet beside them.

Jackie sat across from him in flickering candlelight, her right leg stretched straight out, her left leg crooked beneath it, and her left hand on the floor in a bracing position. She had one of his T-shirts on and a pair of panties, nothing else. The splay of her legs revealed a peek of underwear, more than enough to make him as drunk with desire as he was with wine. She was in one of her moods, coquettish and teasing, running a finger over her lower lip and then slowly pulling the hem of her shirt up her thigh. He reached for her, but she swatted him away. "No," she said. "You can't have any."

Her refusal only provoked him more. "Wanna bet?" he asked. He grabbed her by the arm, but she pulled free of his grasp with a sultry, challenging look on her face. He hesitated, quizzical.

"What's the matter?" she taunted, getting to her knees. "Aren't you man enough to take what you want?"

He rose up on his knees and opened his robe so she could see him, swollen and throbbing. He snaked his arm around her waist and drew her against him; she smacked him about the shoulders—playing, he knew, but barely, just barely. It triggered something in him, like a cougar seeing a rabbit bolt for safety. He shed his robe and toppled her over and forced her onto her back. "Is this what you want?" he said with a curl to his lip. "To be taken?"

She struggled and squirmed beneath him while he pulled her shirt up and squeezed her breasts and tongued her with broad strokes, like an animal licking something he caught. Her chest heaved and her nipples got hard. "You're gonna make me fuck you, aren't you?" she said in a tone she had never used before, a rough, slutty tone. She fought him some more and panted, egging him on.

He pried her legs apart with a knee and shoved his hand inside her panties. She was dripping wet and it made him crazy.

"Make me fuck you!" she cried out, bucking and writhing. He tore her panties off and pinned her wrists and thrust inside her and put his tongue in her mouth. She kissed him back and wrapped her legs around him and moaned when she came.

They found themselves so turned on by the brinksmanship of it all that a bawdy game was born. Ravishing the Queen, they called it: Jackie taken against her will by the cruel and vicious YAF enemy. That she engaged in these sessions with even more relish than he did surprised them both.

Things at YAF intensified, too. Membership and morale sky-rocketed after their successful counterprotest at Walter Library, allowing him to cajole Beldon into mounting the chapter's first-ever offensive operation. David's scheme called for a "liberation" of SDS's regional office at Seven Corners, followed several days later by a huge rally in support of the war. The small but high profile action targeting SDS command and control was intended to generate publicity and momentum for the more crucial event to fol-

low. They settled on the first week of December, before campus
shut down for winter recess.

Liberation morning broke cold and gray, with the thermome-
ter stuck at ten and the city digging out from an overnight snowfall. David and the twenty YAF rank-and-filers he had nicknamed
the Dork Patrol rendezvoused at 0900 on the West Bank, a five-
minute walk from the area known as Seven Corners. Plows had
already scraped and salted the roads, but a fluffy mantle of snow
still covered the sidewalks. He wiped a stream of watery snot from
his nose and clapped his gloved hands together in succession. The
Dorks gathered in front of him with the alacrity of a high school
football team, YAF nerds in earmuffs and stocking caps, not one
of them vaguely reminiscent of what their SDS counterparts
might have looked like. Except for David, hatless in a sheepskin
bomber jacket, his untamed hair falling round his face like the
mane of a lion.

His breath rose up in elegant puffs as he went over the battle
plan one last time. "Don't damage any property," he warned. "It's
imperative that we command the moral high ground. Okay, Dorks,"
he said, grinning. "Time to take our country back."

Unlike YAF, which it dwarfed in size, SDS had grown so large
that in addition to hundreds of campus chapters, it had a national
office in Chicago and various regional offices—one of which the
Dork Patrol now marched on. They walked in silence to the corner
of Washington and Cedar and then followed David to a storefront
office with "SDS" stenciled in black on the window. He glanced at
his watch: 0915, right on time. Beldon would have alerted the press
by now and be on his way to join them. They trooped inside and
encountered a petite woman sitting behind a cluttered metal desk.
She wore wire-rim glasses and had straight brown hair parted
down the middle. Two male staffers stood behind her with coffee
mugs in hand.

"YAF hereby liberates this office!" David announced.

The receptionist's long, plain face was dumbfounded, as if Martians had landed, her world destroyed. "I don't understand," she said. The top of her blouse was unbuttoned and a carnelian pendant dangled from her neck.

"We belong to Young Americans for Freedom," David said, eyeing the two men behind her. They set their coffee mugs down and moved closer. "We are opposed to SDS and its subversion of the war in Vietnam, and are here to occupy this office as a means of protest."

The Dorks sprang into action, first nailing a South Vietnamese flag (three red stripes on a lemon yellow background) to the wall, then tacking up a dozen posters in support of the war. They littered the floor with pamphlets detailing North Vietnamese atrocities before splitting in two, one group going outside to prevent entry to the office, the other remaining inside to block egress.

One of the two male SDSers, a paunchy, sullen-faced man in an army jacket, waved his arms and shouted, "Get the hell out of here! We pay to lease this space. You have no right to be here!"

David closed the distance between them until their faces were inches apart. "Let me get this straight. It's okay for SDS to disrupt classes and occupy buildings, but it's not okay for us? If you try to stop us, I'm going to nail your fat commie ass to the wall alongside that South Vietnamese flag."

The man reached for a phone on the reception desk. "Enjoy calling the shots while you can, you fascist prick. I'll have this place crawling with SDS before you know what hit you."

David glanced down the receptionist's insubstantial cleavage and gave her a wink. "I'm counting on it," he said. "The more the merrier." She blushed and could not conceal an embarrassed smile.

As promised, SDS showed up in numbers, but plenty of others thronged the sidewalks as well, students and locals and reporters, all curious to know who it was protesting the protestors. Beldon joined them inside and waited for the right moment to address the crowd.

David passed the time by trading insults with their two male hostages and flirting with the flat-chested receptionist. Once all the cameras arrived, Beldon, wearing a shirt and tie and London Fog coat, went outside to serve notice that the battle between SDS and YAF had been officially joined.

"Because we in YAF," he said, chin up, facing squarely into the camera, "recognize the sanctity of real property and the right of its enjoyment as granted by the Constitution, we end this occupation in peace, without violent incident or further disruption. We hope it has served to make those in SDS realize that we, too, could trample on the rights of others while making our case, but choose not to, and encourage them to do the same. We hereby consider this SDS office liberated, and as of this moment vacate the premises."

David felt a gush of pride listening to him. Howdy Doody sounded downright Churchillian.

They left waving and mugging, like GIs parading down the Champs-Élysées. David checked the crowd for Levy, his satisfaction incomplete without him. He spotted him near the curb, dark and glowering, pacing back and forth. He walked over to let him know there would be no surcease between them—not now and not ever.

"Glad to see you could make it, Levy." He reached into his jacket pocket and withdrew a pair of torn panties. "Would you mind giving these back to Jackie? She likes to have them ripped off of her sometimes. But then, you probably wouldn't know that, would you?"

•   •   •

Momentum was everything, no less in activism than in war, and YAF had it. In the week following their liberation stunt, the press wrote about them, newscasters interviewed them, and students discovered them. Even the campus paper, *The Minnesota Daily*, ran a front-page story on them: "Conservative Student Group Clashes with SDS Over Vietnam." David was content to work behind the scenes planning their upcoming rally while ceding the spotlight to Beldon—though branding YAF with the face of Howdy Doody while SDS had its sexy Radical Queen only made their image deficit that much worse. Even so, the flurry of publicity they enjoyed gave them their best opportunity yet to make their case that Vietnam was worth winning.

How had it come to this, he wondered, needing to persuade an entire generation of Americans that it was better to win a war than to lose one? He assumed it was mostly conscription that rankled them, having to interrupt their lives: Fight your war if you must, but don't ask me to do it. Still, if YAF could convince one campus of the importance of prevailing in Vietnam, they could convince another, and another, until the entire Midwest was with them, and then the West and finally the East.

The South, he was sure, wouldn't need convincing. The South knew all too well that winning a war was better than losing one.

Things got underway at 2 p.m., with a pale winter sun squatting low in the sky, its feeble warmth just enough to turn the snow on Northrop Mall sticky. Notice of the rally had been posted all over campus and mentioned on TV. Its purpose was to gather signatures for a petition YAF would present to President-elect Nixon, asserting that "peace with honor" was gained through victory—not negotiated defeat. Stacks of petitions awaiting signatures sat atop six metal tables placed end-to-end across Northrop Plaza. Strung up behind the tables was a red, white, and blue banner: Victory in Vietnam.

A late-gathering mob of finals-weary students spilled down the plaza stairs and onto the mall's long, parallel sidewalks, which were lined by the charcoal skeletons of dormant trees. An expectant clamor charged the sharp December air, like the edgy buzz of a prizefight.

David stood beneath the banner awaiting his cue, his head bare, his bomber jacket open. Beldon stepped forward and raised a bullhorn to his mouth, wearing his trademark tie and London Fog.

He thanked everyone for coming and got right to the point. "A country at war," he said, his freckled face all wondrous and Howdy-like, his outlandish ears tipped red with cold, "bears an obligation to its warriors: that of fealty." A round of boos roiled the mall, but some cheers, too, the crowd as yet unwilling to break one way or the other. Beldon went on, saying that the manner in which a nation treated its soldiers laid bare that nation's character. "YAF is tired of the maligning of our troops by SDS quislings who think the war futile. Today we have a Vietnam veteran to tell you first-hand what loyal support back home means to troops in the field—and why troops in the field are willing to die for those back home. Please give a warm welcome to David Noble, one of the heroes of Khe Sanh!"

He accepted the bullhorn to tepid applause. He looked out over the mall, at least a thousand people, a few Dork Patrol look-alikes, but mostly longhairs in army jackets and girls in jeans and boots. He had intended to tell them about Beau—*It ain't love of country that makes men die for one another, it's the willingness of men to die for one another that makes for love of country*—but he never got the chance. Signs sprang up everywhere: SDS Against the War! Next came their jejune chant—"No more war! No more war!"—rising off the plaza and rollicking down the mall, drowning out the few, the paltry few, who were genuinely curious to hear what he had to say.

Oh, the shame of it! That Beau's blood had been shed for this, the craven yammering of a great nation's spoiled children. Had they no respect for his sacrifice, the life he gave? A sacred vessel squandered on foolish honor, they would say: honor, consolation prize for fools and dead men, an illusion of Homeric poets and Confederate generals.

They began throwing snowballs, a few at first, then a barrage, landing with a splat all around him as they found the range, like NVA gunners walking mortar rounds ever closer to the mark.

Beldon took cover from the fusillade by overturning one of the tables and crouching behind it. David laughed and walked to the front of the plaza. They could keep him from talking about Beau, but they could not keep him from paying tribute to him. He stiffened into a military salute and held the pose, shoulders back, eyes unblinking.

They took it as an insult, as if he were giving them the finger. The number of snowballs whizzing toward him doubled and then tripled, hitting him in the chest, ribs, crotch. They called him a killer, a murderer, their eyes bulging, their mouths foaming, like stoning a criminal in biblical times. The crook of his salute shielded his eyes, but little else; eventually a snowball struck him flush in the mouth. Blood streamed down his chin, staining the snow beneath him. The sight of it raised a frenzied howl from the crowd, like a pack of coyotes at the kill, but he held his stance until their arms grew weary and their voices hoarse. Only after they had begun to disperse—the rally ruined, the petition a failure—did he turn to leave.

"Hey, Noble!" a voice called out from the sidewalk below the plaza. It was Kyle Levy, gripping an SDS placard with both hands and thrusting it skyward. A pair of red panties dangled from the sign like a communist ensign, symbolic, David understood, of the politics Levy shared with Jackie. "Nobody gives a shit about Khe Sanh," Levy said. "But then, you probably wouldn't know that, would you?"

He brought his gaze to rest on Levy's face, the molten eyes, the gloating grin. A sudden vision of Levy impaled on his bayonet, David shaking him a thousand times more violently than he had shaken the NVA soldier at Khe Sanh, flashed before him.

He could feel the torque of the blade in his palms as he twisted it.

CHAPTER SIXTEEN

JACKIE EMERGED FROM THE SECOND-FLOOR NICHOLSON HALL classroom where Origins of Western Culture was being taught that quarter to find Kyle waiting for her in the hallway, his tousled black hair flecked with snow. He had an expression of supreme urgency on his face. "The Afro-American Action Committee just took over Morrill Hall," he said, taking her by the hand and pulling her toward the stairs. "We've got to be in on this. Come on!"

He was easy to love like this, in his jeans and knee-length leather coat, rallying against racial injustice, spoiling for a fight. He had a nervous habit at such moments of licking his lips—a mannerism that might annoy her later in life, but that now, when they were still like Bonnie and Clyde, two against the world, Jackie found endearing.

Did time always turn your lover's adorable idiosyncrasies into insufferable tics? Yes, if her parents were any indicator. It was one of the reasons she had so far resisted Kyle's importuning about living together. That, and David, of course—hard to keep seeing David while living with Kyle.

She balked at the top of the staircase. "I've got French in fifteen minutes," she said. "Not a class to cut ten days into the quarter."

Kyle descended onto the first step and looked up at her. "Forget French class," he said, clasping her hand like he was proposing. "We've got a *revolution* to attend."

She giggled and said, "Then let's boogie."

It felt good to be needed again, to have a chance to redeem herself for Walter Library. Kyle hadn't allowed her anywhere near the mall when SDS shut down YAF's war rally last month; he was afraid she'd go soft over David. He was probably right. The sight of David getting hit by snowballs and bleeding all over himself while saluting would have been heartbreaking—even if there were times she too wanted to smash him in the mouth over the war.

She fastened the top button of her coat and raised her collar against the cold as they crunched up the walk between Wesbrook Hall and Northrop Auditorium. It was one of those January days where the sky was as white as the ground, so low you could practically reach up and smear it with your finger. The wind burned like dry ice, searing her cheeks before they had gone twenty feet.

The day before, Kyle told her along the way, seven members of the Afro-American Action Committee had presented President Malcolm Moos with three demands: the creation of an Afro-American Studies program, university funding of a national black students conference, and conveyance of the university's Martin Luther King scholarship program to an agency in the black community. Moos had been given until 1 p.m. the following day to respond, at which time seventy AAAC members had gone to his office in Morrill Hall to receive his reply. When he balked, AAAC leaders Rose Mary Freeman and Horace Huntley had led the others out of Moos's second floor Morrill Hall office and down to the admissions office on the first floor. "They told the staff to leave, then wired the doors shut with coat hangers and barricaded themselves inside with desks and filing cabinets," Kyle said with admiration. "Can you dig it?"

"If they've already made their move," Jackie asked, her words floating up in a cloud of vapor the moment they left her lips, "then what are we going to do?"

"Take over the bursar's office in sympathy," he answered.

"It sounds like they're doing fine on their own. Why do they need us?"

He stopped and laughed into the cold, crystalline air—a patronizing laugh Jackie didn't much care for. "Because we can bring numbers and AAAC can't. They probably scrounged around for a week just to *find* seventy black students, and you could fit the number of white students who care about the Afro-American Action Committee into the back row of an organic chemistry class. The minute SDS is involved it'll be a different story. Northrop Plaza will be overrun with students supporting AAAC's takeover."

The "sympathy" the black students locked inside Morrill Hall were about to receive from SDS made Jackie sad. Sometime around the middle of the decade—she wasn't sure exactly when, for by the time she had joined, the change had already occurred—SDS had evolved from an organization of civil rights workers into an organization of antiwar protestors, and it had never looked back. Kyle viewed Martin Luther King as not only dead, but obsolete: the main struggle in the world as far as he was concerned was between American imperialism and the wars of national liberation—like Vietnam—that opposed it. Jackie didn't disagree, but it saddened her all the same that black unrest in America had become nothing more to SDS than a convenient catalyst to ignite a worldwide revolution against capitalist hegemony. SDS was determined to bring the war home—and had decided to use black extremists to do it. The Morrill Hall takeover for Kyle had nothing to do with civil rights; it was about joining the New Left and the Black Power movement at the hip.

After climbing a set of stairs onto the northwest corner of Northrop Plaza, Jackie looked out over the mall. The trees were brittle with ice and the buildings were piled high with snow. It was dreary and desolate, the essence of hiemal despair. Across the plaza, thirty or so SDS protestors—about a third of them women—had already gathered beneath Morrill Hall's four-columned portico.

She and Kyle joined them and led them inside. The information desk was vacant and most of the offices along the building's nave-like corridor were dark. The admissions office was in room 105. The door was closed, but light filtered through a window over the transom.

Kyle reconnoitered the bursar's office—room 115—and motioned everyone forward. They entered a sprawling, open room with suspended overhead lighting and dark gray carpeting and a multitude of black desks and filing cabinets. An array of phones, adding machines, and typewriters sat on top of the desks. Rect-angular windows took up the wall facing the Tate Laboratory of Physics. A dozen nervous employees looked on while Kyle announced that SDS was taking control of the office until further notice, in sympathy with the Afro-American Action Committee takeover of the admissions office.

They collected their coats and left in silence, appearing grate-ful their day was finally over. Kyle then called the admissions office and informed the AAAC that SDS had taken over the bursar's office in solidarity with its black brothers and sisters. He asked Horace Huntley of the AAAC for a quid pro quo: mobilization of SDS in support of the takeover in exchange for public acknowledgment by Huntley that the AAAC had *asked* SDS to join them. "The phone number here is 373-2103," he said when he had finished. "Ciao."

A series of phone conversations between the two ensued. At three o'clock that afternoon, after yet another call from Huntley, Kyle slammed the phone down in frustration. "Now he wants us to contribute a thousand dollars to their shvartze scholarship pro-gram. Like we have a thousand dollars just sitting around to dole out to them. I'm going to have to call my father and beg him to float us a short-term loan. Horace Huntley is becoming a pain in the ass." He shook his head and turned to Jackie with a sigh of exas-peration. "This weekend, we're trippin' out. I need a break from this shit."

Fine with her; she hadn't dropped acid in a month. She was more than ready for the alternative universe. But calling it a *shvartze* scholarship program? Sometimes Kyle made David look like an enlightened Buddhist monk.

• • •

A short while later, Jackie slipped away to a public restroom in the northeast corner of the building. On her way out, she ran head-long into a young black man shambling into the men's room, head down, mumbling, paying no attention to where he was going. He had shiny skin and a ragged, lopsided Afro. "Sorry," he said, step-ping back with his hands in the air. "My mind's a million miles away."

A full head shorter than her, he reeked of cologne and wore a striped shirt tucked into white corduroys. He looked almost comi-cal. Couldn't she have bumped into Sly Stone, or Jimmy Hendrix, maybe? No, she had to crash into Buckwheat—flipped in Jade East.

"That's okay," she said. "I wasn't paying attention either."

"Are you with the SDS demonstrators in the bursar's office?" he asked.

"Yes, I am."

"I'm with the Afro-American Action Committee in the admis-sion's office. As if you couldn't tell," he said with a winsome smile. "We're considering asking you to join the takeover."

She dropped her gaze, embarrassed by the *Our Gang* associa-tion she had flashed on. "I know. Believe me, I know."

His guileless face lit up with recognition, then gave way to a covetous look that black men often got around her, the blonde with blue eyes: forbidden fruit. "I know you. You're the Radical Queen. Except that's not what we call you. We call you Smokin' Hot Mama."

She laughed and stuck out her hand. "I'm Jackie Lundquist."

"Clarence Madison," he replied, shaking her hand. "I've been on the AAAC since the days it was known as STRAP—Students for Racial Progress. We changed our name a little over a year ago." He shifted weight from his left foot to his right then crossed one in front of the other.

"This is the most important thing we've ever done. More black high school students in Minneapolis go to colleges in the South than their own local university, and it's not because of the weather. The University of Minnesota is hostile to African Americans. We're unwelcome in dorms, the fraternities and sororities are closed to us, and the curriculum ignores our existence. We want it to end. Are you prepared to help us?" He thrust his hands into his pockets and began pacing back and forth.

"It looks like you really need to pee, Clarence," she observed. "We can talk some more when you come back." She liked his intelligence and candor—and willingness to suffer a full bladder to talk to her. He gave a quick nod-and-grin and bolted for the men's room in an awkward canter.

Jackie studied his face when he returned, the megawatt smile, the sentient eyes. It was a face that made her want to restore some measure of equipoise between his civil rights movement and her antiwar movement, the one waning, the other rising, yet her cause no more deserving than his, maybe less so. "If we're going to talk honestly," she said, "you have to promise me that no one will ever know about our little summit."

"I promise," he said with a solemn face.

"SDS has its own agenda. If you align yourselves with us, this will become more of an antiwar protest than a racial protest. My advice to you is to refuse to allow us to join you."

His eyes glistened and he asked if she would mind if he kissed her cheek. She lowered her head to let him, moved by a sudden sorrow for every African man or woman who had ever marched in chains to the dark, fetid hold of a slave ship for a transatlantic voyage to Hell, where the slice of an overseer's whip or the stab of Massah's clapboard penis was all that awaited. It was a soft, grateful kiss that had nothing to do with her being a Smokin' Hot Mama, Jackie was certain, and everything to do with being a white girl who had told him the truth.

They parted in silence, which was just as well, as she did not want Clarence Madison to see her crying.

∙ ∙ ∙

Horace Huntley called Kyle late that afternoon to inform him that the AAAC had decided against inviting SDS to join the takeover. Enraged at being denied, Kyle and some of the others— but not Jackie, who stood idly by—littered the floor with heaps of plundered index cards and documents, years of clerical work strewn within minutes into irredeemable chaos. They then smashed all the typewriters and adding machines into mounds of useless debris, hurled all the phones out the window, and overturned all the desks and filing cabinets, leaving the bursar's office trashed beyond recognition before vacating it. The Morrill Hall takeover ended the following day, after President Malcolm Moos agreed to meet the AAAC's demands.

∙ ∙ ∙

Jackie read in *The Minnesota Daily* later that week that an assistant professor by the name of Matthew Stark had spent the night in Morrill Hall in support of the AAAC takeover. Stark, who was a faculty advisor to a number of African American student groups, the story reported, joined the AAAC in the admission's office that day at approximately four o'clock, in response to a request from campus police to mediate the crisis. The *Daily* credited Stark with having convinced the AAAC to refuse to allow SDS to join its protest—a crucial decision, the article asserted, in that it kept the takeover focused on a limited number of racial grievances, rather than allowing it to degenerate into Columbia-style student anarchy. With Stark's assistance, the AAAC had negotiated with university officials throughout the night and into the next day before prevailing in the standoff.

Jackie tossed her paper aside and smiled. The phone call from Horace Huntley rejecting SDS's participation, she knew, had come at a quarter to four—fifteen minutes before Matthew Stark even entered the building.

•   •   •

That Saturday, Kyle was flattened by a viral contagion that tore through campus like a cyclone, forcing Jackie to improvise her plans for the night. "I have a confession to make," she called out to David from the couch in his apartment, legs drawn up under her, her mohair sweater puddled on her lap. "Promise you won't be angry?"

He emerged from the kitchen with two long-stem wine glasses and an oversized bottle of Yago Sangria. He put the bottle and glasses aside and sat down next to her. "You didn't forget to take your birth control pills again, did you?" he asked.

She gave him a face and dug into the front of her jeans and wriggled about until she extracted a wad of Kleenex that she reverently unwrapped, revealing a single blue tablet that was flat on either end. "It's a tab of LSD," she said, holding it up for him to see. "I want to drop acid with you tonight."

David recoiled as if she had dangled a poisonous snake in front of him. "I'd sooner fall on a grenade."

"Oh, don't get uptight. I mean I want to be with you after I take it. When it comes to dropping acid, who you're with is everything. I need to feel safe."

He sniffed. "Then I'll have you know that my apartment is the single hippest place in the country to drop acid tonight—and *not* because it comes with a battle-hardened marine to stand watch while you do it."

Battle-hardened didn't begin to describe it, she knew. Little by little, he had told her everything about his time in Vietnam: the search-and-destroy patrols, the hand-to-hand fighting, the grinding siege of Khe Sanh. And though she hated the very idea of war, she had listened every time in horrid fascination. She found his manly physicality a turn-on, perhaps to a fault; she was beginning to like their decadent game of Ravishing the Queen more than she should. But that's not what tonight was about. Tonight was about trust—though when she thought about it, so was pretending to have forced sex.

"And why is your apartment such a happening place?"

He got off the couch and padded barefoot to the small stereo he had managed to buy, a Sherwood with DLK speakers, and squatted in front of a stack of albums wearing the outfit she had given him for Christmas: black bellbottoms and a gold sweater shirt with loop-and-button fastening. Seeing him sifting through albums with hair to his shoulders and dressed as cool as anyone almost made her forget how tragically different he was, born a century too late, better suited to the 1860s than the 1960s—her misfit, atavist lover.

He returned with a single album in hand. "Because I have this," he said, thrusting it at her. "I've been waiting all week for it to come out. KQRS previewed it last Sunday, but it was just released today."

On the cover was a black-and-white reproduction of the *Hindenburg* catching fire; Led Zeppelin was printed in red lettering in the upper left-hand corner. It was the debut album of a group formed from the remnants of one of her favorite bands, he told her: The Yardbirds.

She popped the "blue flat" into her mouth and washed it down with a swill of wine. "Just like at a concert," she said.

He shook his head. "How long before you go through the looking glass?"

"Half an hour or so."

"Then I better put this on now," he said, taking the album from her.

It was like nothing she had ever heard before, a dense, distorted amalgam of blues and rock, with overpowering guitar riffs and obsessive drum rhythms. The music was so altered already, she failed to notice the incipient effect of the acid until a song with a brooding bass line and haunting lead guitar spilled itself at her feet like warm mercury.

She made him play it again while she got to her feet and scrutinized the room for evidence that her trip had begun, which indeed it had. The shade of his floor lamp reconstituted itself into an array of undulating orange streamers, like a school of Garibaldi. She had no idea how she even knew of the existence of such a fish; she just did.

He fetched a blanket and unfurled it in front of the stereo. She sat on it in the lotus position, grooving on the vibe around her— David's vibe, calm and strong. A joyous frisson shot up her spine, followed by an odd spasm deep in her pelvis: uterine contractions, she knew from experience, a little-known side effect of LSD.

He touched her arm. "Are you okay?"

The clarity of his voice sharpened, as if the sound waves he generated had somehow bypassed the three little bones in her ear and imprinted directly onto her auditory cortex. Her pulse quickened and her respirations grew shallow. "I'm fine. I'm seeing what you don't, hearing what you can't. It's all too beautiful."

Interlocking geometric patterns bubbled up the far wall, saffron cones and purple cylinders and crenellated cubes of green mica. And the music, so mystical! Led Zeppelin—the band, not the album—seemed to know something no one else in the entire world knew, something revelatory and transformative that she, Jackie, was on the brink of discovering, if she could only decipher the hidden meaning of their chords, the secret of their coded lyrics.

Time slowed, like a Dali clock oozing down the road, or a pteropod gliding above the muck. The carpet was a turquoise sea laving her ankles, David's breath the West wind caressing her cheek. *Led Zeppelin*—the album, not the band: this eponym business was so confusing—took control of her, made her one with the music. She took a sip of Yago—cool, sweet nectar, what hummingbirds sucked from flowers—and walked over to a three-shelf antique bookcase packed with classics: Sophocles and Plato, Dante and Milton, Shakespeare and Hugo, Dickens and Dumas. She pressed her palm against the books' spines. They turned pellucid, their immanent wisdom made visible and manifest. A soothing amber glow penetrated her hand and rose up her arm, universal truths flowing from the books into the chambers of her heart, to be pumped in great strokes to her brain. Knowledge, the elixir of the gods, bathing every fold and sulcus until her head fairly throbbed with epiphanies,

The plateau of her trip endured all through the night and into the dawn when, with a gentle snowfall muffling the world outside, he brought her to a climax that pulsed in color. Afterward she lay dandled in his arms with an acid crash descending over her like a hit of Valium.

How eternal their love would be, she thought, if only she could turn David on, too.

CHAPTER SEVENTEEN

O̶F THE MANY THINGS DAVID HAD VOWED TO DO IF HE SURVIVED Khe Sanh, taking another class from Thomas Devlin was high on the list. He kept his promise by enrolling in a course titled "America after the Civil War: The Reconstruction and Progressive Eras," taught in the same third-floor Blegen Hall classroom as the Manifest Destiny course he took in 1966. He found Devlin little changed, his kinky silver hair no thinner, his stocky frame no less substantial. Though other professors had begun dressing more casual, in obeisance to the times, Devlin still came to class in a jacket and tie and freshly shined wing tips. After taking the entire month of January to cover Reconstruction, he began his series of lectures on the Progressive Era by writing "Of Mr. Booker T. Washington and Others" on the blackboard.

He set his piece of chalk on the aluminum rail and pointed at the board. "Who knows what this is?" He fussed with the sleeve of his tweed jacket while scanning the room for a response.

David had no clue. He twisted around in his seat and saw that no one else did either—save for a rumpled looking black guy in the last row. His arm hung lazily in the air, as if attached to invisible strings. He had a kind face and an unkempt Afro that listed to one side.

"It's a chapter in *The Souls of Black Folks* by W. E. B. Du Bois," he said when Devlin called on him. He pronounced it "do-boys," rather than the French rendering David was accustomed to.

The corners of Devlin's mouth turned up ever so slightly. "That's absolutely right. It speaks to one of the great controversies of the time: how to best address the plight of blacks in the Jim Crow South after the collapse of Reconstruction." He slid behind the lectern and explained that W. E. B. Du Bois and Booker T. Washington were the leading black intellectuals of the Progressive Era, men of breathtaking accomplishments, with Washington best known for helping establish Tuskegee University in Alabama, and Du Bois for his role in founding the NAACP. "In 1895," he continued, "Washington gave a speech on race relations to a mostly white audience at the Cotton States and International Exposition in Atlanta. It became known as the Atlanta Compromise, and advocated blue-collar bootstrapping as the surest way for blacks to secure a toehold amongst the nation's white majority." Rather than give a scholarly exegesis of the speech, Devlin instead read excerpts from it, so that students could form their own opinions of it before hearing his.

> Our greatest danger is that in the great leap from slavery to freedom we may overlook the fact that the masses of us are to live by the productions of our hands ... No race can prosper till it learns that there is as much dignity in tilling a field as in writing a poem. It is at the bottom of life we must begin, and not at the top ...
>
> The wisest among my race understand that the agitation of questions of social equality is the extremest folly, and that progress in the enjoyment of all the privileges that will come to us must be the result of severe and constant struggle rather than of artificial forcing ... The opportunity to earn a dollar in a factory

just now is worth infinitely more than the opportunity
to spend a dollar in an opera house . . .

I pledge that in your effort to work out the great
and intricate problem which God has laid at the doors
of the South, you shall have at all times the patient,
sympathetic help of my race . . . This coupled with our
material prosperity, will bring into our beloved South
a new heaven and a new earth.

He swept the room with his blue-eyed gaze to gauge how effective a fillip his reading had been. Quite effective, David was guess-
ing, what with images of taut-faced National Guardsmen patrolling smoldering cities still fresh in everyone's mind. "It was an
argument for gradualism that saw black upward mobility as a long,
painstaking climb," Devlin said, "similar to what an immigrant
population might expect."

He dealt next with Du Bois's repudiation of the Atlanta Compromise, a gravamen that became fully formed, he told them, in
1903, when Du Bois used an entire chapter in *The Souls of Black
Folks* to make his case. He proceeded to read several passages.

This 'Atlanta Compromise' is by all odds the
most notable thing in Mr. Washington's career . . . and
today its author is certainly the most distinguished
South-erner since Jefferson Davis, and the one with
the largest personal following . . .

But aside from this, there is among educated and
thoughtful colored men in all parts of the land a feeling of deep regret, sorrow, and apprehension at the
wide currency and ascendancy which some of Mr.
Washington's theories have gained . . .

Mr. Washington distinctly asks that black people
give up, at least for the present, three things—First,
political power, Second, insistence on civil rights,
Third, higher education of Negro youth . . .

But so far as Mr. Washington apologizes for injustice
. . . does not rightly value the privilege and duty of voting, belittles the emasculating effects of caste distinc-
tions, and opposes the higher training and ambition of
our brighter minds—so far as he, the South, or the
Nation, does this—we must unceasingly and firmly
oppose them . . . clinging unwaveringly to those great
words which the sons of the Fathers would gain forget:
'We hold these truths to be self-evident: That all men
are created equal . . .'

Devlin stepped away from the podium, his hands empty of all
notes. "Du Bois favored a more confrontational approach to civil
rights, believing that blacks should challenge whites, culturally and
politically. He took to calling Washington 'The Great Accommo-
dator,' and blamed the separate but equal ruling of *Plessy versus
Ferguson* on Washington's acquiescent stance toward segregation.
Du Bois in later years, however, would concede that his approach
of 'educate and agitate' failed to end segregation, and that full inte-
gration was a goal for the distant future—which is precisely what
Washington argued in his Atlanta Compromise speech."

As was his custom, he saved time for a discussion question at
the end. "With all of this in mind, then, whose philosophy should
today's African Americans rely on to overcome the lingering damage of segregation—that of Du Bois or that of Washington?"

David didn't know much about Du Bois or Washington, but he
knew quite a lot about self-reliance. He got a chance to answer
right before change of class, after every single student before him
had picked Du Bois—though not the black guy in the last row, who
said nothing.

"Washington's," he responded. "A philosophy of self-help is always more empowering than one that relies on government decree."

A chorus of boos accompanied someone shouting, "Dude's a
racist, man!" from the back of the room. Devlin silenced their noisy

dissent by saying they were out of time, but the disorderly looking black dude with the cockeyed Afro caught up to David after class and took him by the arm.

"Can we talk?" he asked.

David wondered if he was the one who had called him a racist? If so, too bad: that was the way he felt about things and it had nothing to do with being racist. "That depends."

"On what?"

"On who I'm talking to and what we're talking about."

"Sorry. I'm Clarence Madison." He stuck out his hand, soul–brother-style.

David grasped it and said, "David Noble."

"I want to talk to you about what you said in class," Clarence told him.

Great. If he said no, Clarence Madison would think he was a racist for blowing him off. If he agreed, Clarence would accuse him of being racist for siding with an Uncle Tom like Booker T. Washington. Calling someone racist had become the campus equivalent of pinning a scarlet letter to their chest. Maybe alcohol would help.

"Something tells me we're going to need more than the five minutes I have now. How about tonight at the Equation?"

Clarence proposed seven o'clock.

"Okay then, seven."

Clarence nodded and brushed past him, investing the air with the vanilla-musk scent of his cologne.

• • •

Clarence was waiting when he arrived, a mug of beer in hand, his woolen coat draped over the back of his chair, coattails covered in peanut shells. A pitcher of beer and an empty, frosted mug sat on the table in front of him.

David walked across the bar's pliant wooden floor while

Hendrix wailed overhead and the hounds of winter howled outside, rattling the Quadratic Equation's front window like a
Dickensian ghost. "Colder than a witch's tit out," he said, sitting
down to fill his mug. He felt no chill against his palm, which was
the same temperature as the rime-rimmed glass he wrapped his
hand around.

Clarence stared at him, his face a stern black mask. "Did you
ever notice that only white people use that expression?" he asked.

David took a draft of beer and braced for the worst. He hadn't
even had his first peanut yet and Clarence was all over him about
race relations. He resigned himself to getting what he deserved for
running his mouth in class about something he really didn't know
all that much about.

"It's because black people don't even like *talkin'* about witches,"
Clarence said with a warm grin. "*Rosemary's Baby*, the devil and
covens and shit? Scares the bejesus out of us!"

David broke out laughing, relieved. "So tell me about Washington and Du Bois," he said.

The salient details of the two men's lives rolled off Clarence's
lips like a hero-worshiping nephew talking about legendary uncles
at a family picnic. "Du Bois was born a free man in Massachusetts
and was educated at Harvard and the University of Berlin," he said.
"Washington was born a slave and was freed by the Civil War. He
worked as a salt-packer and in coalmines before putting himself
through college to become principal of the Tuskegee Normal and
Industrial Institute in Alabama, which he built into a full-fledged
black university."

He waited impatiently for a wailing fire engine to pass. David
shelled a peanut and washed it down with a slug of beer.

"Du Bois," Clarence went on, "was no less remarkable. He was
the first African American to receive a doctorate from Harvard, a
cofounder of the NAACP, and the father of the Pan-African movement. The philosophical difference between the two was mostly a

matter of emphasis. What mattered most to Washington was *liberty*, self-determination—an individual's *freedom* to succeed. What mattered most to Du Bois was *equality*, civil justice—an individual's *right* to succeed. Washington said: 'A white man respects a Negro who owns a two-story brick house.' Du Bois said: 'We claim for ourselves every single right that belongs to a free American.' Their argument was—and still is—about the difference between liberty and equality, about showing whites that blacks are equals through personal industry versus *forcing* whites to accept blacks as equals through civil rights legislation."

"Which side do you come down on?" David asked.

"Washington's," Clarence said, in an almost guilty tone, as if confessing to something shameful. "Same as you."

"Then how come you didn't say so in class? I could have used a little help."

His darkly emotive eyes registered a pang of regret. "If I had been the only black in the room I would have, but you'd be surprised how vicious we brothers can be to one another. The black intelligentsia long ago declared Du Bois a hero and Washington a traitor. A black man who favors Washington over Du Bois nowadays is ridiculed as an Oreo, a Tom—a collaborator. That kind of peer pressure is pretty intimidating.

"It's not that I don't believe white racism exists. I do. It's that I no longer believe political activism is the best way to overcome white racism. You know the Morrill Hall takeover last month? I was part of it. But even though we got everything we asked for, I found myself more profoundly moved by a sympathetic white protester who shared some information with me—information that hurt her cause and helped mine—than by the concessions we won. She made me realize that acceptance is more powerful when given voluntarily. You can legislate civil rights, but you can't legislate acceptance. Acceptance has to be earned, one person at a time."

He looked radiant, the burden of his belief lifted. "Besides, De

Bois's confrontation chickens are about to come home to roost. There are Malcolm X disciples in Minneapolis who want a Black Panther chapter in town. They . . ." His jaw went slack and a stunned expression seized his face. "That's her!" he said, pointing over David's shoulder. "The girl from Morrill Hall."

David turned around. Jackie and Kyle Levy were coming down the aisle on their way out of the bar. Clarence got to his feet and bowed. "The Radical Queen," he said.

Jackie's face lit up. "Clarence?" She gave him a hug that made him look like he might faint dead away. "This is Kyle," she said, pulling Levy forward. "Kyle, this is Clarence."

David stood and said hello to Jackie, but ignored Levy. She turned red at the sight of him. "David, what a surprise," she stammered.

"You two know each other?" Clarence asked her.

"We all *three* know each other," Levy mumbled.

David said nothing. The tension was palpable, a living, breathing thing that crowded out all niceties, no matter how hard Jackie tried to keep it from view with her desperate chatter. After what seemed like forever, she and Levy said goodnight and headed out the door.

"That was one uptight white folk encounter," Clarence said after they were gone.

"Jackie is Levy's girlfriend," David explained. "And mine, too. Neither one of us is all that thrilled about sharing."

•   •   •

It may have been the third pitcher of beer that set him off, or the look on Levy's face when he walked Jackie out of the bar, his "I'm going to fuck her tonight and you're not" smirk. Or maybe it was because it had felt so good to finally tell someone Jackie was his girl, to break the emasculating pledge of secrecy she had held him to because she didn't want anyone to know the Radical Queen was balling a YAF ringleader, a marine baby killer, no less.

Marine baby-killer—what an SDS crotchet *that* was. Whatever the reason, instead of going home, he walked from the Quadratic Equation to her apartment and stood on the snow-packed walk, oblivious to the polar blast that threatened to tear his cheeks off. A huge cornice encrusted the top of the building, but a warm flicker of light came through the window of the second floor unit Jackie shared with Liz Bodine, whom David had never met.

Jackie and Levy were inside; he knew they were. He could sense it, feel it, the mingling of limbs, their rising passion . . . He had an image of Levy with his head between her legs, Jackie moaning with pleasure. A wave of nausea gripped him and he felt clammy. He braced himself against one of the hoary elms lining the curb and waited for it to pass. It was the worst thing he could imagine. Because of what it implied, the intimacy of it. The kind of intimacy he had deceived himself into believing she shared with no one but him. His knees wobbled and his stomach roiled and he doubled over and retched up a load of beer and peanuts, but when he was finished, after he had wiped the puke from the corners of his mouth, a rising desire of his own held sway—to maim, like at Khe Sanh, or with Wisniewski last summer.

No good would come of it, he knew, but hadn't it always been this way? He had a storied history of self-sabotage. Was it not more than a little odd that he feared anonymity, yet chose to live alone? And his reason for joining the marines. Was it solely to fight for his country, or had he sabotaged something then, too, by running away from what he feared would only be taken from him if he stayed?

It was a pattern that began during the vagrancy of his childhood, when he was eleven and living in his third foster home. He had become suspicious that foster mother Number Three was going to send him back to the orphanage like Numbers One and Two had done, blindsiding him just when he was starting to believe she wanted him. That Number Three had as of yet done nothing to warrant such suspicion made no difference: neither had the others, in the beginning.

Unfounded or not, his abandonment paranoia got the better of him one night when he and his foster siblings—Jack and Bobby, ages twelve and nine, and Michelle, ten—accompanied Number Three to a local skating rink. After an hour or so of skittering about, David became separated from the others. He lurched around the rink in a panic before finding them gathered around Number Three at the warming house, laughing and drinking cocoa. Had they ditched him? Was she in on it? He decided she was, and vowed he would not be caught unawares again, like the two previous times. When the other children returned to the rink he chased them down one by one, knocking them to the ice over and over, even Michelle, until she sat there crying, legs splayed, her pink jacket spattered with blood from a split lip. When confronted by Number Three, he offered no explanation for his behavior, which at the time he barely understood himself. A week later he was back at the fosterage, his suspicions confirmed. *See, I knew she was going to get rid of me.*

He leaned against the tree he had just barfed on and waited for the mayhem that was singing in his hands to stop, for reason to prevail. Jackie and Levy were safely tucked away in a second-floor apartment; how was he supposed to get at them, by transforming himself into fog and passing under the door like Dracula? Better to go home before he did something stupid.

His wrath had almost dissipated when the sound of chattering voices caught his attention. A couple appeared at the top of the street, coming down its icy slope in a playful glissade. He plastered himself against the tree and waited for them to pass, but they turned up the front walk of the building instead.

A shrill squeal of laughter pierced the night, an annoying peal that carried even above the whistling wind. Liz's laugh could turn back a herd of buffalo, he remembered Jackie saying. The girl heading up the walk was Liz Bodine. And that changed things.

The bantering couple failed to see him fall in behind them. He let them enter the building and start up the first flight of stairs before slipping inside after them. He paused on the landing until he heard them fumbling for keys, then timed his climb so that he arrived at the top of the stairs just as the girl pushed open the door to let the two of them inside. David used his forearm to prevent her from closing it. She stared uncomprehendingly at him, a straight-haired sylph in a parka.

"I'm here to see Jackie." He pushed forward into a small entry-way. The Doors' latest song played from somewhere inside.

The boyfriend—Kevin, he recalled—maneuvered between them. "Who the hell are you?"

He was chubby and soft looking, with curly hair and a doughy face. He posed no threat, so David ignored him. "You must be Liz," he said to the girl.

"Are you David?" Her eyes were wide but unafraid.

"That's me. The imaginary boyfriend. Where's Jackie?"

Kevin took a step backward. "David? Oh, shit."

"Jackie's not here," Liz told him.

David jerked a thumb in the direction of the music. "You always leave the stereo on when you go out?"

"Liz? Is that you?" It was Jackie calling from the next room. Liz shrugged, as if to say, I did what I could.

He brushed past her into the kitchen, which reeked with a feminine scent, potpourri maybe. He turned left in front of a table with a mobile of a parrot hanging over it, letting the sound of the music guide him. Jackie and Levy were sitting across from one another on the living room floor, fussing with a bag of pot. A stereo flanked by turquoise lava lamps sat behind them.

"Well, well, well," David said, standing akimbo, more than a little drunk. "The Radical Queen and Ho Chi Minh, having a little nightcap."

Their heads snapped up in unison. Jackie shrieked his name. Levy scrambled to his feet. "What the fuck are you doing here?"

David felt the craving in his hands, the blood lust in his palms. He wanted to tear into Levy the way he tore into that gook at Khe Sanh, to twist a K-Bar in his liver and gut him, right there in front of Jackie. He went so far as to spin around in hopes of seeing a steak knife on the kitchen table, but all he saw was the wise, sympathetic face of Liz Bodine counseling forbearance, pulling him back from the precipice without a word.

He turned away and impaled Levy with a look that would have made Westbrook proud. "I came to talk to Jackie. But if you piss me off, I could get distracted."

Levy's face tightened and his chest heaved, but he remained motionless. "Go ahead, then. Get on with it."

"No more slinking around," David said to Jackie. "Either see me openly or don't see me at all. It's up to you."

She stood, her face purple. "You follow me home drunk and break into my apartment when I'm with someone else and expect me to keep seeing you? You're a lunatic! You should have stayed in the marines with all the other psychopaths!"

"Call me when you make up your mind."

Liz escorted him out of the apartment and down the hall, warily guarding against an encore. She took his elbow at the top of the stairs and looked him in the eye. "She loves you, David. She always has. She's just not sure if you should be together."

CHAPTER EIGHTEEN

SHE CALLED THREE TIMES THAT WEEK TO BERATE HIM FOR HIS arrogance, his gall at barging into her apartment when she was with Kyle, but each time he held firm. He would be hidden from sight no more. In the end she laid down but one condition for acquiescing to his ultimatum: that he take her to see Zeffirelli's *Romeo and Juliet*, the ultimate primer on the hazards of "being together."

True to her word, they saw it at the Campus Theater on a Saturday afternoon, the Radical Queen consorting with YAF scum in broad daylight. The movie posters in the lobby all sported the same mackled caption: No Ordinary Love Story.

"Whose love story is?" David questioned while standing in line for popcorn.

"If you're going to be critical before we even go inside," Jackie said, "then forget it. The deal's off."

He bent low at the waist and in a conspiratorial voice said, "Too late. There's a pair of apparatchiks behind us who will be reporting your scandalous behavior to the Central Committee. Fraternizing with the enemy—it's Siberia for you, my pretty: no drugs, no music, and no spring break." She whumped him on the arm, a sure sign his drunken raid on her apartment had been put behind them.

He had always regarded *Romeo and Juliet* as a play best suited for callow high schoolers, and had consequently expected the movie version to generate little enthusiasm on campus. What possible interest would the generation of free love have in the ill-fated variety? But he had been wrong. The film was immensely popular with college students.

Two hours and change later, he understood why. Though Zeffirelli eliminated whole scenes and edited entire blocks of text, the smart cinematography, poignant score, and nubile beauty of the leads more than made up for it. What made it so popular with young people, though, he realized halfway through, was Zeffirelli's success at recasting the story's main conflict into one of stasis versus change, order versus rebellion, the sclerotic detachment of age versus the white-hot passion of youth: the Generation Gap, Shakespeare-style.

Was there not an hour's rest from it, not even during a movie version of a play written four centuries ago? How had one generation come to control the dialogue of an entire nation? Was it by sheer weight of numbers, their demographic preponderance a ꞈꞈꞈꞈ ꞈꞈꞈꞈꞈ ꞈꞈꞈꞈꞈ ꞈꞈ ꞈꞈꞈꞈ ꞈꞈꞈꞈ ꞈꞈꞈꞈꞈꞈ ꞈꞈ ꞈꞈꞈꞈꞈ ꞈꞈ ꞈꞈꞈꞈꞈꞈ ꞈꞈꞈꞈ dled complainers of them all in an effort to spare them the deprivation of the Great Depression?

Zeffirelli knew it was so. He showed the youth of Verona that way, slouching toward the *piazza* with time on their hands and rebellion in their hearts. Zeffirelli understood that it wasn't the hue and cry of the striving poor that started revolutions; it was the cavil and tripe of the disaffected well-off.

He said nothing of these things to Jackie, though. She and every other woman in the theater began crying the moment the film ended, its elegiac score seeming to lift the dead lovers toward heaven. She clung to him and snuffled all the way to Lomedico's, an Italian restaurant several blocks away.

They sat at a window table covered with a linen cloth and worked on a basket of garlic bread and a bottle of Chianti that smelled of nutmeg. "So," she said, once their meal had come—

lasagna for him, manicotti for her, the tub of popcorn at the theater having no effect on their appetites whatsoever—"what did you think of the balcony scene?" Her cheek still bore a smear of mascara from her grieving.

David smiled. Even in an age of *The Feminine Mystique*, bra burning, and the Pill, no woman could resist it, Western Civilization's most iconic love scene. "I thought it overemphasized the heavy breathing and rushed some of the most beautiful lines in all of English literature," he said.

To his surprise, she agreed. "I guess Zeffirelli thought the scene spoke mostly to sexual longing, but to me it was more about risk taking."

He had studied the play just last fall, in "Shakespeare I." The balcony scene had been presented as the quintessence of young love, with Juliet the more skillful lover, but he recalled no mention of risk taking. "What kind of risks do you mean?"

"Risks of the heart. Romeo endangered his life by jumping the orchard wall for a glimpse of Juliet. Juliet jeopardized her reputation by being 'too quickly won.' Risks of the heart are what make us human."

He thought back to their Ferris wheel ride at Excelsior, when a single kiss had left him sleepless for a week. He raised his glass. "To risks of the heart. And first kisses, too. Salute!"

A chef in a toque interrupted them, flitting from table to table in search of compliments. "It's the same with us, you know," she said after he had moved on, his ego sufficiently stroked by their raving. "The risks of being together, I mean."

"How do you figure?"

"I'm in danger of losing the approval of my peer group because of you. Isn't that what reputation is, the approval of one's peer group?"

"And you think I'm like Romeo, that my *life* is in danger on account of you?"

She ran a finger around the rim of her glass. "Not in danger of being lost, maybe. In danger of being changed. Your life is definitely in danger of being changed."

She was right, of course. Her influence over him grew stronger by the day, the hour . . . the minute. He felt her washing over him like waves against a seawall, eroding his foundation. "Okay," he said, in a tender voice. "We're a risky couple."

Her face melted into a satisfied smile. "Well, if Juliet was willing to risk her reputation on Romeo, then I'm willing to risk mine on you."

It took only an hour for her vow to be put to the test. A couple walked in the door as they were preparing to leave. "Kathleen, Greg!" Jackie called out, waving over a slim brunette and her ungainly blond companion. "This is David. We just saw *Romeo and Juliet* together. It was fabulous."

She slipped an arm around his waist and gave him an adoring smile, a supererogatory display of affection designed to leave no doubt in her friends' minds as to his status in her life. He could tell from their expressions that this was a big deal, Jackie seeing *Romeo and Juliet* with someone other than Kyle Levy. It wouldn't be long, he knew, before SDS gossipmongers spread the word that the guy draped all over the Radical Queen at Lomedico's was in YAF. Yet as good as it felt to be legitimate again, openly acknowledged as her boyfriend, a competing emotion ruined his satisfaction; for burning inside him hotter than white phosphorus was the desire to be her only boyfriend.

• • •

Jackie didn't make the connection at first, didn't think twice about the temporal relation of it to David's bellicose invasion of her apartment. If not for its vexing persistence, the linkage between the two might never have occurred to her at all. As it was, the actual term for it didn't come to mind until she stumbled across it one afternoon lying in bed reading *Playboy*, which she furtively browsed from time to time—along with *Sports Illustrated*—in an effort to better understand David. Clues to Kyle's inner male she sought in *Esquire* or *Ramparts*. What a shock, then, to see Kyle's Freudian self rather than David's laid bare in an essay preceding the "Playmate of the Month" pictorial.

Premature ejaculation.

It didn't *sound* that bad, like shedding a first-stage booster rocket or something, but in truth it was an invidious thing. At first she had shrugged it off as something all young men suffered from time to time, Kyle more susceptible than most, perhaps, on account of his family background, performance anxiety being practically a Jewish birthright. Even after it happened a third and then a troubling fourth time, leaving her unsatisfied and him deflated, she had still assumed it would be a passing thing. Until she read the article in *Playboy*. It attributed unremitting cases of PE—that's what the article called it, PE: "The Modern Male's Bête Noire"—to a crisis of confidence, either developmental or situational in origin. Since Kyle had previously experienced only the occasional misfire, she concluded that the problem must be in response to some recent trauma in his life. His Quick Draw McGraw issues, she realized, had begun the week after David confronted him in her apartment. It didn't seem like a big deal at the time, but evidently it was.

She thought back to the week before, the scabrous talk and crude manhandling of her that was so out of character for Kyle, a little creepy, even. She had written it off to the black beauties they took that night—amphetamines were a rush, but sometimes brought out the beast. But what had made him think she might like rough sex? They had never come close to trying it before, no matter what drugs they consumed. Maybe poor Kyle thought he could cure his PE that way.

She felt horrible. A part of her—not the part that wanted

orgasms, for that part had suffered greatly—had actually been *pleased* at his untimely eruptions, had taken them as proof of her sex appeal. She had at times even goaded him on to see how fast she could make him come, as if she were some kind of Aphrodite, her beauty making him lose all control. And this despite the fact that she was no prettier or sexier now than the month before, when there had been no problem at all.

She prided herself on never feeling ashamed, even bragged that she didn't believe in shame, but if what she felt now wasn't shame, it was as close to the real thing as she cared to come. She was an idiot. What did she think would come of dating two men who hated each other? That she could keep on screwing them both for as long as she wanted and expect them to be unaffected by it? David's change in status from undercover lover to legit boyfriend was messing with Kyle's head—and worse. She thought back to the old Lovin' Spoonful song and knew the part about having to make up your mind was oh so true.

She resigned herself to having her visibility in SDS reduced on account of being seen in public with David. To expect otherwise would be asking more than Kyle was capable of. But a week later he returned from a trip to SDS national headquarters in Chicago with all talk of limiting her role gone by the wayside. "It's time for SDS to evolve," he told her, "and we need your help to make it happen."

His time in Chicago had reinvigorated a vision he shared with an SDS splinter group born the year before at Columbia University, where it had been known as the "Action Faction." SDS's Chicago-based descendents of the Action Faction saw Vietnam much the way Kyle did: as a surrogate for liberation conflicts worldwide, part and parcel, along with America's racial strife, of a broader, Third World war against neocolonialism. He insisted that she read a book the Chicago bloc had repeatedly cited for intellectual underpin-ning, *The Wretched of the Earth* by Frantz Fanon—which she did, in a single weekend. She found herself greatly moved by Fanon's poignant way of revealing the extreme psychosocial damage caused by colonialism, to individuals and entire cultures alike. But SDS's idea of using the Black Power movement to ignite a racial revolt in America that would trigger a *worldwide* revolution to destroy neo-colonialism—and elevate the New Left to power in its wake—went far beyond anything Fanon proposed.

And why couldn't there be a world free of social injustice, she wondered, free of capitalist conniving and human subjugation for the sake of a dollar? Why not the Summer of Love in every city of every country on earth? The possibility of it, the glorious possibility!

Faith was all that was required. Faith in compassion and peace, in altruism and love, with bounty for the destitute and freedom for the oppressed—and an end to the most vile, evil construct ever conceived by the human mind: the free market, which wasn't free for anyone, especially those on the bottom looking up, the victims. As Fanon had implied, violence as a means of liberation and to discharge pent-up rage at one's oppressors was not only legitimate, but necessary. The victims of white male imperialism cried out for it: violence, just this once.

She was flattered that respected New Left intellectuals in Chicago might need *her*, little Miss Robbinsdale, to help make it happen—and more than a little relieved at not being stripped of her crown, the Radical Queen deposed. So she told Kyle yes, of course she would help him. He rewarded her by making her aide-de-camp of a campaign to convince their local chapter that SDS's mission had changed.

The two of them spent long hours together preparing for and participating in "struggle sessions"—contentious group meetings with ideological control of SDS at stake. Kyle argued that rather than focusing on stopping the war, they needed to dedicate themselves to starting the revolution. He urged them to become "Americong," freedom fighters who would take up arms in support of black revolutionaries like the Panthers. Failure to do so amounted to tacit acceptance of white hegemony, and was therefore racist. Armed with slogans from Chicago—It's Gut Check Time; The Heavier the Better; and John Brown, Be Like Him!—he implored them to show the world that the spirit of Harper's Ferry was alive and well.

"And fuck Robert E. Lee for stopping him!" he would yell, in reference to Lee's squelching—with United States Marines Lee commanded in pre-Civil War Virginia—of Brown's attempt to start a slave rebellion.

"Why would we want to be like John Brown?" someone would challenge. "Brown was hanged for inciting Harper's Ferry."

"Brown's hanging was what made him great," Kyle would respond.

"But what will we do when *we're* in power?" someone else would ask.

"A better job than all who have gone before us," would be Kyle's antiphonal reply. "Because we are the most moral, ethical, best-educated generation ever conceived."

He wanted honky America to shit its pants in fear, and toward that end espoused that the killing of pigs was good, because those who showed no mercy deserved no mercy. On this point, Jackie was ambivalent. Hadn't Pig Piss spared her when he could have torn her face off?

But the push for revolution was all consuming; her time with David dwindled to less than once a week. His skeptical grumbling that Kyle's sudden need of her might have less to do with Jackie's value to the movement than with limiting her contact with him made her sad, but only for awhile.

There was so much to do to make the revolution happen.

•   •   •

She pulled up to her parents' home the Sunday before finals with macadam showing in the drive and patches of grass emerging in the yard. A late March thaw had finally loosened the frozen clench of winter. It was their first dinner together in over a month, and she couldn't vouch for what might come out of her mouth. Her rage and frustration over the war grew stronger by the day, fueled by the pace of events, Nixon threatening to bomb again and U.S. troops in the DMZ for the first time in a year. So much for Tricky Dick's promise to end the war. Kyle was right. The only way to stop the killing was to start the killing.

She felt increasingly cut off from her parents. They didn't understand the *repression* SDS endured, what FBI's COINTELPRO operations were doing to them, the legal harassment and black bag jobs and provocations and beatings. That week alone Tom Hayden and Bobby Seale had been indicted for conspiring to incite violence at the Democratic Convention last summer; maybe she and Kyle would be next.

It used to be that she and her father could at least talk about Vietnam, but lately he had become completely intolerant of what he called her "toxic polemic" on the war—and this despite her watering things down by alluding to *picketing* induction centers rather than blowing them up.

She pulled to a stop in front of the garage and entered the side door without knocking. Her parents were in the kitchen, her father standing by with a freshly lit Dutch Masters while her mother dragged a ketchup-baked meatloaf out of the oven. "Good timing," he said. "Dinner's just about ready."

But for a glimpse of gray at the temples, he seemed impervious to age, his athletic frame as yet unbent, his eyes clear and bright. Her mother, on the other hand, seemed older by the month. Her figure was shot and her face was as brittle and creased as old wallpaper. If not for the brown tint job of her Korean hairdresser, she would have looked more like Jackie's grandmother than her mother. At least her mother cut her some slack, though—unlike good old Pete.

She greeted them from across the room, in no mood for obligatory affection. Her mother set the meatloaf on a breadboard and pulled off her oven mitts. "You should have invited David," she said, brushing a wisp of hair off her forehead. "We haven't seen much of him lately. Your father so enjoys his company."

Jackie peeled off her boots and hung her coat over the back of a chair. "Maybe next time," she said. Or not. Bringing David with her only made things worse—though his long hair *had* thrown her father for a loop last time. They wouldn't think David was so straight and narrow if they saw him playing Ravishing the Queen, a lusty rapist taking their daughter by force.

Out of respect for her mother, whose domestic enslavement she pitied more than resented, Jackie let the meal pass in tranquility, choosing to trade banalities about school or her older sisters— Peggy and Michelle, the childless ones—rather than discuss anything meaningful. But after half a bottle of wine, an overpowering urge to test the true nature of her parents' love got the best of her. Conditional or unconditional, which would it be?

"Kyle and I renounced our white skin privilege," she blurted out during blueberry pie à la mode.

Her father's hand froze in midair, his fork never making his mouth. "You renounced *what*? What kind of privilege?"

"White . . . skin . . . privilege. What you and I benefit from, socio-economic advantage because of the color of our skin."

Her mother bowed her head and made the sign of the cross. Her father put his fork down and glared. "The only socio-economic advantage *I* ever enjoyed was my willingness to work the night shift at Great Northern Railroad to put myself through college. And the only socio-economic advantage you enjoy is my willingness to work sixty-hour weeks at a law firm to put *you* through college. Trust me, tuition doesn't come with a white-skin discount."

She clasped her hands behind her head, leaned back in her chair and sighed. "You can pretend racism doesn't exist, but it does. It's ingrained so deeply in our society we're not even aware of it. You're a perfect example. You cheer for Jerry West and say he's great, yet you call Bill Russell a 'big gorilla' and swear at him whenever he makes a basket. I wonder why?" She had him on that one, she was confident. Unconscious racism—a sign of how bad things really were.

He looked at her as if she'd just tried to climb the dining room drapes. "I cheer for Jerry West because the Los Angeles Lakers used to be the Minneapolis Lakers," he said calmly, "and I call Bill Russell a big gorilla because he's half a foot taller than Jerry West and can jump out of the damn gym. What's that phrase you like so much— mellow out? You need to mellow out, Jackie."

He was mocking her, ridiculing her. "You're a parvenu," she told him, "a racist parvenu. You line your library with leather-bound books you don't read and buy French wines you can't pronounce, and all the while remain oblivious to the injustice around you."

He gave her a look of disgust. "You've had too much to drink. You sound like Kyle."

"You hate Kyle and like David because David thinks like you do, but I'll tell you something. The revolution is coming, and you and David are on the wrong side of it."

His long, rolling laugh infuriated her. "When boys like Kyle look men like David in the eye," he said, "your revolution will be over. Maybe paying your own bills would help you understand why."

She rose to leave and threw a hand in the air. "Go ahead, cut me off. See if I care."

He followed her into the kitchen. She struggled into her boots and coat while he pointed out that since he had already paid her final quarter of tuition, and had transferred title to the Mustang to her the month before, her bravado carried little risk. "But I'd be happy to cut you off all the same, said the parvenu to the radical."

"I'm not a radical," she said on her way out the door. "I'm a revolutionary."

CHAPTER NINETEEN

THEY JUMPED OFF THEIR RENDEZVOUS POINT IN DINKYTOWN WITH fewer revolutionary recruits than Jackie had anticipated. She was used to SDS protests numbering in the hundreds, or thousands even. Tonight she counted twenty, and not a single female besides her among them.

Kyle was sanguine about it. "'Better Fewer, But Better,'" he said, quoting the title of an essay by Lenin. His hair was greasy and unkempt, and he had grown a moustache and goatee. Jackie liked the facial bristles. They made him look dangerous and tickled her palm when she smoothed her hand over them. She wasn't wild about his hair, though. That she preferred clean and fluffy.

He had first told them of the operation earlier that week, at a closed-door session in Nicholson Hall. "The frat houses are throwing a beer bash to celebrate the end of winter finals," he said, "and we're crashing the party. After our national convention in June, things will happen fast. Chapters all across the country need to be ready to foment chaos to bring down Nixon's fascist government. Like Tom Hayden said when they took him into custody on those bullshit conspiracy charges: 'The government, not the New Left . . . is on the eve of destruction.' We need to toughen ourselves, develop physical courage, so that when civil war breaks out our fearlessness attracts others to our cause. We have to show our black comrades we're willing to spill our blood, too." Disrupting a party on Fraternity Row would be their first training maneuver, he told them, an audacious foray into hostile territory. "All revolutions begin with audacity," he reminded them.

Jackie was pretty sure it would take more than crashing a frat party to start the revolution, but she understood what he was try-ing to do. The majority of SDS's membership came from middle-class homes. They were soft and untested, and standing up to Nixon's goons would require sacrifice and hardship—though she was dubious that a beer bash raid would prepare them to face the likes of Pig Piss. Still, she envied Kyle's conviction that it would.

On occasion doubt crept into her mind about what they were doing, and she suffered feelings of guilt over quarrelling with her parents. Kyle suffered no such pangs. Even if his parents didn't always agree with his methods of dissent, they were of one mind about the war. That much she had seen firsthand.

A few weeks before, the four of them had met for dinner at Murray's, Kyle's parents' favorite restaurant. His mother liked the piano bar, his father the restaurant's award-winning Silver Butter Knife Steak. Nathan Levy was a subdued, thoughtful man, with the same slight build and deep voice as Kyle. Sarah Levy was his opposite, overbearing and fastidious, with a shrill voice and quick frown. It was from her that Kyle had inherited his searing black eyes and volatility.

She fussed and doted on him the entire evening, which Jackie found revolting—the Oedipal thing. Halfway through the meal, talk turned as always to politics. Kyle warned his parents that they might one day be paid a visit by the FBI on account of his activity in SDS, which was coming under increasing government scrutiny. His mother patted him on the shoulder and told him not to worry. "Your father and I will be polite, but completely unhelpful," she promised. "And besides, we know plenty of good Jewish attorneys."

Had Jackie said that to *her* parents, they would have told her to start saving bail. But try as she might to deny it, their approval still mattered. Parental encouragement, she was convinced, accounted for Kyle's political certitude—and the lack of it for her own sporadic misgivings.

They moved en masse down University Avenue, Kyle with a furled Vietcong flag tucked under his arm, Jackie with her scarf flapping in the late March bluster. Practically every house on Fraternity Row had a party going on. They targeted one on the other side of 17th Street, a three-story Beaux-Arts faced in limestone. It had a small columned portico and, above that, a pair of filigreed balconies crammed with students clutching plastic cups. Wrought iron palings marked off the front yard, where revelers milled about a silver keg. Music blared from inside, Creedence playing "Proud Mary."

She cupped a hand to Kyle's ear and suggested they all get in line and drink beer first. "Frat boy hospitality," she said. "Can you dig it?" He threw his head back and laughed, his hair windblown and snarled.

He kept the flag under wraps and led them to the keg. They topped off one-by-one, until all twenty of them were standing around sipping beer and listening to John Fogarty. An imposing blond boy in a ski sweater and jeans came over and engaged Jackie in conversation. He reminded her of the Leif Ericson statue in front of the capitol building in Saint Paul. She flirted with him until Kyle leaned over and quashed his hopes.

"She likes cunnilingus," Kyle said, deadpan.

Leif went bug-eyed. "What did you say?"

Jackie placed her index and middle fingers in a V over her mouth and snaked her tongue back and forth between them. Leif stared, agape.

"I said, she likes *cunning linguists*," Kyle answered. "You know, like Noam Chomsky?" Their brays of laughter drove him away, but before he left, his eyes met Jackie's. She felt a spiteful pride at the yearning in his gaze, the longing inflicted by the vision she conjured.

Kyle drained his cup and threw it onto the sooty crust of snow still covering the yard. He then withdrew the National Liberation Front colors (the top half red, the lower half blue, in the middle a yellow star) from his armpit and hoisted the knurled flagstick high overhead. Their band of guerrillas closed ranks around him with the Vietcong flag luffing in the wind. "John Brown, live like him!" Kyle yelled, and led them trooping through the house, chanting as they went.

Leif Ericson was waiting when they reemerged. He came at Kyle with his fist balled in the air like a rampaging Norseman and clubbed him to the ground and dove on top of him. They rolled and grappled in the dirty snow, flinging up bits of mud and ice, but soon Kyle was flat on his back with Leif on top of him, flailing away at his face. Kyle swung his head from side to side in an effort to avoid the blows.

The whacking splat of Leif's knuckles against his face sickened and then enraged Jackie. She flew at Leif and raked her nails across his eyes. He cried out in pain and put his hands to his face. She shoved him with both hands, allowing Kyle to throw him off and scramble to his feet.

Leif recovered and turned to her. "You little cunt!" he yelled, before backhanding her in the mouth. She staggered backward and tasted blood. It was thick and salty and made her feel alive. A general melee broke out, SDS mobbing Leif like villagers jumping on the back of Frankenstein and bands of frat boys wading in to help him.

By the time campus police arrived the revolutionary recruits of SDS had lost more encounters than they had won, but winning wasn't the point. Proving themselves was, gaining combat experience, learning to take a punch. To make it happen. They left more or less intact, a tooth missing here, an eye blackened there, satisfied to a man—and woman—at the fight they had waged. Despite his battered face, Kyle in particular seemed invigorated by it all, his virility newly affirmed—to an extent Jackie realized only later on.

Back at her apartment, after she had balmed his face with unguent and tended to her own split lip, he plowed away at her without stoppage, his PE cured. He lasted fifteen minutes, maybe more, and though Jackie didn't climax, she pretended she did.

· · ·

David had been a cultural phenomenon in YAF ever since joining, the only one in the chapter who had actually fought in the war they supported, and the only one among them who, with his long hair and proletariat clothes, could have attended an SDS meeting without raising an eyebrow. Beldon called his calico shirts and faded jeans "vestments of the counterculture," and wondered why he never wore an army jacket. David told him that in the first place, it was called a utility jacket, and in the second, there was no attraction in wearing what he had already worn during thirteen months of actual combat, as opposed to the pretend kind SDS engaged in.

The only war-related article he *did* wear was Beau's precious bangle, which never left his wrist. Jackie said its constant presence made her feel as if she were in a ménage à trois, sleeping with two redneck marines for the price of one. She would have liked Beau, he often thought. They were kindred spirits, Beau's zest for life the equal of hers—each new day like biting into a Georgia peach was how Beau had put it. Even at Khe Sanh.

His stint as YAF's most intriguing figure ended, however, the day Mark Sipe showed up at their first weekly meeting in April. Tall and rangy, with shoulder-length hair and a black beard, Sipe had confident brown eyes and delicate cheekbones. Beldon made it halfway through the new business portion of their agenda—a discussion on how to respond to campus flag burning—before the bumptious Sipe stood and made his presence felt.

"Lighten up," he said to Beldon. He had on a tie-dyed shirt and maroon bellbottoms that were dusted white with powdered sugar, having evidently hit the donut tray in the hall beforehand. "It's a swatch of material with a government patent behind it. As long as they buy it, who cares what they do with it?"

Beldon frowned, unaccustomed to dissent from anyone other than David. "Desecration of the flag is unacceptable," he said. "It's our most cherished symbol."

"Don't you think we're on the wrong side of enough issues without adding domestic fascism to the list?" Sipe questioned.

Beldon's floppy ears turned red. He loosened his tie and ran a hand through his hair, Howdy Doody coming unglued, his response a sibilant whine. "'Domestic fascism'? How is defending the sanctity of our flag domestic fascism?"

"As long as the flag burner owns the flag," Sipe answered, as unruffled as Beldon was agitated, "flag burning harms no one. Suppressing it is an assault on individual liberty. People are entitled to do whatever they want with their property and that includes burning it."

Beldon flounced across the room. "So this is how we show support for soldiers risking their lives in Vietnam? By remaining idle while homegrown communists defile the flag they're dying to protect? Have you no respect for the traditions of our country?"

Sipe's face darkened. He stepped into the aisle and walked to the front of the room, playing to the crowd, challenging Beldon's primacy. "Flag burning has nothing to do with national tradition. It's a matter of personal freedom."

The piquancy of his argument sparked a fierce debate that raged back and forth until David stood to speak. "A privately owned flag is a unique type of property," he said. "To equate it to a generic piece of cloth is moral relativism of the weakest kind. But burning the flag is not—and should not be—illegal. Free societies do not suspend private property rights in order to suppress dissent.

However, with constitutional rights come civic responsibilities. The right to burn the flag carries with it an obligation to refrain from doing so. It's like saying the word nigger—you can do it, but you ought not to."

Beldon and his adherents stood down. Sipe seemed satisfied, too, middle ground he could live with. Beldon caught up with David after the meeting had ended and pulled him aside. "Libertarians," he said to David with a twisted face. "They're infecting YAF like the plague."

．　．　．

David had an affinity with Sipe that was lacking with Beldon, the natural identification of one longhaired conservative with another. They began talking politics before and after YAF meetings, and on occasion over breakfast at Coffman Union. Over bacon and eggs one morning, Sipe spoke of the conflict brewing in YAF between 'trads' and 'libs' (traditional conservatives and libertarian conservatives). "Trads are obsessed with stopping communism. But their willingness to use the power of the state to wage war against communism makes them just as culpable for Vietnam as the traditional liberals that started the war. We libs are more concerned with domestic statism than international communism, the encroachment of Big Brother on individual liberty."

Only at close range were the pitted scars that his beard concealed at all visible. He took a swig of black coffee and ran a napkin across his lips. "We believe in absolute freedom of thought, speech, and action. This country should legalize prostitution and marijuana, send nine-tenths of the civil servants home, and eliminate the income tax and draft. Government regulation of individuals or their property is a violation of personal liberty, democracy run amok."

"Tocqueville's 'tyranny of the majority,'" David said, recalling the concept from Devlin's class.

Sipe nodded. "Damn straight." He went on to espouse a philosophy of pacifism, laissez-faire capitalism, and unbridled personal liberty, declaiming that the true enemy of liberty was government. Only when he quoted Karl Hess (a former Goldwater speechwriter who had declared common cause with the New Left against the evils of authoritarianism) did David realize that Sipe was not merely a libertarian, he was a *radical* libertarian. It was his radicalism that had attracted David to him in the first place, by affording an opportunity to better understand Kyle Levy's radicalism—and thereby vanquish him.

When Sipe learned how much David liked baseball, he offered him two tickets to the Twins' home opener against the Angels. Sipe's father—a season ticket holder—couldn't get away that day, and since Sipe himself had no interest in going, David went with Clarence Madison instead.

Their seats were ten rows behind the Twins' first base dugout—closer to the field than David had ever been before. The grass was plush and the infield dirt smooth and brown, like chocolate frosting smoothed with a spatula. A gentle breeze blew from left field and the sun peeked timidly through billowy clouds—a perfect day for baseball. The crowd, though, was a disappointment. Met Stadium held over forty thousand, and at least half the seats were empty. Maybe it was the slow start the Twins had gotten off to, 4–4 so far. Or maybe baseball didn't mean that much to people anymore, the national pastime in decline. Along with a lot of other traditions, David thought. Like winning wars.

He wasn't sure what was worse: the public's growing sentiment for ending the war, or the government's feckless manner of prosecuting it. There had been no offensive operations of any kind lately, only anodyne speeches about drawing down troops and negotiating with Hanoi. *We're fightin' for honor, reputation, our good name: what other nations think of us.*

Any concerns about national honor had ended the day Khe Sanh was abandoned to the enemy, dishonoring every marine who had died there, including Beau. They just up and pulled out, left it to Charlie. Hallowed ground. Marine ground. Why not have left when the gooks first attacked if that's what they were going to do? Colucci was right, and that hurt more than anything; it was a fucked-up war.

They settled into their seats and ordered beers from a vendor with crooked teeth and a bulbous nose. Clarence flashed his nacreous smile and sighed. "I haven't been to a baseball game since I was fourteen, when my father took me. There's somethin' about a boy and his daddy at a ball game," he said, his voice wistful, his Afro as askew as ever. "Somethin' special."

"That's for sure," David said.

It was why he had the same pining nostalgia for Met Stadium that he had for Excelsior, the memory of dozens of boys his age sitting next to their fathers—not ersatz versions like his, but the real thing, *Daddy*—learning to make out scorecards. David had learned, too, a little from each of his foster fathers who liked baseball—three out of seven, not so bad, a .429 average.

Clarence looked on in fascination as he entered the cryptic markings onto his scorecard: 6–3 to indicate a groundout to short; K for a strikeout; three vertical bars for a triple. It was a skill he had kept up in hopes of teaching it to a son of his own one day, a sacred totem to forge the bond of baseball between them, at least that much constant in life.

He hit the restroom during the top of the fifth, with the Twins on top 2–0 and Bud draft running through him like a mountain stream. He stepped up to an empty urinal and unzipped, at first only vaguely aware of the person next to him, then more so, beyond the usual awkwardness of standing next to another man with your dick in your hand. He risked a look; it was Kyle Levy, sporting a new goatee. Levy's face turned as red as David knew his was. Neither said a word.

His gaze fell to Levy's cock—to see what he had, what Jackie was getting from the competition. Nothing special, he concluded.

He caught Levy doing the same and thought he looked relieved. What had Levy been expecting? A fire hose David had to hold with both hands?

They zipped up in silence and washed at separate basins. That was when the singing in his hands began, the murderous tension that craved release, like when he split skulls on 861 Alpha or smashed Fu Manchu's face at Moby Dick's. It was a song of hate, the pain of foster drift fully embraced and his jealousy over Jackie, too, the thought of Levy's stubby cock inside her . . .

He wheeled and cut Levy off, trapping him in the corner. Levy crouched beside the towel roller, his eyes darting around the latrine for help that would never come in time. David thought of the beating Sergeant Garland had laid on Zbikowski in boot camp, leaving him blind with pain within seconds. He moved to do the same to Levy, but stopped short when he noticed something sticking out of his shirt pocket. He pointed and asked, "Is that a scorecard?"

Levy managed a weak smile. "It's an old habit. I score every game I go to."

"Who taught you?"

"My father. Why?"

"Is he here today?"

Levy straightened up. "What's it to you if he is?"

"Answer me, goddamn it! Is he here?"

The fear returned to Levy's eyes. "Yes, he's here! We go to every opening day together!"

The mortal humming in his hands ceased. "Enjoy the game," David said. The soles of his shoes made a tearing sound as he trod out the door.

•   •   •

Oddly enough, it wasn't Vietnam that ate away at him as April turned to May, but something else, something unexpected: Kyle Levy's dick. Seeing it had the same effect on him as the accidental witnessing of parental sex might have had on a young child, a visual he could have done without, the implications beyond troubling. By night it was a one-eyed spitting snake barging into his dreams, capering up from the depths of his subconscious. By day it was a malevolent serpent of doom, crowding out all that was hopeful.

He struggled to understand why the image was so disturbing, why it had such staying power. The obvious explanation, that it made him fearful Jackie might prefer Levy's cock to his, made no sense. As cocks went, Levy's wasn't much to look at, and thanks to Number Six and the street whore education she had given him, he was supremely confidant in his ability to keep Jackie satisfied.

No, seeing Levy's penis had raised insecurities not about his cocksmanship, but about his future, the possibility that Jackie might choose—for reasons that had nothing to do with sexual gratification—to spend her life with Levy rather than him. The thought of it threw him into a cold sweat. When he was with her he felt like he was part of something, less separate, less alone—less *anonymous*. That's what love did; it made you whole.

His abandonment paranoia relapsed stronger than ever. Soon he began spying on her, suspicious that she was easing him out of her life. One such foray came after she declined to meet him for lunch in Dinkytown; she claimed she had an appointment at the Student Health Service. He became convinced that she was lying to him, having lunch with Levy instead. He decided to expose her deceit by staking out the entrance to the Student Health Service fifteen minutes before her alleged appointment. At five minutes to one, there was still no sign of her. She had deceived him, he was sure of it.

"David?" a voice called out behind him. "What are you doing here?" It was Liz Bodine, wearing a chintz top and a look of puzzlement on her narrow face. "Jackie should be here any minute. We're getting our birth control prescriptions renewed together."

He felt like he'd been caught rifling through Jackie's purse. He invented a story about needing a tetanus shot and escaped before she arrived, but the next evening at his apartment, over white wine and cheese fondue, she mentioned the incident to him.

"Liz said I just missed you yesterday, that you needed a tetanus shot or something?" She extracted a dipping fork from the *caquelon* she had brought over and blew on a piece of cheese-coated bread while awaiting his answer.

He stalled for time by fiddling with the Sterno, adjusting the flame. "Oh, yeah. I stepped on a nail in the parking lot outside my apartment."

"I'm sorry," she said with bathos, fondue fork poised near her mouth. "You don't seem to be limping, though."

He took a sip of wine. "It was pretty small. A three-penny, maybe, like a lath nail or something."

She slid the piece of bread off her fork and into her mouth in a suggestive manner, all lips and tongue. "Let me see it," she said, waving her empty fork at his foot.

"There's nothing to see. The puncture was so small it's already closed."

"Really? You must have tremendous healing capacity."

He acknowledged that he did.

"Either that," she said, "or there was no nail. Were you at Student Health to see if I was lying about having an appointment there?"

He hung his head. "Yes, I was."

He looked up expecting her to be livid, but she wasn't. Instead she gave him a contented smile and smoothed her mane of hair, like a cat preening after a satisfying meal. "If you're jealous it means you love me."

He felt no sense of relief—only humiliation at what Levy's runt of a dick had somehow provoked. "Othello was jealous, too, you know, and look how that turned out."

To make amends, he capitulated to something she had been bugging him all week long to do: let her pierce his ear, so that he could wear the silver hoop earring she bought him for his birthday.

She did it right there in the kitchen in her choker and tube top, a slightly pornographic Florence Nightingale, her surgical congeries laid out in front of her: ice to anesthetize him; a sewing needle and cigarette lighter to sterilize the needle; rubbing alcohol to disinfect the site; and the cork from their bottle of wine, to drive the needle into after passing it through his ear. She pinched the needle and aimed it at his left earlobe as though she had done it dozens of times before—which she had, she assured him, as a teenager with girlfriends at piercing parties. He barely felt a thing. She threaded the silver hoop into place and held up a mirror to see what he thought. He talked himself into believing that it made him look like a pirate, but when he dragged her into the bedroom to play Ravishing the Queen, he wishboned her legs and slammed away at her with such force that for the first time ever she yelped in pain rather than pleasure.

The bruises he caused left him feeling worse about himself than when the night began.

CHAPTER TWENTY

DAVID STEADIED THE SHALLOW-HULLED RED CANOE THEY HAD rented for the day while Jackie climbed inside. He passed a Styrofoam cooler full of beer and sandwiches to her and stepped down off the dock into the canoe and took the rear seat, she in the bow, the cooler between them. A few clouds floated high overhead, cotton balls in a powder blue sky on the first day of June.

They pushed away from the dock and paddled across Lake Calhoun's smooth silver surface in tees and cutoffs, dressed exactly alike except for the yellow swim top Jackie wore beneath her tee. A pair of towels, two straw hats, and a bottle of Coppertone rested on top of the ice chest. Within minutes they came to an irregular channel along Calhoun's north shore. They cruised onto it and passed beneath a span of road onto the southern edge of Lake of the Isles, which was shaped like a fist with an index finger crooked north. The middle of the lake afforded a clear view of the nearby downtown skyline, with the Foshay Tower standing supreme—though not for much longer, construction on the fifty-seven-story IDS Center having started the year before.

They peeled off their tees, raided the cooler, and drifted. The wake from passing canoes laved against their hull, quivering Jackie's bosom like a mold of Jell-O.

It was their first placid moment in weeks, Hamburger Hill and People's Park having strained things between them like never

229

before. The Battle of Hamburger Hill had been fought the previous month, near Laos, in terrain not unlike Khe Sanh's. Except this time the bad guys controlled the high ground. It took five battalions of the 101st Airborne ten days—seventy killed and over three hundred wounded—to secure the redoubt the 101st had dubbed Hamburger Hill.

The press's handwringing over the offensive made David's stomach turn. Some idiot AP correspondent had started the second-guessing by questioning why infantry were used in the assault rather than arty and air. "Because bunker reduction requires boots on the ground, you moron!" David had yelled at his newspaper. Next came a series of anguished *Time* magazine articles disputing the need for the operation in the first place. Their effect on public opinion was devastating.

The People's Park incident occurred at the same time the Battle of Hamburger Hill was being waged, when a group of Berkeley locals expropriated a few acres of land from the University of California and turned it into a "free speech" park. Governor Reagan ordered law enforcement officers in riot gear into the park to reclaim it, but when a confrontation broke out, Alameda County sheriff's deputies fired double-ought buckshot into the crowd, with the death of a student resulting. National Guardsmen had occupied Berkeley ever since, barricading streets and imposing a curfew on the city.

Jackie treated Hamburger Hill as a cause célèbre, something SDS could use to weaken the nation's stomach for war; David viewed it as proof that national honor still had a pulse. On People's Park they were even further apart. He applauded the sheriff's deputies for imposing law and order on a rogue campus; she accused Reagan of reprising the Democratic Convention, with Reagan in the role of Mayor Daley and the Blue Meanies of Alameda standing in for Chicago's Finest. David was counting on their chain-of-lakes canoe trip to heal the rancor.

They made their way west toward Cedar Lake under the sway of a mellow beer buzz. That and the prickle of sun on their skin and ache in their arms from paddling pushed Hamburger Hill and People's Park to the back of their minds, just as he had hoped. The long, narrow canal connecting Lake of the Isles to Cedar Lake was in many ways the prettiest part of their excursion. Tree-filled yards of gracious homes sloped gently toward the canal, oases of coolness and greenery tinged with the scent of clematis and chiming with birdsong and the voices of small children. It was what David wanted for himself someday, a settled family in a grand home on the shores of a city lake.

They beached their canoe and ate tuna sandwiches and drank more beer and necked. He pawed at Jackie's breasts, but the non-stop parade of gawking canoeists gliding down the canal left him frustrated. He thought about doing it in the bushes, but the prospect of being rousted naked from somebody's yard was too daunting for him. He dealt with his stymied horniness by shoving off again and quickening the pace, propelling them down the canal and onto Cedar Lake at twice their previous speed.

They drove northwest to Brownie Lake's hidden entrance and emerged from a tunneled waterway lying beneath a railroad over-pass panting and sweating, having come nearly two miles from their original departure point on Lake Calhoun. Brownie Lake was a sylvan triptych of woods and water, a diminutive oval pond offer-ing them nothing much to do other than drink more beer and soak up the scenery. The dense growth of trees encircling the lake made it feel like they were in the Boundary Waters rather than the shadow of downtown, though there were plenty of other canoeists to shat-ter the illusion.

A quick swim in Cedar Lake on the way back provided only temporary relief from the heat. They were hot and exhausted by the time they reached Lake of the Isles again. David's lingering sex-ual frustration and falling blood alcohol level made him irritable enough to get baited into talking about People's Park. "Now that's my kind of demonstration," he said, in response to Jackie's description of topless female protestors placing flowers in the gun barrels of National Guardsmen. "A pair of tits in your face and a daisy in your muzzle."

She swung her legs over the bow seat and turned to face him. "I'm surprised they didn't shoot them anyway. And rape them first."

Troop quality *had* deteriorated, but still . . . "One protestor died at People's Park," he said. "*Seventy* soldiers lost their lives on Hamburger Hill. Seventy. Maybe you could muster up a little sympathy for them, too."

His gaze fell to her bosom, where a fresh tan line had appeared. She gave him a look of disgust and pulled her tee on, his leering at her breasts done for the day. "James Rector wasn't one of the protestors," she said. "He was sitting on the roof of a theater, watching. They just gunned him down."

David thought of Cavanaugh, decapitated making a water run. Fucking new guy. And she was going to lecture *him* on life's brutal inequities? "They're lucky the deputies showed as much restraint as they did. Those people didn't own the land, you know; the university did."

"The protestors at People's Park got what they deserved, is that it?" she said with an angry moue. "Then the soldiers on Hamburger Hill got what they deserved, too."

"Oh, come *on*. How can you compare the deaths of American soldiers to a death at a fucking protest rally?"

She dug into the cooler and tattooed his chest with pellets of ice. "You think your friend Beau died an honorable death and that James Rector died an absurd one, don't you? Well you're wrong," she said, cold and hateful. "It was *Beau's* death that meant nothing."

His hands sang like never before, worse even than when they were dripped in blood at Khe Sanh. "Take it back."

"Never! Vietnam isn't a failure of national honor, you fool. It's a failure of national conscience!"

He tossed his paddle aside and stood up. "Take it back."

"Fuck Beau!" she screamed. "And fuck you, too!"

He scooped her off the seat and over the side in one agile motion, his effort so smooth and powerful the canoe barely twitched. He then sat back down and dug his paddle into the water, leaving her thrashing and sputtering while he stroked toward the channel leading to Lake Calhoun.

● ● ●

He tossed his coffee-stained Sunday paper onto the kitchen floor and picked up the phone, then slammed it down halfway through dialing. It had been the same every time he sat down to call her, those despicable words detonating inside his head: *Beau's death meant nothing.*

Finals had come and gone, and Jackie's commencement, too; yet here he was, not close to apologizing for tossing her in the lake, a perfect cannonball, her ass-splash sending a geyser of water three feet into the air. He had attributed his fury to her disrespect for Beau, but now he wasn't so sure. Something else was driving his anger, something even worse. What if she was right, her words trenchant but true?

The possibility was becoming difficult to ignore. Just last week Nixon and South Vietnamese President Van Thieu had met on Midway Island—*Midway* of all places, scene of the most sacred ten minutes in American naval history—to announce that twenty-five thousand U.S. troops would be withdrawn from Vietnam immediately. David didn't believe it at first, assumed it was a canard, a shrewd negotiating ploy. But it wasn't. "Vietnamization," Nixon called it, transferring the burden of war to the South Vietnamese.

In truth it was a euphemism for "We've had enough and we're getting out," a presidential ablution leaving South Vietnam to fend for herself. And everybody knew it, especially the enemy. If this was peace with honor, then maybe Jackie was right; Beau's death meant nothing.

But in his heart he knew she wasn't, and he realized that he was angry not with her for what she had said, but with himself, for what he had *failed* to say—to the people for whom it mattered most. He swallowed the last of his Folgers and vowed to honor Beau's sacrifice the way he should have to begin with, instead of wrapping himself in his grief, as if the loss of Beau were his and his alone to bear.

The following morning he called the roofing company and told them he wouldn't be able to start his summer job that week as planned. Something had come up, a personal matter that required his presence in Atlanta.

•   •   •

Late the next evening, Jackie gave up after letting the phone ring a dozen times, David either not in or not answering. She sighed and left her bedroom for the living room, taking with her a joint she had fired up to keep copasetic while talking to him. She sank into a big beige armchair in the corner of the room and looked up at a poster of Janis Joplin tacked to the opposite wall. After making a mental note to tell Liz they needed one of Dylan, too, she took a drag off her joint and for the thousandth time replayed getting heaved into Lake of the Isles by David.

The ferocious power in his hands when he snatched her up and whisked her over the side of the canoe had taken her breath away. What damage they could do, yet what pleasure they could bring. The trip back to Lake Calhoun wasn't all that bad, really, a short swim to shore and a twenty-minute walk down a grassy path that connected the two lakes. She found her shoes, hat, cooler, and even her bottle of Coppertone piled next to her car, David having evidently found another way home. Fortunately, her keys had stayed put in the front pocket of her cutoffs when she hit the water.

It took her a week to get over the indignity of being pitched overboard like so much jetsam. At first she was glad David didn't call, glad he missed her commencement, too, which at the last minute her parents attended. Some healing there, at least, her father beaming and proud while she grasped her diploma and threw her mortarboard in the air, his threat to cut her off for calling him a parvenu an empty one, as she had known it would be. He stomped and blustered and did his Republican thing, but in the end Pete Lundquist denied his favorite daughter—well it was true, she was, even Peggy and Michelle admitted that—nothing in life, and never would. Unlike that ass David, throwing her out of a canoe. She eventually got over it, though, and was even prepared to tell him she had it coming. She never meant to insult Beau. She was just upset over People's Park and Reagan and Nixon and COINTELPRO and all of it, the Man coming down on them. What she meant to say was that Vietnam wasn't worth Beau losing his life over.

So when a second week went by she called him, but he wasn't there, even at this late hour. Now she would have to wait even longer to get straight with him, because she and Kyle were leaving for SDS's national convention in the morning.

Which reminded her: she still hadn't finished reading the sixty-page mission statement of Kyle's Chicago coterie, the eleven SDS mandarins from the national office who had aligned themselves with the Revolutionary Youth Movement (RYM) faction of SDS in anticipation of a convention floor power struggle with the Maoists of the Progressive Labor (PL) faction. The manifesto's opening words had spelled out the elite committee's core beliefs in no uncertain terms: "The main struggle going on in the world . . . is between U.S. imperialism and the national liberation struggles against it . . . Prevailing in this struggle means collaborating with . . . the

American Black Power movement, in order to start a revolution to reject racism and economic exploitation in first America and then the world."

It was the same riff Kyle had been laying down for months, years even. The manifesto's dreamy metaphysical verbiage made her proud to belong to SDS, but what she *really* got off on was its title. She went over to the stereo and put on "Subterranean Homesick Blues," the song the title had been lifted from. Even in '65, Dylan's frenetic lyrics were already predicting the gathering whirlwind. She headed into the kitchen to satisfy a sudden craving for something sweet and glutinous—like gelato, or a finger full of honey out of the jar, maybe—while keeping an ear cocked for the line that spawned the manifesto's title.

She broke out in a wide grin. She just *had* to remember to tell Liz about that Dylan poster.

·   ·   ·

The convention was held at the Chicago Coliseum on Wabash Avenue, a mile or so south of where Jackie and Pig Piss had tangled the year before. Its crumbling brick façade resembled an old castle, complete with turrets and battlements and crenellated walls with portholes cut at regular intervals; Jackie half-expected to see archers lining the parapets. The inside was dingy and capacious, with ocher-colored cement-block walls. A rostrum with a podium and microphone sat at one end of the main hall. Row upon row of chairs for delegate seating stretched to the other. Literature tables jammed the perimeter, representing various splinter groups: Wobblies, Spartacists, Marxists, Maoists, and more.

All sixty pages of "You Don't Need a Weatherman to Know Which Way the Wind Blows" were included in the convention issue of *New Left Notes*, the SDS paper, which each of the fifteen hundred delegates in attendance received. The other delegates promptly began referring to the authors of the manifesto in aggregate, calling them Weatherman.

Weatherman's vision for SDS as articulated in the manifesto was anathema to the PL delegates at the convention, who, like the Weatherman/RYM coalition, numbered around five hundred. PL's supporters believed that class rather than race should be SDS's main priority, and that SDS needed to align itself with the proletariat rather than with Black Nationalism. PL also objected to Weatherman's endorsement of armed resistance as the only acceptable means of revolution. They called it reckless, lunacy even. "You don't need a psychiatrist to know who the psychos are," Jackie heard them grumbling before the gavel fell to get things underway.

She and Kyle sat right of the rostrum, amongst a bloc of Weatherman/RYM supporters. PLers occupied the left side of the hall. "They look like they belong at a YAF meeting," Kyle said. "Wait until they see what we have in store for them this afternoon."

Weatherman's section was full of men with long hair and beards and women in butterfly-print blouses, PL's section was comprised of shorthaired geeks with collared shirts and pressed pants, clutching Mao's *Little Red Book* like a missal. And their women no better, so *austere*. Each side sought to recruit enough uncommitted delegates to their cause to forge a voting majority, with control of SDS at stake.

PL made a motion to expel the press, since most of the interviews would be given to members of the national office, meaning Weatherman; Weatherman defeated the motion by arguing that freedom of the press was indispensable. Weatherman claimed that the multitude of workshops at the convention provided an unfair forum for PL to recruit new members; PL prevailed in preserving them and complained that there weren't enough workshops scheduled. Much of the jousting was over the role feminism and the women's liberation movement should play in SDS. Weatherman viewed feminism as important, but subordinate to the evils of racism and imperialism, whereas PL saw the problem of sexual inequality as a subset of capital's exploitation of labor.

The debate left Jackie cold. She had encountered more interesting dialogue on the matter in *Playboy*.

Late in the day, Weatherman trotted out a string of minority speakers—representatives from the Puerto Rican Young Lords, the Mexican Brown Berets, and the Black Panthers—who were critical of PL. Their intent, Jackie knew from Kyle, was to damage PL in the eyes of the other delegates by painting them as racists. She awaited the Black Panther speaker with giddy anticipation, like ramping up the excitement at a rock concert before the headline act. The New Left was in thrall to the Panthers, but other than for Bobby Seale at the Democratic Convention the year before, this was her first chance to actually see one up close and personal. The group had yet to establish a chapter in Minneapolis—an unforgivable failure of the local black community, in Kyle's mind.

Rufus "Chaka" Walls, Minister of Information of the Illinois Black Panther Party, took the podium with a strutting, swaggering walk, appearing at least a decade older than the delegates he had come to address. He had a well-tended Afro and was of medium build—not nearly as imposing as the detail of muscle-bound, black-shirted foot soldiers who trailed him. Despite the Coliseum's murky lighting, he wore dark wraparounds with thick bows. His bodyguards took up positions behind him, scowling beneath jauntily worn tams, their arms folded across their chests.

"I have seen a lot of things around here I don't like," Walls said. "People sayin' blacks don't have a right to choose as blacks. You PL motherfuckers better get yourselves together, because blacks have the right to self-determination!" The Weatherman/RYM section cheered while he mocked PL as armchair Marxists, saying that while Panthers were out shedding blood, the white Left had yet to fire so much as a rubber band. He had them in the palm of his hand—until his eyes found Jackie in her third row seat. He removed his glasses and stared, long and hard. She fidgeted in her seat and wished she had worn a different top than the one she did, an orange-and-white-striped, low-neck sleeveless pullover with slits in the sides. That she had deliberately bought it a size too small made things all the worse.

"For you ladies in the crowd," Walls said, knocked completely off message and sounding more like a cocktail lounge crooner than a revolutionary, "just let me say that the Panthers believe in women." He shot Jackie a wolfish grin that made the row in front of her turn around to see who he was leering at. "We believe in freedom of love," he went on. "And we believe in *pussy power.*"

Her head snapped back as if someone had popped her between the eyes. Pussy power? Did he really say he believed in pussy power? "I think Brother Walls has the hots for you," Kyle leaned over and said, sounding untroubled by it all, proud even.

Someone in back, a woman, yelled, "Fight male chauvinism!" The PL delegation left of stage picked it up. "Fight male chauvinism! Fight male chauvinism!"

Walls used the microphone to shout them down, clueless to what he had unleashed. "Looks like we've got some puritans in the crowd," he said, his head bobbing up and down. "Well let me tell you this: Superman was a punk, because he never even *tried* to fuck Lois Lane!"

What that tripe had to do with the price of eggs Jackie had no idea, but she had heard enough. She joined in, as did most of the convention, RYM included: "Fight male chauvinism! Fight male chauvinism!" Kyle fidgeted and said nothing, an attitude that was beginning to piss her off.

There was no way Walls could continue. He shrugged and loped off the stage with his menials in tow. The national office leaders—Weatherman—tried to salvage what had turned into an utter disaster by rushing another Panther to the dais, a thickset brother named Jewell Cook. Cook took a few shots at PL and then crawled into the same sexist sewer as Walls. "But you got to know," he said, "I'm for pussy power myself. My brother Chaka was only trying to say you sisters have a strategic position in the movement."

Jackie knew what was coming next. They *all* knew: Stokely Carmichael's misogynist rant, the line that haunted him still. "And that position," Cook said, defiant, "is prone!"

The convention hall exploded, sheer bedlam. Jackie stood and yelled, "You mean supine, you dumb son of a bitch! Unless you're a butt fucker!" She bounced up and down, palms raised, as if she were back at Robbinsdale High School cheering on the Robins basketball team. "*Fuck* male chauvinism! *Fuck* male chauvinism!" she shouted, leading PL and RYM women alike in the chant.

Their mantra reverberated off the coliseum walls like cannon shot, drowning out all else. The Panthers had humiliated not PL, but their Weatherman sponsors instead. Kyle tugged at her arm, his angry stare cutting through the cacophony, a greasy lock of hair plastered on his forehead. Though she could not hear a single word he said, she read his lips without difficulty: Sit down.

It was too much, man after man trampling on her, David throwing her into a lake, Chaka Walls publicly drooling over her pussy, and now Kyle, completely insensitive to Walls's sexist remarks, worried only about the politics of it all, his needs over hers—always and forever, men and their needs. She jerked free and slugged him in the mouth, drawing blood.

Her awkward punch set off a chain-reaction, fights between blacks and whites, women and men, PL and RYM, the shambolic first day of the 1969 SDS national convention hereby adjourned.

CHAPTER TWENTY-ONE

SHE HEALED HER RIFT WITH KYLE BEFORE MORNING, MAKE-UP sex in the same Clark Street hotel they had stayed at during the Democratic Convention doing the trick. Foreplay consisted of cooing apologies all around, Kyle for failing to condemn Walls, Jackie for her bout of temporary insanity. That her flailing, girlish right hand had been intended as much for David as for Kyle she kept to herself.

SDS underwent no such reconciliation, but by Saturday, the fourth day of the convention, it was clear that PL, not Weatherman/RYM, held a voting majority. At Kyle's behest, Jackie agreed to take part in a secret plan to deliver SDS to Weatherman. What that might be, she could only imagine. If Weatherman lacked sufficient delegate votes, what could they do, stuff ballot boxes like Daley? Skeptical but willing, she joined eleven other RYM women late that evening in a starkly lit caucus room down a corridor off the dais. Twice as many men were present, Kyle among them. Various national office leaders circulated about, giving last-minute instructions and fastening green armbands on the men. Jackie's orders were to march out front with the other women and look stern until the men came out and joined them to form a cordon around the stage. What was to happen next, she had no clue. And neither, it seemed, did anyone else—with one exception.

Bernardine Dohrn whirled around with an energetic purpose unmatched by anyone in the room, her appealing face taut with tension, her brown, cover-girl eyes not missing a thing. She wore a black leather jacket and jeans and parted her long, dark hair down the middle. She whizzed past Jackie and did a double take, stopping dead in her tracks.

"Are you Kyle's lady?" she asked. "The one they call the Radical Queen?"

Jackie nodded.

"The name suits you. You're gorgeous."

There was no envy in her voice, and Jackie liked that. But what reason did Bernardine Dohrn have to be envious of her? She was an SDS figurehead, window dressing to pull in fresh recruits; Bernardine was a prominent national office leader, Weatherman's sexy martinet. The entire room deferred to her, male and female alike subdued by her insolent charm, her brigand's grin. Jackie smiled and shrugged, a little nervous—and when's the last time *that* happened around another woman? "Thanks," she said, "but I'm just here to do my part."

Bernardine's upper lip retracted into a provocative snarl. "Then let's get it on," she said. "First we remake SDS; then we spit in honky America's eye."

She spun away, leaving Jackie in her wake. In a flash of intuition, a photon of extrasensory information conveyed from Bernardine to her, she understood exactly what she and her RYM brothers and sisters in the caucus room were being tasked to do: secure the convention stage for Bernardine—beguiling, cajoling, unrelenting Bernardine. She wondered briefly, though, why an organization established on the principle of participatory democracy found it necessary to commandeer a stage?

She and the others marched down a short corridor and entered the main hall left of the dais, a dozen women wearing Levis and grim faces. They took up positions around the stage shoulder-to-shoulder, silent, thumbs looped in their jeans. Jackie was grateful for the formless navy sweatshirt she wore, no distracting décolletage to upset things like on Thursday, when her too-small vented top had incited the pussy power riot.

The men followed in two columns of equal length, their green armbands disturbingly reminiscent of Hitler's *Feldgendarmerie*. Kyle wore his over the gift she had given him in case he was called on to give a speech—a gold shirt with a straight hem and barrel cuffs. His goatee and wild black hair—and shirt, of course—made him look like a beat poet about to do a reading on the hustings. She fought off a proud smile to avoid breaking character.

The cavernous hall hushed to a whisper, everyone waiting. Cigarette smoke hung in the air like backlit fog. Jackie stole a glance down the corridor; there she was, Bernardine, materializing in the haze, jaw firm, heels clattering as she ascended the stage. Jackie resisted a temptation to crane her neck and instead stared straight ahead into the crowd. Bernardine began by establishing the legitimacy of Weatherman's cause.

"For the last twenty-four hours," she said, "our caucus has discussed matters of principle. We support the national liberation struggles of the Vietnamese, the American Blacks, and all other colonials. We support all who take up guns against U.S. imperialism. We support the governments of China, Albania, North Vietnam, and North Korea. We support women's liberation."

From there she launched a tirade the likes of which Jackie had never heard, decrying PL with back-alley vitriol one minute and employing soaring rhetoric worthy of Daniel Webster the next. She backed it all up with specific quotes and unimpeachable logic, a tour-de-force aimed at every undecided heart and mind in the hall. She kept it up for nearly half an hour before drawing a breath, closing remarks all that remained.

"SDS can no longer live," she concluded, "with people who are objectively racist, anticommunist, and reactionary. Therefore, all

Progressive Labor Party members, people in the Worker-Student Alliance, and all others who do not accept our principles are racists and counter-revolutionaries. From this moment forward, they are no longer members of SDS."

An awkward silence ensued. Did Bernardine just expel Progressive Labor from SDS? A disorganized outcry left of stage coalesced into a thundering condemnation that rocked the hall. "Shame! Shame! Shame!"

Jackie turned around. Bernardine glowered at the PL section and yelled, "Long live the victory of People's War!" She balled her fist in the air and exhorted the entire Weatherman/RYM contingent—and any other delegates sympathetic to her cause—to follow her out of the coliseum. Nearly half the convention hall, Jackie and Kyle included, trailed her into the street, taking up her full-throated cry. "Ho! Ho! Ho Chi Minh! The NLF is gonna win!"

Jackie failed to comprehend the full measure of what had transpired until she and Kyle were marching beside Bernardine in the thick night air, the muggy Chicago night clinging to them like cheesecloth. They were on their way to SDS's national office on West Madison Street, to take control of their mailing lists, files, names of contributors, and checkbook. What they had just taken part in, she realized, was a coup d'état by a minority against the majority, a Beer Hall Putsch that succeeded.

If this was Bernardine's way of remaking SDS, what did she have in mind for honky America? Concentration camps? A great rush of sadness and regret swept over her. She had not only witnessed the death of participatory democracy, she had helped Bernardine Dohrn twist the knife.

.   .   .

The long ride back from Chicago was even more disturbing than the convention. Just outside Eau Claire—ninety miles to go, the final leg of interstate before them—Kyle told her he had been accepted to grad school at Berkeley. "You should have seen me opening the letter," he said. "I was so nervous I almost tore it in half."

The news blindsided her. He had already been offered a spot in Minnesota's Poly Sci program, which she had assumed he would accept, leaving things unchanged, no need just yet for a solution to her Rubik's cube of a love life.

"Congratulations," she said, in a flat voice. She took her eye off the road long enough to give him a sideways glance. His lip was purple and swollen from the shot she had given him at the convention. "Why didn't you tell me you were applying there?"

"I wanted to surprise you."

She didn't believe him. It felt devious, calculated, intended to force her into making choices she was as yet unwilling to make. "Move over!" she yelled at a black Lincoln in front of her. She looked over her shoulder and gunned into the right lane and then pulled back sharply ahead of the Lincoln. "Is that where you want to go?" she asked. "To Berkeley?"

"Are you kidding me? A chance to leave the frozen tundra for California? Why wouldn't I go?"

"What am I supposed to do?"

"Come with me. Be my lady."

"I'm already your lady."

"You know what I mean. To live with me."

"Why can't you go to grad school here?"

"Because Minnesota isn't Berkeley, the 'Frisco scene. Everyone knows that's where the revolution will start. I want to be there when it happens. I want us to make it happen."

A horn honked beside them. "Watch it!" he said. She yanked the wheel to the left to avoid hitting a dirty red pick-up in the lane next to her. The driver gave her the finger and sped up to get away from her.

"Is that what life with you would be like?" she asked after she recovered and had them cruising smoothly again. "All my important decisions made for me in advance? Why are you so selfish?"

"I'm not selfish. This is an opportunity for us to start a life together. You just need to get used to the idea, that's all."

She harangued him about it the rest of the way home, but his mind was made up; he was going to Berkeley and he wanted her to come with him. "Think it over," he said, after wrestling his suitcase onto the front walk of the house on Sixth Street that he shared with two roommates. "Take all the time you want."

She eased away from the curb and strained into the rearview mirror. He stood there waving, his face blurred by the weather-beaten plastic window of her Mustang's retractable top. She shifted her gaze from his slowly receding figure and punched the accelerator.

Try as she might to make it stop, an endless loop of John Sebastian imploring her to make up her mind played over and over in her head.

. . .

David steered his aging Skylark through downtown's empty streets on the way to meet Jackie at Loring Park. It was a lazy, sun-splashed Sunday, the last in June. A full month had passed since Lake of the Isles, time to set things right between them. Past time, really, but before his pilgrimage to Atlanta there was no way he could have forgiven her for insulting Beau—never mind apologize for throwing her in the lake. Now he could do both, fully and sincerely.

It had taken two-and-a-half days of hard driving to get there, the Skylark pinging and rattling the entire way. Finding Woodfin and Annabelle Beauregarde—who could forget names like that?—however, went much more smoothly. Beau had actually lived in a small town ten miles northeast of Atlanta, and there was only one Beauregarde listed in the Clarkston phone book—Woodfin.

David came to the door of their stone rambler early that evening. The front shrubs were redolent of honeysuckle, and an American flag hung over the threshold. He reached for the bell but hesitated. He knew nothing about these people. What if they were superstitious and went to mediums and séances and the like? They might mistake his appearance on their stoop for an apparition, some kind of message from Beau. It might push them over the edge. He had already failed the Beauregardes once. *The next time you write home, you tell your parents you've got a blue-bellied devil from the First Minnesota watching out for you.* What if driving them insane was his doing, too? What would living with that be like?

He lost his nerve and turned to leave but thought better of it and punched the bell with his heart galloping. A plump, smiling woman with limp brown hair and a pair of glasses looped around her neck opened the door. Her lashes were thick with mascara and her cheeks were dusted with rouge.

"Can I help you?" she asked.

"My name is David Noble, ma'am. Your son Linton and I were at Khe Sanh together. I was hoping we could talk."

Her face momentarily took on the expression of a hooked bass, as if he were a revenant summoned by her Ouija board, but her look of shock quickly melted into the tender countenance of a loving mother. "Red!" she called, without taking her eyes off him. "Come quick! David is here, our Beau's David, here, on our step. Hurry!"

A short, wiry man with a comb of orange hair and tobacco-stained teeth appeared beside her, bouncing up and down, a Bantam rooster if ever there was one. "Pleased to meet you," he said, offering a hand. "My name's Red, and this here's my wife Annabelle. Beau wrote us all the time about you. We'd be plain honored if you'd have dinner with us."

David began bawling like a child, a lusty heaving that left him weak-kneed and on the verge of toppling over. "I'm sorry," he said, over and over, his nose running snot. "I'm so sorry."

Annabelle took him in her arms. "Why, whatever for?"

"That Beau died instead of me," he answered, sniveling, shamed anew by his failed vow to protect their son.

"Oh, you poor boy!" she cried out. "You poor, dear boy. You come inside with me."

He wound up staying a week, even slept in Beau's old room, from which all of Beau's belongings had been removed, Red and Annabelle not the type to wallow in sorrow. "Better to move on," they told him.

Not that they weren't hungry for details of Beau at Khe Sanh. Which David willingly supplied, night after night in the backyard, the three of them drinking mint juleps beneath a berry-laden dogwood tree, Red with a copper spittoon at his feet for runoff from his chaw of tobacco. David was particularly fastidious about Beau's death, taking care to relate as accurate an account as possible so as to spare them the pain of wondering, the unknown being worse—always worse—than the real thing.

They took it hard, to be sure, such a gruesome death for a son, shot through the eye for God's sake, but their lack of bitterness and refusal to ascribe their loss to anything other than God's will was almost beyond his ability to comprehend. They spent more time making sure he forgave himself for not saving Beau's life the way Beau saved his—an act of heroism he made sure Red and Annabelle Beauregarde would revel in for the rest of their lives—than they did agonizing about why the Ghost Patrol had strayed so far from base.

They even insisted that he not despair over Vietnam. "Southern men know somethin' 'bout lost causes," Red told him, "and Vietnam is not a lost cause. It may be a lost war, on account of the mo-rons runnin' it, but it ain't a lost cause. The cause remains worthy." And that cause, David knew, from the words and deeds of this southern man's son, was honor. Beau's death meant something.

His last night there, after finishing Annabelle's meal of fried chicken, sweet potatoes, black-eyed peas, sweet tea, and pecan pie, he presented the bracelet to them, swathed in excelsior inside a small cedar box. They cried and comforted each other and thanked him a dozen times before solemnly placing it on the mantel beneath a portrait of Robert E. Lee.

After strong black coffee and bacon and grits, he left early the next morning. Annabelle kissed him and made him promise to write, and Red pumped his hand and told him there would always be a place at the table for him—even if he was a blue-bellied devil. He arrived home that weekend with a light heart, forgiven for Beau by his parents, and who could ask for more than that? He discovered the cedar box concealed in his gear the following day. The bracelet was inside with a note: Wear it proud and wear it always.

It was at that moment that he had called Jackie to ask if they could talk.

Loring Park was an urban reserve in the tradition of New York's Central Park, though smaller of course, at best thirty acres, David estimated. Its perimeter formed a five-sided polygon shaped like a house, with a northernmost apex and southernmost base. A short channel spanned by an iron footbridge connected a large pond in the lower half of the park—generously named Loring Lake—to a smaller body of water in the park's northwest corner.

It was on the footbridge—graced on either end by heavy plantings of yellow evening primrose—that Jackie had instructed him to meet her. She stood with her hands on the rail, looking down-channel toward the larger pond, which was brimming with waterfowl. He paused before disclosing his presence, taking her in: the spill of blonde hair, the pouty lips in profile, the swell of bosom beneath her clinging fuscia V-neck, the sleeves oh-so-stylishly frayed. The morning sun turned her hair to spun gold; she had never looked more alluring, not even in the desperate fantasies that sustained him at Khe Sanh.

She turned at the sound of his voice and stepped to the middle of the bridge as he approached, making no move to embrace him. "Let's walk around the pond," she said. "See if you can refrain from throwing me in."

He looked to her eyes for the twinkle that augured forgiveness, but got only blue ice. "I was getting to that," he said. "You beat me to it."

They crossed over the footbridge on a counterclockwise amble around Loring Lake, stopping frequently to observe the geese and ducks and herons and painted turtles and goldfish that inhabited the pond. After apologizing for heaving her into the lake, he blamed his eruption on unresolved guilt over Beau. "I'd probably *still* be beating myself up over it if I hadn't stayed in Atlanta for a week with his parents. I know it's no excuse for not calling sooner to say I'm sorry, but I had to get my head straight first." A turtle broke water five feet from shore to have a look around before submerging again.

"That's where you were? With Beau's parents?"

He could feel the wronged-woman indignation draining from her voice. They resumed walking while he told her about Red and Annabelle, how they had convinced him that no matter how Vietnam turned out, Beau's sacrifice was worthy, because it wasn't Vietnam that Beau had died for; he died for the honor of his country. "I decided that if Beau's parents could come to terms with Vietnam, it was time I did, too."

He promised that the war would cease to be a flashpoint between them, but as they rounded the southern edge of the pond and worked their way up Loring Lake's eastern shore, Jackie grew increasingly melancholy, morose even. They stopped near a pergola with fluted columns and a bum with brindled skin lying in the grass beside it. David tried to lighten things up by pointing out some of the wonders of the pond. "Look over there, near the bridge. A pair of loons, right here in the middle of the city. How great is that?"

"Those aren't loons," she replied.

Why was she being so contrary? "Yes they are."

"Those aren't loons," she insisted. "They're cormorants."

He shaded his eyes and took a better look. "They look like loons to me."

She rolled her eyes and groaned. "Loons are black with white spots and their heads are shiny green. Cormorants are pure black. Those are cormorants. Didn't you ever go camping, stay on a lake?"

He shook his head. Distinguishing cormorants from loons had somehow been omitted from Number Six's rather unusual recreational agenda. "What difference does it make? The point is, whatever they are they're beautiful."

She stamped her foot and shouted, "It makes all the difference! To you those are graceful, stately loons; to me they're greedy, rapacious cormorants. To you Vietnam is a matter of national honor; to me it's an abomination. To you Holden Caulfield is a spoiled reprobate; to me Ivanhoe is a dangerous chauvinist. We're incompatible!" She was crying, huge tears rolling down her face. "I tried to call you, but you weren't home and now it's done!"

He moved to hold her, but she shook her head and put a hand up to ward him off; the other was clamped over her belly, as if she were ill and about to vomit. "Kyle is moving to Berkeley and I'm going with him," she said in a rush. "I had to choose, so I did." She backed away from him, holding her head with both hands and sobbing.

Kyle is moving to Berkeley and I'm going with him. The words thundered at him, bludgeoned him. A wave of black, viscous grief oozed from organ to organ inside him, smothering his soul, extinguishing his future. It was as awful as being told he was going back to the fosterage, the panic he felt, the fear of dying anonymously stronger than ever.

His chest tightened and his eyes welled. "I don't believe you!" he told her. She had broken up with him before and come back; this time would be no different. Jackie was always complaining that they were incompatible, like oil and water, their constant fighting too much to bear. *She's just not sure if you should be together.*

She turned and ran toward the footbridge. He started after her, but she spun and stopped him dead in his tracks. "Get away!" she yelled. "It's over, really over!"

He watched her disappear over the bridge and out of his life, helpless, like a forsaken child again. *Why don't you want me?*

In the weeks to come, when she would refuse to take his calls or answer his letters, he would grow angry and bitter, and come to think of her as one of the cormorants ducking and diving in the pond, cold-blooded, insatiable, swallowing their prey whole. But for now he thought only of himself, and how like a turtle *he* was, poking up above water from time to time, but mostly gliding silently beneath the surface, retracting his head into his carapace at the first stab of pain.

• • •

Three days before Jackie backed her Mustang down her parents' driveway to leave for Berkeley—her mother and father tearfully waving from the stoop, gamely trying to hide their distaste for Kyle, who rode shotgun beside her—the *Minneapolis Tribune* reported the shooting death of a Minneapolis policeman.

Police officer Dennis Burchette was shot and killed last night on the 1200 block of Fremont Avenue North. A lone gunman fired on Burchette with a high-powered rifle at a private residence where Burchette had been dispatched to investigate an emergency

phone call. An unidentified female caller told opera-
tors that her boyfriend was beating her, but the home
at the address given by the caller turned out to be
occupied by an elderly widow, who slept through the
entire incident. Homicide detectives believe the call
was placed in order to lure law officers into an
ambush. The motive for the slaying is unknown.
Burchette was a Vietnam veteran who served two
tours of duty before returning home to work for the
police department. He is survived by his wife and two
daughters, ages one and three.

She mentioned the story to Kyle, but he showed little interest
in discussing it.

CHAPTER TWENTY-TWO

David picked up a winter quarter registration packet at Morrill Hall the day before Thanksgiving and stepped outside into the biting afternoon air. A fresh layer of snow topped Northrup Mall, beading its barren trees like carefully applied white frosting. He zipped his bomber jacket and descended a short flight of stairs, eager to select his classes and get on with his life.

Without Jackie, his world had contracted, collapsing unto itself like a black hole, ever denser, void of light. He had skipped fall quarter to work at the roofing company and dropped out of YAF, too. An absence of joy marked each day, each hour, each minute, the oppressive crush of time worse even than at Khe Sanh, no end in sight to his anonymity—only intolerable separateness.

His mood vacillated between anger and despair, with anger finally winning out. At least with anger he was still fighting, still alive. Despair was like death, cowardly capitulation. *A rattlesnake never surrenders. And neither do marines.* He became furious at having remained so relentlessly faithful to someone who had rewarded him by breaking his heart.

He displaced his anger by engaging in a string of desultory one-night stands, mindless revenge sex with stewardesses and secretaries he picked up in downtown bars. He never stayed the night and never called them back, making sure he tore up their phone

numbers the next day. The only exception was a dental receptionist he met one night at the Outer Limits, a girl named Diane
Peterson. She had straight brown hair, green eyes, and a slight case
of strabismus that marred an otherwise pretty face. For whatever
reason, he had neglected to throw away her number after sleeping
with her. Two weeks later, on a Wednesday evening at the Outer
Limits, when he was getting shot down by everyone he approached,
he accidentally came across it in his shirt pocket. He recalled the
hopeful look on her face when he left her apartment, so willing to
fall in love. It was a shitty thing to do, calling a girl you had used
for sex and pretending you liked her in order to get laid again, but
what the hell. Everyone else had said no that night, what was one
more? He went to a phone booth on Hennepin Avenue and dialed
her number, using the neon light of the Gopher Theater's marquee
to see by.

"Hello."

She sounded sleepy, already in bed, having to get up early for
work. She would probably make a responsible wife and mother
someday. But that's not why he was calling.

"Hi, Diane. This is David. From a couple weeks ago?"

"What time is it?"

"I don't know, midnight maybe."

"Where are you?"

"Downtown. Out drinking. Can I come over?"

"You never called me back. How come?"

"I was afraid."

"Of what?"

"That I might like you."

The line went silent while she struggled to decide if he was serious or about to use her again. "You can come over if you promise
me one thing," she said.

"What's that?"

"That you won't lie to me once you're here."

"I promise."

"Ring the buzzer in the lobby when you get here and I'll let you in."

He sprang an erection before leaving the phone booth. There was something tremendously arousing about a woman you barely knew consenting to sex on five minutes' notice. He felt a little ashamed though, too, for he did not love Diane Peterson and knew he never would. What seemed to be there for her was not there for him: that spark, that irresistible attraction that started the age-old dance. The mating dance.

Her apartment was in St. Louis Park, just off Highway 100. She opened the door wearing a red silk negligee and smelling of lilac, having clearly decided to hedge her bets by leaving the truth for later. She made no attempt to stop him when he backed her against the wall and kissed her and ran his hand up her nightie. The inside of her thigh was warm and smooth and tensed when he touched it. He could feel her venereal heat on the back of his hand.

She led him into the bedroom and gave herself to him yet again, no questions asked, a sexual lark with an emotional cipher, the dubious legacy of Number Six manifest in his every loveless kiss and stroke. She did her best to reel him in, to conquer him with her trump card, genuine passion, but it made no difference. After they had finished and were back on the couch, his brain no longer clouded by lust, his seed spilled in her for the second time that month, he did as he had promised.

"You're not going to call me again, are you?" she asked.

"No. I'm not."

Her lip puffed and her eyes filled with tears that ran down her cheeks. She wouldn't wipe them, just let them run, which made him feel like the coldhearted bastard he knew he was.

She finally blotted herself with a Kleenex and sniffed. "You love someone else. Someone who hurt you."

His mouth fell open. "What makes you say that?"

"I have a knack for attracting men who have been burned by other lovers. They know they're running to a safe place, someone who can't hurt them. Guys don't fall for me like they do other girls. I keep thinking that if I have sex with them they'll want me more, but they never do. The sooner I sleep with them the faster they leave. I don't know what to do. Maybe the only way to get them to stick around is by not going to bed with them, but what good is that? I might as well be a nun."

"Find different men," he told her. "If you keep going like this you'll be a professional mistress someday."

She nodded and said, "Or a prostitute."

She stopped crying and seemed over it. He couldn't quite put his finger on it, but she looked different, more attractive somehow. "Your eye," he said. "It's straight."

She blushed and put her head down. "It happens every time I have an orgasm. It's the weirdest thing. For an hour or two after I get off, I'm not cockeyed. No one can explain it, not even my doctor."

"Is that why you invited me here?" he said, pretending to be suspicious. "To fix your eye?" She laughed, and so did he. "At least I was good for something then, wasn't I?"

He got up to leave, but she turned serious and stopped him at the door. "You gave me some good advice, now let me give you some. Whatever she did to you, get over it. Stop being afraid of love. How many women like me will you pass by before you decide to take a chance again? Five? Ten? Twenty? How many before it's too late? Open your heart, David, or you'll end up a lonely man." She put her hand on his cheek. He kissed it and said goodbye.

After that he began to shrug off the bitterness that for five long months had left him incapable of loving again. He stopped sleeping around and enrolled in school in time for winter quarter. Maybe by the time class started, he'd be ready to give love another try. Maybe he'd even give Diane a call.

A hand gripped his forearm and yanked him off the last step onto the sidewalk below. "David! How are you?"

Clarence Madison stood grinning before him, bundled in a greatcoat and stocking hat, his catawampus Afro shaved clean off. David took his gloved hand in a soul-shake and grinned back. "Hey, Clarence." He pointed to the greatcoat. "You look like a black Russian Cossack."

"There's African blood in these veins, brother. Might freeze up."

"Hard to believe it's been almost a year since you guys took the place over," David said, gesturing to Morrill Hall behind him. "With Kyle Levy's help, of course," he couldn't resist adding.

Clarence's face clouded over. "A lot has changed since then. You got time for a beer?"

David said he did.

"Grab us a table at the Equation, then. I'll meet you there in fifteen minutes."

True to his word, Clarence pushed through the doors of the Quadratic Equation fifteen minutes later. David flagged him to a table in back, away from the belches of cold air that were gusting into the bar with every exit or entrance. Clarence picked his way through a snarl of raucous students and sat across from him to munch peanuts and chug beer while they caught up on things. Though they hadn't seen each other since spring quarter, they talked politics and current events with an easy camaraderie. David waited until they had nearly finished their pitcher of beer before telling him that Jackie had moved to Berkeley with Levy.

Clarence sighed and shook his head. "That's what I heard. How could she do that, man? He's got her under his spell, like Rasputin or some shit."

David rolled his eyes. "Oh, Jesus, not with the spells again. You don't have to invoke a hex to spare my feelings, you know. She preferred Levy to me, what can I say?"

Clarence's eyes cut through the smoky haze like a pair of

headlamps. "You don't understand. Levy really *is* like Rasputin. Remember that cop that was killed last summer? The one that got set up by a fake emergency call?"

He nodded and said, "They arrested some guy and his girl-friend for it just last week, didn't they?"

Clarence leaned forward and lowered his voice. "The shooting took place four blocks from my home. I know the guy that got arrested. He's from our neighborhood. We call him Tweeter. Word is he did it in hopes of attracting a Black Panther chapter to Minneapolis. Thing is, Tweeter's not too smart. There's no way he thought that up on his own. People say white radicals put him up to it by convincing him the Panthers would reward him if he took out a pig. They say Tweeter's coach was Kyle Levy."

David's stomach lurched, the peanuts and beer and cheap intrigue making him queasy. "And Levy moves to Berkeley to ingratiate himself with Panther leaders. Won't Tweeter finger him?" he asked.

"Like I said, Tweeter's not too smart. Levy never really *told* him to do anything. He just put ideas in Tweeter's head."

After they paid their bill and parted company, David did something he had promised himself a thousand times he would never do. He walked over to the apartment Liz Bodine now shared with her boyfriend Kevin and asked her for Jackie's phone number in Berkeley.

Liz made him swear he wouldn't tell where he got it.

. . .

"There it is," Kyle said. "On the right, with all the cars in the drive."

Jackie pulled to a stop in front of a Craftsman two-story on Hillegass Avenue south of People's Park, about a mile from their apartment on Dana Street. An off-plumb, clinker brick chimney

pierced the home's front eave. She locked the Mustang and followed Kyle up the walk to a porch on the south side of the house.

Stewart Burris, a rotund, bearded poly sci professor who had
wasted no time in making Kyle his protégé, met them at the door
and welcomed them into the entryway. An unlit Menorah sat
beside a posy of red poinsettias on a console table of vermiculate
black oak. Burris and his wife Cindy were hosting a private fund-
raiser for *Ramparts* magazine, where Cindy worked as a writer. A
crush of eccentric entrepreneurs, civil rights attorneys, polymath
professors and authors, and a handful of Sutter Street art dealers
milled about with *Ramparts* staff, Berkeley radicals, and a bevy of
Black Panthers in berets and *dashikis*—David Hilliard and Geron-
imo Pratt among them. Burris took their coats and needled Kyle
about spending more time at Panther headquarters on Shattuck
Avenue than in class.

On most nights gatherings such as this would have reminded
Jackie of the thrill of living in the Bay Area, the Haight and
Berkeley at her feet, epicenters of the cultural and political revolutions that had shaped her life. To more thoroughly acquaint herself
with the vicinity, she had taken only a twenty-hour-a-week job as a
medical records clerk at Alta Bates Hospital, to leave plenty of time
to explore.

Kyle, meanwhile, had devoted himself to grad school and getting established in the local radical community, which in Berkeley
meant currying favor with the Black Panthers. The group's
shootouts with local police had made the New Left's strategy of
using the Panthers to foment armed revolt seem not only plausible,
but on the cusp of being fulfilled—even with Huey Newton in
prison and Eldridge Cleaver in exile in Algiers. Given the degree of
competition for Panther affection, Kyle's meteoric rise to promi-
nence with the group—and thus with Berkeley's New Left—had
been nothing less than astounding.

But her proud wonderment at the swiftness of Kyle's ascent

through the ranks of Berkeley's New Left had vanished that morning. David's phone call—while Kyle was in class, thankfully—had caught her completely unprepared, the sound of his voice, *Hello, Jackie, it's me, David*, dredging up a torrent of heartache only recently stilled by time and distance.

Leaving him had proved much tougher than she thought, impossible at first. The rapture of David, she had realized with a growing sense of panic and regret, was a once-in-a-lifetime event, a shooting star whose radiance was unlikely to ever be eclipsed— by Kyle or anyone else. The loss of it hit her hard. For weeks she mourned it, snapping capriciously at Kyle and doing way too many drugs in the Haight, her mind constantly lapsing into tingling reverie, the indescribable pleasure of being held in David's protecting arms and entwined by his sturdy legs.

But the trauma of losing him—like a death, really, as bad as losing a parent, maybe worse—had finally slackened, her mental image of him growing more indistinct each passing week, her bereavement at last abating. Until the sound of his voice resurrected all the old longings, the tender crush of his body, the practiced touch of his hand. And who gave him her number, anyway? Her parents, probably, to undermine Kyle.

She had fantasized briefly that he had called to beg her to come back, but instead he told a wild tale about Kyle instigating the slaying of a cop who had been ambushed last June, right before they left for Berkeley. A shooter and an accomplice had been arrested, he said, and a motive determined—to attract the Black Panthers to Minneapolis. An idea put in their heads by Kyle, David claimed.

She didn't believe him at first, but her skepticism faded when she learned the identity of his source: Clarence Madison. Clarence wasn't the type to spread groundless rumors. If true, it made Kyle's instant cachet with the Panthers easier to comprehend. In their eyes, killing pigs, the soldiers of white oppression, was an act worthy of the highest esteem, no different than the French

Underground killing German soldiers, as Huey Newton had famously said.

Was Kyle really so ruthless as to have planned all this, their move to Berkeley, assassinating a cop, solely to forge a bond with the Panthers? And if he was, how did she feel about it? Throwing urine-filled balloons at cops was one thing; contriving to kill them was quite another. In the end, she had accused David of trying to discredit Kyle and told him not to call her again, but she hung up more than a little resentful that he failed to confess his undying love for her—though he did warn her to be careful. Better than nothing, she supposed.

She had waited until just before they left for the party to confront Kyle, saying that Liz Bodine had called after hearing about it on campus. Instead of snorting and saying that Liz did too much LSD, Kyle said it was true, that he did instigate it. "The Panthers respect action," he told her. "Doing it. I had to prove myself to them."

The joint she smoked in response to his admission had done little to calm her jangled nerves, so after being introduced around the party by Cindy Burris, a petite redhead ten years her husband's junior, Jackie headed straight to a wet bar in the den. She noticed too late the beeline a burly Panther made in her direction, her preoccupation over all that had transpired leaving her less vigilant than usual.

She had given Panther males in Berkeley a wide berth, her pussy power humiliation by Chaka Walls in Chicago still fresh in mind. What contact she did have with them reinforced her belief that to a man, the Panthers enthusiastically embraced the vainglorious notion set forth by Eldridge Cleaver in *Soul On Ice*: that sex with white women, consensual or otherwise, was an insurrectionist act against white male oppression. Their lewd stares—undressing her with their eyes, testing the water to see if she was yet another fair-skinned radical seeking to establish her racial bona fides by humping a black revolutionary—were to her as much a Panther trademark as were their shotguns and berets.

"My name's Earl," he said, pulling up beside her at the bar, invading her space. "What's yours?"

His biceps were huge, the biggest she had ever seen, rippling beneath the sleeves of his orange *dashiki* like a stallion's haunches. His beret was pulled low over one eye and he smelled of cologne, English Leather Lime, maybe. She slid imperceptibly away and did her level best to not antagonize him while he placed generous pours of Southern Comfort in front of them on the bar's soapstone inlay. They traded stories about where they were from, Minneapolis and Detroit, which led to talk of Motown, nothing provocative there, common ground. Safe ground.

She began to relax, the liquor and pot mellowing her out. Earl wasn't so bad, more like a fatuous bodybuilder than a blonde-obsessed Black Panther. Or so it seemed. Out of the blue he raked his eyes over her organdy dress and flashed a Chaka Walls grin, an Eldridge Cleaver grin.

"The ladies call me Tripod," he said. "Wanna know why?"

She tensed and looked around for help. "No, I don't think I do."

He leaned over and told her anyway. "Cause my black dick is ten inches long," he said, cooing in her ear, brazen, emboldened by the absence of Cleaver and Newton, no longer having to settle for leftovers, going straight for the high-end white pussy instead. "And somethin' tells me you'd like it if I held you down and fucked you with it."

She spotted David Horowitz and Peter Collier standing with David Hilliard. "See those two guys over there talking to your boss? They're editors at *Ramparts*—you know, the magazine that keeps printing nice things about the Panthers so the pigs lay off? If you don't get the fuck away from me, I'm going to tell them you threatened to rape me. And since the guy I live with is a friend of theirs, they won't be too thrilled. Half the brothers in Oakland would kill to be a Panther bodyguard, and most of them aren't stupid enough to proposition a woman they don't know at a party full of people they need. I'm sure David Hilliard would have no trouble replacing you after he cuts your sorry ass loose for pissing off *Ramparts.*"

Earl put his drink down and stood up with a dismayed look on his face, as if he'd just been told he had the clap. He left without saying another word.

Did he use that line with everyone, she wondered later on, or had he somehow sensed her penchant for Ravishing the Queen? Whatever the case, his come-on triggered a throbbing in her limbic system that persisted all through the night. Not for Earl, of course, but for David. She surrendered to it by sneaking to a pay phone the next morning to call him with a scheme to meet that weekend in San Francisco.

· · ·

The Pan Am 707 bearing David to the tryst wheeled to the gate at San Francisco International right on schedule. He retrieved his seabag from the overhead and disembarked to the treacly farewells of a pair of stewardesses giving Rose Parade waves. A series of well-marked overhead signs directed him to ground transportation, where he got in line for a cab to Union Square.

Meet me in front of the clock at the St. Francis Hotel at 4:30 on Friday. Bring enough clothes for two nights.

Oxygen. That's what it had felt like when she called back to tell him she had to see him. Like sweet, fresh oxygen, bubbling into his lungs, relieving the most horrible air hunger imaginable. Whether his phone call had spooked her about Levy or not was hard to say; all he knew was that he had forty-eight hours to convince her that leaving him had been a mistake.

He flagged down a dented-up yellow cab piloted by a talkative cabby with silver hair buzzed close to the scalp. A crusted lesion at the tip of his right ear trailed dried blood. He draped an arthritic hand over the wheel and maneuvered away from the curb, his fingers so deformed by bony spurs and protrusions it was hard to identify a single normal joint. A registration card clipped to the front visor identified him as Patrick O'Rourke.

They left the airport in muted sunshine and headed up Highway 101 talking football, David's Vikings playing the Rams in LA on Sunday in a possible preview of the playoffs and the 49ers the following week, back in Minnesota.

"I don't imagine you're in town scouting the Niners, though," O'Rourke said, eyeing him in the mirror. "You're probably here for the concert. They want it to be a West Coast Woodstock—like that's something to aspire to, for Christ's sake. Two days before Pearl Harbor Day and all they talk about is the Rolling Stones. Mark my words, a hundred years from now nobody will know the Rolling Stones from the Flintstones. Even Kennedy will barely register by then. And Vietnam? Lucky to rate a single paragraph. Trust me, there's only one thing in this whole fucked up decade that's fit for posterity: 'The Eagle has landed.'"

David tensed at his dismissal of Vietnam, but conceded he had a point about the mind-blowing images coming from the surface of the moon last July: Neil Armstrong in the Sea of Tranquility, Homo sapiens transcendent. Apollo 11: the one pure note of a discordant decade.

"I'm here to see a girl. I didn't even know there was a Stones concert."

O'Rourke's cockeyed grin was full of broken yellow teeth. "Nothing like a woman to make a man feel alive. But take it from me, sooner or later, time extinguishes the flame of passion. And don't think you and your young piece of tail are going to be any different."

David frowned. Of all the cabbies at the airport, why did he have to hail the most cynical one in all of San Francisco? "Jackie.

Her name is Jackie," he said, annoyed. "How come so many people stay married, then? Why don't they just move on and light the flame all over again with someone else?"

"Because as passion fades," O'Rourke answered, his eyes shifting back and forth between David and the road, "something stronger takes its place: devotion. If your Jackie's high-riding tits fell to her knees tomorrow and her pussy went dry as sawdust, would you still be flying halfway across the country just to get a sniff of her? No, you would not, because you don't truly love her. Not yet, anyway. Passion is an imposter; devotion is the true face of love. When you can change the colostomy bag Jackie has on account of her colon cancer and in the same breath kiss her cold, pale brow, then maybe you'll know what I mean. That's Candlestick Park to the right," he said, pointing. "You can see Willie Mays play there for three bucks. Best deal in town."

David gave a reverent nod. "The Say Hey Kid. Greatest all-around player in the history of the game."

O'Rourke smiled and winked into the mirror. "For a longhair with an earring, you're all right, you know that, kid?"

They pulled up to the St. Francis a few minutes past four. He paid his fare and laid a hand on O'Rourke's shoulder. "I hope your wife's cancer is cured."

"My wife never had cancer," O'Rourke said before pulling away. "She's healthy as a horse. You give Jackie a stiff one for me, okay?"

CHAPTER TWENTY-THREE

JACKIE GOT ON THE UPPER DECK OF THE BAY BRIDGE WITH FRIDAY rush hour beginning to swell. The late-afternoon sun waned low in the sky, leaching color from the bay and turning the liquid palate around her an opaque shade of perse. A weekend with David awaited, and it gave her gooseflesh just to think about it.

As lovers' alibis went, hers was as good as any, simple yet plausible, as bulletproof as such things could ever be. Which was to say not bulletproof at all, only a chance meeting or intercepted phone call away from blowing up in her face, the vagaries of circumstance beyond all control. She had told Kyle that she was spending the weekend in the Haight with her friend Peggy, dropping acid and going to the Fillmore, which was what one did with Peggy. More often than not, the quantity of drugs they ingested on their Friday night bacchanals left Jackie so incapacitated it took until Sunday to recover, so staying two nights instead of one was not at all unusual. To bolster her story, she had kissed him goodbye that afternoon wearing her favorite Fillmore garb: a floppy orange hat and a checkered poncho and jeans.

Kyle disliked Peggy and vice versa, so when she told Peggy that she was going to spend the weekend in San Francisco with a lover, Peggy had been more than willing to sign on to the deception. As for Kyle, he was probably grateful to be rid of her; he had a paper due the following week and wrote best in solitude—not an option

with her around. Besides, he had another Panther-*Ramparts* event
to attend that evening. This time to plot against Reagan, in hopes
of avenging People's Park. Did he plan on ambushing Reagan next,
she wondered? In light of the Earl incident, it was understood that
Kyle would be going to Panther headquarters alone from now on,
anyway. This way he wouldn't have to feel bad about leaving her
home on a Friday night.

She had instructed David to meet her where generations of San
Franciscans had met—in front of the master clock in the lobby of
the St. Francis. From there they would walk around the corner to
the King George Hotel, where prices were more reasonable and the
rooms adorable, like something out of Dickens. They would fit
in some sightseeing—Chinatown, Fisherman's Wharf, Lombard
Street, the Haight, everything that had delighted Jackie when she
first arrived—around long stretches of lovemaking in their cozy
room. She felt no guilt over the assignation she had arranged, but
knew from the schoolgirl flutter in her stomach that it was about
far more than satisfying a craving for wild sex; it was about decid-
ing if she had jilted the wrong lover.

She emerged from the Yerba Buena Tunnel with her radio
tuned as always to KSAN. "The venue of the Rolling Stones free
concert tomorrow has been changed from Sears Point in Sonoma
County to Altamont Speedway in Alameda County," the dulcet
voice of the afternoon DJ announced. "Other bands scheduled to
play include Jefferson Airplane; Crosby, Stills, Nash, & Young; and
the Grateful Dead. To reach the concert site from San Francisco,
take Interstate 580 east out of Oakland to Highway 50, near the
town of Livermore. Parking will be available at the speedway and
along Altamont Pass Road and Grant Line Road. Water enough to
float a battleship will be provided at the concert, but the Alameda
County Sheriff's Office is recommending that fans bring their own
food and blankets. A huge crowd is expected, so arrive early. Gates
open at 7 a.m."

She had completely forgotten about the Stones concert. It was going to be like Woodstock, a transformational happening. She had wanted to go, but Kyle had balked, claiming they wouldn't get anywhere near the stage without sleeping there the night before, which he was unwilling to do. But sleeping on the ground would be nothing to David, not after Khe Sanh. If they left now, they could be among the first to arrive, and come morning have their pick of spots.

She clicked through a list of things that would be necessary to make it happen. The reservation under her name at the King George would have to be changed from two nights to one, so they would have somewhere to stay tomorrow night when they returned to San Francisco from the concert. They would need to buy some woolen blankets at one of the downtown department stores and stop at a grocery store along the way to pick up some food. And to be on the safe side, she would have to call Kyle, to tell him that she and Peggy were going to the Stones concert at Altamont instead of the Fillmore. She would also have to phone Peggy to make sure they had their stories straight—just in case.

She crossed Market Street and headed to Union Square with KSAN playing wide open, singing and pounding rhythm on the steering wheel. She and David were going to Altamont.

●　●　●

David spotted her pushing through the lobby's revolving door, a hippie-angel in an orange hat and poncho, blonde tresses flying this way and that, wild, untamed: gorgeous. A uniformed doorman next to her craned his neck to get a better look, allowing the heavy steel door he was holding to swing into the face of a heavily powdered older woman in a fur coat, knocking her glasses clean off of her. Jackie turned and shrugged at the doorman, giggling at the wreckage she had caused.

The helpless expression on his face made David wonder if that's how he would look, too, when she came across the lustrous marble floor to greet him. He waved her over, so in love it hurt.

She threw her arms around his neck and kissed him. "I missed you," she said in a husky voice, smelling of jasmine and lemon.

It was what he had come two thousand miles to hear, three words that changed everything. He looked around the lobby and dragged her down a deserted corridor, into a darkened nook. She wrapped herself around him, the press of her lips and caress of her hands blowing him away, like at Excelsior so long ago. Had it really been only three and a half years? It felt like thirty. He tore at her with a beastly impatience, desperate to get at her. "Let's go to our room," he said, panting.

"Not yet, baby," she murmured, touching his lips with her finger. "Change in plan. We're camping out tonight."

The idea of spending the night outdoors left him unenthused at first; his preference would have been to spend the next twelve hours naked in bed, coming up only for air and room service. But when she told him what she had in mind, seeing the Stones and making love under the stars, it didn't sound so bad. He had waited this long to be with her again, to ask her why she had left him for Levy—another hour would be nothing.

After she had finished making a series of secretive phone calls from a booth in the lobby (one to Levy he supposed, but who gave a shit?), they redid their hotel reservations, bought four woolen blankets and a sack of food: lunchmeat, a loaf of bread, Swiss cheese slices, bananas, and a jug of orange juice. Then they spent the next three hours snaking through the foothills east of Oakland, part of an endless, crawling caravan of cars and VW buses and Harleys and Chevy vans and flatbed pick-ups, as if all of San Francisco were evacuating, an entire city on the move.

"Are you sure this Altamonty is only forty miles away?" he asked. "This is taking forever."

"Altamont, she said. "Altamont Speedway. It's going to be famous."

"Famous or not, this is painful. I've never *seen* so much traffic."

Finally they arrived, the speedway grandstand looming in the distance, silhouetted by countless headlights stabbing the night, car upon car pouring into the racetrack's dirt parking lot to see the Rolling Stones for free. Jackie rolled to a stop in the middle of a muddled congeries of cars, not an attendant or parking cone in sight. "I can't believe how many people are here already," she said. "We better get going."

She turned off the ignition and jumped out of the car. David met her at the trunk to help unload their blankets and food. "Where's your airline ticket?" she asked.

He patted the back pocket of his jeans. "Here. In my wallet."

"What if you lose it? Lock it in the trunk."

He withdrew two twenties and stuffed his billfold inside his seabag, which Jackie then stowed beneath a small suitcase. She slammed the trunk and they were off, with her carrying their blankets and him their food. They followed a mob of people toward the grandstand, where a small Hooverville had formed in front of a black-and-white sign hanging over the racetrack's padlocked front entrance: Altamont Speedway Ticket Office. They weren't first in line, but they were close enough. All they had to do now was avoid freezing to death to be assured a prime spot when the gates opened at daybreak.

The first order of business was a trip to the portable toilets set up right—or south—of the entrance. Following this, they spread their blankets as close to the front gate as possible and snacked on sandwiches and fruit while drinking beer with a group of college football players—most of them linemen, David guessed, from their size and the high numbers of the gold jerseys they wore. Rejuvenated by the food and beer, Jackie decided that she needed to commune with the tribe, so they began circulating amongst the rest of the squatters on Altamont's stoop, taking full advantage of the pot and wine offered at each campfire they visited, David as usual passing on the weed, Jackie as usual refusing nothing. He found himself surprisingly moved by it all, the generosity of so many strangers.

Their wanderings eventually brought them to an area that afforded a glimpse of some low-lying flatland north of the race-track, where stage lights cast a netherworld glow over a rudimentary stage. Half-erected scaffolding reached into the inky sky like spires of a medieval church and hundreds of stagehands swarmed about, flanked by dozens of trucks and generators, the steady clack of their effort resounding into the chill night air. The concert, it seemed, would be held not at the racetrack, but on the grounds outside the speedway.

Jackie steadied herself on their way to the next campsite. "I've never met so many beautiful people in my life. I want to smoke a joint with every one of them." She looked fetchingly mysterious beneath the soft, wide brim of her hat.

David scanned the parking area and surrounding hilltops and blinked to be sure he wasn't seeing double—or triple, or quadruple, or whatever exponent was high enough to account for the number of campfires that lay burning before them. "That's a whole lotta reefer," he said, with a grand sweep of his hand. "You'd be high for a week." It looked like a massive military encampment, like Mead or Lee at Gettysburg, reinforcements pouring in by the hour. An *invasion*.

Their last stop was at a gathering of about twelve, not far from where they had begun. David sat cross-legged and tipped a jug of wine to his lips while Jackie knelt and waited for a joint to come around. Before it did, a willowy figure in a loden coat emerged from the darkness near the grandstand and stood at the edge of their circle. "I'm 'avin' a bit a trouble sleepin' tonight," he said with a sly grin and British accent. "I was wonderin' if any a you blokes might 'ave a little somethin' to help me out? Somethin' mild, you know, like a spot a chamomile?" A shag of jet-black hair fell over his brow and ears and onto his shoulders. A dozen people stared dumbfounded at his long, defiant face and soft poet's eyes, the crackling fire their only response.

"You're Keith Richards," Jackie finally said.

"Ay am?" he said, patting his chest and thighs in mock surprise. "Are ya sure?" Someone stood and gave him a joint. He took a drag and smiled. "Bless yer 'eart, mate." He turned out to be witty and thoughtful, not at all the fey crackpot David would have predicted. He stayed for ten minutes, telling stories and promising a show they would never forget. "Get high and come together," he said, before moving on to the next campsite, communing with the tribe like Jackie.

The encounter made David wonder if he had judged his generation too harshly, been too critical of his coevals' sybaritic ways. Maybe they were on to something, that new vibe Jackie kept harping about, a way of life predicated on kinship rather than competition, harmony rather than strife. Even two world wars hadn't ended all the killing and hatred, and now there was a Cold War, leaving them all a Cuban Missile Crisis away from extinction. Maybe Keith Richards was right, that the healing power of music and love would pull them all back from the precipice. Maybe J. D. Salinger was right, too, and Walter Scott wrong, the age of Ivanhoe obsolete, the Age of Aquarius truly dawning, personal authenticity the thing, getting real. Coming together. Here, at Altamont.

It was after midnight by the time they found their way back to their gear. The pop and hiss of fire and buzz of voices around them was white noise, something to help them sleep. But before sleep came bliss, making love beneath a scrim of stars with the sweet smell of dope lacing the cold, crystalline air. She opened herself to him and took him to a loving place where life and death were indistinguishable, her dominion over him so complete he would gladly have crossed from this realm to the next at the mere nod of her head. And though surrounded by a tatterdemalion throng of strangers, he had never felt less anonymous.

. . .

Jackie awakened an hour before dawn, shivering, the football team having failed to tend the fire once a certain level of intoxication was reached. She put herself together as best she could, smoothing her hair and clothes, dusting off her poncho and hat. She bent to kiss David but hesitated to study his face, the cleft of his chin, the strong line of his jaw, so content now, so serene. Last night, the way he responded to her . . . she realized how much he loved her. And she him. She nuzzled him awake so they'd have time to prepare for the mad dash inside. Already people were milling about; soon a pressing mass of bodies would be jockeying for pole position.

They took turns at the portable toilets and organized their belongings as darkness lifted and the rest of the bivouac stirred to life. A pair of lines formed almost instantly, so they hastily queued up in front of the ticket office and stamped their feet to stay warm as a crescent of coral and orange forced its way over the eastern hilltops.

The gates opened just before seven. They funneled everyone north of the grandstand and down a steep grade that sloped to a barren hollow. The stage was a football field or so away, backed up against the freeway they had arrived on the night before. She took David's hand and sprinted toward it with all the others, yelling and hollering like a child let out for recess, grinning with delight. They staked out a piece of ground a few hundred feet from the stage and stood there panting, their breath hanging in the chill, visible. After pausing to catch her wind, she spread their blankets and had a look around.

The stage was at the northernmost end of a valley bounded by three pale yellow hills. One formed the eastern wall of the valley,

another its southern wall, and a third—confluent with the grandstand—the valley's western border. She inferred from the unoccupied grandstand that the concert's "seating area" was to include
the valley floor and surrounding slopes and summits, providing
clear lines of sight to the stage for however many people showed
up—something the limited seating of the grandstand could never
have done.

"Doesn't exactly drip bucolic charm, does it?" David com-
mented.

In his blue work shirt and jeans, and with the earring she had
bought him dangling from his earlobe, he looked like he fit right
in, another mellow stoner come to Mecca.

Her instinct was to argue the point, no bummers allowed, but
he was right. The valley was harsh and desolate, not a blade of grass
in view. And the treeless hillsides were no better, monotonous and
dreary, the color of straw.

It wasn't long, though, before the sun began to penetrate the
haze and brighten things up a bit. David took his bomber jacket off
and she stopped blowing into her hands, but even so, things still
looked filtered and indistinct, as if she were afflicted with cataracts.
More people poured in and helicopters began landing on the racetrack, ferrying in equipment that legions of stagehands worked
furiously to position.

Soon the valley floor behind them was packed and the surrounding slopes had turned black, as if infested with insects.
Frisbees and soap bubbles filled the air, and someone tethered a
rainbow-colored hot air balloon to the ground; it hung over the
parched valley like psychedelic tapestry, warm and familiar. A mus-
tachioed man in a leather coat and jeans came on stage and tested
one of the microphones. He had a Cockney accent and an imperi-
ous manner about him, the Stones' majordomo, Jackie guessed. He
told a bunch of teenage boys climbing the scaffolding to show
some reason and come down. Following this, he made an appeal on
behalf of the Red Cross for more ace bandages, gauze, and sponges.

"What's that about?" David asked, frowning.

"Minor mishaps are bound to happen," she said, sitting down to slap together a couple of sandwiches.

"Minor mishaps?" he echoed, still standing. "We'll be lucky if we don't all self-immolate once some of these nutters get juiced up."

"Don't be so judgmental. You have long hair, too, you know."

He sat down beside her and lowered his voice. "Long hair has nothing to do with it. This place looks like a carnival freak show: 'Step right up and see the scaled lady; she walks, she talks, she crawls on her belly like a reptile!'"

She laughed at his barker imitation because she knew it was true. The teeming farrago around them defied characterization: Hare Krishnas with shaved heads and flowing robes playing finger cymbals and flutes; bikers in leathers and chains popping black beauties; fresh-faced groupies in halter-tops drinking wine from the same vile jug as a toothless tramp in bare feet; a bony white woman in a surplice passing a collection basket for the Black Panther Defense Fund (Jackie refused to give so much as a dime); a young mother changing her baby's diaper with one hand, and smoking a joint with the other; and mimes in face paint riding unicycles.

They consumed drugs and booze like chips and dip, and with intoxication came an urge to disrobe, males and females alike shedding their clothes and strutting their stuff in a contagion of stripping. One enormous mound of blubber pranced through the crowd completely nude, his hand pressed to his mouth like a ballerina who had made a misstep during rehearsal. He had saggy breasts, a tattoo on his left arm—Oscar, it said—and flaccid buttocks that slapped from side to side as he ran. Next a topless brunette with marabou-braided hair appeared, carrying a basket full of long stem roses and plastic love beads. She presented a rose to Jackie and draped a set of beads around David's neck before moving on without uttering a word, her eyes bloodshot and glassy, totally wasted. Jackie felt a stab of envy at the Rose Queen's perfect breasts and was about to make a snide comment when a leather-faced man with a sun-bleached moustache and a corncob pipe clenched between his teeth came on the scene. He wore a green Tyrol hat with a white feather in it and had a harsh, croaking voice.

"Acid, pot, magic mushrooms!" he called out, like a ballpark vendor. "Acid, pot, magic mushrooms!"

His words found their way to the nest of neurons in her brain that was responsible for craving: *I want,* they said. *I want.* After telling David she would be right back, she chased after the gravel-voiced peddler and was quoted a price of two dollars a tab for LSD and five dollars a lid for marijuana; she had no interest in psilocybin, magic mushrooms not her thing. She paid him and slipped enough acid into her jeans to launch a rocket.

The idea of turning David on hit her when she got back to the blanket and was laying out their breakfast of sandwiches and fruit. It was something she had wanted him to experience for the longest time, that most sacred of tribal shibboleths: the consumption of mind-altering drugs at a rock concert. So that he would finally understand the healing nexus of music and drugs and long hair.

An acid trip for David would be transformative, like the conversion of Saint Paul on the road to Damascus, exposing American power and materialism for the false gods they were. LSD would enlighten him, as it had Huxley and Leary and Kesey before him, allowing him to see through the fog of herd conformity and government repression. He would finally comprehend that imperialism and mass consumerism were incompatible with brotherhood and tolerance—and he would reject the emotional alienation of capitalism. All from the wonders of dropping acid in the microcosm of love and harmony that was Altamont.

She waited until yet another helicopter landing at the racetrack distracted him before furtively dissolving the tabs of LSD she had bought into their bottle of orange juice. He'd be upset at first, but soon enough he'd thank her for it.

CHAPTER TWENTY-FOUR

DAVID DRAINED THE LAST OF THEIR ORANGE JUICE FROM THE bottle—even unchilled it had tasted so much better than out of a carton—and disposed of it along with their other refuse in an over-flowing garbage can near a bank of portable toilets right of stage. Don't Be a Litterbug, a sign said. He shook his head; do drugs and go nude, but don't be a litterbug.

On his way back he paused in front of the stage to take things in, the tableau before him smudged like an Impressionist canvas by the morning's feeble sunlight. The valley and surrounding slopes and hillcrests were dense with people, half of San Francisco crammed into a gigantic, open-air theater in the round. Marooned among the endless sea of bodies were dozens of vans and chartered buses, their roofs jammed with people seeking a better vantage point from which to view the stage. The grandstand remained unoccupied but the infield had been pressed into use as a heliport, copters coming and going, the whir of rotors leaving him slightly unnerved, Khe Sanh still only twenty months behind him.

He returned to their blanket and took a long pull from a brown jug of wine that was making the rounds. He caught Jackie watching him with a sly look on her face, but before he could question her about it, the Englishman in the leather jacket took the micro-phone again. "We're working as fast as we can," he said, "but if everyone could be patient just a bit longer, that would be really groovy."

A bunch of young girls sitting beside them gifted a purple bottle of Mr. Bubbles (Magic Wand Inside, the label said) to Jackie, who challenged him to a bubble-blowing contest to pass the time. The object of the game was simple: to see whose bubble floated the farthest before bursting. After ten minutes or so, David noticed something peculiar going on. Their bubbles had begun to emit refulgent hues of green and yellow and red and blue, like Fauvist balloons floating over the crowd. Their texture had changed, too, their smooth surfaces replaced by complex networks of ridges and rills. The word "surfactant" popped into mind, and he seemed tantalizingly close to comprehending the mathematical mysteries of surface tension. His face felt warm and flushed, and his hands were tremulous. The next bubble off his wand left an orange contrail.

"The bubbles," he said. "They're so beautiful!"

Jackie draped an arm around his shoulder and kissed his cheek. "Isn't it wonderful?"

He stared at her, uncomprehending.

"I put LSD in our orange juice. Don't be afraid. Kick back and trip with me."

A doubt-laden shiver rattled his teeth. If a single joint had convinced him he could fly, what would a hit of LSD do to him? He shut his eyes to make it go away, but a coruscating explosion of chartreuse erupted behind his eyelids and a wave of euphoria seized him. He opened his eyes and giggled. "You shouldn't have done that," he told her.

He took her hand and embarked on a magical mystery tour of intense distortion, where inanimate objects escaped their borders and oozed into a variety of unlikely visions. The latticework of the scaffolding transformed into a rete of capillaries throbbing with blood pumped by the stage, which had become cordiform and contractile, a surreal approximation of a human heart. His hearing became exquisitely acute, parsing the garble of conversation around him into distinct words and phrases, like a conductor capable of hearing every instrument in the orchestra.

He rode an acid wave that colored the morning's pale sunlight lemon yellow and turned the clods of earth beneath his feet into creamy chocolate and painted Altamont's flaxen landscape gold as a newly minted doubloon. His thinking grew complex and philosophical; he seemed on the verge of great insight, secrets of the universe at hand. Fictional characters from literary works with a common theme of deceit inhabited human bodies: Jackie was Lady Guinevere before the betrayal, loving and true; the Englishman giving orders on stage was Hamlet, directing his play-within-a-play to expose the treachery of Claudius; and David was d'Artagnan, come to save the Queen. The Radical Queen.

His only shaky moment occurred when a long line of motorcycles arrived, intruding on the surrealistic bubbles and prismatic light of his trip like a loud, angry fart. The crowd parted to let them through, scowling faces on rumbling machines reeking of oil and gas. Huns, come to pillage and rape. They parked their bikes and clambered onto the stage. 'Frisco Hell's Angels, the backs of their vested jackets said. Suddenly the lemon-yellow light bathing the stage went dark, as if suffused with coal dust, and a young boy sitting atop one of the equipment trucks turned into a crow—an ugly, cawing crow. David stood and clenched his fists and told Jackie not to worry, that he would protect her.

She coaxed him back down. "It's okay, baby, it's okay. They're cool, part of the scene, sort of like the pigs, only ours. And no guns. See? No guns."

He calmed down and cruised into the concert, Santana kicking things off just before noon. Their guitar licks were clean and tight at first, every note a joy to his ears, but halfway through their set, time compressed and all sound receded. The stage and scaffolding transformed again, this time into a Doric-columned Parthenon, with detailed friezes and pediments. A mellifluous voice sounded inside his head: Man is by nature a political animal. It was Aristotle, speaking to him across centuries of time. He had a powerful presentiment that the New Left was in jeopardy and that Altamont had something to do with it.

Jackie's voice prized him from the mirage of the Parthenon, and as his body and mind reconnected, he became painfully aware of a full bladder. He headed for the portable toilets to relieve himself but encountered lines too long to even consider, so he made for open ground, beyond the palings that marked off Altamont's northeast boundary. He picked out a patch of unoccupied scrub pasture and whizzed away while gazing at a nearby curl of water snaking southwest. An odd kind of river, he thought, what with everything around it so parched and withered, not a lick of riparian greenery in sight.

Jefferson Airplane was being introduced by the time he made his way back. He got to within thirty feet of Jackie when a commotion broke out, a group of Hell's Angels scuffling with the crowd. One of the Angels, a short, well-built harelip, shoved somebody in the chest. A clear line of sight opened up to the combatants; the man Harelip had shoved was Kyle Levy. He spit in Harelip's face, but a strawberry blond with sideburns like Elvis cracked Levy over the head from behind with a pool cue, dropping him to the ground. David moved toward the fray, his drug-addled brain struggling to process it all: Levy, struggling to one knee; Harelip, reaching into his jacket and clicking open a switchblade; Grace Slick's powerful contralto, a song called "We Can Be Together" grabbing him by the nuts.

His eyes found Jackie, the woman he loved gaping at Levy, a horrified look on her face. All he had to do was stand down, let Harelip bury his knife in Levy's chest.

He ripped Blond Elvis's pool cue from his hands and brought it down hard on Harelip's wrist, causing him to yelp and drop his

knife, then swung it like a baseball bat across the bridge of Blond
Elvis's nose. Elvis howled in pain and clamped his hands to his face,
blood pouring from his nostrils. David considered holding his
ground, but decided against it; instead he upended a pair of motorcycles and stomped on them before hauling ass past the toilets and
into open pasture. He looked over his shoulder and broke out
laughing when he counted half a dozen of them giving chase. He
had done this before. This would be a lark compared to luring a
bunch of bloodthirsty gooks off a downed fighter jock.

He barreled east as fast as he could, his stamina amazing, like
that of a racehorse. He could run for hours, twenty-six miles if
need be, like Pheidippides at Marathon. Fuel-injected Pheidippides. *Acid-powered* Pheidippides. He reached the river with the
bikers still in pursuit. Except it wasn't a river. At least not like the
Rao Quan, with its inviting green water and lush banks. This was
ugly and manmade, with dun-colored water and a chain-link fence
around concrete embankments.

He scaled the fence and slid feet first into the canal, eluding the
Angels the way he had eluded the NVA at Khe Sanh. He fought
through the paralyzing shockwave of cold and dove under, letting
the current propel him to safety. It was stronger than he expected.
He opened his eyes and saw nothing, only blackness, not a ray of
light. He stroked toward the surface for air, but the swirl and pull
of the canal sucked him under again. Time and again he battled his
way up only to be yanked back down, as if some unseen hand had
ahold of his ankle.

He struggled mightily, nursing the same stale breath, thrashing
and flailing until his arms and legs burned like fire. He held out as
long as he could, refusing to open his mouth to that fatal tide of
water, until he drifted in darkness, alone. So alone.

For a terrible moment he regretted his choice, saving Levy for
this. But then the darkness lifted and he was no longer face down
in a murky stream. He was in a green glade ringed by magnificent
oaks, wearing gleaming silver mail made of interlocking rings and

plates and a plumed helmet that glinted in the yellow light that
came slanting down in broad beams. In his one hand was a sword,
tipped red with blood, and in the other a shield, dented and coated
with dust. Colucci was on his right and Beau on his left, unhorsed
as he was, fighting with Ivanhoe against the Norman usurpers, outnumbered twenty to one, no way they could prevail. But as the
trumpets blared and the clank of swords and thud of axes drew
close around them, he grew peaceful with it, for he would take from
this life something humanly essential, craved by heroes, lauded by
poets, immutable by time.

And he soared toward the brightness.

• • •

It happened so fast she hardly knew what to think, Kyle beside
her and David gone, as if some magician had made one disappear
and the other materialize. How did that happen? LSD shenanigans?
Not that it hadn t always been that way, the two of them swapping
places in her life at a dizzying pace, a romantic revolving door. She
forced herself to try and reconstruct things—no easy task, considering the load of acid she dumped in their orange juice.

After David left to pee, Kyle had emerged from the mass of
newsmen and roadies jamming the stage and begun waving at her.
Was this real, she had wondered, or some kind of guilt-wracked
hallucination? Kyle or his LSD specter, whichever it was, jumped
off the stage and came toward her with a pair of binoculars swinging from his neck and a self-congratulatory grin on his face,
pleased he had found her, she supposed. Then came the fight, right
in front of her, Kyle getting tangled up with a bunch of Hell's
Angels and cudgeled to the ground with a pool stick. An evil-faced
gnome with a harelip had pulled a knife to stab him, but then
David appeared and kicked the crap out of everyone, until the
Angels forgot all about Kyle and began chasing David through the
crowd and out of sight. And so here she was, sitting next to Kyle

fussing over a goose egg on his head, telling him how surprised she was to see him, trying to sound elated.

It took her a moment to realize Kyle hadn't the slightest inkling that it was David who had rescued him. He attributed his survival to the surge of the crowd pushing the Angels off of him in the nick of time, "Before that little bastard with the knife really messed me up."

His head was throbbing, he told her, but other than that he was ready to party. "And judging by the trippy look on your face," he said, withdrawing a joint from the pocket of his jean jacket, "I've got some catching up to do." He lit it and took a drag before explaining his preternatural materialization on stage. "I met a reporter from *Ramparts* last night who had been assigned to cover the concert. He had stage passes and invited me to go with him. We rode out this morning on his Harley."

"How did you find me?"

"You said you'd be up front, so I looked for your orange hat. It was easy with these," he said, patting his binoculars. He massaged the knot on his head and asked where Peggy was.

His face split into half a dozen distortions, as if reflected by a fun house mirror. Jackie rubbed her eyes and succeeded in reducing the number of talking heads confronting her to two. "She met up with an old boyfriend. They're around here somewhere."

Kyle didn't like Peggy and was no doubt glad to be rid of her, so it seemed to satisfy him. What she would say when David showed up, though, was another matter. Act like it was coincidence, maybe. Half the country was at Altamont—why not him, too? It would be asking a lot of David to play along, though; he had already saved Kyle's life. How much more could she expect him to do?

More violence broke out when the Airplane began playing "Another Side to This Life." This time the band tried to stop it. Grace Slick, wearing an aqua blue pantsuit and looking strangely like a Vegas chanteuse, pleaded with everybody to quit fucking up, but a few minutes later, Paul Kantner announced that the Angels had just knocked out their band mate Marty Balin. There was a stoppage in play to resuscitate him, during which Jackie's loving groove dissolved into a terrifying bummer of a trip.

She became profoundly sad, but not, as she led Kyle to believe, over Marty Balin. If the Angels were attacking musicians they were supposed to protect, what would they do to David if they caught him? The stage transmogrified into a giant rice paddy and she had a horrific vision of David dying in Vietnam. The fans around her became Vietnamese peasants being mercilessly slaughtered, their cheers the anguished cries of the wounded. Where others heard wailing guitars and pounding drums, she heard shells whistling and grenades bursting.

She found herself fantasizing that Pig Piss and the Chicago Police would come to save them, anything to stop the carnage. But no one came, not even David, and as the afternoon unraveled and the violence stripped away Altamont's brotherly hippie matte to reveal the face of the beast, her tears ran like rain. She cried for Oscar, the nude fat guy who came too close to the stage and got pummeled by a host of Angels until blood streamed down his face. She cried for a shirtless man in jeans, whom the Angels pitched off the stage into the crowd after battering his eyes into a swollen, purple mess. And she cried for David, who had survived the blood red clay of Khe Sanh to go MIA in the mellow yellow grass of Altamont.

Kyle was convinced that she had gotten into some bad acid, so he took her to a first-aid station for a shot of Thorazine, but the sheer volume of bummers had long ago exhausted their supply, so he tried to talk her down instead. She thought briefly about telling him the truth but decided against it; Kyle was the only thing holding her together. She couldn't risk having him freak over David. Not yet, anyway. There would be plenty of time for that when David showed up. If he showed up. Where was he? Was he staying away to avoid a scene, accommodating her capriciousness yet again?

Nightfall and Mick Jagger singing about the devil only made things worse, her hallucinations a nonstop parade of Hydras and gargoyles. But nothing the acid conjured up held a candle to Altamont, the grisly horror of seeing a long-bladed knife plunged between the shoulder blades of a young black man ten feet away from her. That and David's failure to return made her come completely unglued. She raved like a lunatic all the way back to Berkeley and deep into the night, which she spent rolled in a ball at the foot of her bed, Kyle trying to soothe her, an impossible task.

The following afternoon, with Kyle out making a grocery run, she sat at the kitchen table leafing through the Sunday paper's coverage of Altamont, her head on fire, her stomach pitching, hoping she wouldn't vomit. A single-column story below the fold grabbed her attention. It reported that a white male in his twenties, wearing a blue work shirt, love beads and jeans, had, despite the warnings of a nearby state police officer, climbed a chain link fence, entered the California Aqueduct near Altamont Speedway and drowned. The man had no identification on him, the story said, only a bracelet on his wrist with an ironic inscription: Too bad, oh, too bad!

She tore the page in half again and again and again, ripping it into smaller and smaller and smaller pieces, as if there were a size she could reduce it to that would nullify everything on it, void what she had just read. And she screamed, a full-throated, demented shrieking that prompted the couple in the next apartment to call the police. She kept it up, tearing and screaming, screaming and tearing, until the pieces of paper were too small to hold and she was rendered mute, her vocal cords ground raw and bloody, incapable of even a whisper. Kyle and the doctors at Alta Bates Hospital would assume that bad LSD caused her psychotic break, but it was something else, something Jackie had until that moment believed she was utterly insusceptible to.

Shame.

PART IV

By heaven, methinks it were an easy leap
To pluck bright honour from the pale-fac'd moon,
Or dive into the bottom of the deep,
Where fathom line could never touch the ground,
And pluck up drowned honour by the locks.
—Shakespeare, *Henry IV, Part I*

CHAPTER TWENTY-FIVE

It was nearly 3 a.m. by the time my mother finished her account of David's death and composed herself. She sat across from me in a leather swivel chair, her eyes red, the front of her jogging suit wet with tears. The blown-out photo of them at Altamont loomed large on my screen, damning proof of her culpability. Even my action heroes—at least the ones she hadn't knocked to the floor earlier—seemed to stare down in denunciation of her. But despite the toll her lengthy avowal must have exacted, a girlish softness ruled her face. Her eyes gleamed a dazzling shade of blue, as if a gloomy film had been scrubbed from her corneas.

Or soul, maybe.

She brushed a lock of hair off her forehead and sighed.

"I should have come forward to identify him, but I couldn't bring myself to do it. The sight of his cold, lifeless body would have finished me off. Instead, after I got out of the hospital, I bought a dozen white chrysanthemums and an American flag and drove to the pier. His seabag was still in my trunk. I weighted it with rocks and wrapped it in the flag and carried it to the end of the pier. Then I threw it into the bay and dropped the chrysanthemums into the water. 'I love you,' I said as it sank. 'I'll always love you.'

"I never told anyone the truth, but living with the shame nearly destroyed me. The only thing that saved me was you. I had gotten careless about taking my birth control pills, and a couple of months later discovered I was pregnant. Kyle was upset at first—we were in no position to have a child—but after a few weeks he warmed up to the idea and we decided to get married. We could barely afford to feed and clothe you those first few years, so we delayed having more children until he finished his PhD and took a job at UCLA. But by then I had trouble getting pregnant again."

I thought of the "moral trespass" she had long refused to talk about, the "unpardonable sin" that had destroyed my parents' marriage. "Is that what caused your divorce? Infertility? I always thought you split up over an affair."

She slid to the edge of her chair, her eyes moist and bright, her voice hushed. "We did. I went to a fertility clinic and found there was nothing wrong with me. The problem was Kyle. He was diagnosed with a form of congenital sterility."

She came over and knelt in front of me with her hand on her heart and a supplicant look on her face, like a penitent Magdalene.

"Kyle Levy isn't your father. David was."

.   .   .

I slumped in my chair and stared at his photo. I couldn't take my eyes off him, not even when my mother jumped to her feet and clasped me to her bosom.

"I'm so sorry," she said, over and over, crying again, her tears wetting the top of my head. "My beautiful, darling boy, please forgive me."

Kyle Levy isn't your father. David was.

That she used the past tense shattered me into a thousand pieces. In the course of one night, I had learned that the father who spurned me was not my father at all, and the pathetic antihero I had intended to pillory the sixties with to renounce him was. The bitter resentment of Levy's cold abandonment of me, the pain of being a forsaken son—a scab I picked for over two decades—began to dissipate, only to be replaced by a new heartache.

David's death seemed somehow fresh to me, in some ways worse than if he had been alive all this time and then abruptly taken by a car accident or heart attack, keeled over in the yard with no warning. At least then I would have had some memories of him, something familiar to cling to. This way I had nothing: no recollection of the smell of his aftershave, the sound of his laughter, the touch of his hands. Hands that might have thrown me in the air and caught me while I screamed with delight or clapped at my first home run—or held me down and tickled me before tucking me into bed. For as long as I lived, I would have no memory of the remarkable champion my mother had revealed this night. Only broken fantasies of what could have been.

I came undone, bleating and shaking like a child even though David had died thirty *years* ago. My mother held me, but it wasn't the healing catharsis she might have hoped for. The paternity bomb she had dropped would take some getting used to; already I felt a creeping anger over her deceit. Forgiving her would be more complicated than she thought. Though still the magnificent woman who had raised me alone, she was now also the Clytemnestra who had killed my father—even if unintentionally.

I stood and pulled away to a neutral corner of the room. "I need some time alone with this."

Her lip quivered and she bowed her head to cry, but didn't. "I always knew I'd answer to you one day," she said, raising her gaze to mine. "I suspected from the moment you were born you were David's son. Whatever you decide, I want you to know that all these many years, I never stopped thinking about him. He's still my David. My marine."

I looked away and swallowed hard, the depth of their love tearing me apart. She rescued me from losing it again by saying good night and letting herself out, leaving me alone to digest it all.

I walked over to the monitor and studied his face, the strong brow, the defiant chin. "Why didn't you just walk away?" I shouted.

But there would be no Oprah moment for me, no joyous father and son reunion: only celluloid silence. I sat in my chair and put my head in my hands and noticed the action figures my mother knocked to the floor when the night began. Unable to suppress the neatnik in me, I got on my hands and knees and began collecting them, so as to put them back where they belonged, restore them to their rightful places.

And that's when it came to me. David had been an action hero, too, and deserved to be restored to *his* rightful place the same way I was restoring the plastic figures in my hand to theirs. I toyed with Green Lantern and smiled. If my mother was Clytemnestra, then I would be Orestes, the son who set things right. Not by killing my mother, of course.

By saving David from his greatest fear.

*   *   *

It would take six years to fulfill my promise, though I reconciled with my mother in days, forgiving her completely. Instead of the fictional *Altamont Augie* I had intended to make, I set out to make the real thing. But David's story as related by my mother was incomplete, limited to her point of view. With her tireless assistance, I tracked down and interviewed everyone else whose voice I still needed to hear: Rocco Colucci, who was still running the same body shop in Queens he had started after returning from Vietnam; Woodfin and Annabelle Beauregarde, who were still living in the same house David had visited outside Atlanta; Kenneth Pipes, who knew more about Bravo Company's role at Khe Sanh than all the reference books I read combined; and Westbrook, whose near photographic memory of Marine Corps Recruit Depot San Diego, circa 1966, was invaluable. We even found Clarence Madison, by then a prominent Minneapolis psychiatrist, and David's drinking buddy Wisniewski, the owner of a successful Minneapolis roofing company.

I saved Kyle Levy—whose duplicitous silence on the matter had been due to my mother's threat to implicate him in the shooting death of the Minneapolis policeman if he told me about David—for last. He broke down and cried into the phone when I told him I had learned the truth about things and forgave him for walking out on me. When I mentioned I wanted to make a movie about David, he offered to meet about it anytime. More than merely willing to help, I got the feeling he was eager to.

I arrived at his office on the campus of the University of Wisconsin at Madison a few weeks later, on a brilliant blue morning in May. After an awkward greeting and embrace, we headed over to Memorial Union, a four-story campus landmark that, with its graceful limestone walls and green tile roof, was vaguely reminiscent of a Venetian palace. We trooped around behind it and sat beneath an umbrella on one of a suite of mostly occupied yellow and orange and blue tables speckling an open-air terrace overlooking Lake Mendota. A solitary yellow-hulled sailboat glided across the lake's placid water while the sizzle and smell of bratwurst cooked on an open grill assaulted us from nearby: Memorial Union Brat Stand, an orange sign with green lettering said.

Over twenty years had gone by since I last saw Kyle Levy; had we passed on a city street, I would never have known him. He had a sallow, churlish face, wispy gray hair, and stooped shoulders, appearing (unlike my mother, who had an ageless, if Botox-enhanced, elegance about her) a good ten years older than his age of fifty-four. Only his eyes retained the luster of youth, the dark, fissile passion I most remembered him for.

Over bratwurst and beer, he talked of my father deep into the afternoon, beginning with the day David first challenged him by singing "The Ballad of the Green Berets" at a protest rally. Some of what he told me I had already heard from my mother—the debate over Manifest Destiny in Thomas Devlin's history class; YAF's disruption of SDS's blockade of Walter Library; the night David forced his way into my mother's apartment in Dinkytown—but much of it was new. Like his account of the terror he felt when David cornered him in the men's room at a Twins game. Had he not just emptied his bladder into the urinal, he confessed, he would surely have wet his pants, so terrifying was David's countenance that day, like Achilles confronting Hector.

"Yet seven months later," he went on, "he gave his life to save mine—though I didn't know it 'til I flunked the fertility test your mother told you about. I've asked myself a thousand times since if I would have been capable of doing the same had our roles been reversed. I have little faith I would have.

"It's a humbling thing—humiliating, really—to live each day knowing your most hated rival eclipsed in death anything you could ever hope to achieve in life. But with the passing of time, I've come to think of him differently, like opposing soldiers years after the enmity, geriatric Japanese and Americans at Pearl Harbor, tears streaming down their cheeks with their arms around one another as they stare down at the *Arizona* thinking, 'My God, how could we have done such things?'

"After your mother went to pieces over him, she kept repeating the same phrase over and over in the hospital: red clay and yellow grass, red clay and yellow grass. At the time I thought it was just tripped-out gibberish, but I know now she was referring to Khe Sanh and Altamont: red clay and yellow grass, metaphors for the senseless slaughter of Vietnam and the folly of utopian fantasy. Red clay and yellow grass, a battleground and a rock festival, repositories of my generation's honor and shame, our shame and honor.

"But which resides where? I once told David no one gave a shit about Khe Sanh, but I was wrong; in the end, it was Altamont no one gave a shit about. His death made me realize this: Honor is a vital human instinct, without which human beings and the societies we form cannot endure."

The film précis of my father's life that Levy's testimony helped create would be nominated for an academy award, but neither the box office success of *Altamont Augie* nor the doubts about my self-identity it resolved meant anything to me compared to the satisfaction of knowing that David Noble died not in nameless obscurity, but in glory, now and forever an honorable man.

BIBLIOGRAPHY

The author wishes to cite the following as sources of ideas, inspiration, factual incidents, and general information.

BOOKS

1. Andrew, John A. III. *The Other Side of the Sixties: Young Americans for Freedom and the Rise of Conservative Politics.* New Brunswick, N.J.: Rutgers University Press, 1997.

2. Bowman, James. *Honor: A History.* New York: Encounter Books, 2006.

3. Collier, Peter and Horowitz, David. *Destructive Generation: Second Thoughts About the Sixties.* San Francisco: Encounter Books, 2006.

4. Corbett, John. *West Dickens Avenue: A Marine at Khe Sanh.* New York: Presidio Press, 2003.

5. Drez, Ronald J. and Brinkley, Douglas. *Voices of Courage: The Battle for Khe Sanh, Vietnam.* New York: Bullfinch Press, 2005.

6. Eisen, John. *Altamont: Death of Innocence in the Woodstock Nation.* New York: Avon Books, 1970.

7. Klatch, Rebecca. *A Generation Divided: The New Left, The New Right, and the 1960s.* California: University of California Press, 1999.

8. Murphy, Edward F. *Semper Fi Vietnam.* New York: The Random House Publishing Group, 1997.

9. Sale, Kirkpatrick. *SDS.* New York: Vintage Books, 1973.

10. Sauro, Christy W. Jr. *The Twins Platoon.* St. Paul: Zenith Press, 2006.

11. Schneider, Gregory L. *Cadres for Conservatism: Young Americans for Freedom and the Rise of the Contemporary Right.* New York: New York University Press, 1999.

FILMS

1. Maysles, David, Maysles, Albert, and Zwerin, Charlotte (Maysles Films, Inc.). *Gimme Shelter.* Los Angeles: The Criterion Collection, 2000.

PERSONAL INTERVIEWS BY AUTHOR

1. Pipes, Kenneth W. Captain, Bravo Company, 1st Battalion, 26th Marine Regiment, Khe Sanh, Vietnam, 1968.

2. Ross, Earnest. Drill Instructor, Marine Corps Recruit Depot San Diego, 1966, and Staff Sergeant, 1st Battalion, 9th Marines, Khe Sanh, Vietnam, 1968.

The songs below are listed in the order they appear in *Altamont Augie*, and when considered together, help tell the story of late 1960s America.

"Eight Miles High" and "Dazed and Confused" were musical game-changers, the former launching the genre of psychedelic rock, the latter heavy metal. Four other songs on the list had great social significance: "Ohio," in reaction to the Kent State shootings of 1970; "Sky Pilot," one of the most critically acclaimed Vietnam War protest songs ever written; "The Ballad of The Green Berets," a highly unlikely 1966 hit in support of the war; and "Subterranean Homesick Blues," notorious for having inspired the name of the Weather Underground.

Listen to them all at www.altamontaugie.com and let the music of *Altamont Augie* transport you to a Sixties state of mind.

1. "Ohio" / *Crosby, Stills, Nash & Young*
2. "The Ballad Of The Green Berets" / *Staff Sergeant Barry Sadler*
3. "Turn Down Day" / *The Cyrkle*
4. "Eight Miles High" / *The Byrds*
5. "Itchycoo Park" / *The Small Faces*
6. "Sky Pilot" / *Eric Burden & The Animals*
7. "Sunshine of Your Love" / *Cream*
8. "Fire" / *Crazy World of Arthur Brown*
9. "Dance to the Music" / *Sly & the Family Stone*
10. "Ball and Chain" / *Big Brother and the Holding Company*

11. "Rock & Roll Woman" / *Buffalo Springfield*
12. "Dazed and Confused" / *Led Zeppelin*
13. "Touch Me" / *The Doors*
14. "Romeo and Juliet (Love Theme)" / *Henry Mancini*
15. "Subterranean Homesick Blues" / *Bob Dylan*
16. "We Can Be Together" / *Jefferson Airplane*

ACKNOWLEDGMENTS

The author's heartfelt thanks to:

MARK SPENCER, Dean of the School of Arts and Humanities, University of Arkansas at Monticello and past winner of the Faulkner Award for the Novel and Omaha Prize for the Novel

CAROLE J. GREENE, Simenauer & Greene Literary Agency

GAIL M. KEARNS, To Press & Beyond

EARNEST "GENE" ROSS, who passed away 12/4/09. Though I never went through boot camp, you made me feel as if I had.

And

My wife GAIL, who has read this story more times than all of the above combined.